# ANGEL CHILD

## A NOVEL
## BASED ON A TRUE STORY

## JACQUELINE AUSTIN & ZOE PARRY

POCKET BOOKS
New York   London   Toronto   Sydney   Tokyo   Singapore

This book is a work of fiction. Names, characters, places and incidents are products of the author's imagination or are used fictitiously. Any resemblance to actual events or locales or persons, living or dead, is entirely coincidental.

An *Original* Publication of POCKET BOOKS

POCKET BOOKS, a division of Simon & Schuster Inc.
1230 Avenue of the Americas, New York, NY 10020

ISBN: 0-671-70917-8

First Pocket Books printing August 1996

10  9  8  7  6  5  4  3  2  1

POCKET and colophon are registered trademarks of Simon & Schuster Inc.

Front cover photos courtesy of the author
Text design by Stanley S. Drate/Folio Graphics Co. Inc.

Printed in the U.S.A.

## *Meet some residents of*
## *Zoe Parry's inner hell . . .*

### The Demon

I entered Zoe's body when she was a baby! It was a little tender innocent I wanted . . . I possess that body! I am in control! It is ME you have to deal with!

### Donnie/Donna White

I came out with rage beyond rage. I would take the hitting without tears, and even laugh at the mean old mother.

### Jamie Roberta

Nothing my Daddy says or does is wrong. What me and Daddy do in private is none of your business.

### Selina

For once, on this day of power, let me be myself. Give me my own skin, my hair, my amulets crafted well. I pray you! Give me myself!

### And then there is Zoe . . .

I am alone—dead and in Hell—foaming in my own decay. I have lost the battle. I give up, God. Take your child home. . . .

# ANGEL CHILD

*To all those struggling to build a better self.*
—JACQUELINE AUSTIN


*To my mother,*
*whom I've come to know, understand, and love*
*better through the writing of this book.*
*Your journey was as hard as mine.*
*And to my father, who died in 1978.*
*One does not cause pain*
*unless it has been experienced.*
*Through the rugged road of this book I find peace,*
*enough so I can say, "I forgive you."*
—ZOE PARRY

# Contents

## PART FOUR

# JUDGMENT MORN

■

# List of Personality Maps

# Part One

# THE
# FALLEN
# ANGEL

# A Cave in the Woods

There had been a dry spell in Florida on February 3, 1992—the day I was to meet Zoe Parry. Continued sun had been forecast. But it was pouring. Out my window it looked as if the world was about to wash away. And so it was. My world of assumptions was about to wash away.

I had always assumed I was an outsider. Now I was about to meet someone who was more of an outsider than even me, and who was the perfect insider as well: a multiple personality.

Multiple Personality Disorder, MPD, is by definition a condition in which many personalities—what therapists call "alters" (short for *alternates*)—share a single body.

Are alters truly separate people? That depends. Today, most of us believe in one body to a customer. If somebody says she's a "they" and that "they" are many, we think she's very, very sick, although in other places and other times, we might have comfortably accepted those assertions.

What MPD is today, is a disorder of plenty. Multiples have great imaginations and they are often geniuses— Zoe's IQ is 170. Most are female. Roughly ninety-eight percent have a childhood history of severe psychosexual abuse. They were strongly forbidden in youth to be themselves, and perhaps they lacked (or were not encour-

3

aged to grow) the part of the brain that creates a unified self-perception. They had no place outside themselves to turn their massive creativity.

Like good gardeners in a drought year, most multiples try to preserve what they can of nature's bounty. Their forbidden emotions and capabilities, they stick into jars in the pantry of the brain. These preserved selves, alters, later pour forth in all intensity when some event or stress causes the opening of the jar.

MPD is a disorder of waste. The jar is opened, tasted, and then dropped in panic, because the weak surface self can't allow any strong tastes. If the surface person is to maintain its relative stability, the alters can't feel each other: but they do. The alter evoked by a stress grows powerful as that stress goes on, eventually bursts the walls of repression and takes over. The result is a chaos of impulsive activity, which the surface self can't remember. Over time—especially if the body is strong, healthy, and young and receiving new impressions—as each new surface self tries to defend itself, takeovers by rejected, vital, and mutually exclusive parts of self will become more and more violent.

Eventually I would conclude that without a center that could take responsibility for her actions, Zoe Parry was not exactly a person. She was a country unto herself, a country fighting a civil war. I thought of Benjamin Franklin's words on signing the Declaration of Independence: "We must all hang together, or assuredly we shall all hang separately." Zoe was a fragmented, revolutionary country: one under constant threat of coup.

Sprawled on my couch that morning, oblivious to the interview I needed to—and had not enough data to—construct, I watched the rain stream down outside my window. Rain drummed the glass, melting its flatness into a mess very unlike my usual sunny view of Florida. There were no kids outside. No lawn mowers. No jolly joggers with dogs. One timid smeary car ventured by, tried to brake at a stop sign, and skidded, screeching, into the neighbor's garden, in a rattle of dead sugarcane.

I had no idea what to ask Zoe Parry.

Frankly, I was scared. Sure, I'd read up on multiple

personality, thought I understood what it was about. Terror. Magic. Flight. Escape from death. Some of the same problems that had affected my own family—Holocaust survivors—and myself. My own struggle with the past was far from complete. But it was nothing, next to Zoe's.

I'd heard about Zoe from a close friend, a psychiatrist named Sarah Freed. She had dropped by a month before to tell me about this patient of hers, this multiple personality, who was burning to tell her story. "For years she's been trying. She's desperate. It's a great story. She just can't seem to get it out."

So this Zoe must either enjoy failure, I deduced, or love keeping her secrets. Or maybe MPD was bogus. But Sarah had argued: wouldn't a brilliant MPD survivor with a sense of humor be interesting? As I demurred, she suddenly smiled. "Forget it," she said cheerfully. "It's obviously too challenging for you."

Hmmph! I demanded Sarah's facts.

■

Zoe had been born June 22, 1945, in the Chicago home her parents, Dave and Zoe May Bryant, shared with her maternal grandparents, Anne and Luke Adams. Both Zoe's father and mother came from what Sarah called unstable southern families. Dave had been the youngest, shortest, and least successful son in his birth family. Zoe May, also the youngest and the runt, was prone to nervous breakdowns.

Illness, however, was unacceptable. The Bryants and Adamses were staunch Christian Scientists. To them, illness was error, a denial of God's perfection. "Knowing" an action (feeling it strongly in their soul, "capital $K$") was tantamount to doing it.

Zoe May's worst breakdown, both of nerves and faith, had occurred during pregnancy. She just Knew she'd die giving birth. The bed in which she'd spent her nine months was the same in which her eldest sister had died in childbirth; the same in which her crazed great-grandfather had died years before, chained to the posts. When the infant was born fine, a tiny blonde girl with hazel-green eyes, her mother reportedly burst into tears. She wailed that only one of them could live, either her or the baby. Zoe May gave the child her own name and then spent her days, not cuddling tiny Zoe, but staring at the walls.

In the Bryant family, said Sarah, people ignored such negativity, following the biblical proposition that all things must pass. Another proposition, that all children are born perfect, they also accepted, with a new twist. Zoe was a real baby, not the angel God had supposed advertised. This creature gulped and kicked and screamed for care, so perhaps (Sarah said ironically) she wasn't God's Perfect Child after all. Dave Bryant changed her often; he was hyper-clean and she continually cried.

In September 1945, the Bryants turned over the baby, age three months, to her maternal grandmother, Anne Adams, who lived downstairs.

Mrs. Adams had had eight children of her own—seven girls and a boy. Luke Junior was off in the Philippines, fighting World War II. The family feeling was, boys were not fragile like girls. Luke, they felt, could take care of himself.

A week after baby Zoe was placed in the care of Mrs. Adams, Luke Junior jumped or fell from a hospital window. Her beloved son's death came as an unbearable blow to Mrs. Adams. She, seconded by everyone else in the family, comforted herself with the thought that Zoe must have been sent by God to replace her Luke. She clutched the baby and rocked her incessantly. The infant drowsed to her sobs and prayers, and to the grief-stricken screams of all five living aunts.

Soon Dave and Zoe May Bryant reclaimed Zoe, who by now had experienced three months of hysterical neglect and two months of fulsome death-denying fussing.

They called her their Angel Child, their "doll in a box." It was no easier for Zoe May to take care of her this time than it had been before. All day Dave Bryant would sell typewriters; when he came home, his wife would be staring and his "doll" would be lying in her own excrement, also staring. Gradually, the baby sank from screams into long spells of listless passivity. Still Bryant, living up to his standard of godliness, denied the negativity in his household. He'd clean his "doll"—she took a lot of cleaning—and feed his "doll"—she took a lot of feeding—and rock his "doll" in his beefy arms. Dave Bryant's "doll" took a lot of love. A whole lot of her father's love.

The Bryants taught Zoe right from wrong. An angel doesn't wet her pants. Dirt comes from the Devil, who must be denied our attention. The Devil often got a diaper rash.

As Zoe grew she was trained to deny the bad, crying girl; she spent her waking hours being perfect.

In 1947, at age two, the story went, little Angel Child had healed the sick with silent prayer. Most Christian Scientist toddlers aren't encouraged to do this, but the Bryants knew Zoe was cut out to serve God. Perfection, she learned, brought her praise and attention. When she was bad, someone might have thrust her hand into a burning stove once, but the Devil's Child probably deserved it.

About 1950, Sarah told me, the Bryants moved from Chicago to St. Petersburg. Their best friends were a couple named Perret. John Perret was like Bryant, righteous, a pillar of the church. Except on Sunday afternoons, about which only Zoe knew.

Zoe, who had nightmares, begged her father to sleep in her bed. Her mom didn't mind, so until 1955 Bryant would turn off the TV each night, tiptoe into Zoe's frilly pink room, and crawl into her bed among the stuffed animals. Each morning he'd stroke her golden hair and kiss her awake. The nights, only Zoe knew about.

Somebody's father sometimes drank himself sick, but it couldn't be Dave Bryant—everyone knew he was a teetotaler.

Somebody's mother sometimes hit her silly, but not Zoe's—everyone knew Zoe May was a perfect mother.

Zoe's fear at age seven of her grandfather, the family termed rudeness, Sarah said; her talking to saints at age eight, holiness. Her uncanny stillness at eleven was delicacy, and her attempt to see a psychiatrist half a year later, ungodliness. Her love affair with a girl was not to be discussed, because it would fade away (and so it did). Zoe's marriage to a sailor at age seventeen was romantic; her delivery two years later of a son, whom she named Davey after her father, was a sure sign that the skittish colt had settled down. But she hadn't—and the reason was a universal mystery.

Currently, Zoe was as fragile and tempestuous as ever. She was seeing two therapists: my friend Sarah Freed, and Dr. Gwynn Fischer, a hypnotherapist. Seven years back, said Sarah, after Zoe had consulted a lifetime total of forty counselors and a hundred doctors, Gwynn Fischer had finally correctly diagnosed Zoe as a multiple personality. (The average amount of time it takes to diagnose MPD is seven and a half years, from the start of therapy. Zoe's strangeness had variously been attributed to anxiety, phobias, hysteria, immaturity, and schizophrenia.) Therapy for Zoe had been, to put it mildly, arduous.

On the date of our first conversation, Zoe lived celibately with her husband, Carmine Parry, and with her best friend, an ex-nun named Janet Moore. Also in the Parry household were her son, Davey, twenty-seven and troubled, and her mother, Zoe May. Doctors had labeled everyone in the household mentally ill; the Parrys were still, however, rigidly pursuing perfection. Dave Bryant had died in 1978, of an illness he'd denied to the last.

"Is that all?" I asked.

"Nope." Sarah had sipped her coffee and set it down.

"What's she done for the past fourteen years?" I asked.

In 1978, a few months before her father's death, Zoe had done something so outrageous, Sarah said, that even after years of self-examination, she could barely acknowledge it. She and her household were still suffering the consequences. But Zoe could tell me herself, Sarah said.

She sipped more coffee. The heart of Zoe's story, she added, lay in the ways Zoe had used and abused her relationships with self and others. Why not let Zoe call me?

Maybe, I thought. Okay.
"Is she dangerous?" I asked Sarah.
"Are you?" returned Sarah.

■

Isn't everyone? I thought, wading to Sarah's office through the rain, a danger to self and others? Sometimes? Zoe and I were about to meet, and I was trying to decide how loose a cannon she might be. Was Zoe a danger—today, February 3, 1992? What had she done in the past? What might she do in the future? Was MPD for real? Might it not be just a form of self-hypnosis?

As I sloshed through the flood, I reviewed my facts—aside from Sarah's summary, there were precious few. Zoe and I had by now spoken twice on the phone. She whispered. She seemed to be one person, not the eighteen she claimed to be, but maybe alters cut loose only with people they knew. She had impeccable manners but had referred to herself as a "wimp" and a "doormat." Our meeting had been put off twice, because she'd had a severe cold and thought she might die of it.

From my reading, I expected the surface personality to be depressed and amnesiac, somebody who might lose large chunks of time and be scared about it. She would be scattered, creative, and possibly suicidal. I'd decided Zoe must be a pretty fragile creature.

Big mistake. I was to come to the conclusion, after this one meeting, that if there were a nuclear war, Zoe would be around after to talk about it. Multiples evolve for one purpose only—survival.

My next mistake was equally naive. Wanting to meet at some reassuring location, I'd arranged to meet at Sarah's, an hour before Zoe's regular appointment. That way if I asked anything awful that caused Zoe to disintegrate right then and there, Sarah could come galloping to the rescue. As I would find out, Zoe usually stayed composed. Multiples are constructed to stay composed. If anyone would fall apart, it would be me.

Sarah's waiting room was open, hospitably set with pitchers of tea and ice water. I didn't want to wait. I hung up my soaking raincoat, walked into the office, and considered. There were three choices—the shrink's chair, the patient's chair, and an uncomfortable wooden chair. I sat in the wooden chair, waiting impatiently, reviewing a landmark book in this field, Frank Putnam's *Diagnosis and Treatment of Multiple Personality Disorder*.

On page 43, Putnam quotes the therapists' bible, *The Diagnostic and Statistical Manual*, in defining MPD as:

A) The existence within the individual of two or more distinct personalities or personality states (each with its own relatively enduring pattern of perceiving, relating to, and thinking about the environment and one's self); and B) Each of these personality states at some time, and recurrently, takes full control of the individual's behavior.

Putnam links MPD to other kinds of altered consciousness—fugue states, out-of-body experiences, apparent reincarnations, hypnotic states, dissociations . . . and demonic possessions.

Demonic possessions? During my interviews?

The door cracked open. I looked up with a smile. There stood a slender middle-aged woman with the largest head of hair I'd ever seen. Ash-blonde—and not one strand out of place. This was a capital *L* Lady, with that 1960s look, a suburban housewife dolled up for church. She had big, wet, blinking innocent eyes and was smiling shyly.

"Zoe?" I managed, holding out my hand.

"Jackie?" Giggling nervously, she stepped inside.

"Are you as scared as I am?" I asked.

She looked up in surprise and blinked. A faint scar on her forehead, artfully half-concealed by wisps of hair, wrinkled as she nodded and looked away. Her delicate, foxlike jaw clenched tightly, and a vein corded and quivered at the side of her thin, tense neck.

Our fingers met awkwardly. Zoe's hand was dry and cool; mine had begun to sweat. The black fabric covering her extended wrist bulged slightly, and as she withdrew her hand, the fabric snagged, revealing a tidy, flesh-colored bandage.

Zoe noticed my glance and blushed. "Sometimes somebody does things to the wrist," she said.

*The* wrist? Didn't it belong to Zoe?

"Things—?"

"Scratches."

"What kind of scratches?"

"Deep ones."

"With—?"

"Fingernails or whatever." Zoe blushed.

"Oh."

"Somebody wants to kill the body."

I nodded. We both sat. Zoe took the patient's chair, crossed her—no—*the* legs at *the* ankles. She folded *the* hands in the lap, waiting with the poise of a queen.

"I don't want to pry," I began.

"I don't know where to start," she said just then. We laughed and snuck peeks at each other.

We were members of different species. About two inches shorter than my five-four and at least thirty pounds lighter, Zoe wore a conservative black dress with a collar that went up to the neck, sleeves that went down to the wrists, and a hem that skimmed the knees. Prim as it looked, the tight-knit fabric clung in all the right places, especially at her tiny waistline.

It looked like an expensive dress. The shoes were expensive Ferragamos; the stockings appeared to be silk. Zoe had mentioned her husband worked for the post office and that she did odd jobs. How did she pay for all of this?

The one strikingly false note was the jewelry. Zoe was wearing a ton of it, and it clashed. A huge crucifix banged against an Egyptian ankh, a Jewish star, and an enameled yin-yang sign; she wore two wedding rings, plus gold astrological earrings, which soared like flying buttresses. Nervously, she twisted her largest bracelet, a heavy gold bangle, on and off, off and on, and smiled again, blinking at me through what might be false eyelashes or merely a very generous application of black mascara.

Despite the torrential rain, Zoe's perfect makeup hadn't smeared. She wore full foundation, shadow and liner plus the vampish lashes, brown eyebrow pencil, demure pink lipstick, and blush. Her short, polished nails looked as though they couldn't scratch anything, let alone a wrist. Her hands were the only uncovered part of her body.

We chatted about the storm. Though the surface personality could take the rain or leave it, others in the system—and Zoe gestured down "the body"—adored the rain, would dance naked, daily, in the rain if they had the opportunity. The more violent the storm, the better. "Someone," as she put it, loved lightning, though "the children" were terrified and would dive under the bed at every crack of thunder, if . . .

Suddenly she switched the subject. With tears in her eyes, Zoe said she doubted that anyone could write, let alone understand, her story.

"Why not?" I asked.

"It's overwhelming. It's confusing."

"To you, maybe," I agreed, "but how about the others?"

She sat up even straighter and looked panicky. I think she'd forgotten I knew she was a multiple.

"Can the others speak?"

Zoe smiled tightly. "They can speak, all right."

"How?"

She looked almost angry. Her smile showed her teeth, a little. "They pop out all—by—themselves," she said. This alter, whomever, seemed to hate that loss of control.

"Who are they? Do you know them?"

"You wouldn't want to meet them," she said, her voice much harder and, curiously, deeper.

"Is that why the story's overwhelming—because you don't want to meet a lot of your, uh, the system's alters?"

"Oh, dear, this is so confusing. I just don't know."

"Is everybody listening? Can everybody hear me?"

"I don't know. I think they might. Possibly not."

"What would be the foundation of a book about you-all?"

"What?"

"The theme, the thing that ties your story together?"

"It would be about me, about us."

"What ties you together?"

This alter began to cry. "I don't know. We don't have a foundation. We don't have a support. That's what we've been looking for. We live in hell. Nobody understands."

"No, I don't understand. But maybe you—all of you—can begin to explain. Who are *you*, in relation to the others?"

"I don't know!"

"What's your name?"

"The Patient. Also someone named Elizabeth is here."

It doesn't hurt to accept an interview subject on his or her own terms. She believed in her MPD; I suspended my skepticism, for now.

"Hi, Elizabeth. What do you look like?"

"Something like Zoe." She didn't trust me.

"How do you come into and out of awareness, Elizabeth?"

"I float in and out. I'm asleep and, why, here I am."

I got a sudden image of someone holding a bunch of helium balloons. They floated up, up, attached by long strings, so distant from the person who held them that they seemed to have no connection at all.

Large eyes blinked at me as I thought, *if this woman's alters don't know each other, won't work together, I'm never going to be able to do this. I won't be able to trust that some alter won't do something* outré—*to other alters, to me—won't lie, at least by omission, and then blame the lack of truth on me.* The surface seemed terribly nice, but who knew what was inside? Then again, this was so interesting. And fantasy, selective perceptions, weren't these at the heart of everybody's self-image—including mine? Getting that shiver we get when confronting a mystery, I took a deep breath while I considered Zoe. I finally said, "Let's try something, to see if we can work together.

"Meeting you and knowing there are others, I feel like

a tourist. Tourists might poke around where they're not wanted—unless they're prepared."

She looked stricken. "Prepared?"

"They carry maps. They know key phrases of the language."

"What exactly does that mean?"

"If I'm going to visit your country, I'll need a map of who's inside. Names, descriptions, and dates. When they were born. And who they are."

"Dates? We don't think like that."

She looked horrified. This was thin ice, trying to quantify her soul. I realized that I was also being unicentric—acting as if she were one.

■

Ultimately—though I had no idea at the time—I would end up asking for a personality map every six weeks for a year and a half. I researched six generations of family history. Zoe and I spoke for an hour and a half a day, five days a week, from February 1992 to July 1993. Zoe's alters produced hundreds of often contradictory, piecemeal accounts; I'd patch these into a story.

The points at which alters couldn't answer my questions, the times when Zoe's personality system broke down, or fell silent, I learned to see as markers.

I eventually decided that multiplicity is indeed real, that it is to some degree a universal condition. According to one psychiatrist, Dr. John Beahrs, who has written extensively on the subject, all of us have multiple selves, which he likens to the instruments in a symphony orchestra. But unlike Zoe, most of us have a conductor.

Zoe's alters don't believe they are one, but from outside, they look and sound quite ordered. Via Zoe's maps, I saw the changes in one personality system over time. New alters came out at each crisis in the story. Old alters kept reorganizing, into changing cliques with differently charged consciousness, function, and power. As her story unfolded, Zoe's world changed. Her inner structures, her "tunnels," shifted. Some alters went from the Tunnel of Hell into the Tunnel of Watchers; some spent their energy in the telling and went into the Tunnel of Limbo. In this book, the names of Zoe's inner tunnels change in each chapter, to reflect these movements of alters.

Zoe's story raises more questions than it answers.

■

So at our first meeting, after saying, yes, dates and names, and realizing that specifics can be threatening to a multiple, I continued more gently.

"I'll make our conversation as manageable as I can. Your story will be like a house; we'll enter one room at a time. I'll respect your privacy outside these limits, and you'll respect mine. We'll arrange circumstances"—and I paraphrased Frank Putnam, thanking God he'd assembled a contract for use with multiples and that I'd read it—"circumstances safe for yourself or -selves and for me, which encourage health in everybody, both internal and external."

She sat back and relaxed a little. We all relaxed, except for her internal watchers, who never relax. "That sounds good," she said.

"What is it like, being multiple?" I whispered.

Zoe's breath caught. "Say you wanted to go to the store and get some milk." Her voice sharpened. "You'd get your money and your purse, and go outside, and go in the car and start driving. The store is only five blocks away and you only have to turn once. You make the turn, and a, a bird . . ."—her voice got higher, her breathing labored—"a bird flies under the tire, and bam!"

"What is it?" She seemed to be reliving some trauma.

"M-m-my feet don't reach g-g-gas pedal. I only two years old. I two. Daddy kill Zoe if I break car. Where the thing you press to stop the car? Way down there!"

Oh, no.

"What I gonna do? I can't see! I'm gonna crash!" She clutched her chest. I'd heard she had heart problems. "I can't breathe!" Her eyes darted frantically to one side.

"It's okay . . ."

"You bet your sweet ass it's okay." The voice was hard, alert, lower, older.

"Who are you?"

The unconscious, I'd always felt, was much smarter than the conscious mind, and here was someone with a nation of the unconscious. This could be anyone. Or everyone.

"Who are you?" I repeated.

"I'm Zoe," she said archly, "of course." This was the alter I would later know as Angel Child. Watching me. Angel Child sees herself as perfect. Perfectly powerful. Invincible. And always right. Later she would state that she is a fallen angel. She has the power to kill with a thought, she says—and she's used it. "Do you know today's date?" she now said, softly, mockingly, melodiously.

"February third? Is it significant?"

She smiled. "Yes . . . It's an anniversary, of a kind."

"What are you celebrating?"

"What is the worst thing you've ever done?" she purred.

We were there to speak about her—not me. "What's the worst thing *you've* ever done?" I countered.

She didn't answer.

Later, she would.

■

Abuse. We blame it on others—bad parents, bad children, the wealthy, the poor, the mentally ill. We do not blame it on ourselves. In America, the reports of MPD are on the rise. Forty documented cases in 1980. Seven thousand cases today. Hundreds of thousands of cases of dissociative disorders. Victims at every corner, on every talk show, in every column of the newspaper. If we really are such a nation of victims, we must also be a nation of abusers.

Every man, woman, and child in this country shares with Zoe some dissociative skill. When's the last time you saw something that outraged you and immediately put it out of your mind?

A multiple can tell us a lot about ourselves.

Most multiples won't tell you a thing about what they've suffered or what they've done. These things are often secret even to their many selves, buried deep within. They don't know, won't see, are too wrapped up in their inner whirlwinds, to undergo the second-by-second self-confrontation it takes to find and tell the truth.

Zoe Parry wants to prevent the further misuse of power. She has delved deep to find the truth.

So have I. In persuading Zoe's alters to speak, I have had to leave both the land of dreams and the land of logic, and to go to meet them in the land of the psyche.

I've listened to Zoe's voices, one hundred and thirty-five of them and more, each clamoring that they know the only truth, each contradicted in some spots and bulwarked in others, by facts.

Of one fact I am certain: Zoe has lived in hell.

She is willing to let you tour hell if you listen to her message.

For her, the message is "Use power wisely."

■

"What anniversary was February third?" I ask the Angel Child, a.k.a. God's Perfect Child, the Golden Child, and the Devil's Child.

It is March 25; we're sitting in my living room. It is a sunny day; all the colors glow. On the surface, Zoe Parry is a forty-seven-year-old woman decked out in a dark red suit and matching makeup. She smells very clean. She is smiling. She has just dropped off an enormous box of journals, letters, and legal documents. We're chatting about filing systems. She looks like anybody's neighbor.

The Angel Child, though, says she's thousands of years old and has been reincarnated many times since her first lifetime in ancient Greece. *She* does not look like your neighbor. No, indeed. She can shapeshift at will, says the Angel Child, from a blonde little girl with banana curls to a ravening beast.

In a singsong the voice begins:

"Far away there is a forest. In the forest is a cave."

"A forest?" I asked the Angel Child inside Zoe's body. She nods. "Inside or outside?"

An enigmatic smile. "Within."

"Are you there right now?"

A shrug.

"What is the cave?"

"The entrance to hell."

"What is the forest?"

"The way within."

"Where is this forest, Angel Child?"

"Look beyond my eyes," says she.

■

Zoe Parry has hazel-green eyes. Past them, far, far back—so far within, she claims, that you might as well be outside—is a forest. Silent. Vast. Lit by the sharp rays of a setting sun.

She describes the inner country. "As you walk, your feet crunch dead leaves. The trees form a pattern above you. You could easily get lost. The only way out is down and through the caves."

"The caves? Where are they?"

Another shrug. "I could guide you there."

In his journey through hell, Dante had a guide, Virgil. Virgil was not as tricky as the Angel Child. He was created by art. The Angel Child was created by pain.

■

This is what Angel Child described to me that day:

You enter the forest with her and walk for several miles. Beyond a thicket are two tall trees sticking up like legs. Between them, the dirt is packed hard, as if many have stood there for a second while they caught their breath. There is a rock between the trees. If you look beneath it, you find a small black hole, just big enough to admit one. One way.

This entrance to hell looks ominous. But you wouldn't want to imagine things—to interpret trees, underbrush, rock, and hole, for example, as the entrance to Mother's womb. So you take a deep breath and you plunge into the hole.

It's pitch black. You can't see. With each step you take, there are echoes. Somewhere, water drips—the *blap, blap* multiplied by a thousand. From a far distance away comes the crying of a child.

Someone laughs. You jump. But don't run! You don't want to fall into some pit and die. You put your hand on the oozy wall and inch forward. Your feet squish sand. Drums are beating somewhere. Your breath goes in and out, damp and hot. Was that another laugh, right by your ear?

Groping, finally you see a far, dim gray light. Voices drift to you, muddled by distance. You hurry up a wide tunnel, burst out, and see a Georgia mansion, white pillars and all. Children play tag on a sun-dappled lawn. Their caretaker, a pretty nun—Sister Zoe Ann—stares at you, with eyes as hard as agate. You do not belong here. You beat it, fast. "A guide could tell you this was the Tunnel of Light," adds Angel Child, sweetly.

Back in the dark you go. After what seems like an age, your hand penetrates fog. The Tunnel of Dreams. The surface Zoes—"poor things," Angel Child sneers—live here, "if living in a gray mist is living at all." You hear words. "The mist speaks," says Angel Child. Shutting her eyes, she hisses in a cold voice, "A visitor, isn't that nice. What land shall I dream for you?"

She opens her eyes again. "You're shivering," she says (it's Angel Child's light, metallic voice again, with false compassion). She continues the story. "Now you proceed once more. The black brightens; the rough walls grow smooth. Now you're squinting down a long red hallway. This is the Tunnel of Lost Souls."

You're not a lost soul—not one of Zoe's, anyway—so you hurry on. You pass through a door. Wrong again. You are not at the exit but at an underground lake. A beached whale gasps out its life on a stretch of hard gray stones. But this is not a whale. Says the voice, "It is two hundred and fifty pound Mary Cora." Those are not stones, but candy. Mary Cora has fallen asleep eating candy. "This is the Tunnel of Limbo. Don't wake Mary Cora—she needs her rest."

Again you find the chamber. The drum is faster, louder. You stumble up to another pit. The hiss warns you—snakes. "This way lies the Tunnel of Hell."

There's a laugh, in a different voice, low and purely evil. She's putting you on? The low voice whispers, "I've done in real life what scares you in your dreams." This is not someplace or someone you'd care, just now, to stop and investigate.

Next is the Tunnel of Darkness and Death. "Will this be better?" says Angel Child. "Who cares?" Throwing caution to the winds, you race down, down, and find white-hot sand. Paradoxically the Tunnel of Darkness is a desert. If you left the wall, you would die of thirst.

The guide voice leads you on and on. Eventually you come to steps, leading down to a pillared courtyard.

"This is the temple of the Sun God, Ra," says Angel Child with the intonation of a guide on a tour bus. "Notice the fine stonework. The temple is covered inside and out with stone scarabs. These are the sign of Ra. If you had a guide," says Angel, "and if you were clean," she adds, "down the steps you might go, past two guards wearing loincloths. Past the pillars, you'd find the inner sanctum. There you'd see a priestess tending something on a slab of stone. If you were very quiet, you might be allowed to see what was on the slab. Since you won't be, I'll tell you. It's a baby. Three months old. Named Frozen.

"What has caused Frozen to be this way? If you asked in the Tunnel of Waiting and Secrets, they might tell you. Probably they wouldn't. They're too bad, like the Bad Girls Ronny and Roberta, who'd as soon spit in your face as tell you. Or too scared, like the Zoes, those wimps. Or too strange. The Dark Ones, and Heather, and Markus, and Paul, were created to be mysteries—and they are."

Where is the way out? You have come three hundred and sixty degrees around the chamber—"without your guide," snickers Angel—"and here you are exhausted, poor thing, but you're almost done. This is the Tunnel of Watchers." And you think with relief, here are the ones who know, who could tell you, how did the baby get that way? You've taken an L-turn, you know. Now you're haunted by that baby, rather than worrying about the way out. You're lost in this country, one step inside the border, here before you've even passed customs. Or perhaps you've given up on the baby. Because now you've remembered to ask, "Is this real?"

The earth groans, shifts. Rocks crash down, threatening to crush you. All is noise and choking dust and laughter.

In the quiet after the system's realignment, you realize that the tunnel structure has changed. "You're trapped," laughs Angel Child. In this cave within the forest. One step inside was too deep for you to go. The way out closed when you crawled in. The Watchers note this from their place of rest. The Observer sees you squirm. And so does everybody else. Because now, besides watching Zoe-the-Host and the other citizens of this nation, the Watchers are watching you, the intruder. Will you kill them or help them? Hang separately, or together? It better be B, because if it's A, friend, you don't stand a chance.

"This nation has powerful protectors." One of the Watchers is Oya, the goddess of storm. Sometimes Oya *becomes* a storm. At this moment, you begin to annoy Oya with your gropings. You feel a drop on your face. And another. Rain floods the tunnels. Beats you down. Now you turn tail. Flee. Splashing and sloshing through the blackness. Swimming. Sinking. Water above, around, rushing black, sucking you down into your final panic.

Dispassionately, Oya watches as you drown.

■

From February 3 until today, March 25, with the approval of Zoe's therapists, I'd set foundations. I'd introduced myself to each alter. I'd found a way to say "you" that could mean one alter or Zoe's whole system. We spoke each morning by phone. Or rather, whichever alter was out spoke; I asked questions.

Revelations—or creations?—trickled out. A few at first, then a flood. There were not eighteen alters (Zoe's first count). The first map showed fifty, the second eighty, the third, ninety. Then one hundred, one hundred and twenty. By August 1993 we peaked at one hundred and fifty and a host of Nameless Ones. Some personalities considered themselves alters; some did not. Several said they received each other's thoughts or saw others within the tunnels, some apparently close, others farther away. There was a lot of one-way communication, which alters variously termed "mind control," "thought impressions," "amnesia," and "blocking." Though Zoe-the-Host considered the infant dead, she seemed very much alive—though encased by protective alters. The frozen energy that Zoe-the-Host described during her panic attacks matched her descriptions of this fundamental self: the baby rigid in fear. I began to wonder how the evils Zoe-the-Host so feared were fed by her fears.

Many alters seemed built to serve a purpose—Dr. Silverstein, Aunt Sophie, Rebecca Gwynn, and others were clearly introjects of an esteemed or hated companion, often a therapist. Scarier alters seemed to be substitute parents (the Demon) or beings powerful enough to take on introjects (the Angel/Devil/Golden Child). Others said they were reincarnations—Cynthia, Ronny/Lillian, Martin Caine. Many called themselves "observers," "spirit guides," and "teachers"—Black Wolf, Cassandra, Heather, Paul. These were not quite Internal Self Helpers (ISHs), alters who reputedly can see the whole shebang, who supposedly pop out (say certain theoreticians) to help not just the self, but the questioner. While all of the alters were helpers, their help tended to boomerang. The number of tunnels stayed fairly constant, at seven, eight, or nine. The forest never changed, but the tunnels, dark and mysterious, shifted with each change in the tide of my questions.

I went through Zoe's papers and made a sixty-page time line. I reconstructed events, filling in each alter's amnesias by having other alters report on activities during so-called lost time. Through decades of therapy Zoe had not yet managed this, and seeing how long a process this was, how Zoe took on crises to interrupt it, and how obliquely she presented facts, I understood why.

At first I was afraid of interfering. Gwynn Fischer, Zoe's hypnotherapist, said she didn't want to reify personalities by showing too much interest in them. Might the concreteness of my approach harm Zoe—emphasize fantasy at the expense of integration? Later I settled down. If my enthusiasm and insight—and even my stupidities—were going to harm Zoe, then we shouldn't work together. But that was a possibility we could only discover in the doing.

I sent Zoe the time line and asked each alter to annotate events during which he/she/they'd been awake. From the responses, I constructed questions. I also contacted Zoe's husband and son, and other key figures who could corroborate her story. Who are you? What do you look like? Feel like? When were you born? How do you perceive the body? What's your tunnel like? Can you see other alters? Do you ever know what others are thinking?

Some questions were historical: What was your mother's family like? Your father's? When did you marry? Can you tell me what happened during this gap in the time line?

Some questions were fantastic: Greetings, Priestess. I have heard many things about you from others. Perhaps you can elaborate . . .

Some questions were emotional: Oh, no, I can't believe you would let someone stick a coat hanger up you! Why?

Some were factual: Who is this person—someone in your system or someone outside?

Some were narrative. And from these came the structure of this book.

On the evening of March 25, a few hours after Zoe's visit to my home, my phone rang.

"Hello, Miz Jackie. You don't know me. My name be Eleanora. I'm gonna answer your question."

It took me a few moments to figure out that my "question," asked repeatedly for seven weeks, was, "What happened on February third?" and that this Eleanora was one of Zoe's alters. She surely didn't sound like anyone I'd met to date. Not that the others were similar. In fact, Zoe often suffers from laryngitis, the result of a human voice box straining to produce superhumanly separate effects.

Eleanora described herself as a gracious black woman in her forties. Soft, smooth, and religious, Eleanora had been a hell-raiser in her youth. "They called me the Shady Lady. Before I got religion, I pimped for some of the others."

I bought time while I tried to figure this out.

"Pimping, that's pretty dramatic," I said to Eleanora.

"That's so."

"How, uh, did you do it?" I couldn't begin to visualize how two alters, sharing one body, could have this particular relationship.

"Of course, I wouldn't do such a thing now," said Eleanora, veering off the subject. "But it was dramatic."

"I guess people in the system have done some pretty dramatic things."

"Oh, yes," said Eleanora, amused. "You could say that."

"What's the most dramatic thing you-all have ever done?"

"That's easy, child," said Eleanora. She paused. "In 1978," she continued, "someone kidnapped a child."

"What? Who?"

"I don't know," said Eleanora. "But the State of Florida claimed it was one of us, though it surely didn't feel like one of us. They said we went along with this woman, Crystal. The lawyers said it was a *folie à deux*. That Crystal was crazy and that we-all was even more crazy together. But we don't know who inside would do such a thing. Not one of us, surely. We would never do anything so dreadful, no matter how confused. Some of us surely do get confused. But we're creatures of God. It's a mystery."

"Who was the child?"

"Jennifer King. Age of one and a half. A child Mother Zoe was baby-sitting for. Her and this friend I told you about, Crystal. Many of us adored Crystal. She was beautiful. And so was the child. It was a beautiful time. And a beautiful child. Baby Jennifer. Sweet as pie. Mother Zoe and Crystal loved playing with that child. They were thrilled to go each morning over to the Kings' home on Orchid Drive . . ."

"What was the date of the kidnapping?"

"February 3, 1978." So this was the anniversary Angel Child had been celebrating!

"Who kidnapped Jennifer King, Eleanora?"

She still didn't know. But soon—from this one alter would come a trickle of other alters, and then eventually a flood—soon, I got the most extraordinary answer.

# Part Two

# HER
# BURNING
# GRACE

# Zoe Parry: Inner Structure

*February 1992*
*Discussing the kidnapping.*
*57 Personalities.*
*7 Tunnels.*
*Each personality is present in one tunnel only.*

The Tunnel of
Light and
Wisdom

The Tunnel of
Hosts

The Tunnel of
Waiting and
Secrets

**CAVE
ENTRANCE**

The Tunnel of
Lost Souls

The Tunnel of
Darkness and
Death

The Tunnel of
Limbo

The Tunnel of
Hell

# Zoe Parry: Inner Structure

## February 1992

In Zoe's personality map of February 1992, seven tunnels form a circle around a cave entrance—Zoe's hollow-feeling center. There are fifty-seven names on the map. Each name appears in one tunnel only. The host Zoe is in the Tunnel of Hosts, at the middle left of the page. That's where Zoe usually places the names of alters who are "out"—relating to society—at the time of mapping.

On this map, and on all subsequent maps, Zoe's inner geography faces left. Put in terms of the right brain/left brain dichotomy, Zoe, when remembering how she kidnapped a child, faces toward logic and away from buried intuition.

On either side of the Tunnel of Hosts are the Tunnel of Light and Wisdom and the Tunnel of Lost Souls. To Zoe's social alters, the alters in these two tunnels feel good and wise. To Zoe's system, the Tunnel of Hosts feels forward, out in the weather. The Tunnel of Light and Wisdom feels higher up and brighter, like heaven. And the Tunnel of Lost Souls feels deeper in and redder, like a womb.

Farthest away from the Hosts, on the right-hand side of the page, are the Tunnel of Waiting and Secrets, the Tunnel of Hell, and the Tunnel of Darkness and Death. These contain the alters who are most blocked from the social Zoe when she recalls the kidnapping. In these memories her demons, her witches, her priests, and her frozen baby (her original, abused self) are blocked from the social Zoe. She is terrified and believes these alters to be inhuman, mysterious, or evil. Screams, growls, chants, drumbeats, and gut-wrenching sobs emanate from these tunnels, as do deadly silences: the social Zoe can't bear them.

# 2

# The Kidnapping

It was four A.M., February 3, 1978. The town, which I'll call Huerta Vista, slept. On the empty crosswalk at Oblicuo and Main, a traffic light changed from green to yellow.

Halfway up a cul-de-sac of old ranch houses, 5724 Gardenia also slept. The curtains were drawn tight. The doors were locked. In the yard, hanging from the high fork of an ancient eucalyptus, a child's swing creaked softly back and forth.

The swing belonged to twelve-year-old Davey Parry. He'd never used it—he'd been too old and too troubled for such a thing even three years back, when the Parrys and the woman they all called Aunt, fifty-five-year-old Crystal Moon McGuire, had moved in. Zoe had begged her husband, Carmine, to hang up the swing, begged in the wistful voice of a child. Now the swing shivered, twisting in the wind.

For the past nine months, the longest she'd ever kept a job, Zoe had earned four hundred dollars a month baby-sitting. Zoe had told her husband, her parents, her priest, her therapist, and her neighbors that she loved George King, realtor, Lillian King, teacher, and their two little daughters, Taffy and Jennifer, but in fact this job would

31

have challenged Mary Poppins. The hours were long. The rules were rigid. And there was the matter of Taffy's screams.

Taffy, four, got headaches. She also clutched her eyes and bumped into walls and fell down staircases. Though the Kings were staunch Christian Scientists, and thus strongly believed in healing through faith and correct visualization, they'd been so distressed by Taffy's symptoms that they'd recently taken her to a doctor. Tests had shown a brain tumor, which had spread to the child's optic nerve and blinded her. The pain was excruciating. The doctors could not prevent more pain; the Kings, then, had returned to constant prayer.

That would have been hard enough for Zoe, whose parents were also Christian Scientists who placed all their conscious hopes on healing through the Lord, would have been hard enough even if Zoe could have thought through the dynamics of the situation. But all day at work Zoe was busy cleaning house, making meals, and chasing Jennifer. The Kings' palace was crammed with precious antiques, which Jennifer, one and a half, yearned to stuff in her mouth or "make go-boom."

The Kings set off weird echoes within Zoe. Voices, ghosts, kept drifting across her senses. She'd catch a glimpse of a shadow in a mirror, hear a fugitive voice, smell flowers that weren't there. She strongly felt the presence of two ghostly children, which she linked to the King children. Today, Zoe can identify these ghost selves. Baby Frozen is Zoe's fundamental alter, a cold, corpselike infant with staring eyes. Mazie is a scared child-alter with golden banana curls who lives to take care of Mama.

In 1978 Zoe was weaker and she didn't acknowledge any other selves. She felt them, though, as hot bubbles of demonic energy pressing up, like lava, trying to burst her brittle surface. Whenever they broke through, whenever her polite rationalization that they were the King children exploded for a moment, she'd blank out. When she would come to again, she'd have lost time—unconscious of what awful thing she might have done.

Since Zoe had started working at the Kings' house in June 1977, whenever the real child, Taffy, screamed in pain, Zoe's ghost children, Mazie and Baby Frozen, had screamed too. Zoe (as much as she wanted to) could not repress the screams.

Though therapists would later articulate Zoe's anxiety and anger, feelings that a perfect angel must not have, at the time Zoe had seemed delighted with her job. The cash went a long way toward supporting the Parrys. "The Kings were such a nice young godly couple. And Taffy and Jennifer," Zoe adds, "were darling."

Under the bland surface though, Zoe's secrets were ticking away, ready to "go-boom" in everybody's face. Her Aunt Crystal was, in fact, Zoe's lesbian wife. Zoe's recent three-week trip "to a religious meditation center" had been, in fact, a doctor-recommended stay on a psych ward. But these secrets paled next to the most important one.

Crystal and Zoe planned to kidnap Jennifer King.

The surface Zoe did not know that others had spoken through her mouth, telling Crystal that Lillian was a bad, evil mother and pledging to rescue the holy baby.

Not only would they save Jennifer by stealing her, as had insisted a rasping voice that named itself to Crystal as Mrs. Patterson, but the kidnapping would serve another purpose as well. It would lift a curse that had been placed on Crystal and Zoe by a notorious local witch named Isis Bergeron, someone they'd originally consulted for herbal healing. Why alter Mrs. Patterson, who claimed to hate Zoe, cared to lift this curse, the voice did not say. Crystal is dead now, so the only one who remembers is Mrs. Patterson—and she refuses to state her reasons.

Within the previous two years, Crystal and Zoe, in certain moods and voices, had been drawn further and further into witchcraft. They'd joined Isis's coven and had later ("without my knowledge," Zoe adds) split off a coven of their own, raiding Isis's group for members. Taking Jennifer from Lillian, Mrs. Patterson repeatedly promised Crystal, would liberate "all" from Isis's spell.

The late 1970s marked a rise in witchcraft in Florida.

Several thousand New Agers, utopian lesbians, and spiritualists were at the time exploring everything from biorhythms to hypnosis. The thirteen-member ladies' club that regularly visited 5724 on Carmine's night out with the guys was, in fact, Zoe's coven. Zoe's voices do not agree on the nature of this coven, or on Zoe's role in it.

One alter, Cynthia—who sees herself as a tall blonde with powerful green eyes—says she ran the coven, using nature-based Wiccan rituals and wearing Zoe's body, a black robe, and a huge blonde wig. Her motive for kidnapping Jennifer was to save her coven's rebirth festival, Imbolc. February is a holy month for Wiccans; with the impending return of spring, they celebrate rebirth, the budding anew of nature's cycle. On the evening of February 2, Cynthia had found herself unable to celebrate Imbolc; the songs had died on her lips. Taking Jennifer—a baby represents spring—would thwart Isis, the crone, the woman winter. Cynthia felt she could in this way regain her power.

Another alter, Selina—who sees herself as tall, copper-skinned, half black and half Hopi Indian—insists in broken English that it was she, not Cynthia, who ran the coven. She used voodoo ceremonies; in proof she sends me a photo of a dark-skinned Zoe (face dye) wearing a black wig. She says, in a strong, thick accent, "I was the one who take Jennifer. To save a child from bad mother, yes, I take."

A third alter, High Priestess Oya, sends a photo of Zoe in a white robe, a red wig, and a vacant stare. In a harsh, powerful voice, she says it is she who ran the coven. She considers herself the avatar of the mother goddess Oya—an African goddess who brings life but who can also unleash the storm. Her motive for taking Jennifer was to prevent evil from flooding the earth, by making a holy sacrifice.

A fourth, rasping voice, Mrs. Patterson, says no, it was she who was in power, she who ran the coven for Satan. She is not obliging about describing herself. Her motive was to take the child for Satan—to corrupt her. "Just as"—she laughs harshly—"I took the child Zoe, long ago."

The only one of these alters who admits she's evil, who revels in glorious badness, is Mrs. Patterson. This badness paradoxically serves Zoe's system, just as the others' vaunted goodness or weakness also serves the system. Until Zoe's badness publicly showed itself on February 3, 1978, via Mrs. Patterson, Zoe had been unable to get help.

The kidnapping plan felt necessary to Zoe's alters, even reasonable, on many levels. Crystal and the rasping voice, Mrs. Patterson, had it all figured out.

At four A.M. on February 3, 1978, Zoe was not asleep. Her body was awake; Zoe-the-Host, the surface self, was too, anxiously awaiting the hour when she could get dressed for work. Another alter, Mother Zoe, tells me that she was out, too, sitting shivering in the dark by her phone. Waiting for the courage to dial.

Mother Zoe sees herself as delicate, ash-blonde, twenty-four. She says her heart was racing, her head was spinning, and she could barely catch a breath. To this day Mother Zoe panics at the thought of bad mothers. That day she felt lost and heartsick. She ached for a magic mommy to come make it all better. She longed for her therapist, Dr. Magda Hoff.

At many levels of self Zoe needed magic mommies. The witch selves had found Isis. The Christian Scientists were happiest with Zoe's own mother, grandmother, and Lillian. The Catholics relied on the Virgin Mary; Mother Zoe, on Crystal. Zoe was always with one of these magic mommies. Even her therapists were magic mommies, and the more maternal they were, the more she wanted to sleep with them. But they had sublimated their longing for their Catholic psychiatrist, Magda Hoff.

Ever since Zoe's three-week hospitalization, the magic mommies had fled like lemmings. Even Dr. Hoff had pulled back from caring for her as the Patient felt doctors ought to. Zoe's complaint on entering the hospital had been that she was possessed by Satan. Hoff—who dreaded Satan—was now quite slow about returning phone calls.

Today Zoe's voices were screaming. The surface person could hear that the night was really peaceful and still.

But though she knew it was quiet and could tell that her lips weren't moving and nobody was making a sound, she felt swamped in noise. She could hear so many voices, screaming in vain, so many that she couldn't think.

"I knew I was about to do something awful," says Mother Zoe, "and that I couldn't stop it."

She sounds soft, remorseful, fearful, lonely. She thinks nobody will hear her now. "My only thought," she adds paradoxically, "was that I must save the child."

She's avoided thinking about the kidnapping ever since it happened. Now, as all the alters tell the story together, each adding a bit to the whole mosaic, Zoe—the entire system of alters that is Zoe—listens and experiences the chain of events for the first time. And as the alters listen together and speak together (even though they speak in turn, the chorus of voices tells a single story), they begin to share consciousness. They acknowledge each other. They begin to develop a common history.

A multiple's re-creations are even more intense than are her original experiences. Years of unconsciously repeating "I don't know what happened, I must not look," actually make the memory more intense. When recall finally bursts through, it isn't perceived by Zoe as something past and done. It is now, it is always, it is pure revivified horror.

Zoe moaned. No one heard. In the master bedroom, Carmine lay snoring. Davey was two rooms away. Zoe's dogs, in the guest room, snapped at bones in their dreams. Both beds in the guest room were rumpled from lovemaking.

In the bed nearest the open doorway, a figure lay awake. Crystal Moon McGuire had been up all night with Zoe, planning the kidnapping and making love. A schizophrenic and manic-depressive, who had been getting worse lately, she probably could not hear Zoe's moans. By all accounts she was listening to her own voices.

Though many schizophrenics hear things (their voices, unlike those of a multiple, seem to come from outside), few manage to find lovers who can hear the voices too. Crystal's voices dovetailed neatly with Zoe's.

The two women even shared a few. The most frightening of these was Beatrice Patterson. Zoe channeled Mrs. Patterson: she felt her presence as the Devil and blacked out with fear every time Patterson rose to the fore. The strange, multilevel, rasping speech and Mrs. Patterson's coded journals, only Crystal could interpret. Her translations had grown increasingly bizarre in the four years she'd lived with Zoe. The two sets of voices must have fed each other, heightened each other. Lately, Crystal carried out Mrs. Patterson's every command.

Yes, their illnesses dovetailed. Each was accustomed to acting alternately as the other's mother or the other's child. Each was so in need of the other, and so unable to accept help except from the other, that they had shut out everyone else. Patterson's notes and Crystal's symbiotic responses to them would later be found by the police and used as evidence against the pair, though to this day Zoe-the-Host protests, "That was not my handwriting."

Mother Zoe reached again for the phone. The inner presence watched her, sneered as her hand crept toward the dial, and then suddenly snatched the hand away. Very visibly alone, the woman shrank back into the pillows.

She was dry with cold. Two wedding rings—one from Carmine, one from Crystal—kept slipping off; she jammed them back on again and again. By now her lips were sore from nervous licking. In her narrow chest her heart pounded arrhythmically with each jagged breath.

In times of stress, Zoe's alters switch rapidly.

If you'd been there, on February 3, 1978, possibly you would have seen a woman standing up, talking, sitting down, talking some more, and standing up again.

Mother Zoe raised her nightgown and glimpsed her dark reflection in the mirror. Five feet four, one hundred and ten pounds, ash-blonde hair and eyes, twenty-four years old (to the body's thirty-three). Her gaze swept right past a mark on her left side. It was invisible to her. Some alters can control others' perceptions.

Mother Zoe came to with a start, realizing that she was standing looking at her naked body in the dark. The nightgown fell. "I'm totally losing my mind. I've got to get to the phone. Right now."

Came the alto voice of her grandmother, "You are not losing your mind. You cannot lose your mind. You are Mind.

"You are Something. You are God. You are Truth."

■

**MOTHER ZOE [Zoe I] (the Tunnel of Light and Wisdom):** *I did not feel like Something. I felt like nothing wrapped in nothing. Only when imagining myself loving my mother, and my mother loving me back, did I feel I was something. That may be childish but it's true.*

*From 1972 till 1978 I'd been something with Crystal. She was so lovely. So maternal. So warm. So open. Crystal and I were a universe of Love.*

■

Zoe cried as she remembered what she could of the past night. Davey and Carmine had gone to bed. Crystal and she had then stayed awake, making love.

Mother Zoe feared this was her last time with Crystal. And so did another alter—Martin Caine.

Martin Caine sees himself as a gentleman of 1865, a Confederate soldier with sandy hair and beard, wearing Confederate gray. According to Martin Caine, he and Crystal had been spouses in former lifetimes. He'd been reincarnated into Zoe's body to live out karma from these past lives.

■

**MARTIN CAINE (the Tunnel of Lost Souls):** *Crystal and I shared a secret bond through the centuries. Our vows predated Zoe's vows to Carmine. Carmine hated that—but he didn't have much choice. He'd learned he couldn't control his wife.*

*Lately I had felt Crystal drifting away. Isis had come between us, and so had Mrs. Patterson.*

*That day, I would lose my love, for this lifetime.*

▪

Mother Zoe stood. Her shadow flared out ahead of her. The living room had been dark. Now it was ablaze with the light of candles—red and yellow and black. Burning on the bookcase, smutting the walls. Hot, bright, dancing flames!

Howls of laughter. Zoe shuddered and suddenly, quickly, fumbled the phone from its cradle. She glanced at the clock: 5:30. She'd lost an hour and a half since she'd last tried to call, time in which an alter, Selina, had performed a ceremony with candles and paper cutouts. Mother Zoe feared that Dr. Hoff would be angry if she called so early, but what was Hoff's anger compared with damnation.

An accented voice started to chant. The phone fell from Zoe's hand. The strange voice touched off more shivers. Then followed visions: a tall coppery woman, half-nude, whom she now identifies as Selina; a faceless figure robed in black, Mrs. Patterson; a blonde, green-eyed witch similarly robed, Cynthia; a red-haired, blue-eyed goddess in white, Oya. She did not know that these people were part of herself, but remembers feeling that each was real, and powerful. She says the candle flames flared high, releasing bursts of incense-laden smoke.

▪

**MOTHER ZOE [Zoe I] (the Tunnel of Light and Wisdom):**
*Selina approached, her muscles rippling. Her black hair, shining skin, and dark eyes appeared alien—evil.*

▪

Though each says she was in charge of the coven, these four, Selina, Cynthia, Mrs. Patterson, and Oya, rarely shared awareness. Usually, each tried to snatch control whenever she could and blocked the others. On February 3, 1978, the switches were frequent, and the flow of power between the four coven leaders and the other alters was complex. Mother Zoe and Martin could see each other and interact. Selina could take over from them or from any of the child alters. Cynthia could take over from Selina; Mrs. Patterson and Oya could take over from Selina or Cynthia.

■

**MOTHER ZOE [Zoe I] (the Tunnel of Light and Wisdom):**
*Selina knelt in front of the candles. She was naked and sweating. I listened but could not stop her.*

*"Lend me strength, O my teachers. I must battle mother who let children suffer. I must destroy the evil of Lillian King!"*

*Lillian! What did this witch have against dear Lillian? She had enough on her hands, with her job and her afflicted child. I realized I must call Lillian now, warn her not to leave baby Jennifer, not to leave poor brave blind Taffy.*

*Who to call first? Lord! Lillian needed help. The children needed help! But I did too! Who needed help the most? If this kept on, I realized, I could die.*

■

Mother Zoe took her pulse. The vein jumped under her fingers.

But as she tried to reassure herself, another alter grabbed control. Flat, rasping, the voice dripped fire. Zoe tried to run away, but the voice held her pinned.

"I am Mrs. Patterson. Don't you want to see me?"

"No," said Mother Zoe. A vision formed: the faceless, hooded, black-robed figure. Zoe could see candle flames through the robe. Suddenly the figure turned. And horror—the face was Crystal's.

■

**MOTHER ZOE [Zoe I] (the Tunnel of Light and Wisdom):**
*"Get thee behind me, Satan!"*

*"Lord," I prayed, "save the child." With agony, I realized that poor Taffy might be beyond saving. But Jennifer must stay innocent! Jennifer must be saved!*

*Lillian was such a good Christian. But how could any mother*

*worth her salt leave a blind girl and a baby not yet potty trained
with a sitter? Even when the sitter was me!*

*Lillian is perfect. Her faith. Her hair. And her job? Just what
I should be doing, if I weren't such a nothing! She saves holy
innocents from child abusers!*

Selina interrupts: *"She bad mother! We teach her big,
bad lesson!"*

■

Zoe leaped up and switched on a lamp. The shadows flew
forth. Drumbeats pounded at her heart. It was too much.
She fled. Down the hall, whispering, "Crystal!" Past
Carmine's door, and Davey's. Down the long, long hall.
"Save me, Crystal!"

The bathroom door was locked. She rattled the handle. Inside, water hissed. Crystal was in the shower. Zoe
rested against the cool, smooth door.

"I heard Crystal washing away our love," she says,
"could imagine her white hair and skin glowing in the
steam, and her beautiful blue eyes. For a second, the
ghost of Martin brushed me. I heard him whisper, 'It's
the end, dear heart.'

"I felt Martin dissolve into tears. Now it was just me
against the voices. The voices told me that Lillian didn't
care about her kids. That Taffy could die and she didn't
care. But I knew Lillian cared. She did. She does."

Dial tone. Her ears echoing with the voices, Zoe
punched Dr. Hoff's number. To this day she says Lillian
was perfect. "She just believed Taffy's illness was an
error, and according to Christian Science, she was right."

Finally an operator answered.

Zoe's alters reconstruct the conversation:

"Dr. Hoff's service. Whowez calling?"

"It's Zoe Parry. I need Dr. Hoff! I keep hearing voices
that want me to—"

The operator interrupted crisply. "Yes, Miz Parry,
number, please, and state the last time you've seen
Doctor?"

"Mrs., Mrs. Parry. I've seen her for years. Dr. Hoff
has prayed with me. She's heard the Demon—"

"And what seems to be the problem today?"

"I'm going to do something awful! Tell Dr. Hoff I need her to sign me into the hospital—"

"We will pass your message on to Doctor."

"Please—I need help now!"

"Doctor will call you just as soon as she checks in."

"Mommy!"

Time folded. An eternity passed—or an hour.

"Now, look, ma'am," said the operator. She sounded no longer crisp, but weary. "It's seven ay-em—"

"It is not!" said Zoe indignantly.

"—And I've told Doctor all four times you've called."

"Just get Dr. Hoff."

"Bother her again?" Now the operator got upset. "You wanna get me fired? Forget it, lady."

Zoe couldn't understand why this idiot refused to do her job. "This is the first time I've called! It's an emergency! Why won't you help me? Why!"

Click. Dial tone.

The receiver hung buzzing from her hand. "Four times?" The thought was a shock. (Later, the child alter Mazie would tell me that, in a panic, she'd tried to reach "Mommy" again and again.) Zoe got up and pulled the drapes.

Early daylight flooded in, splashing over the orange couch, the matching easy chair, and dozens of well-tended plants. The lamplight sickened. At five-thirty in February, it is dark out. It was seven. She had lost more time.

What might have happened in one and a half lost hours? Zoe searched for clues. Intent on her innocence, she had already forgotten the blazing candles, the visions of inimical robed figures. Now she saw with fresh horror that her shelves, under the candles, were piled with crude paper figures. She saw a ragged, black-paper woman doll and two paper girls. Selina tells me that the paper dolls symbolized Lillian King and her daughters, and that if Mother Zoe hadn't meddled in a perfectly useful voodoo ceremony and destroyed her candles and cutouts, the whole day might have turned out differently.

"Dear Jesus!" Mother Zoe exclaimed. There was her crucifix, weighted with stones, upside-down. The stones rattled to the floor as Zoe righted the cross and snuffed the candles.

"Whatchew doing, hon'?"

Mother Zoe can see, as though it's happening right now, Crystal in the doorway, fresh in navy slacks, a white blouse, and a soft gray sweater.

"I feel so awful—been up since four."

"Y'mean all night," said Crystal from the doorjamb.

"All night?—I forgot."

"Yep. Lovin'. And plannin' and prayin'."

"Oh, Lord, I've got to rest."

"Rest as much as you like, as long's you don't forget our plan." Zoe looked vacant. "Sometimes you got a brain like a sieve, baby doll. Strip off that rag. Maybe it'll help your recall if we get you dressed."

As Crystal approached, Mother Zoe felt an inner force burst through. Soundlessly she dropped into blackness.

"That better," said Selina, stretching. She felt Mother Zoe's presence yammering, screaming: she pushed it down.

Zoe's body is a tight fit for Selina. She says she is much taller and rounder than Mother Zoe, whom she derides as "a clump of dried-up clay." With her wiry golden hair and glowing red-brown skin, she sees herself as the exact opposite of Zoe's concept of beauty.

"You more yourself now?" asked Crystal.

"I always myself." She hummed a power song as Crystal helped her into the starched, white nurse's uniform, hose, and sensible shoes that Lillian had bought her servant.

"Selina?" Crystal said, cautiously.

Five of Zoe's alters—Mrs. Patterson, Selina, Oya, Mother Zoe, and Martin Caine—had identified themselves to Crystal during their four-year relationship. Apparently Crystal could recognize them.

A multiple's alters each inhabit the body differently. Research has shown that alters measurably affect unconscious processes such as heartbeat, the five senses, muscle tone, allergies, and digestion. Zoe suffers food allergies; Selina does not. Zoe slumps; Selina stands two inches taller. Zoe walks; Selina paces. Selina has sharp, bright eyes. And that out-there accent.

If the 1978 Selina was the same as she is today, either Carmine and Davey must have had to work hard not to notice her or Selina must have hidden when Carmine and Davey were around. I believe that she was there, that she hid from Carmine and came out with children and Crystal, and that Davey (who loses time, just like his mother) worked very hard not to notice her.

"Y'all recollect the plan now, Selina?"

"Silence," commanded Selina. "Respect."

"Sheesh," said Crystal, and shut up.

Selina's hand, in the sheath of the pale pink body, was firm as she wiped off Zoe's makeup.

■

**SELINA (the Tunnel of Hell):** *I say to myself that day, I no need paint. No mask. This the mask, this ghostlike body. I pray, "For once, on this day of power, let me be myself. Give me my own skin, my hair, my amulets crafted well. O my teachers! I pray you! Give me myself!"*

*Nothing happened.*

*"Teachers," I say, "Selina accept this, your test."*

■

The baby-sitter looked the picture of classy, competent domestic help, from her sprayed bouffant hairdo to her leather-clad toes. She got in the Parrys' beige Plymouth Duster and started it. Leaning out the car window, she cautioned Crystal, "Stay here. Wait. I be back soon."

"We sure are gonna teach that Lillian a lesson." Crystal tossed a plastic bag through the open passenger window, then jumped back as the Plymouth zoomed away.

"This my truth, this my way," thought Selina, driving.

"Yes," agreed Cynthia. Her gold hair sparkled with electricity; her eyes held so much power today, she says, they could kill. She knew Selina could see her only as a dim and faraway vision, but she enjoyed leaking warnings. "But I have the power. Today we do things Wicca's way."

Cynthia remembers a jolt of shock then, as though someone were smiling nastily at her. And Mrs. Patterson boasts, interrupting Cynthia on tape, "They thought my name, Mrs. Patterson, was just a label for fear. Well, guess again." She fondled certain objects, ceremonial objects, through the thin plastic bag next to her thigh. "Today we save Thy child," said Mrs. Patterson. "For Thee!"

The sun burst through the clouds. The woman—Selina again—squinted as she drove north.

■

**SELINA (the Tunnel of Hell):** *Yellow light strong today. Cars move slow. Time move slow. Bird fly slow, ocean wave crash slow on beach. Is good. There much time for ceremony with child.*

■

"Stupid Selina," interrupts Cynthia. "Time is slow because I have made it slow." She explains that during the second stretch of lost time, from five-thirty to seven A.M., she'd performed magic of her own. Unlike Selina's magic, aimed at people, this had been a sun ceremony, aimed at time itself.

■

**CYNTHIA [The Blonde] (the Tunnel of Hell):** *I spelled forgetfulness on the body. Then I went outside. There I found a stone perfectly round, perfectly white. Uttering words Isis had taught me in another lifetime, I climbed up on the swing and plunged the stone in the fork of the tree. Immediately the sun rose. Its light grew hot and thick. The swing broke with a loud crack, and I fell. "You try to prevent my work," I challenged the evil ones. "But my spell will hold."*

■

Mrs. Patterson snickered, watching Cynthia. So Cynthia thought she was so powerful! She laughed, until Cynthia dissolved, and the body's heart seized up in violent, irregular rhythms. Then Mrs. Patterson stopped laughing. It wouldn't do to destroy the body, she decided, until it had stolen the child.

Zoe's car turned off into the Kings' private road. Rows of eucalyptus trees made a whispering green tunnel.

At the end of the road the trees opened out into air. The driver slowed as she spotted an eagle floating high above.

Quartz chips crackled under the tires as the car pulled into the Kings' driveway. The driver studied the house. Set in a beautifully landscaped garden, built of old brick, Casa Paloma projected age and peace. Casa Paloma was a liar.

Snatching the plastic bag, Zoe slammed the car door and hurried up the walk.

■

**SELINA (the Tunnel of Hell):** *The haze thickens. It yellows the flowers and the windows. There are evil faces in the windows. I pray to gods and goddesses, don't let bad spirits come alive.*

■

Selina spat, let herself in with Zoe's key.

The Kings' house was dark and cool. Persian rugs stretched past antiques from a hundred countries.

She set down the bag. Passing the living room, she stood at the foot of the grand staircase. From the depths of the house came the ticking of clocks and the loud, jolly music of cartoons. From upstairs, no sounds. In the family room, Jennifer laughed. Deep within an animal-like alter growled.

"Zoe—is that you?"

Zoe jumped. A trim brunette swept elegantly downstairs.

"Zoe, please announce yourself when you come in. I'm so jumpy I'm liable to call the police!"

"Sorry, missus."

"Now, dear, must I beg you to call me 'Lillian'? Aren't we friends?"

"Two year we meet," said Lillian's servant.

"My dear, you're talking hoarsely. Are you ill?"

Lillian came the rest of the way downstairs and felt her servant's forehead; her servant twisted away. "I fix food."

"Good," Lillian agreed, then changed the conversation to recent events. "George and I are so happy the dog was returned."

Selina was not happy, but smiled as Lillian went on.

Two days ago, all the Kings' downstairs windows had been smashed. Allie, their golden retriever, had been dognapped. Lillian had called the police. The dog had then been returned. Newspaper articles, the next day, would report these as mysteries. Neither the Kings nor Zoc's weak surface self, nor any of the reporters, realized that Crystal had smashed the windows or that the alter Selina had dognapped Allie or, indeed, that there was anything going on but vandalism.

■

**SELINA (the Tunnel of Hell):** *Person who return dog very stupid. Allie agree to die. This was Mother Goddess Oya's plan to save the children. In times like these there must be a sacrifice—to open the door between the worlds.*

*Now a child might have to die. How to save the child, while keeping Oya's trust? Oya is a terrible one to cross! When Oya want sacrifice, she get!*

*Lillian King stupid, like all fanatics. Bad prayers do not fix brain tumor. Dry prayings to pale God no can save real child! I know! I see!*

*Child is animal, red with life. White with power. Child need power animal, red-as-blood, white-as-flame, black-as-mud. Child need Selina's Goddess to be saved!*

■

"George and I just want to thank you for finding Allie."

The woman's eyes narrowed. "I?" Up to this moment, she'd been unaware that an alter had returned the dog.

Lillian talked on. "Now, I know your aunt handles your schedule. Would she object if you stay till eight tonight?"

Crystal and Zoe had lied about their relationship to Lillian, too. This enabled Zoe, who couldn't bear separations, to bring "Aunt" Crystal to work. Crystal spent the hours reading Charles Dickens. She had just finished *Martin Chuzzlewit*.

The baby-sitter frowned. "Eight?"

"Dear, it's the earliest I can get back. Now, will you call your aunt Crystal, or should I?"

Mother Zoe weakly surfaced for a moment. She said, "Oh, Lillian, I don't know if I'd be up to it. You know I just got out of the hospital—"

"You'll be fine," said Lillian. "You've had a good rest and, dear"—she patted her servant, with whom she'd had many spiritual discussions—"you know I believe in your health." Belief is a tenet of Christian Science: healthy belief equals godliness. "I do appreciate your struggle, and also, how very much you need the money."

"I feel very weak."

"You are not. You are strong. Down in the depths where the Good Lord sees you."

"I do believe."

"I know you do, dear, because all else is error."

Christian Science *treatments* are silent, powerful prayers. The object of Zoe's regular treatments of Taffy was to dispel (unsee) the essential misinterpretation (error) which Lillian thought caused Taffy's brain tumor and her blindness. A Christian Science *practitioner* is not just a faith healer, but one who rejects matter and materialism—the earthly world—for God.

"Dear Zoe, I so appreciate the way you treat Taffy. The error is rooted so strongly, sometimes even my belief wavers. Oh, Zoe"—Lillian was sobbing—"it's so hard day after day to clear your mind when it's your own child's error you're trying to unsee!"

Zoe hugged Lillian. "Are sin, disease, and death

real?" She was quoting Mary Baker Eddy, the founder of Christian Science.

"No!" Lillian smiled. "Thank you so much, dear." Composing herself, she pulled vitamin-shake mix and fruit from the refrigerator.

"I fix," offered her servant.

"No, do the children's breakfast." Lillian then prepared her shake as the baby-sitter filled the mugs and bowls.

"Now, if Taffy gets cranky, I want you to call Joan Halliday. Weak as you feel, I couldn't ask you to do a treatment."

■

**MOTHER ZOE [Zoe I] (the Tunnel of Light and Wisdom):** *It's really difficult to work for Mrs. King. She expects me at eight-thirty and doesn't return till night. I have to keep the whole house clean, the children happy. I also work Saturday nights. I don't want to, but can't say no. She's real nice, but I'm scared. I have to do what she says.*

*How Taffy screams. I wish I could give her aspirin. Listening to the screaming, even Jennifer starts to cry. She's only a baby and needs a lot of attention. I hold Taffy's hand and try to quiet Jennifer and tell Taffy she's God's Perfect Child and he didn't make a sick child, so she can't be sick. I tell her, again and again, the Scientific Statement of Being. I say, "This tumor is a false belief, an artifact of your mother's fears."*

*She keeps screaming, and I have to call Joan Halliday, the CS practitioner. Joan prays and calls Lillian, and from their offices, they both pray. Meanwhile I'm here.*

*When everything's quiet, Lillian calls. "That's why I like you, 'cause you have such deep knowledge of Christian Science." And my entire body begins to shake.*

■

**SELINA (the Tunnel of Hell):** *When you do not help a child, do not call healer, that is BAD! So take child away. Make the mother suffer! You ask why I take baby instead of the child in pain? The baby is helpless! Innocent. I like the baby. So we took.*

◾

All children in pain, external or internal, present, past, or future, are the same to Zoe. The outer children, Taffy and Jennifer, were somehow herself. It thus seemed logical to Selina to strengthen the innocent child at the expense of the bad mother. If past, present, and future were one, then taking this baby would prevent the ruination of baby Zoe. As a baby, Selina knew, Zoe hadn't been saved: today, February 3, 1978, perhaps she would.

◾

"Ooops," said Lillian, glancing at her watch. She set down her drink. "Gotta go. I'm late. Have a nice day."

"Good-bye, missus," said her servant.

Far away, the front door slammed. The children wandered into the kitchen. Taffy moved uncertainly because of her new blindness. Selina's heart expanded. "Beautiful children," said Selina, as Jennifer ran to her.

Alone, Taffy wailed. "Jennifer, wait up!"

"I here!" said Jennifer, hugging Selina. Her red-brown curls glinted in the light.

"Where?" said Taffy. Groping, she bumped her head on the table; sat. "Oya—I hurt myself!"

If Zoe's alters remember this correctly, Taffy's calling her baby-sitter Oya has substantial implications. High Priestess Oya must have come out often at the Kings'.

"Oya?" Selina whispered. She knew of only one Oya: the African mother goddess. She concluded that the goddess herself must have visited this house, in this body. That explained the feeling of having been possessed. Joy overcame Selina. Oya had been here! Not the Devil after all!

The baby-sitter picked up Taffy and embraced her, alongside Jennifer, carefully avoiding the shunt in Taffy's dark, silky hair. This was an implanted tube from which doctors could drain the constantly accumulating fluid. To allow Taffy time to correct her error, Lillian had, after much soul-searching, approved the shunt. Her daughter would have died without it.

Many of Zoe's alters felt that Lillian didn't wash Taffy's hair, didn't stay home, because Lillian was afraid of her own error, as materialized in the objectionable, painful, lifesaving shunt. Human pain, career demands—these they judged trivial.

Now, Selina repeated to herself, this pain must stop. The bad mother must learn the error of her ways.

The phone rang and she answered it.

"King house," she said.

"God's sake, baby doll, where are you?" hissed Crystal.

"Mrs. King just leave," she responded. "She late."

"Well, y'all gonna get that little thing on over here, or leave me to sit around playing with myself?"

"*Shh*, I bring," came the answer. "Soon. Wait. Calm self. I bring when sun at top of sky."

"Y'know y'all can be some kind of a—"

Gently, Selina hung up the phone.

Zoe says she heard the accented voice, faintly, and felt her skin crawl with the thought that what humans begin, Satan often finishes.

Dusting the front hall, Selina picked up Crystal's plastic bag and put it by the stairs. Then entering the family room, she summoned Taffy. "We play game now."

"With Jennifer?" Taffy said a little distrustfully.

"No. You and me. We play tea party."

This was what Taffy liked to do more than anything.

"Tea party. With doll for guest."

Upstairs, the baby-sitter filled her arms with dolls and led Taffy into George King's closet, which was roughly the size of an average walk-through kitchen. A hundred suits lined the walls, color-coordinated with rows of matching pressed shirts and ties. In front of the full-length mirror in which Mr. King admired himself daily, the sitter pulled out boxes for chairs and tables and covered them with scarves. She seated the dolls.

Selina patted Taffy. "I leave now. Be good. Door not locked, but you stay here."

"Okay," answered Taffy, groping for and picking up

a plastic teacup. Her sitter shut the door, leaving the blind child in blackness. Taffy's voice sounded little and lonely as she asked, "Aren't you going to play, too?"

A moment later, the sitter reopened the door, clicked on the light, and kissed the child gently. Taffy repeated, "Oya, are you going to play?"

"Maybe soon. Stay here. Not move." The sitter left, closing but not locking the door.

Any observer might have told the competent-looking woman in the nurse's uniform that leaving a blind child alone in a closet, never mind in a huge house, was not a good idea. But there was no observer. Mrs. Patterson twisted Selina's already unusual judgments: Taffy seemed content. Selina even recollected, "Little Mazie like being in closet, to pray."

Moving like a robot under remote control, Selina dressed Jennifer in a fresh diaper, warm clothing, and a matching jacket, got the baby's car seat, bundled it and Jennifer into her car, and drove off.

Under great stress, some of a multiple's alters can seem to others to be outside the body. If you had been driving on the Flagg Highway next to the Duster that day in 1978, you might have seen the driver taking turns talking to herself and to the baby in an infant seat next to her.

But inside the car, this is how it seemed to Zoe's system: While Selina steered—Jennifer had fallen asleep—in the backseat materialized Rona, a lank-haired, preadolescent waif in denim jeans. Her white shirt was puffed at the waist to simulate pregnancy.

■

**RONA [*the Waif*] (the Tunnel of Waiting and Secrets):** *I am outside the body. Lost. The yellow haze is so thick I can hardly see. What is Jennifer doing here? The car turns off the highway, heading for Zoe's house.*

*Crystal stands on the curb, spitting mad, checking her watch. As we pull up, she yanks open the car door. "Y'all better stick to the plan now, or you'll spoil ever'thang." Selina answers calm down or she be the one to ruin plan.*

*Scowling, Crystal gets in and sits down. I don't say hello. She scares me. I hunch up and try to make myself invisible. As we drive off, Crystal laughs. "We sure gonna show boss-lady which end is up!" I never like it when Crystal talks that way.*

■

Five minutes later, the Duster swung into the carport of the Hacienda Gardens, whose sign proclaimed it "Florida's Family Resort." The ground was muddied by the recent rain. In front, four cacti lay, flattened like road kill. The "gardens" consisted of one yard-square patch of dichondra. The "hacienda" was a gray shed, faintly reminiscent of a chicken house, containing fourteen *salas* to rent by the hour. "Florida's Family Resort." Baby Jennifer's new home.

■

**RONA [*the Waif*] (the Tunnel of Waiting and Secrets):** *All of a sudden Cynthia, the Blonde, takes control. At the time, none of us understands Cynthia. She seems totally crazy and evil. We call her Animal or Eyes, because she only speaks in growls and because of her piercing gaze. She glares at me, then goes into the office to register.*

■

Later, the Hacienda's manager would tell the police that the blonde woman could barely walk, let alone sign in—she seemed to be in another world.

■

**RONA [*the Waif*] (the Tunnel of Waiting and Secrets):** *Now I'm at the open door to room 13. Inside, I can see Jennifer asleep on the bed with her thumb in her mouth, under a painting of Mexican hat dancers. Crystal swats mosquitoes with the Bible.*

*Crystal strips off her sweater and uses it to cover the baby. "You scat, now," she tells me. "We'll be fine. Call me when the bitch gets home."*

*I say I don't want to do the plan now.*

*"You tryin' to chicken out? Well, you can't."*

*"I never—"*

*"You sure did. So you-all just hear me and listen to me good. We keep Jennifer till Lillian knuckles under!*

*"Now, I'm like to starve from worryin' and waitin'. You just go fetch me some lunch,"* stormed Crystal.

*Suddenly the yellow dust drags me back to the car.*

■

If you'd been out that afternoon on the highway, you might have cursed the Duster whose driver seemed drunk—honking, erratically weaving through traffic. Once the car nearly drove into the sea! Well, perhaps the woman in the white nurse's uniform was going to some emergency. She was certainly driving as though possessed.

On the road back up to Casa Paloma, Selina found herself aware and driving again. This time, though she once again felt she had lost time and had been possessed, she was no longer certain that the mother goddess Oya had been the one doing the possessing. After the actual kidnapping, she was almost certain that demons were trying to possess her—and perhaps had done so already.

■

**SELINA (the Tunnel of Hell):** *At front door, suddenly I am under attack by demons. Yellow swirls around me, rising in a choking dust. The faces in the windows come alive. They are evil spirits in the windows. I know they will try to get me. I must break glass, let spirits out. I go get broom from garage and break windows.*

*But attack not stop. Spirits have trick me. They sweep into body—all around. I run to house. In kitchen, I get knife to protect self and Taffy. Too late I remember the words of my teacher. "Be wise with power, or it turn on you."*

*The knife clatter to the floor. I have been fool. I have allow enemy to enter. Today the power, it turn on me.*

■

With that, Selina felt herself black out. Another alter, one of the strongest Catholics in the system—today she's an actual lay nun in the Third Order of Franciscans—felt herself burst into consciousness, her crucifix almost burning on her neck.

■

**SISTER ZOE ANN (the Tunnel of Light and Wisdom):** *I was suddenly out, fumbling through the phone book.*

*From inside came a vicious laugh. "Go ahead. Call your priest. He has no power over me!"*

*I groaned. It was true! You cannot imagine my agony. Damned. Damned.*

*"Get thee behind me, Satan!" I cried. And that laugh . . .*

*Voices accused me of the vilest deeds. I couldn't deny them. I was damned.*

*The voices formed into a vague shape. Dear Lord, it looked like Crystal. "Who are you?" I whispered.*

*"Call me Mrs. Patterson, my dear," it mocked. "For I have been weaving this pattern for a long, long time!"*

*"What do you want?"*

*"The child!"*

*"Hail, Mary, full of grace," I prayed.*

*"Go ahead! Say your prayers. Call your priest! I'll take you both to hell with me!" A black hand whizzed past my eyes. It ripped the phone right off the wall. I ducked. The phone narrowly missed my head and smashed into Lillian's wallpaper.*

*Voices chanted. Shadows formed. I crossed myself. But horror—the shadows solidified into zombies. Burning like ice. Cold as the grave. Three pairs of glazed white eyes stared at my body. Three times ten fingers fumbled for my soul. The coldness clutched my heart. My hands dropped. I screamed. That is the last thing I remember.*

■

Selina was back, but it was a defeated Selina.

■

**SELINA (the Tunnel of Hell):** *I now sitting on kitchen floor. I have no clothes on. Nothing. I am naked, the way I came into the world. I feel oh, so tired. There is a hole in wall. Telephone is smashed to bits. Zoe's clothes are crumpled in a pile. The* *dress they make her wear, the shoes. So weak I am. I must have let my mind get weak, else how could Demon take it over?*

*I look up and see Demon in corner. She burns. She watch me. Her eyes red dots. She lift her hands and open them. There is the flame of my life, burning low. She smile. And then she blow flame out.*

∎

Now Mrs. Patterson opened the plastic bag, the bag she had brought to the Kings' house that morning. Nestled within were a wig and two thick coils of rope.

The naked woman crammed the blond hair over her own and slammed out into the garden.

∎

**RONA [the Waif] (the Tunnel of Waiting and Secrets):** *Now I float away. But then I look back. Stupid.*

*Cynthia stands in the roses. Her legs are wide apart and her hands stretched up to the sun. Her hair crackles, like she's gotten a jolt of electricity. She howls, "Come and do me, Satan! Fill me with your child!" Her womb glows golden through the shell of her skin. A bolt of yellow light comes down from heaven. A bolt of blue light comes up from hell. They meet within in her womb. Thunder cracks. I can see the baby, deep within, start to stir with evil power.*

*Cynthia trembles. She is sweating. She bites her arms and gouges long wounds in her belly.*

*But suddenly Cynthia sniffs deep. She can smell me! Furiously, she charges. Midair, she changes into the Devil! He comes straight at me, hissing with his snake tongue. "You dare to defy me?" I turn tail. Dash back to the house, with the Devil at my heels.*

∎

Cynthia rampaged naked through the house, smashing mirrors.

According to Zoe May, as a child Zoe would smash mirrors when she was angry. When it was all over, her mother would ask, "What possessed you, to do such a thing?"

Her father would say, "The Devil"—and open his Bible.

■

The alters were switching rapidly now. None could stay in possession of the body for more than a few moments. Any such consistency was prevented by a wash of conflicting emotions: triumph, rage, terror, guilt. Some of the alters must have been aware of the blind child still shut away in the closet, no matter how safe other alters insisted she was. Other alters must have wondered what was going to happen to Zoe, now that she and Crystal had taken Jennifer. Still other alters must have dreaded internal retribution even more than they feared being found out by the police. The alters in Zoe's system are not stupid, and they know on some level that what half the system does has to be answered for by the other half.

■

**RONA [the Waif] (the Tunnel of Waiting and Secrets):** *The green bathroom. There it's safe. I run upstairs. Taffy's bathroom is like a garden, with flowered walls, potted plants, and pretty smells. I used to sit there and pretend that Taffy's house was mine.*

*I look into the mirror. My eyes are big. Tears stream down, wetting my hair. I'm a ratty mess. In the mirror I see people who followed me in. Cynthia. Selina. Naked. Both possessed. And zombies. One is Henry Owens.*

■

Henry Owens had been an orderly at the mental hospital where Zoe had first met Crystal, in 1971. Zoe'd had sex with Owens as early as seven years before. Later, Crystal and Mrs. Patterson had brought Owens into the coven.

Now that the kidnapping was over—Zoe says she knew Jennifer would be safe with Crystal—Taffy's crying suddenly penetrated into Zoe's befuddled awareness. Zoe does not know for how long Taffy had been crying. She wants to believe that the child felt safe, that she wasn't terrified. With all her heart, Zoe wants to believe that she and all her system's alters have done everything they've done for good purposes. Zoe adores children and would do anything she could to prevent child abuse anywhere and at any time.

■

**MOTHER ZOE [Zoe I] (the Tunnel of Light and Wisdom):**
*"Oh, honey, I'm coming!" I whisper.*

*I rush to the closet. Tell Taffy she's been very, very good. While I hug her, I hear chanting and see coppery hands touching Taffy's eyes. Taffy shrinks back.*

*"It sounds like monsters!"*

*"You're safe. No one can get you."*

*Safe? There's a sudden, blinding blow on my face. I stagger, trying not to scream.*

*"I'm scared!" whimpers Taffy.*

*"You'll be fine, " I say. I mustn't terrify the child.*

■

Selina says that she gathered her own strength, in one final burst of energy, in order to magically heal Taffy of her blindness.

■

**SELINA (the Tunnel of Hell):** *I go in closet with Mother Zoe. I see Taffy. Start to perform ritual to free her eyes, to let her see. And then I feel something strange! It feels first like an animal. Not my power animal. Different. Cold. Is fear. Mother Zoe and Rona, they hold on to Taffy. I stand in the middle. I feel Demon behind me. I want to protect.*

*But Demon overpower me and Cynthia, too. Her face is contorted. The green eyes turn red and blaze dark, dark as the night! Snarling and growling, a horrible voice says it is going to take Taffy, going to take Mother Zoe; we're going to take all the children and give them to Satan.*

■

From outside, you would have seen a sweating, naked woman trying to hold a child who was backing away from her, straining with her freshly blind eyes to see what was going on. The baby-sitter alternately reassured the child and growled at her. Sweat poured down her body. She had a golden wig half on, half off, and one hand held ropes. Intermittently she crossed herself and yelled, "Get thee behind me, Satan!" The child was shaking her head no, backing into her father's suits, and whispering, "Mommy!"

■

**SELINA (the Tunnel of Hell):** *There is a battle then! Mother Zoe is thrown against door. Hard she is thrown. Zoe thrown, too! Is many people. Children. Demon. Calls itself Patterson. It is Legion. It is Evil. It is many, one. The closet become cold. Foul odor come. Not like anything I smell before. I have been in many ceremony. This different. This thing comes out of the bowels of hell.*

■

This Demon wreaked its fury on Zoe.

■

**RONA [the Waif] (the Tunnel of Waiting and Secrets):** *The Demon doesn't touch Taffy, but it keeps hitting Mother Zoe. Real hard, in the face. And it bites her on the arm, again and again. Blood runs down the body. Then the body gets picked up and thrown. "You dare . . . rrrrRRRRR!" growls the Demon, and leaps. The body and mind shatter and there we all are, running, running to get away, climbing up the walls, hiding, struggling to reach the door, as the Demon enters the wound within.*

■

Here, during the telling, Zoe's entire tunnel structure changes. Selina leaves the Tunnel of Hell and joins herself now with Black Wolf, an alter who sees herself as an ancient, Native American shaman.

All over the house the clocks chimed three. In the bedroom, you would have heard the noises stop. You would have seen George King's closet door open and the naked baby-sitter, streaked with blood, come out. She moved robotically. Shutting the door, she sat, not feeling the carpet's luxurious softness against her bare bottom. She transferred the two ropes to the other hand, opened her legs, and lay the ropes beside her.

The baby-sitter's shoulders jerked up and back. Her mouth opened in a silent scream.

■

**MARIE MARTIN (the Tunnel of Watchers):** *Now Cynthia and Selina are prisoners. Mrs. Patterson stands behind them with one hand on Cynthia's right shoulder, the other on Selina's left.*

*I float out of the body and hover near the ceiling. Everything is very bright. The air smells rank. Selina and Cynthia's faces freeze. Mrs. Patterson chants to Satan. Her legs open wide. Under her, between Cynthia and Selina, now appears little Zoe, five, who we all call Mazie.*

*"Neeeya, nyanyanya . . . Here is the child!" She hungrily licks the lips, which look today like Crystal's. Suddenly the lips peel away to reveal huge yellow teeth at the center of a pointed black beard.*

*"Save the child!" call the weak ones. "Here she is," call others.*

*The Demon crushes them. Chuckles. His beard wags up and down. Above Mazie's head, his penis stirs. His round black eyes gaze down at her.*

*From the closet, I hear the cries of Taffy. In between the Demon's legs Mazie sits frozen with fear. He touches her hair. "Lie down."*

*Suddenly Mazie darts up for the door. The Demon is faster. He lifts his hands. That is all he has to do. Calmly, Selina and Cynthia stand and corner Mazie. Selina holds her. Cynthia slaps her. Then they bind her hand and foot with the rope.*

■

The naked, bruised woman twisted her body into an almost impossible position. It takes superhuman force and coordination to tie one's feet and then, tightly, one's hands. These ropes were so tight they burned lines into the skin. The woman's flesh began to swell. That night, the police would have to cut into her flesh, to free her.

**SELINA/BLACK WOLF (the Tunnel of Watchers):** *Demon tie Mazie. Strong, much stronger than Cynthia or I. He tie our minds as well. Cynthia is numb. I am numb. Mazie's circulation is cut off. She feel much pain in hands and wrists and ankles. More pain in mind.*

"Mommy," wailed the woman. "Mama . . ."

**MARIE MARTIN (the Tunnel of Watchers):** *Now Selina and Cynthia vanish. The Demon vanishes. And Mazie's body grows. It is seven years old, then ten, then twelve. Breasts sprout. Beyond terror, her eyes rolling back in her head, Mazie becomes Mother Zoe—Oya's sacrifice.*

*The harsh voice of the mother goddess comes from the air. "You must die, to open the door between the worlds."*

Over the past few months, Zoe's internal chaos had built up unbearably. Now, says the high priestess Oya, she intended to restore the balance.

The real little girl, Taffy, sobbed in the closet.

Zoe had been just Taffy's age when she'd been raped for the first time. All her inner pain and rage now coalesced: revivifying her memories, she acted out the rape. To this day, Zoe is not sure exactly what happened—what an outside observer would have seen as real. But on one thing we can all agree: her pain.

**MARIE MARTIN (the Tunnel of Watchers):** *Downstairs, a door slams. Mazie jerks rigid against her bonds. Footsteps come up the stairs—thud, thud. The footsteps pause outside the door of the master bedroom. Then suddenly, the door crashes open.*

*There in the doorway is a round black man with a thin*

*mustache, naked except for round eyeglasses. It is Henry Owens. The man from the coven meetings. The high priest.*

Though the surface self did not know this, according to other alters, including Rona, Owens had sexually used Zoe's body many times at the mental hospital, in the most degrading ways. To control Owens, the Oya personality had, with primitive logic, invited him into the coven as the high priest.

Zoe has an extremely hazy memory that before the last meeting of some coven, a blonde woman had told Henry Owens about the Kings, about all the fancy jewelry and the expensive art. "Great," she vaguely remembers Owens saying. Apparently he had decided to chloroform and rape Lillian King and burglarize the house. Apparently Zoe begged him not to. Now her conscience took on Owens's form.

**MARIE MARTIN (the Tunnel of Watchers):** *Henry kneels to check the ropes, and laughs. Mazie looks up. In his glasses jiggle twin reflections of her face. As he approaches, the child gags on his breath.*

*Suddenly, he lunges, grabs Mazie's hands in one of his, and flings them over her head. With the other hand he yanks the rope off her feet. Pushing the child's legs open, he lowers his head and, with his long tongue, opens her crotch. He licks, trying to penetrate the tight, resistant openings.*

*Bored, he shoves two fingers inside the child's vagina. She screams.*

*Bam! Henry Owens slaps her, hard. "Open your legs."*

*"No."*

*With his fingernails, he rips her stomach.*

*"I'm gonna get a little."*

*"No no no."*

*He spits in her face. "If you don't open your legs, I'm gonna break your legs." He shoves her open and rams himself in.*

To a multiple personality, rape seems eternal, as though it happens now and now and now. Zoe's unacknowledged memories replayed themselves as she both kidnapped, and became, a child.

Had you been in the Kings' master bedroom, you might have seen a woman, alone, writhing on the floor, and heard only silence from the closet.

■

**MARIE MARTIN (the Tunnel of Watchers):** *He jams it in and out, in and out. She goes limp. He moans and groans and growls. The seed goes in, as if someone had put a hose up in her and all of a sudden turned the warm water on. It tears her to pieces. Her insides are on fire. And he looks down and calls her "Bitch!" and "Whore!"*

*Henry stands up and shakes what's left of the fluid onto the woman's and the child's body. They look dead. The woman's eyes open. And they're just staring.*

*Henry walks into the bathroom, takes one of Lillian's white washcloths, puts soap on it, and cleans his penis. And he puts his T-shirt on, his black pants, his shoes and socks. He's ugly. He looks in the mirror and smiles at himself. He walks down the hall and down the stairs and the door slams.*

■

"Mrs. Parry?" said a petite brunette whose badge identified her as Deputy Lori Skye. Flashbulbs popped. As a police photographer took closeups of the ropes, Deputy Skye tapped her on the shoulder. "Mrs. Parry? Can you speak?"

Police officers and firefighters had crowded into the Kings' bedroom, hunting for the baby. They stared at the nude, filthy baby-sitter tied up on the floor, her blonde wig sprawled next to her like a dead animal.

Suddenly Zoe's mother, Zoe May Bryant, rushed in. "Zoe!" she gasped, rushing to her daughter. "What are you willywagging at?" she scolded the officials. "Cover her up!"

Zoe lay there like a deflated balloon, like someone who's just given birth. Skye took the paramedics' scissors, and cut the cords from the victim's flesh. The victim whimpered as blood began to flow back into the rope burns.

Zoe May yanked off the silk bedspread and used it to wrap up her daughter. "You should be ashamed!" she said to no one in particular.

She tapped her daughter. "Honey. Did a man—?"

According to her mother, patting was the most physical attention she ever gave to Zoe. Zoe's eyelids flickered up and down—a "yes" response.

"They violated my daughter!" whimpered Zoe May.

"What did he look like, miss?" said Deputy Skye.

The dry lips parted and Zoe whispered. "Three of them . . . One blindfolded and tied me, one chloroformed me . . . and one . . . did it." And that was all they could get from her.

As paramedics brought the stretcher downstairs, Zoe called to Taffy. "Taffy, Taffy, are you all right?" She seemed to be raving. The paramedics exchanged glances. The stretcher went outside with a lift and a slam.

Outside there was a crowd. Police dogs, firefighters in two red engines. An ambulance. Even a search helicopter. On a multiband radio, the police directed Explorer Scouts to search the local playgrounds. Through the sound of beating helicopter blades, a loudspeaker broadcast the missing child's description. Later, army reserves were called in to aid with the search. The newspapers published a photo of the missing child.

Suddenly George King's face hung above the stretcher. He had just found Taffy in the closet; she clung silently to his side. "Zoe, please? Where's my other daughter?"

■

"There's no evidence of rape," said Sheriff Billy Brownstein to Deputy Lori Skye. They were in the emergency room with Zoe Parry.

"How about chloroform?" Deputy Skye asked.

"No evidence of that, either."

"How about the wounds, the bruises?"

"Coulda been self-inflicted."

Lori Skye asked Zoe again, "Where's Jennifer?" Four hours later in the Brooke sheriff's station Skye's face was gray and desperate.

Brownstein's was sly and meaty. "If you tell, we could maybe get you a lesser charge. Less bail for your folks."

The child alters burst forth. "Mommy!"

"She's pissed herself." Deputy Skye looked disgusted.

"Goddamnit, lady, where's the child?"

"Let me try." This new voice belonged to Dr. Magda Hoff, who'd just walked in waving a large yellow pass. With her smooth black haircut and red wool suit, her metal glasses and her bluff manner, Hoff looked as though she could get information from anyone. She'd been trying to return Zoe's calls all day. It wasn't until Carmine had returned from work—he'd been summoned back by Mrs. Bryant—that he'd picked up the phone. Carmine had sent her to the police station. He did not come to the station himself. He was busy, he told Zoe later, taking care of Davey and fending off reporters.

■

**ZOE 2 (the Tunnel of Light and Wisdom):** *I tell Magda, Mommy, I so glad you here. I need to go poopie real bad, and this bad lady won't let me!*

*But Mommy Magda turn out as mean as the others. She take me to bathroom. But then she take me back to mean man and woman. They ask me and ask me about Jennifer. I don't know. I want my ba-ba. I wanna go night-night. I cry.*

■

"How did they find Jennifer?" I ask Zoe Parry, on April 26, 1992.

"They didn't," answers Zoe. "All those searchers, they couldn't find a child right under their nose. At two in the morning, after the body had been up for forty-eight hours, Beth popped out. Little Beth loves to tell the truth."

Little Beth saw herself in 1978 as nine years old, thin,

earnest, and honest. Today she sees herself as in her early twenties, a champion of truth who acts as a teacher and spirit guide to Zoe's system.

In a high, serious voice, Little Beth told Skye and Brownstein about the Hacienda Gardens. She gave explicit instructions on how to get there. "Bring something to eat," she added. "They're probably very, very hungry."

■

**RONA [the Waif] (the Tunnel of Waiting and Secrets):** *Down the hall outside the room, a man was crying from joy. The door was open, with officers running in and out. They read me my rights. And out the doorway, I could see.*

*Crystal was pushed down the hall, screaming. I tried to say hi, but the deputies said, "No talking."*

*Down the hall, Lillian held out her arms, and Billy Brownstein handed her Jennifer. Jennifer reached up and hugged her mother. Lillian stroked her. George King shook Billy Brownstein's hand and patted him on the back.*

*I tried to run to Lillian. I was so glad they'd found Jennifer!*

*Deputy Skye grabbed me. "Stay put." I told her let me hug Lillian, and she said I'm nothing better than a murderer.*

*"Honey, that lady will never wanna talk to you again."*

*Then she whipped out handcuffs and slapped them on.*

■

Zoe wailed, high and soft. "Wanna go night-night."

"I'll bet," snorted Lori Skye.

At four A.M., almost exactly one day after Crystal and Zoe had made love for the last time, they were marched up a concrete walk. A gate slammed behind them. Crystal and Zoe entered what we'll call Anderson Prison.

■

**MAZIE 5 (the Tunnel of Light and Wisdom):** *In the holding cell a huge woman grabbed me. I was crying. She held me. Her breath was awful, rotting. "Shut up before I shut you up."*

*I shut up. "Now gimme the jacket. I cold."*

*I handed her the jacket.*

*"You lucky, bitch. Later I want more."*

*I peed again.*

*"So what, so you pissed. You think you impress me? You just sit still and shut up. Stinkin' bitch."*

<br>

Zoe sat real still, just like the big woman told her, even when the woman stole her breakfast. She watched as the woman ate it up.

"Whatchew staring at?" said the woman. "Close your eyes and shut up like I told you."

Zoe succeeded in this so well that soon she was catatonic. She stayed still and shut up when they carried her from the holding cell. She stayed still and shut up—say her child alters—when they stripped her for the body search and when they pushed the body into the shower and hosed it off. She stayed still and shut up when they shoved their fingers into her vagina, routinely searching for drugs. She could not stay still and shut up a few hours later, when her heart medications and tranquilizers wore off and she went into acute withdrawal. Zoe Parry began to scream.

By February 8, after five days of questioning and withdrawal, Zoe's body was twisted into a knot, her head and arm twisted to one side. She had lost ten pounds.

"Help me, help me," her child alters whimper.

"Did they help you?" I asked Zoe.

"The people said something. I couldn't understand what anyone was saying. Even the voices. Especially them. They were still there, talking in a way I couldn't make out.

"No, nobody helped me. Nobody knew how. And my father didn't even visit."

<br>

Dr. Gwynn Fischer, Zoe's therapist in 1992, traces the demonic possession to Zoe's early anger that had no words, only growls—anger at her mother and herself. She tells me that Zoe's account is sketchy and distorted, that we will never know what really happened on February 3, 1978.

I look over my newspaper clippings, the police reports, Zoe's records of a hundred psychiatric sessions, and two hundred pages of transcripts. I decide, it doesn't matter. What Zoe described is real enough. Perhaps it's sixty percent of what was and forty percent of what might have been: but it's one hundred percent of what it's like to have undiagnosed MPD.

# Zoe Parry: Inner Structure

April 1992
*Discussing Dr. Sidney Altman.*
*72 Personalities + 8 acknowledged other "Dark Ones" = 80.*
*8 Tunnels.*
*Each personality is present in one tunnel only.*

The Tunnel of
Watchers

The Tunnel of
Light and
Wisdom

The Tunnel of
Waiting and
Secrets

The Tunnel of
Zoe of Dreams

The Tunnel of
Darkness and
Death

**CAVE
OPENING**

The Tunnel of
Lost Souls

The Tunnel of
Hell

The Tunnel of
Limbo

# Zoe Parry: Inner Structure

*June 1992.*
*Discussing Dr. Sidney Altman.*
*Approximately 92 personalities.*
*8 Tunnels.*
*1 personality—Selina—present in all the tunnels;*
*the others are each present in one tunnel only.*

The Tunnel of
Watching and
Secrets

The Tunnel of
Light

The Tunnel of
the Lost and
Blind

The Tunnel of
Faraway Dreams

The Tunnel of
Walk-ins and
Lost Souls

**FLOATING
ENTRANCE**

The Tunnel of
Dreams

The Tunnel of
Darkness

The Tunnel of
Hell

# Zoe Parry: Inner Structure

## April 1992 and June 1992

Ninety-two alters and two personality maps are needed to convey who Dr. Altman was and is to Zoe.

In Zoe's map of April 1992 there are eight tunnels and seventy-two alters. By June 1992 the number of alters grows to ninety-two. The alters who speak about Dr. Altman are fear alters, lovers, mothers, observer-guides, healers, and rage alters. Some names are new to me: the Observer, the Dark Ones. Some are not. Names are added, but none subtracted.

Some of the alters I first met switch tunnels in the time from April through June. The act of narration changes Zoe's brain. The Tunnel of Light and Wisdom splits off a new tunnel, the Tunnel of Watchers. The Tunnel of Hosts mutates into the Tunnel of Zoe of Dreams (April 1992) and then changes again into the Tunnel of Faraway Dreams (June 1992).

The Tunnel of Hell shrinks. Cynthia (the Blonde) drifts into the Tunnel of Lost Souls and gets ready to die. To the child alters, Cynthia is no longer a bogeyman. By April 1992 some say that they've met Cynthia and pity her. The act of confessing to me, a stranger, has given a once alienated part of Zoe a chance at redemption.

In April the center of the map is called the Cave Opening. By June, it is the Floating Entrance.

The host Zoe is still at center left; and two alters—Bobbi Jo and Danielle—have combined with her. By June there are dozens of alters at the left, in the social part of the map. There are even more in the new Tunnel of Watching and Secrets. And alter Selina suddenly appears in all the tunnels.

# 3

# *Daddy Sidney*

Ten-story, sixteen-year-old 11933 Coral Way is a professional building in plush Arsdale. Today, April 30, 1992, the Way's century-old coral trees are in bloom. Right by St. Peter's Hospital, catercorner from St. Peter's Church, 11933 epitomizes the word *patriarchal*. Eighty percent of the tenants are older men—doctors, psychiatrists, lawyers, and a priest. The concierge says most have rented since 1976; now in their fifties and sixties, they've reached the top.

I ride the elevator to the floor Zoe has described. The ninth-floor hallway buzzes with activity. Parents drag kids to the orthodontists' suite at the back. The optometrist's door opens and shuts rapidly.

One door remains closed—sealed, perhaps. There is a white rose stuck in the keyhole. The half-outline of a doctor's name, removed long ago, reads "Dr. Sidney Altman." Lipstick faintly smudges the *A* of *Altman*.

Dr. Altman reached the top in 1978—the year Zoe and he met. He hit bottom in 1981.

Most of what follows occurred behind closed doors. Altman's notes, if he kept any—and I can't see why he would have—are not available. We have Zoe's word against that of a dead man. It can be neither substantiated nor disproved.

Some of Zoe's story, though, is public record: police reports, depositions, court transcripts, the rather credible testimony of a priest and two nuns, and complaints filed with and investigated by the Board of Medical Quality Assurance. This set of facts was enough to cost Dr. Altman his license, and more.

■

"Babysitter Raped Self, Stole Child!" screamed the headline on February 7, 1978. "Kidnapped Toddler Found Safe in Motel After 'Raped' Sitter Leads Way." Under a rain-soaked umbrella, forensic specialist Diane Timothy of the Tampa police department, a petite redhead, whistled in disbelief. She retrieved the dripping paper from her stoop. Running through the rain, she scanned the story.

As Diane remembers, it was seven A.M. on a workday. She'd intended to drive downtown. But now, she slammed the paper on her car. *Zoe Parry?* Her childhood friend was the wacko? No. Please! Maybe it wasn't true.

Zoe was hardly the criminal type, Diane reassured herself. Giggly, liked fun, sure; but a good girl. In childhood everyone had called them The Odd Couple, because popular Diane had at times bent domestic law, while Zoe had seemed straight as an arrow. They'd been good for each other. Even their parents had liked the friendship.

They wouldn't have if they'd seen Diane's hurt at age eleven. It wasn't just the crushes Zoe had on anyone with two legs, thought Diane. She could understand boy craziness. It was the on-again, off-again rejection. She'd actually seen sweet, supportive Zoe giggling with a gang of kids about her, Diane. And then she wouldn't even admit it!

Now Diane remembered Zoe's eyes, so innocent and hurt when accused. She'd been a good little liar, thought Diane. They'd drifted apart. When Zoe married Carmine Parry, that clinched it. Diane hadn't seen her again.

But Zoe in Anderson Prison? With the toughest gals in the county—and that was just the wardens! Once she hit the general population, two-thousand-snarling-ladies strong, they'd cut Zoe's heart out and eat it on a bet. At Anderson, Zoe would be horse meat.

Why hadn't the Bryants bailed Zoe out? Diane realized: they were as innocent as mooncalves about such things. She'd better go see what she could do.

"I got there," Diane says, "an hour later. Mrs. Bryant opened the door. Gosh, she'd shrunk. I remember thinking, had she always been this frail?

" 'Diane? Thank the Lord!' she whispered. She took my umbrella and led me in. I asked what had happened. She said darned if she knew, but it sure was a tragedy for little Davey. 'That poor, poor boy,' Zoe May kept saying. 'Little Davey is the apple of Dave's eye, more than Zoe ever was.' I was floored. Didn't the kid have a mother and father? Okay, Mrs. Bryant cared about Zoe's son, but she sure didn't show much concern for her daughter. I found out later she was scared to, because she was afraid Dave Bryant might fall apart.

"Mrs. Bryant stopped talking as an old man shuffled up. I wondered who he was. I'd thought both Zoe's granddads were dead. Then I realized it was Dave Bryant!"

In place of the pillar of the community stood a small man gnawed by bitter gall. "We shook hands. He didn't seem pleased to see me, though I'd been a favorite back in the old days. I told him I was there to help. He blew up at me. Zoe was charged with two counts of kidnapping and false imprisonment. Like 'What can you do with that, Miss Expert?'

" 'Well, what have you done so far?' I asked him.

" 'So far,' he shouted, 'I've given Zoe life, given her everything, put up with a lot. What have I done? I've prayed for guidance, on bended knees, like a good Christian!'

"Mrs. Bryant fluttered around, saying God had answered Dave's prayers by bringing me here. He brushed her off, sat, and opened his Bible. He wasn't reading. He was shaking. You could tell his heart was just about broken."

Within three minutes, Diane had called Carmine Parry at his job and discovered that Zoe's bail was only five

thousand dollars. The reason that nobody had bailed
Zoe out was that Carmine had been both frenetically
busy—working, fending off reporters, taking care of
Davey—and furious at his wife; the Bryants hadn't
thought of bail.

As she drove Dave Bryant to the bank and back,
Diane got an earful. Apparently Zoe had gone to the
dogs—abandoned Christian Science for "the RCs"—
what Zoe's folks called Roman Catholics. "It's Parry's
fault. He's no kind of a man. The only thing good to
come out of that marriage is Davey—and her lasagna, I
admit she can cook. The damned RCs corrupted her.
Under their influence, she's fornicated, changed her hair-
style, and even gone to psychiatrists! This is what comes
of abandoning your faith. Now she blames us for her
problems." Dave Bryant turned red. "Her problems!
The power of the mind can be used for good or ill! As
she's sown, so shall she reap!"

Back at Zoe's parents' house, Diane called a Tampa
police friend, who gave her the names of criminal lawyers. At the top of the list was Mitchell Cox. He liked
newsworthy clients. She phoned him. Having seen the
media coverage, Cox seemed eager to take this case.
"After she's examined. By an expert—we're going to
need a great psychiatrist on our side. Her emotional state
will be the critical question. Her best chance may end up
being a folie-à-deux defense—that's two people jacking
off each other's craziness—where I'll have to prove Mrs.
Parry was heavily influenced by the McGuire woman. A
crack psychiatrist—that's the ticket."

"Do you know a crack psychiatrist?"

"Sure. Sidney Altman. He's the best. Been practicing
twenty years, all kinds of honors. Writes about the socially disenfranchised, I believe. Has traveled—Canada,
Europe, you name it. Has given expert testimony enough
times to be credible and not enough to be a whore.
Admitting privileges at St. Peter's."

Diane handed Mr. Bryant the phone.

"Nope," she heard him say. "We Christian Scientists
don't hold with . . . No, sir. Oh, I see. Tomorrow. Thank
you, Mr. Cox." He jotted down an address—11933
Coral Way.

"Right next to the hospital," he said. "See you then." He hung up, returned to his chair, and reopened his Bible.

"Don't you want to call the psychiatrist?" Diane asked.

"Let her mother do it."

Zoe May put her hand to her mouth. To the Bryants, psychiatrists were the agents of error.

In the end, Diane called Altman. His wife set up Zoe's appointment for the next day, right after her meeting with Mitchell Cox.

■

Three figures approached. Between Dave and Zoe May Bryant, carrying a bag from which a wig kept spilling, was a skinny woman with glassy eyes. She moved awkwardly; her pants were damp. "There's Diane," said Zoe May, pointing.

The head turned. Like a junkie's, the eyes rolled up, then focused. Then, horrifyingly, from this wrecked woman came the young voice Diane remembered—Zoe's voice. "Hi, Diane."

"Hi, Zoe. How ya doing?"

Zoe blushed. She looked at Diane's car: lime green on the bottom, forest green on top. "Gee, a Caddy? You've sure come up in the world."

Diane hugged Zoe. She felt like wood.

"You know those slippers they give you? Couldn't keep 'em on. I'm thinkin' I'm gonna catch my death of cold. And the guard comes in and you know what she says?"

"What?" said Diane.

Zoe started to cry. " 'Get your shoes on, Cinderella. You're goin' home.' "

■

Zoe May says of her husband softly, "He couldn't face it. He was strong in a lot of ways, but not about this. I was able to face it somewhat, with the help of God. But because of it, he went down under and could never be himself again."

■

**ZOE 2 (the Tunnel of Light):** *He sad. He just say, "Let's go." I wanna hug him. But I can't. Somebody won't let my little arms reach up to hug my daddy. He not talk. Even in the car. Nobody talk.*

■

Says Diane, "No, I didn't see or hear evidence of other personalities. She was quiet. Sheepish. Staring out the window. It was about five when we pulled up to the Bryants'."

An adolescent boy ran out to greet them. "Mom!"

Dave had already gotten out. He hugged Davey and ruffled his hair. "How'd you get here, son?"

"Mrs. Wallace. She picked me up from school."

"Kids still sassing you?"

Davey kicked the sidewalk. "I guess. Not much."

"Where's your father?"

"Work, I guess. Uh—I got to go help Mom." He ran to Zoe's car door and opened it.

"I felt sorry for him," says Diane.

"The kid needed time with his mom. So I started up. He tries to hug Zoe. But she brushes right past him and runs after me, screaming, 'Diane! Don't leave me!'

"Poor guy stands there. Fighting back tears. I bet they'd been awful to him at school about his crazy mom. You know kids. The story was all over town. That kid must have had no one to talk to about the kidnapping.

"Dave put his arm around the boy and led him inside."

■

One feature of MPD is a huge gap between emotions and actions. Zoe adored her son. The child alters identified with him. Watching Dave with Davey, Zoe felt through her dead haze a tinge of comfort. Unconsciously she was intensely, almost murderously jealous. As she saw Dave's arm go around Davey's shoulder, Zoe blanked out.

■

**AGNES CAINE (the Tunnel of the Lost and Blind):** *I couldn't face that boy. Or anyone. Mrs. Bryant had cooked up a big southern meal. Corn bread, sausage stew, and orange-pecan cookies. I couldn't eat. I went to her bedroom and sat and rocked. After dinner, Davey came to see me.*

Smiling, Davey's mother held out her arms. He ran to her. He was now asthmatic; he panted when he asked, "Why'd you do it?"

"I didn't. I don't know who did."

He hugged her. Something sharp bumped his thigh.

"Careful. That could hurt you." She smiled, picking up the knife. "Honey, Mom's gotta go."

"No, Mom!" His voice cracked.

"Gonna go, gonna go away." She rocked him, making him her baby again. Her words were soft as a song. He half pulled away, half held her. "Away, up to heaven. Can't take you along. Don't cry, honey. I'm gonna rock with the child in the bosom of Mary."

"You can't." He was angry. "C'mom, Mom, get serious."

"Hand me that pen."

As Davey watched in horror, his mother transferred the knife to her left hand. With her right hand she wrote on a piece of scratch paper.

**AGNES CAINE (the Tunnel of the Lost and Blind):** *"Give me a Catholic funeral," I wrote, "at St. Peter's. Have my own Father Kirkland do the ceremony. Say the Rosary the night before. Bury me in white, like a bride, with beads in my hand and a Bible in the coffin. And finally, make sure my hair is real pretty."*

*Then I said, "Go in your room, shut the door, and hug your dog. I don't want you to see the knife go in my belly."*

*"Nonny!" Davey shrieked. "Grampa! Come here quick!" Zoe's parents rushed in and that was the end of it.*

*This was the tenth time I had tried to kill myself since 1956. I didn't mean to do bad to the boy, but when he was there, it all overwhelmed me.*

*Murder is wrong. Since I found out about the others, I don't try it. But then I thought I was better off dead.*

In spite of themselves, the Bryants were impressed by Altman's building. Their near-catatonic daughter didn't notice the classy lobby, the mosaic depicting doctors of the ages, but they did. Still, they were silent as they rode up in the elevator.

Suite 904. Dr. Altman's name, in gold leaf, sparkled against the mahogany.

Inside, a man was positioning an Oriental lamp on a side table. He switched it on, rose, and approached them. Tall, with wavy black hair and deep blue eyes, he smiled and held out both hands. "Hi, I'm Dr. Altman. Sorry about the confusion—we're redecorating."

"Hello," said Mrs. Bryant, and shook his hand. Mr. Bryant did not; he sat, drew a small green book from his pocket, and began to read.

"You just go on in," Mr. Bryant said to his wife. "You know where to find me."

Dr. Altman turned toward his new patient. "And you must be Zoe," he said, very gently.

In his office, Zoe May sat on the couch; Zoe, on the floor. Talk—gibberish to her—flew over her head.

On a small chair close-by sat a porcelain bride doll, beautifully childlike. A hand reached up and stroked the spun-gold hair, the fragile lace dress.

**MAZIE [Zoe 5] (the Tunnel of Light):** *There I was, playing with a doll that looked like me!*

*"Do you like her?" A big man squatted down, so close I could smell him. Mmm, candy canes. His clothes—mmm, clean. He kissed the doll and gave it back.*

*"Hi. I'm Dr. Altman."*

*I asked him what that meant. His eyes crinkled. He told me that in German, Altman means 'man on high.' "*

*I asked him if he was German, and he said no. "Well, don't fall down from on high," I told him. He said he wouldn't, thanks, and did I know where I was? Could I tell him why I was here?*

*I hugged the doll. He was nice, so I told him. "They say I took Jennifer. And left her with Mommy Crystal. They bring-ed me to jail. There are animals all around." I begged him, "Don't let them get me!" I dropped the doll.*

*Dr. Altman didn't get mad. He just picked it up and said I had to go to the hospital—I was actively blocking. I looked for the blocks, but they weren't there to play with.*

*He hugged me and said he'll take care of me. Everything will be OKAY. I cried. I didn't want to leave my mommy.*

*You know, my nickname is "Little Mama." I always take care of everyone. For once someone promised to take care of me. Now I could stop worrying. I could leave it all to him.*

▪

Mazie had found a new magic mommy—Altman.

Hospital records state that Altman phoned St. Peter's, reserved a bed, ordered Valium, Mellaril, Inderal, Dalmane. He evaluated Zoe as having an acute psychotic reaction, probably schizophrenic, over an underlying hysterical personality organization. This was a respectable evaluation; MPD was not yet recognized. To ask if a patient's voices seemed to come from inside rather than outside—an indicator of dissociative rather than schizoid thinking—wasn't yet a common diagnostic question.

▪

**MAZIE [Zoe 5] (the Tunnel of Light):** *At the door, he said, "I will see you at the hospital. Every day." He winked at me. And I fell in love.*

▪

**The DEMON (the Tunnel of Hell):** *I was watching. Fuck all psychiatrists! And fuck the body! You thought you were rid of me, you stupid bastards and bitches. I was there all along. Laughing. I could see Dr. Altman was a bastard from Day One. Two-faced, like all Christians and psychiatrists.*

▪

Zoe spent her first month at St. Peter's curled in a ball or sitting at a table while nurses lifted a rubber fork to her rubber mouth. She forgot Crystal, still locked up; her family had refused to post bail. All she saw was her new pain and her new Altman. Other patients gossiped: the new girl got all his attention.

■

**ZOE-THE-HOST (the Tunnel of Faraway Dreams):** *At meal-times Sidney would bring a tray up to my room and feed me, bite by bite. He was so fatherly! So loving!*

*From the family I got no attention. The father wouldn't visit; the mother, who feared hospitals, only came once a week. Davey was too young. Carmine was at work. Crystal, in jail. The one bright spot was Sidney.*

*He came into my room like a god, like angel and savior rolled into one. Every day, often twice. He'd sit on my bed and take my cold hand in his warm one, and we'd talk. I told him about my dogs, and he told me about his daughter, Edie. He'd smile at me, and I'd feel he loved me, too.*

■

Supportive therapy is one standard treatment for a patient who's out of it, as Zoe was. There is no way to corroborate how frequently Altman visited. If he did drop by twice a day for more than a few days, that's unusual. It might mean he was already getting too emotionally involved.

The only other persistent visitor was Diane Timothy, whose take on Altman is revealing.

In our phone interview early in 1993 I ask, "What did Zoe and he do?"

"We were in the dayroom at St. Peter's. She was sitting at a table with me, hanging her head. Dr. Altman and she had no chemistry that I noticed. He was at the next table, with another patient who kept looking us over."

"What did Dr. Altman look like?"

She breathes out. "Crazy! His eyes had a far-off look. He was overly animated. He looked crazier than his patients, and I told Zoe so."

"Did she respond to him?"

"She smiled at him. I got worried. Though he had on a white coat, I thought, 'He's the doctor?' He looked weird. He had a lot of hair."

"So does Dustin Hoffman, and nobody says he's crazy."

"Dr. Altman's hair stuck up in two points. It looked—now this sounds nuts—exactly like the horns of the Devil."

＊

" 'Raped' Sitter Charged!" On February 9 Zoe was arraigned at the Brooke County Courthouse. Coplaintiffs Lillian King and the State of Florida accused Zoe of kidnapping and false imprisonment. As Altman recommended, Zoe did not have to appear in person.

On February 17 the headline read, "Judge Denies Gag Order in Kidnapping Trial!" Cox claimed that Zoe couldn't get a fair trial in the midst of the press's salacious gossip party. Nobody else agreed.

February 28's headline: "Women Enter Pleas of Insanity!" Crystal's lawyer and Cox independently found their clients to be out of touch. Each now asserted that the other's client had evilly led his own poor client astray.

On Altman's orders, Zoe was refused newspapers. Reading them, she'd go catatonic.

＊

**MOTHER ZOE (the Tunnel of Light):** *After the arraignment, Mr. Cox badgered me. I wanted to know if Lillian was okay, and Jennifer and Taffy, but he wouldn't tell me. He kept rolling his eyes. I couldn't take it. I got hysterical.*

*Sidney chased Mr. Cox away, and held me in his arms.*

*We'd have sessions in a little room away from the ward. He would prepare me for the doctors. I couldn't understand why I had to see so many doctors.*

＊

It's been eighteen years since the Parry trial; Judge Wood, who presided over Zoe's trial, has died. However, lawyers unanimously agree that he was the best kind of judge: thorough, compassionate, wise, and no-nonsense. He began each case by meticulously reviewing the material before him.

In six weeks Judge Wood ordered three evaluations, each with a psychiatrist who'd never before met Zoe. The judge had three purposes: to discover Zoe's condition when she took Jennifer, to determine her present readiness for court, and to cut out what he saw as a lot of dang-fool, contradictory, fancy shrink-talk. He'd just discount any assertion on which the three psychiatrists disagreed.

Prognoses for Zoe varied widely, depending on who was out of her inner tunnels. A Dr. Doug Buck reported to Wood that "this woman of average build with a huge blond wig and flattened affect . . . functions on a low-average level, distorts simple proverbs, and expresses an anxiety ridden with paranoid content." The alter Cynthia had done the interview; she had nothing but contempt for Buck, whom she addressed as "Dr. Doodlebug." According to Buck, Zoe freaked out whenever anyone mentioned Crystal. She was a danger to self and others. If she regularly received talk therapy and medication, he wrote, commitment to a state hospital might not be necessary.

By mid-March, Zoe had progressed. Though she was very confused and ill, at least she'd showered. In occupational therapy she'd written poems, depressing, to be sure, but connected. She recalled that someone had kidnapped Jennifer. Not her—a demon. This was progress.

Since two out of the three psychiatrists now agreed she was somewhat in contact, Zoe was summoned in March to Brooke County Courthouse.

Judge Wood presided. The hall filled with reporters and with a curious, half-angry public. Zoe was rushed inside by Mrs. Bryant, Cox, Altman, and Diane Timothy. Dave had stayed at home, Carmine was at work, and Davey was nowhere to be found.

**MOTHER ZOE (the Tunnel of Light):** *Holding my hand was Dr. Altman. His presence made up for Father's absence. Father blamed me, you see, for his own bad health. He said I'd infected him with toxic thoughts.*

■

"Order!" Judge Wood banged his gavel. About seventy, Judge Wood held court from a wheelchair. He had a reputation, many lawyers agree, as one of the best judges in Florida. "Mr. Cox, Mr. Hadley, please approach the bench."

He hitched his wheelchair forward. "Okay, boys, let's talk turkey. No one will win by dragging this on." He tapped his heavily underlined summary of *The State of Florida vs. Zoe Parry.* "The tot's mom just wants privacy. Everyone agrees the sitter needs psychiatry not jail, and certainly not more media hoo-ha. And folks, the doctors' bills are mounting as we speak."

"The facts aren't as simple as they seem," said the DA, Mark Hadley. He whispered something to Judge Wood.

The judge nodded. "What's all this about her being a witch?" he asked Cox.

Zoe overheard. She leaped up, pounded the table with her fist, and screamed "I object!" On the other side of the courtroom, Crystal, unseen by Zoe, also began to yell. The reporters went wild with joy. Cox rolled his eyes, raced to his client, and told her to be quiet.

Judge Wood cleared his throat.

Altman soothed his patient and apologized for her. Judge Wood squinted sharply at Zoe. "Can we cut the dramatics?" he said, not unkindly.

■

**MOTHER ZOE (the Tunnel of Light):** *I managed a nod, and he smiled. I sighed. The men were going to take care of me.*

*But then the judge said, "I'm gonna stipulate that you two gals better stay apart. You hear?" I said yes. And Crystal said yes! And I saw her, for the first time!*

*She looked terribly haggard. But her eyes blazed at me. I must see her! Soon! But how?*

*Finally, Crystal told me. At the end, when everybody stood up to leave, neither of us was watched: and Crystal mimed speaking on a telephone. I shrugged: I don't know where to reach you! And Crystal circled a finger by her ear.*

*I realized Crystal must be in a hospital too!*

■

Back at St. Peter's, Zoe was about to put on her nightgown, when the door swung open without notice and Altman walked in. She muffled a shriek. He averted his eyes.

"Excuse me," he said, backing away. "I was just going to congratulate you. I'll return in half an hour." His eyes flickered. Weeks of semistarvation had left Zoe as slender as a teenager. It seemed Altman liked the prepubescent look. So had Mr. Bryant. Zoe smiled.

Now the Stupid One names herself: Sherry.

■

**SHERRY [*the Stupid One*] (the Tunnel of the Lost and Blind):** *I r-r-realized that Dr. Altman was just like Mr. Bryant! Lord, now what were we g-g-going to do?*

■

What they were "going to do" was clear. They would continue. When Altman knocked later, Zoe sat on the bed, demure and neat in a hospital robe. They had their session in her room, with the door wide open.

■

**ZOE-THE-HOST (the Tunnel of Faraway Dreams):** *He asked, how did I feel about Judge Wood's idea?*

*"What idea?" I had to admit I hadn't listened.*

■

Altman summarized Cox's plea-bargain and Judge Wood's response to it. Clearly Zoe had taken the child. It remained to be established whether or not, at the time, she'd been legally insane. Cox claimed yes, that Crystal and she had been under each other's spell, and this folie-à-deux explanation had seemed to please Judge Wood. If

Zoe changed her plea on one count to guilty, Mark
Hadley might drop the other charge. Then Judge Wood
might sentence her to probation with psychiatric care,
instead of to jail. This would take work, said Altman, lots
of it, but in this case justice might triumph.

"Plead guilty?" said Zoe. Her voice trembled.

"To just one charge. But then you wouldn't go to jail.
You would report every so often to a probation officer."

"Who?"

"Whomever Judge Wood chooses."

"Could you be both my psychiatrist and my probation
officer?" Zoe wondered aloud. "It would save a lot of
work—for you and the judge."

"Zoe, that's brilliant!" said Altman. "I don't think
they'd agree to it at first, though. Maybe after sentencing.
Why don't you ask your lawyer?"

"I don't have the money to call."

Someone should have recognized an issue of account-
ability here. No one did. Zoe's flattering, expedient request and Altman's evident agreement would eventually
make Altman answerable to no one but himself.

Dr. Altman reached into his pocket, pulled out small
change, and pressed it on Zoe. This might be interpreted
as human kindness or, with twenty-twenty hindsight, as
an improper crossing of boundaries.

"I bet I never see you again," Zoe said suddenly.

"I wouldn't miss seeing you for anything," he answered.

"That week he came in even on Saturday and Sun-
day—usually dead days on the ward," remembers Zoe.
"But every day would have been dead for me, without
Dr. Altman."

He gave Zoe money every so often. Grateful for the
windfall, she did call her lawyer; she also called every
hospital in a twenty-mile radius to ask about the status of
patient Crystal Moon McGuire.

Zoe located Crystal and managed two long, tearful
talks. They pledged to escape. But the third call back-
fired. When Zoe hung up, there stood Altman!

∎

**MOTHER ZOE (the Tunnel of Light):** *Apparently he'd listened to our entire conversation!*

*He left and didn't show up for two days. Life without him was hell. When he returned, I cried. He said he never wanted to hear Crystal's name again. I was so afraid of losing Sidney now that I apologized for calling and for my misuse of his trust.*

*"You're in such an improved state," he said, squeezing my hand. "I'm proud of you. Soon you'll go home."*

In April 1978, she did. Altman released her on a Saturday, not to Carmine, but to her parents. Carmine was working overtime.

In her childhood room at the Bryants', with cooking aromas wafting under the closed, locked door, Zoe listened to voices rumbling from down the hall. Carmine and Mr. Bryant were discussing how the Parrys could get out of debt. Zoe was in shock: she'd just been told she no longer had a home.

**MOTHER ZOE (the Tunnel of Light):** *How could Carmine have left Gardenia Circle, sold my dogs and furniture out from under me, burnt Crystal's and my journals, all without a word? He just sprang it on me.*

*"Kids were beating on Davey. I had to get him away. I couldn't pay rent. I had to get a smaller place."*

*"Where?"*

*"Camino Real."*

*"But that's a hellhole."*

*Carmine glared at me with such rage that I whispered, "Please, just go."*

She heard a car pull up outside. Running to her window, she looked out. A yellow cab pulled away. Crystal, pathetically skinny, tottered up to the screen door and banged on it. Zoe heard the door slam, then approaching steps and a knock.

She opened her door; Crystal all but fell inside. From

the doorway, Zoe May watched them embrace. "Well, I guess . . ." she started.

"Why don't you go finish dinner?" said Zoe. "We'll be down in half an hour."

"Fifteen minutes?" amended Zoe May, and, in answer to Crystal's glare, shut the door.

Crystal turned its key. "There." She looked awful. She was clutching her purse as if it were a shield.

"How'd you get out?"

"I walked." She opened her purse and dumped it on the bed. There were two big bottles of pills and a pack of brand-new razor blades. "Hold out your hands." Opening one bottle, she poured out what seemed like one hundred brown M&M's. "Thorazine. The other bottle is for me."

"No," said Zoe."

"What's our choice?" said Crystal. "Jail?"

"We're mentally ill. We were not responsible."

"Bull doody."

"My doctor told my lawyer and my lawyer told the judge."

"So we're gonna end up chained to a bed in a loony bin. We might as well end it." Crystal opened her own bottle and unwrapped the razor blades. "You with me or not?"

This was the Inquisition; they were prisoners. "Yes."

Crystal picked up a glittering blade. "Here's what we do. We swallow the pills. Then I make sure."

"Okay," said Zoe. Her hands shook. "I can't."

Crystal pushed in the pills. Zoe held them in her mouth. Then her friend gulped her own pills down.

Suddenly Zoe spat. Wet pills flew everywhere. A child's voice shrieked, "Mommy! Daddy! Save me!"

Crystal let out a bloodcurdling yell. Her eyes glazed with fury. She grabbed the blades and hissed, "How could you?"—just as Davey and Carmine broke down the door.

Davey looked at his mother, his chest heaving asthmatically. The past few weeks had changed him. He laughed. "Get real, Mom."

"Out of the room, young man." Carmine was furious.

"Just watching Mom kill herself again. What is that brown glop? Ca-ca? Oh—it's Thorazine!"

Carmine raised his hand. Davey beat it, fast.

Carmine looked at the two women. A tense, tragic man, he'd already been pushed to his limit. He was working like a horse, paying for St. Peter's, desperately trying not to blame his wife for the havoc he felt she alone had wreaked. Carmine also came from a troubled home. His mother had gone insane, was still locked away in a state mental hospital. What had kept Carmine alive through his own miserable youth was the thought that he'd have a family someday, people he could stick by. He believed he had stuck by Zoe.

Carmine's wife took one long look at her husband's uplifted hand, shrieked, and ran out the door and down the hall to her father. Silently Carmine chucked the suicide supplies, sat Crystal down and called her doctor, as Zoe sobbed to her father about how awful Carmine was—to sell her dogs and furniture like that. Bryant patted her; he looked green. Zoe May was in the kitchen, feeding Davey.

Carmine picked up the phone again and dialed Operator.

"Do you have a number for a Dr. Altman?"

Altman's second hospital admission for Zoe states, "Schizophrenic reaction, chronic undifferentiated type with acute exacerbation." Crystal Moon McGuire, the exacerbation, was hospitalized under restraint, twenty-five miles away.

■

**SISTER ZOE ANN (the Tunnel of Light):** *An hour later I was back at St. Peter's. I was told I'd have a roommate. I was not pleased. But when I walked in, there was a motherly-looking woman on one of the beds, reading her Bible and holding a little silver cross. My roommate's name was Janet Moore.*

*When the nurse left, Janet said, "Here, I got something for you!" She tossed something over, which I caught. I opened my hand. There it was—the cross. This was so kind, it brought tears to my eyes.*

*We opened up to one another. We went daily to mass.*

*Strangely, our observance was not encouraged. Once I was lying on the floor, with my forehead pressed to the ground and my arms outstretched in a cross, and Janet was kneeling, saying the Rosary. A psych technician walked in. By the reaction, you might have thought we were making love! Within ten minutes Dr. Altman was there, calling me out for a session. Janet's doctor took her into another room.*

*I guess they thought we were really bananas. They said ever so carefully, "What are you doing?" I told Dr. Altman, "Praying." You know, it seemed quite logical to me, to be praying in my situation!*

■

According to Janet, from her therapy room she could hear Zoe in hers, crying to Altman about her dogs and plants. His responses were so melodious, she says, he might have been singing.

Later, as the roommates lay in bed perusing the Bible, came a knock; Janet watched Altman approach. "That man was way too handsome." He bore a huge red plant, wrapped in gold cellophane and a purple bow, which he set on the night stand.

Janet watched incredulously as Altman knelt by her friend's bed, whispered, "Zoe?" and gently touched her.

Zoe shut her Bible, saw the resplendence, and wept.

"It was just too much," says Janet. "He stroked her. And she liked it. At the time I couldn't help myself, let alone her; I turned my back until he'd gone."

In psych wards, patients can form substitute families. Janet and Altman were Zoe's: her new sister/friend/mother and her father/mother/priest/lover/God. But the new family did not get along. Janet and Altman hated each other. They were, however, both attentive and loyal; seemingly more so, to Zoe, than her true family, which was drowning in stress.

The new family was exclusive. Altman told Zoe not to trust any other therapist. "I have no respect for most therapists. No faith." The message was to trust him alone.

Zoe improved: she became more coherent. Janet

helped her to see that Crystal and she were bad for each other; Altman simply forbade contact. "No discussion."

By May, Zoe was planning to leave the hospital.

When Janet told her she'd miss her, Zoe laughed.

"What's funny?" said Janet.

"Oh, Janet! What if you moved in with me and Carmine?" This would solve everyone's problems, thought Zoe. They could move—with Janet's help—to a good apartment. Janet would not sink into depression and alienation with friends around. Excitedly, they sketched out a plan and laid the foundation of a friendship that continues to this day. They also laid the foundation for extreme conflict: smashing this new family up against the old.

May came. With Altman's approval, Carmine took off a personal day. He didn't let on that being ordered around, supervised, by Altman made him feel impotent. Carmine often tries to blend with his background. He can agree, in this state, to things he may later violently regret.

When Carmine arrived to pick up Zoe at St. Peter's, Janet clasped her forearm, whispered good-bye, and fled.

Carmine kissed Zoe's forehead and packed her bags. She took one look at the empty side of her and Janet's room, and switched to an alter that can't feel a thing. Carmine checked her out and quietly drove her to what he called home. To Camino Real—Zoe's "hellhole."

▪

**MOTHER ZOE (the Tunnel of Light):** *Dark, dirty, my apartment filled me with despair. It all rushed in on me. Crystal, my dogs, my plants, all gone.*

*It was, to give Carmine justice, all he could afford. With him at work and Davey at school, I'd sit in the dingy living room and wish I were back in the hospital.*

*To top it off, in June, Mr. Bryant's prostate problem became worse. He also developed heart trouble. He blamed it all on his daughter and her toxic thoughts.*

▪

**CYNTHIA (the Tunnel of Walk-ins and Lost Souls):** *When Zoe visited on June fifth, Mr. Bryant came out of the bathroom,* *naked. His genitals had swollen to the size of a pumpkin. He couldn't pee, and he was whimpering with pain.*

*I did not feel sorry for Mr. Bryant.*

■

Zoe panicked severely; she did not return to Camino Real. In her mother's bed that night, lying rigidly awake next to the rigidly sleeping Zoe May, Zoe listened to her father's soft noises of discomfort, and agonized.

On June 6, Zoe had an emergency session with Altman. Bryant, sitting on a cushion, drove her. His reflexes were not what they had been, and they had a near miss on a turn. She arrived completely regressed.

■

**ZOE 2 (the Tunnel of Light):** *I look at the stuff on Daddy Siddie's desk: little dolls, and a big rock so his papers don't blow away. He hugs me. Then he says lie down. There's a birdie toy hanging from the ceiling. He says watch the birdies and just let everything go. I do, but I say stuff he don't like. He's mad. He says Mommy Crystal is bad and Mr. Parry is bad and that the Bryants are real, real bad. He can't say who's baddest. He says I am the only good one in the family. He likes me just the way I am.*

■

Suddenly a low, accented voice said, "Grasp the sword, or it strike you, Warrior." Altman's patient sat up and eyed him. She stretched, her body sinuous, sexual.

Recently Altman had contacted Zoe's former psychiatrists to do a thorough review of her care; none had mentioned this kind of change. He had reviewed a report from a Dr. Patricia Wald. "Zoe Parry is a complex individual. Schizophrenic. Sexually confused." At this moment, his patient seemed neither. "Good. Flirty. Phobic. Manipulative. Sociopathic. Suicidal. Dependent. Once, I was late, she thought I was dead and was about to jump from the office roof when I came up to find her." While reading this, Altman had thought Wald must be a ding. Now he stared at his patient. Her breasts rose and fell. She was as contradictory as Wald had said.

"Now, Zoe—" he began.

"I not Zoe. I—Selina."

Perhaps Altman found himself drawn to her out-there Indian accent, and to her earthiness. Perhaps he couldn't tell if Zoe was faking or not. The chess game of psyching her out may have appealed to him. Perhaps he enjoyed not knowing what to expect; possibly he entertained himself by playing at controlling this bright, strange woman.

They discussed methods of healing. The patient delighted Altman with her acuity. She guessed his most particularly troublesome problems—a rocky marriage and a cardiac condition. She did not tell him she'd overheard him complaining to Elyse Altman.

Says Selina, she promised to brew him healing tisanes, which they'd drink together. "Not like booze. These good for you. Help heart." Altman laughed and looked defensive. Lately his breath had smelled of alcohol. She nodded significantly at his bottom right-hand desk drawer, where he kept a supply.

From now on, while Zoe, sheeplike, followed her doctor's every implicit or explicit word and gesture, Selina happily dominated Altman. They arrived, Selina felt, at the understanding of equal partners.

On June 9, Zoe was to attend a pretrial hearing; Judge Wood had ordered more examinations.

Dr. Buck pronounced Zoe "still suicidal."

A Dr. Kowalski found Zoe insane within the M'Naghten test rules, both now and when she'd kidnapped Jennifer, too insane to go to court. She might be dangerous. Mindful of the last hearing, after which Crystal and Zoe had attempted suicide, Cox and Altman had the hearing postponed.

■

Three months later, Zoe was still popping Mellaril five times a day, Valium and Inderal four times, and Dalmane at bedtime; but her domestic situation was better. Carmine and Janet were polite to each other. As soon as they could move in together, Carmine reasoned, he might be able to cut his workload—no more overtime. With

Janet's disability pension and Zoe's insurance, they'd just squeak by.

Part of Zoe began to anticipate leaving the hellhole. Another part wanted to stay. If she left hell too soon, this part felt, the punishment would have to continue in the next place they moved. Not that locations mattered.

As soon as Janet was released from St. Peter's, they all moved into a large, sunny apartment two blocks away from the Bryants. As in Camino Real, there were few trees or shrubs; but at least here there were front and back lawns, and windowboxes to fill with flowers. Zoe set up a routine based on therapy, daily mass with Janet, and studies on healing. On the surface, her new family had joined the old.

She and Janet even had a family of churches. They started going to St. Ann's for meditation. St. Ann's was more intimate than the larger, patriarchal St. Peter's, which they associated with hospitals. They attended St. Peter's on feast days, Sundays, and for confession; but daily prayers, they said at St. Ann's.

Since her father had become so ill, Zoe also attended Christian Science meetings with her parents. At these times, she couldn't stop her guilty ruminations. "What if my thoughts really are poisoning Father?"

At one Wednesday night prayer meeting, Zoe spotted Lillian King. Lillian saw her, too, got out of her seat, and ran.

One morning two weeks later, Zoe had Janet drive her to her local Christian Science Reading Room, to study orthodox healing in a clear atmosphere. Alters felt both like double agents and like straight loyalists. She'd been there two hours when she sensed hostility. Twisting in her chair, she encountered the angry glare of Lillian King.

Zoe went red. Though she believed she had not kidnapped Jennifer, she still felt overwhelming remorse.

■

**CAROL SEEMORE** and **VIRGINIA ZION** [*the Christian Science Girls*] (*the Tunnel of Faraway Dreams*): *That they met was Divine Providence. Lillian is a true Christian, a good, good woman. When she saw Zoe looking so wan, her anger melted.*

*God's Presence was there. It was a complete healing. Lillian
forgave Zoe and, little did she know, the whole system.*

■

It was true—Lillian did forgive. By her strict standards,
the mentally ill are not responsible for their deeds, no
matter how heinous. And once sane, they're to be treated
as though they'd never hurt you. Lillian judged that Zoe
had been punished enough. At the next meeting, Lillian
went up to Zoe and invited her out to see the children.
This exchange is too painful for Zoe to discuss, except
for her awe and gratitude—and resentment.

According to a court document, on August 25 Zoe
met the Kings at McDonald's. The children were quite
friendly. They'd grown. Taffy's tumor had receded. Both
Zoe and Lillian agreed this was a demonstration of Divine
Spirit. Secretly Selina felt that the kidnapping had
shocked Lillian into projecting healthy instead of toxic
energy; that she had thus helped Lillian.

Zoe answered Lillian's guarded questions. Lillian felt
psychiatrists were dangerous, but she also commented
on how well Zoe looked. "This Dr. Altman sounds quite
nice." Then she laughed. "Gosh, Zoe—wouldn't it be
funny if the police walked in and saw us together?"

Zoe's heart sank, but she smiled. Lillian laughed nervously. After that Wednesday meeting, Lillian says, giggling, she'd been so scared, she'd called the police.
Later, she'd remembered how close she and Zoe had
been. How hurt she, Lillian, had felt after the kidnapping.
She had had to find a good Christian way through the
problem. To turn the other cheek without being a sucker.

At the restaurant her clear, strong voice grew dark
with anguish. "Tell me frankly, Zoe. I know you took
Jennifer. But did you break our windows? Did you take
my dog? Did you make those phone calls? Why? Why!"

By now all the Kings were crying. Zoe wanted to hide.
Was Lillian just curious, or had she been put up to this
by Mark Hadley, the DA? "Lillian," she began, "I
hadn't been myself for a long, long time . . ."

She told the story as she knew it. She did not include
the coven, the satanic rites, or Henry Owens—about

whom she had no conscious memories. She did include her remorse, which was genuine. Couched in polite language, smoothed over, the story did not sound half as crazy as what had happened. It did sound sad.

After Zoe finished, there was silence. Then Lillian said, "Zoe, now I have just one more question. It's the most important one of all."

"What would you like to ask?" said Zoe, dully.

"Would you like to come with the kids and me to the beach tomorrow—and just have fun?"

■

When Zoe told Altman about reconciling with Lillian, and how later the Kings had dropped all charges, Altman said, "Zoe, you never cease to amaze me." For months now he had been writing letters on Zoe's behalf to Cox, Hadley, and Judge Wood, and now he urged that Lillian do the same.

And she did. Repeatedly. Lillian begged Hadley to drop his end of the case. The DA responded, he could not. That was up to the State of Florida, the coplaintiff, which was not quite as easy to persuade as she.

There were other serious problems in addition to what Zoe perceived as Hadley's intractability. Dave Bryant's health had deteriorated rapidly. Davey was now sleeping around—at age thirteen—and hanging out with a tough crowd from Camino Real; two moves had hardened him. Getting meals on the table from Carmine's inadequate salary, juggling the flood of bills, were impossible for Zoe, even with Janet's aid. Plus Cox, her lawyer, unhinged her: his continual eye-rolling made her feel strained and berserk.

By Judge Wood's order, Zoe returned to Dr. Buck for a third evaluation. His report states that the patient now wanted to live. But she also blurted out seemingly paranoid statements about some witch's curse. Spirits talked to her, she insisted, all the time. When he asked her her goals, she said "to be a good wife and raise children." Buck pronounced Zoe semi-marginally fit to stand trial.

Mark Hadley wrote to Zoe May: "I can certainly

understand your desire that the People dismiss the case against your daughter. Unfortunately, an infant was kidnapped. . . . If, as you say, your daughter was legally insane . . . I am certain that the jurors will so find.''

On November 24, Janet and Zoe went up to Osceola Springs, near Lake Kinnara, on a spiritual retreat; Zoe wanted to prepare for her coming trial. This was the first time Zoe had been away since her hospitalization.

**MOTHER ZOE (the Tunnel of Light):** *Kinnara Lake is so beautiful and peaceful. When I got there and looked at the water, I just knew God was with me.*

But Zoe's vacation was cut short. On November 27, while praying, she was summoned to the phone.

**MOTHER ZOE (the Tunnel of Light):** *Mr. Bryant said, ''I'm dying, and you're going to be sorry for the rest of your life that you left.''*

Dave Bryant's kidneys had failed. He was dying of uremic poisoning. Comments alter Cynthia, there was fear in his heart, fear in his mind. He could hardly breathe.

**ZOE-THE-HOST and CAROL SEEMORE (the Tunnel of Faraway Dreams):** *I was home within two hours. I called in a doctor, who warned me that Father had sustained irreparable damage. I rode with Father to the hospital and held his hand until they put him into intensive care. He pleaded with me not to leave him, but the nurses made me go.*

*Mother and her sisters and I were in the living room, denying Father's illness, when at ten-thirty the doctor called to say he had died. My mother screamed. I tried to rejoice in his eternal life. Then Aunt Rae asked how I could look so calm. ''The kidnapping unbearably stressed your father. His death was all your fault.''*

■

Two Christian Science practitioners, Joan Halliday and Dave Bryant's old friend Paul Barnaby, drove Zoe to the hospital. As they pulled onto the freeway, Zoe got down under the dashboard and hid.

■

**DONNA WHITE (the Tunnel of Light):** *At the hospital I signed the papers; Mrs. Bryant couldn't. I arranged the funeral; Mrs. Bryant wouldn't. I arranged the payments; Mrs. Bryant hadn't. And I arranged for the mausoleum. Mrs. Bryant mustn't hear one word about putting her husband in the ground.*

■

At the funeral home, Zoe found a bathroom and hid. She could not bear the sight of the open casket. Paul Barnaby pounded on the door. His voice quivering, "Zoe Bryant Parry, you get out here right now and represent your father." She did manage to open the door as the service started.

■

**MAZIE [Zoe 5] (the Tunnel of Light):** *At the funeral, so many of us were out, we never cried. We just tried to get through it. Davey wasn't there; he was with friends. He couldn't take it. He loved his grandpa more than anyone. His grandpa had loved him too—much more than he'd loved any of us.*

■

At the funeral, the Kings asked Zoe if she could baby-sit for them once again.

Even Zoe sensed this was an unusually Christian request. She felt awed at such forgiveness. She also felt terrified at the thought of returning.

Now four of Zoe's families would clash: her family of marriage, her hospital family, her inner family, and her old family of ghost children and bad mothers—the Kings.

She prayed that week at three churches: at the church she considered her father church, St. Peter's; at her mother church, St. Ann's; and at her child and grandmother church, the Christian Science meeting house.

Altman was particularly tender. At first Zoe just sank into his warmth and sobbed; Mr. Bryant had been a pillar of the community, a perfect father. After a week, she told a less idealized story. Mr. Bryant used to hurt her, but she couldn't remember when or how.

Altman was especially interested in a recurring dream Zoe had had since age seven. "I am frying a penis in hot oil—my father's penis."

"Do you always have this dream?"

"Not during the funeral week."

"When did it return?"

"Last night," she whispered. "But the person the, ah, organ belonged to had changed."

"Whose organ was it?"

"Last night—yours."

"Can you talk about that?"

"Christian Scientists believe in a God that is both father and mother. You are both father and mother. And my father was, too."

"Your father was like God?"

She blushed and was silent.

"You don't like men, do you?"

She shook her head, then shot a stricken glance at him.

"Have you ever liked a man?"

She blushed; her eyelids fluttered. "Not Carmine." She'd always wished for a man at once perfectly strong and perfectly nurturing, and if she couldn't find him, she wanted a woman perfectly nurturing and strong. Altman suggested that Zoe bring Carmine in for family therapy. When she asked could she bring Janet and Davey, he said yes to Davey but no to Janet.

■

**MOTHER ZOE (the Tunnel of Light):** *He was possessive. He hated Crystal and my mother and father, but especially he hated Janet. He told me—now this is awful—he'd looked up her records at St. Peter's Hospital and that he had the power to destroy her. He was jealous of Janet, because I liked her.*

■

He was not jealous of Davey. Zoe brought Davey to see him. Consciously, she wanted to help her family solve its problems, under expert supervision. Unconsciously, she pressured Davey to accept Altman in place of his father.

Davey could not articulate his rage in words. Zoe's families had moved from border skirmishes and were now clashing in an escalating, senseless war, from which the child suffered the most. He toilet-papered Altman's bathroom and outer office, proclaimed the therapist "a jerk," and said he never wanted to see his ugly face again. And at home, he ate. He started small—cookies, doughnuts. But soon he ate anything in sight. Davey's weight ballooned abruptly.

That Saturday would be Zoe's first visit to Casa Paloma since the kidnapping. Her therapy that week was aimed at desensitization of fears. Night and day, she had flashbacks—mysterious and terrifying to the acknowledged self.

The actual meeting was anticlimactic. George was out playing tennis. Dressed in their Sunday best, Taffy and Jennifer politely said hello. Lillian set out games and snacks, kissed them, and marched out for a walk.

When Lillian returned half an hour later, the girls and Zoe were laughing over Candyland. Jennifer had helped Taffy. Lillian relaxed. God had taken care of them all.

She asked Zoe to baby-sit regularly. Why Zoe accepted, she cannot say, except that she loved the children and wanted to do what was best.

■

Altman let Zoe peek at his report to Judge Wood, titled "Record of a Successful Treatment." "I've adjusted the defendant's medications until the combination works. In talk therapy I've emphasized reality issues. Defendant has voluntarily severed contact with the McGuire woman and is concentrating on her own family. Under my care, she has substantially improved." The report concluded, "I think the defendant is an extremely sensitive person who'd react badly to jail. I urge you to recommend probation."

Altman invited Lillian King to his office during one of

Zoe's sessions, hugged her, and cried because he'd never seen such forgiveness.

Late in 1978, by Judge Wood's order, a board of seven psychologists ran a battery of tests on Zoe. They recommended that she find something to do outside of therapy: work in a children's facility under constant supervision or go to college. They recommended permanent separation from Crystal, continued care, and a stable home life. Judge Wood ordered Zoe to achieve these objectives by her next court date four months away; this became Altman's therapeutic goal.

Altman decided that with her record Zoe would have a hard time landing a child-care job. So he had her train to become a nurse's aide specializing in geriatrics. Under his supervision, she attended and completed training.

Altman may not have been a Svengali, but he certainly did not encourage his patient to achieve autonomy around men. Between her godlike doctor and father, her judge, her husband, and her temporary probation supervisor, a stern man named Martin Ellbaugh, Zoe achieved almost total passivity. She went through the moves her doctor prescribed for her, and did almost nothing else.

In February 1979, one year after the kidnapping, Martin Ellbaugh reviewed her case. "Charged with a 207 and 236," reads the report, "intending to plead guilty to the 207, defendant now spends her time doing housework and going to church. What are the chances that she will commit another crime?" Ellbaugh decided: zero percent. "I recommend a three-year grant of probation, stipulating that Mrs. Parry be closely monitored by the court through a probation officer skilled in psychiatric evaluation."

Except that Zoe had not yet pled guilty to kidnapping, Judge Wood's orders had been obeyed. The next step, Zoe and her doctor agreed, was to get the judge to name Altman her permanent probation officer. In November 1979, Altman accompanied Zoe to her next hearing.

■

**MOTHER ZOE (the Tunnel of Light):** *At the hearing I broke down and could not plead guilty. We agreed—Judge Wood,*

*Mr. Cox, and myself—that I would accept the bargain, as soon as I could get through the plea.*

■

From late 1979 through 1980, Zoe tried to plead guilty half a dozen times. Each time, she'd break down; Altman would end up escorting her from the court. Her days were an endless round of continuances, prayers, and therapy sessions, all under the cloud of her inability to complete the plea.

It troubled Zoe that she could not remember sessions. She would start up from the couch at the end of the hour, feeling exposed. Altman linked Zoe's shame at pleading guilty to her shame at paternal abuse, as yet consciously unadmitted and for which she blamed herself. This was a good hypothesis; Altman was smart.

But Altman often had alcohol on his breath these days. His color was bad. His blood pressure was sky-high, he told Zoe (the records agree). He was on pre-scribed antihypertensive, diuretic, and antiarrhythmic drugs.

Though Altman prided himself on balancing combinations of drugs with Zoe until they worked, perhaps in his own case he was not as careful. Zoe says she saw many medications in his office, and he seemed to take them irregularly.

"We've got to wrap up your case," Altman kept saying. Zoe's feeling of being controlled by him increased. She responded automatically—yes, wrap up the case, at any cost.

In late November 1980, in profoundest shame, Zoe pled guilty to a kidnapping she was sure she had not done "because," she tells me, "Dr. Altman advised me to do so." Judge Wood immediately sentenced her to three years of probation. He named Altman her probation officer.

Within a month Zoe found a part-time job caring for a bedridden old lady. Though Carmine's insurance still paid for therapy, the Parrys' bills were soaring, along with everyone else's: inflation and basic costs had both recently hit record highs. Zoe, though, felt safe at work.

Lottie Tanner was the quintessential pink-cheeked grandma. Her bedroom was stuffed with Christmas cards and letters going back half a century. When she got lonely, which was often—her family had abandoned her—Lottie would read a letter and fall asleep. That's what Lottie did, pre-Zoe. Now, afternoons, as she sat in her recliner, clean, fed, and prettied up, Lottie recounted stories of her youth.

Three mornings a week, Zoe went to therapy. Staring up at the bird mobile, she'd stammer out her feelings. She loved Lottie. Lottie was a saint, just as Anne Adams had been (she'd recently died). Zoe's grandmother had been so strong! "She's a saint," repeated Zoe. "Up in heaven."

Dr. Altman leaned forward and laughed. "A saint!" His breath was metallic today; his body smelled sweaty. "A saint," he repeated sadly. "Tell me your sins."

Since becoming Zoe's probation officer, Altman had seemed to be in more pain. One moment he'd be jovial, alert; the next, he'd wince. He'd talk swiftly to cover it up.

Submissively, Zoe began. "My grandmother lived by her principles. More so than my mother or I."

"What principles have you broken?"

Zoe whispered, "Sexual ones."

Altman seemed to like this. "Stupid," a voice said inside Zoe, "nothing's wrong. All psychiatrists have sex on the brain."

According to Zoe, Altman then made her replay specific sexual abuses by her father.

Many doctors include reenactment of traumatic childhood scenes in their therapies. This isn't just so patients can discover how they got to be the way they are. They can also find what the episodes meant to them and transcend the old meanings once and for all. The point is that this time, the patient will win.

This time, Zoe would lose.

■

In 1980 Carmine went in with Zoe for four sessions of family therapy; he says Altman was totally eccentric.

Carmine is not an unusually self-assured man. Altman was confident—magical, to the Parrys. Carmine is wiry, arthritic, and broke; Altman was tall, wealthy, and cultured. Carmine was miserably married; Altman seemed happy. Carmine was part of Zoe's old, rejected family; Zoe had for months praised Altman to the skies—at her husband's expense.

When he first went in, Carmine says, Altman was sitting behind his huge desk playing with his big gray rock. They shook hands. "He looked at me like I was smaller than small. He was handsome, as my wife had mentioned," says Carmine.

Altman affably took a history and then got to the point. "Your wife," he told Carmine, "has an unfulfilling sex life. With you.

"In sessions," Altman's bass voice smoothly continued, "we've explored how her problem with sex is related to paternal abuse she suffered as a child, which caused her—I don't know if you're aware of it—both to hate men and to have some unhealthy relationships with women.

"Now, I care about your wife. I want to help her."

"Uh, terrific," responded Carmine. He remembers looking at his watch. He was due at work in forty minutes. He had the afternoon and evening shift. Altman had kept him waiting half an hour.

"The reason I'm asking you is, I need signed consent forms from you both."

"I'd consent to—?" Carmine said.

"To my having sex with your wife."

"Say what?" Carmine couldn't believe his ears.

Zoe says she felt like a piece of meat. Altman cracked a joke, and he and Carmine laughed.

Carmine says Altman smiled at his ignorance. "Haven't you ever heard of sex therapy?" he said, as though everybody not only had, but knew it went like this.

Carmine remembers shaking his head. "I couldn't agree to that." Zoe remembers Carmine saying, "I've never heard of anything quite like this."

"But she hates men."

"She's a pretty good wife to me."

"According to your so-called wife, sometimes she's brought home a woman and they've used the bedroom while you slept on the couch. How does that make you feel?"

To his dismay, Carmine felt his eyes fill with tears. "I love her dearly," he said.

"Aw, come on, Mr. Parry."

"You never know what to expect!" Carmine burst out. That was the understatement of the year, but Carmine's an understated guy. "One minute she comes on strong, the next, she cries like a baby. But, Doctor, all the same, I can't take what you said seriously. It's in very bad taste."

"Then we won't say any more about it," said Altman, rising and holding out his hand. And he didn't—to Carmine Parry.

"There was something unprofessional about Dr. Altman's request," Carmine says. "Unusual." His eyes dart around, as if looking for something that life can't give him. "However," he adds, "I did not feel I could do a thing about it. He didn't say nothing like that again. So I stayed out of it. I didn't take it seriously."

By the end of 1980, Altman appeared disoriented to more people than just his patients. Later his widow would testify that he was physically and emotionally imbalanced.

In one session, Zoe rebuked Altman: she said that medicine doesn't mix with even one sip of alcohol.

"I'm in control," said Altman. As an example, according to Zoe's journal, he confided to her his strong sexual feelings for his nine-year-old daughter, Edie. "Since she was small I was fascinated with her female organs, whenever I bathed her." Zoe's father also used to bathe Zoe. "Unlike your father," declared Altman, "I controlled myself. I could fully take advantage of Edie, but I haven't."

"So you can feel safe with me," Altman continued.

"Oh, I do!" enthused Zoe. "Extremely safe." She was hiding strong panic. Had she heard him right? The session had started with her criticizing Altman's lack of control; he'd twisted it so she felt both guilty and aroused.

"But? There is a *but*, isn't there?" Altman laughed. Today he reeked of alcoholic sweat. "What would make you feel the safest in the whole world? Keep your eyes shut. Say the first thing that comes to mind."

"Mother's breast."

"Good," said Altman. "Good. We're getting someplace. Now, as your doctor I am here to nurture you. Even a man has something that is the equivalent of mother's breast. Keep your eyes shut. What pops into your mind?"

"The penis."

"Precisely," said Altman. "Symbolically. Take mine home. Carry it with you. My penis will keep you safe."

"Like a baby," whispered Zoe 2.

Altman laughed. "Sometimes I feel like a baby, too. But the difference is, I know I don't have to grow up. I can fool everyone, and so could you."

"Don't have to grow up, never-ever?"

"Nope." A piece of paper fluttered over Zoe's face. She opened her eyes and took it—her probation report. She read it. "Wow," she said. "I been a good girl?"

"My good girl."

She stood. They hugged good-bye. He kissed her. She put her finger in her mouth and turned in her toes. She told no one about this conversation, just wrote it down.

From her tunnel, Selina saw things were going wrong. She did spells to save Altman, whom she genuinely loved. But she was angry. She hissed, "This white doctor better not cross Selina or hurt children!" Deep within the tunnels, drums began to beat, faster and faster.

The last Saturday in January 1981, Zoe went to Casa Paloma to baby-sit as she had for the past year. She was exhausted at the Kings'. Her heartbeat was irregular; she'd taken extra Inderal. Her bra seemed oppressively tight. And February 3, the anniversary of the kidnapping, was fast approaching.

Inside Taffy's green bathroom she locked the door, took off her shirt, and unclasped her bra so as not to suffocate. Images flickered in the mirror—a waiflike girl with brown hair, a leering black man behind her. Dave Bryant, his flesh eaten by maggots, reached out from someplace just out of sensation, trying to clasp her close. Suddenly Zoe was flooded with such fear that she found herself moaning, with her cheek against the mirror.

On February 4, Zoe confessed her bra phobia to Altman. He did not connect the phobia with the anniversary of the kidnapping, with her fear of her own dark potency, or with her increasing fear of therapy with him.

**MOTHER ZOE (the Tunnel of Light):** *I wore the bra day and night. I felt too afraid now to take it off. Sidney hypnotized me. His voice was so warm. I found myself telling him about the bra, how tight it was, how oppressive.*

*"Would you mind taking it off?" I heard Sid say.*

*"No. . . ." As if underwater, I reached up under my blouse and undid the snaps.*

*He sat by my side on the couch. "Would you mind pushing up your blouse?"*

*"No. . . ."*

*I lay there with my breasts exposed. He gently examined me with his stethoscope. Then he put his hand across my chest and massaged me. "Where do you feel the tightness?" he asked in a very soft, professional voice.*

*"Up top. You know I had tuberculosis as a child."*

*Until then it had been like a doctor's exam. But now he touched my nipples and said, "I want you to feel good."*

*I felt embarrassed, but thought, "He wants to help."*

**SERENA (the Tunnel of Dreams):** *Help, my ass. I got straight out of there and phoned Patricia Wald.*

The alter Serena is a teenage "California" blonde; Zoe can't decide if she's a free spirit or an evil sex maniac. Serena likes women and hates men, most of whom she sees as rapists. She split off from Zoe at age five, during a rape.

Wald was Zoe's ex-psychiatrist—the one who'd told

Altman that Zoe was manipulative, sociopathic, flirty, phobic, good, bad, and suicidal. She was one of two therapists Zoe had seen from 1969 to 1974; the other was a Dr. Frederick Small. For Zoe, they'd been surrogate parents. Wald, who'd flirted with her and then dumped her, she'd thought warm and maternal. Small, who'd treated her kindly if not brilliantly, she'd found cold and impersonal.

On February 23, Zoe told Wald about Altman. Wald, slender, with her hair in a flip, violet eyes, and huge round plastic eyeglasses, saw Zoe in her serene and very pink office.

"Help me," begged Zoe.

"Help you what?" said Wald, looking owlish and a bit cross. She'd agreed to the session because she felt curious. Now she didn't know quite what to do: she hadn't meant to revive Zoe's interest. "I mean look, the man's a professional, right?" Wald giggled uncertainly. She'd been a debutante in her youth, what people call a Daddy's girl. Now in her late forties, she still preserved the manner. "He's one of the most highly respected psychiatrists in the community. He travels, writes, teaches, he's a member of all the associations. *Merde,* the man would have a lot to lose."

"I guess you're right," said Zoe. "Patty, I could hug you. I'm so glad to be here. It's like coming home."

"I'm glad, too," said Wald, and they embraced.

On March 7, Lottie had a heart attack. Doing first aid till the paramedics arrived, Zoe had palpitations, too. On March 9, when they had not subsided, she went in for an emergency session, Altman once again massaged her chest. "How do you feel about what I'm doing?" he asked.

■

ZOE 10 (the Tunnel of the Lost and Blind): *I knew it was nasty. But I was honest and told him I felt it down there. He asked me to show him. I thought, "Oh, no, now what do I do?"*

*I thought I was going to choke. But she pulls down her jeans and spreads her legs. She's blushing. I can see she's scared that if she doesn't do exactly what he says, he's gonna lock her away. He's her probation officer!*

*"Could you show me with your fingers?" She puts her hand on, you-know, and he goes, "Move your fingers?"*

*Then he asks, "Do you mind if I—?"*

*She whispers, "No," and he does. She melts. He doesn't force—he's gentle, like a woman.*

*"You remind me of a beautiful, sweet child," he says. He has this real dreamy look in his eyes.*

*I feel her start to explode, from her head to her toes. We children are there. And we feel really embarrassed about this, but we have a climax, too. And then he puts his head on my shoulder and kind of blacks out.*

*Downstairs, I almost passed out. Janet asked what was wrong, and I told her. She yelled at me to tell someone. I said no. Who was going to believe us—convicted felons?*

*"Then let me tell someone." I said no. He'd promised to destroy Janet if she got in his way.*

*I was being suffocated, stifled, imprisoned. I prayed to Our Father. "Lord, help me bear this cross!"*

On July 3, Zoe came to her session in a white silk dress with matching slip and bra. They took their usual places under the mobile. Under Altman's direction, Zoe dreamed an old fantasy. "A beautiful golden man named Mark swooped down and flew off with me to a place called the Golden Beach World. The sun was shining. Salt spray tingled on my skin; the sand rushed forward—"

She fell with a thud. Back into the office.

". . . why I'm rewriting the Bible," Altman was saying.

"Poor God," she thought. There was silence.

Suddenly she felt warm weight on the couch next to her. She thought, "If I don't open my eyes, this isn't real."

Soft fingers gently rubbed her forehead. "Would you mind," said his golden voice, "taking off your clothes?"

"No." Without opening her eyes, she pulled off her dress and slip. Her fingers fumbled with the bra and he helped her with it—the first and only time. Then she lay naked, silent. "I felt no shame," she says. "It was strange, on that couch I never did; only when I left was I a wreck."

"Would you mind touching yourself?"

"No."

"Would you mind—?" he said, a little later. "Oh. Just relax." He sighed. Her eyes were shut. "You are safe."

"And I was! I felt quick touches on my nipples, forehead, lips."

Suddenly she felt the weight lift. She opened her eyes. "There he was," she says, "naked. Through the blinds one ray of sunshine touched him. He was so handsome. He lay down on the couch and pulled me on top of him. We kissed each other. He told me that he loved me.

"I wanted to run and hide. I wanted to stay and be loved."

■

**SELINA (from Every Tunnel):** *Both of us were very primitive. We both like touch, smell, rub. That why I like him. He like me for myself.*

■

**MOTHER ZOE (the Tunnel of Light):** *As Dr. Altman was dressing, he apologized about his underwear, which was torn. I said, "That's okay." He reached for his calendar. "Next Saturday at nine?"*

*"Sure."*

*He hugged me. "Will you forgive me?"*

*"Sure," I said.*

■

"Forgive me, Father, for I have sinned." The priest at St. Peter's, handsome Father Kirkland, recognized the voice in the confessional: that very troubled lady who'd threatened to jump off the steeple.

"Father, I feel so dirty, so confused."

He murmured, "God is love." Then the young, fresh voice spilled out an appalling confession. Worse, the poor thing was terrified that her "mortal sin" had damned her forever. "You are ill, my child, and not responsible."

"But, Father . . ."

"Your doctor's behavior is wrong. He has violated a sacred trust. Please sit and pray until I can join you."

Kirkland came out after half an hour. "Zoe. I feared it was you. I am sorry."

Father Kirkland urged Zoe to leave so-called therapy immediately and to call the parish counselor, Sister Johanna.

That month, Zoe told an amazing number of people about Altman. Besides Janet and Father Kirkland, she told her mother, her physician, her husband, Lillian King, Pat Wald, and Davey, who was now fifteen.

An MPD sufferer cannot easily discriminate between appropriate and inappropriate confidantes. For example, Zoe told Davey. Conspicuously, she did not report any problem to Judge Wood, Cox, the Florida Psychiatrists' Association, or the Board of Medical Quality Assurance. Each could have taken action, each could have gotten her away.

Carmine's reaction was less than protective. "I'm only gonna make things worse if I interfere. Let the nun handle it. You're doing fine." He soon left the house to look for Davey.

"Pat," she sobbed five minutes later on the phone, "Carmine doesn't care. He's just like my father. And Dr. Altman doesn't like me either, not really."

Wald prided herself on her ability to take patients' fantasies with a giant grain of salt. "He sounds like a real nut case, but you're taking it too hard."

"Mommy," said a regressed little voice, "he really don't like me." If Wald had actively taken control at this point, she might have averted two tragedies. But she didn't.

Wald giggled. "Mommy? Tee-hee!"

■

ZOE 2 (the Tunnel of Light and Purity): *Siddie and me have a secret game—Apeman. He swings his arms and yells, ''Ooogh ooogh.'' He jumps around and touches my chest and legs. Then he narrows his eyes like an ape does and says, ''Take off your clothes. I'm gonna get you!'' When he catches me, he puts his mouth on my peepee. He's Mr. Ape, and I'm the little girl. He says, "You'll always be my girl!" And when he gets too much like a big rascal . . .*

■

**ZOE 10 (the Tunnel of Secrets):** *. . . then he says, tell him, "Down boy, down boy, down." He gets on all fours and starts to bark. He has cheese crackers in his office. He says, "Throw the dog a cracker." He catches the cracker and eats it, and then he licks us.*

*And then he wants to play the Kidnapping Game.*

■

**SELINA (the Tunnel of Guides):** *I very angry. I warn him, if you do this, I put spell on you. And he say, "Go right ahead."*

*"This is your therapy," he say. "This good for you." He tie up the children and put them behind the couch and watch them scream. And then he wish to make love. He very sick. Nobody know but me.*

*So soon I make my spell. One time, I bring candles, black and white. I chant, and I make him chant. Soon Sidney is howling like a wolf. He want a power animal so bad. He think his power animal be wolf. So it easy to make Sidney into a wolf, my poor Warrior of the Sky. I turn him into a wolf. And I want to teach him lesson, not to hurt children. So I take his belt from pants, and I hit him hard, so.*

*And then my poor Warrior, he throws up.*

*After this, my poor Warrior goes away on vacation.*

■

"Zoe, you've got a hell of an imagination," said Wald, laughing, when she heard Zoe's story. She traced with Zoe how these fantasies recapitulated her childhood. "You have to realize you are making this up."

"Goodness," said Sister Johanna. It was July 13, 1981. They were in the parish offices next to St. Peter's, on Coral Way catercorner from St. Peter's Hospital. Sister Johanna was the counselor whom Father Kirkland had recommended. Zoe had called her the day after Sidney went away.

Seventy years old, stooped and slightly plump in her

# Zoe Parry: Inner Structure

*July 1992*
*Discussing Dr. Sidney Altman.*
*Approximately 105 personalities.*
*9 Tunnels.*

Personalities God's Child (the Golden Child, Angel Child), Selina, and Mary Cora are present in more than one tunnel.

Some personalities seem to share consciousness for certain types of experiences.

Mother Zoe seems to share consciousness with many.

<br>

The Tunnel of
Careful
Observation

The Tunnel of
Power

The Tunnel of
Light and Purity

The Tunnel of
Dreams

**GOD'S
CHILD**

The Tunnel of
Secrets

The Tunnel of
Eternal
Protection

The Tunnel of
Guides

The Tunnel of
Limbo

The Tunnel of
Hell

well-worn navy blue suit, Sister had a kind, brusque manner. "Now, Zoe," she said roughly, caught herself, and smoothed her voice. "Zoe, please help me. How can I convey to you how wrong this conduct is?"

"I'm afraid I deserve it," Zoe said.

The nun nodded, recognizing the sincerity, and then shook her head, disagreeing with the sentiment. "You certainly do not. He is your servant, you are not his."

"My servant?"

"He's agreed to help you in your search for health, just as you've agreed to be guided by his recommendations."

"Guided?" Zoe smiled.

"What's funny?"

"Sidney doesn't guide. He orders."

Sister reached across her desk and took Zoe's hand in both of hers. She spoke earnestly and slowly. "Zoe, dear. You must report this man. Just imagine if he went from you to someone else."

Zoe blanched. "I can't betray him."

"What if I called Dr. Altman and spoke to him as professional to professional? This might deter him."

"I don't know," Zoe whispered. "I'm afraid. He can put me in jail and throw away the key."

"What if I called Judge Wood?"

"And ruin Sidney? Please, Sister, don't make me destroy Sidney."

Sidney, according to the public record, was already destroyed. He was in the hospital, his practice shutting down, his behavior so wild that even his colleagues were beginning to notice.

Altman must have known that with Zoe, he'd smashed his career beyond any hope of resuscitation. Her descriptions of his subsequent conduct also make a pretty good case that he'd developed acute paranoid schizophrenia.

During their session in September, according to Zoe's depositions, Altman started shouting he was being followed. Pacing, he cursed Governor Graham. "He's been after me for a long time. When this story breaks, it will be bigger than Watergate." Then he described strange messages left with his answering service. "Death threats.

Someone's out to get me. Do you know about these messages?"

Zoe, still standing, froze.

Altman's hands rested on the gray rock paperweight. He stared at Zoe. Suddenly she blushed and hung her head.

"Aha," said Altman. He hefted the rock and flung it at Zoe's belly.

It hit with a thud. Zoe fell backward, then lay still on the floor. She was very good at pretending to be dead.

"That's all," said Altman officiously, sitting down and reaching for his book. "Until the ninth!"

"The ninth," Zoe said, and got up to leave.

That evening, after Zoe summarized this session, Sister Johanna begged Zoe to leave Altman. Zoe refused. "I have to abide by the rules of the court."

Victims of severe abuse subsequently can stubbornly pretend perfect submission to authority. While showing perfect obedience in her sessions, and without betraying the man she internally called "Father," Zoe started making appointments and breaking them. She would call in sick, forget the date, run out of gas.

Altman's license to prescribe drugs was revoked; the public record does not explicitly state why. According to his widow's deposition, he was behaving erratically. Soon he would be placed under the care of a twenty-four-hour-a-day nurse.

In another deposition, Altman's neighbor, a university professor named Jasper Kirby, described how Elyse Altman had sought his help in getting Altman to see a doctor. He also testified that he'd been called to the police station once to fetch Altman, who'd been picked up driving under the influence of alcohol and jailed.

When asked by the lawyers whether he was aware that Altman had been a patient at a psychiatric facility, Kirby said yes, adding that Altman had signed himself out against medical advice. The lawyers then described five in-patient facilities at which Altman was held in the period from August 1981 to February 1982. The last hospital was St. Peter's, from which Altman had just been suspended by Dr. Earl Chasen, his supervisor.

On September 15, Carmine demanded a divorce.

"Why?" Zoe whispered. "Why!"

"I can't get the picture of you and him out of my mind. Doing those things. I keep seeing it."

■

**MOTHER ZOE (the Tunnel of Light and Purity):** *Not only did Carmine sue for divorce, against all our religious beliefs, but my court report was due October 1. Dr. Altman would not write it for me. Every second, I thought the police would come and put me in jail.*

*On October 10, I entered Dr. Altman's office to find it in total disarray. Papers all over, stale food, dirty cups. He looked worse than ever. He pointed up to the ceiling.*

*"We're being bugged by the FBI. Come on. Or they'll get me."*

*He pushed me into the elevator.*

*Outside, he pointed at one car after another and said, "This is an FBI car." At his car, he opened the passenger door and threw me in.*

*We took off with a squeal of tires. As we drove he pointed out "secret agents." "Your friend Janet is one." He stopped at a red light, crammed a candy bar into his mouth, and wrote on the wrapper, "That produces ultrasound, which usually jams the bugs." Fortunately, I kept that piece of evidence.*

■

That candy wrapper is now in a box in a yard-square stack of boxes in an Arsdale storage room, leased to the firm of Bertrand and Bertrand, medical malpractice lawyers.

■

**AGNES CAINE (the Tunnel of Secrets):** *Then he went up Flagg Highway and took us high on a cliff. He said he would run the car over, and I said, "Do it! Hurry!" But everyone else inside was screaming, "Stop!"*

*Suddenly he slammed on the horn, did a U-turn, and drove back to Coral Way at seventy miles an hour. When we got back to the parking lot, he said he would be having patients visit his home from now on. He stopped talking for a moment and*

*passed his hand across his forehead. For a second he looked at
me with the saddest expression in his eyes.*

■

**SISTER ZOE ANN (the Tunnel of Power):** *Janet drove us to St.
Ann's. I walked through the door, and it was like someone
saying "Welcome!" The sun streamed through the stained-
glass windows. I began to pray . . .*

■

The stained-glass windows at St. Ann's include the forgiving, gentle countenances of the Virgin Mary, St. Ann,
and St. Thérèse. The haloes are yellow ovals, in contrast
to the spiky, austere-looking crowns that grace the
blessed at St. Peter's. The congregation is young. No
hollow-eyed patients from a hospital next door. Next
door to St. Ann's are a preschool and an ice cream parlor.
Zoe begged God to take control, and says he answered.

After, Zoe called Mitchell Cox. The next day she sat
in his office, told her story, and watched him roll his
eyes. "I think it's very important," she said, "that you
tell Judge Wood and find out what effect this will have on
my probation."

His voice was very cool as he disagreed. "I don't
think it's that important."

On October 14, the next time she saw Cox, she
brought out her only piece of evidence—the candy wrapper. Cox nervously said, "Don't see this man any more."

Zoe's court report was now two weeks late. She had
called Altman repeatedly, and now, in desperation, she
agreed to see him at his house. On October 17, Janet
reluctantly drove her to Cypress Estates.

The doctor and his family lived in an immaculately
restored Spanish colonial revival house above a river.
Elyse Altman opened the door. Her black hair was tou-
sled, and her brilliant, alert eyes looked troubled.

They nodded; they'd met at the office. Elyse escorted
her to the living room and left. Zoe examined the deep
velvet sofas, the concert-sized Steinway, the huge granite
fireplace, the wet bar. One wall was filled with original

oil paintings signed "EA." French doors looked down into the river.

But the living room was marred by stacks of files. Papers spilled onto the coffee table and over the couch. This was obviously Altman's temporary office.

On the coffee table was the portrait of a young girl with Sidney Altman's curls and Elyse Altman's brilliant eyes. Edie. "She doesn't seem like an incest victim, but then," thought Zoe, "who does?"

Her therapist entered, looking relaxed in a plaid shirt and clean chinos. "Hi, Zoe. You look nice." She was wearing tight jeans, a white shirt, and spike heels. "Gosh it's chilly." He lit the ready-laid fire, then went to the bar. Pouring a vodka, he offered it; she declined, and he gulped it down.

In the fireplace, the fire roared to life.

■

**ZOE 10 (the Tunnel of Secrets):** *He came over, took my hands and held them tight, real close to the fire. He said, "If you tell, I'll—" And he pushed my hands down.*

■

Zoe says her hands were sore for a week. Her voice quavers with stress. A bevy of alters comes out to describe the session.

■

**ZOE 10 (the Tunnel of Secrets):** *Then he laughed and released me. "It was just a game."*

*"Nice game." I started asking about the stuff in the room. There was an old fencing sword above the fireplace.*

*"Nice game!" Sidney repeated. Grabbing the sword from the wall, he ran up to me, grabbed me again, and put the sword to my throat.*

■

**DONNA WHITE (the Tunnel of Power):** *The sword came closer. "Nice sword," I said.*

*"Ha!" said Dr. Altman. "You didn't flinch. You must not be guilty! Congratulations. You pass the test."*

■

**MOTHER ZOE (the Tunnel of Light and Purity):** *Sidney dropped the sword and dragged me out the French doors and down the hill. I was stumbling and tripping. High heels aren't meant for a hike through weeds.*

*He stopped near the river. "Isn't this lovely?" he said. I looked into the river. It was full of rocks and racing along. I prayed like never before. "Wouldn't we like to be swept away? It's human, a wish to die." He was holding me over the water. . . . I have no idea how we escaped.*

■

**GIOVANNI PARRY (the Tunnel of Careful Observation):** *I know how. Man, I fucked his brain. He'd told Zoe in a session about a neighbor of his that got killed. So now, I started talking about Carmine's connections amongst an organization Sidney feared. "Close family members high up," you know the type of thing. He knew all about it, Sidney did. He lapped it up. I loved it. He was so fucking paranoid.*

*But, man, I didn't know. I was just out to scare him. I didn't have a weapon. What could I use but my mind?*

■

**THE GOLDEN CHILD (the Tunnel of Careful Observation):** *That's right, Giovanni, you did a very good job. We have to protect the system, right?*

■

**GINO PERRONA (the Tunnel of Careful Observation):** *I'm the one that called his answering service.*

■

**THE GOLDEN CHILD (the Tunnel of Careful Observation):** *And left the message—that you'd blow him away if he fucked with Zoe. Thank you for the message, Gino.*

*If there's a threat, I strike! With madness. Then with death. Just look at John Perret, at the father, and now, at Sidney darling. Cold and rotting in their graves.*

■

Back at the house, Zoe asked if Altman would mind giving her that probation report—now.

"Oh, time for work." He sighed. Getting out his tape recorder, he mumbled a few lines. Then he dashed into the kitchen for cookies, ice cream, cake, and fruit.

Mrs. Altman came running. "What are you doing, Sid?"

"Curing Zoe."

"I'll bet." She sighed. "Sid, other patients are waiting." He handed her the recorder, and politely asked, "Elyse dear—would you be so kind as to transcribe a letter?" She nodded and left.

Later, Elyse Altman would reluctantly testify that her husband was taking Dyazide and Inderal for his high blood pressure, plus Lopressor. "They couldn't quite figure out what was wrong with him. We felt that Lopressor disoriented him." When asked about her husband's decline from September to November, she said, "He was disoriented. He couldn't remember facts. I don't know, it just wasn't Sid."

When asked if his behavior had deteriorated more after his release from the hospital, Elyse Altman said that was a hard question, since she'd been at work full-time and had hired a full-time nurse. When asked if Altman had delusions that people were trying to kill him, she answered, "Yeah. That was part of the disorientation. A friend of his was killed when we were on vacation. And so was the so-called drunken behavior, part of his disorientation."

The loyal wife returned and handed Zoe her report and walked her to the door. They said good-bye. Zoe looked back. Altman was gazing into the fire and rubbing his hands through his hair until it stuck up in two points.

This is Zoe's last image of Altman.

At home, though, the next day, Zoe's phone rang. It was Altman. He pleaded with her to let him move in—that day. "I need to escape," he said. He promised he'd stay out of the way. He'd sleep in the living room, under the coffee table. "Please take me in. Please don't leave me."

"I'm sorry, Sidney," Zoe found herself saying.

"And so I fail him," alter Selina comments. "Ride into sunset. Farewell, Warrior of the Sky."

Dial tone. Zoe looked at the phone in her hand. Slowly, she dialed Sister Johanna's number. Then she called Barry Bertrand, a lawyer she'd seen on a TV talk show, whose firm specialized in psychiatric malpractice lawsuits.

*Letter, December 11, 1981, Sister Johanna to the Florida Board of Medical Quality Assurance:*

In July 1981 Zoe Parry was referred to me because of extreme anxiety and guilt regarding sexual acts between her therapist and herself. The acts were described as mutual masturbation and attempted coitus. . . . My present concern is twofold. First, that steps be taken to ensure that Dr. Altman does not practice psychiatry until and unless he is competent to do so; second, that Mrs. Parry be spared any further anxiety over the matter. He has repeatedly threatened her, and she is understandably afraid. I therefore request that in any communications with him, her name be withheld.

On January 5, 1982, Zoe called Altman's answering service and told them she would no longer be coming in. They said another doctor had taken over Altman's practice. "When?" she asked.

"Three weeks ago," the service operator said.

Calling the doctor, she asked why Altman had left.

"He had a chemical psychosis, high blood pressure, and alcoholism. He may never practice again."

■

**THE GOLDEN CHILD (the Tunnel of Careful Observation):** (In a sweet, melodic voice.) *I fell from grace. By a man's ugly face! Well, I regained my power quite nicely, a thousand plus years ago, my dear. It came back in a nice little form, a golden girl with big green eyes.*

(In a harsh, witchy voice.) *When I put the curse on a person, it stays! I am the Golden Child. Very old, very young. I*

*had it planned, when John Perret touched the body—He died in
a few weeks, didn't he? And it didn't take long for Dr. Altman.*

*There was a little girl, who had a little curl, right in the
middle of her forehead. When she was good, she was very very
good. And when she was bad—SHE WAS HORRID!*

■

On January 10, 1982, Zoe met with Barry Bertrand. Then
she met with Patricia Wald. According to Zoe's journal,
Wald held Zoe in her arms, promised to take care of little
Zoe Parry and make her all better—the same words that
Zoe records as having been said by Altman, on February
9, 1978.

Sister Johanna wrote to Judge Wood. After describing
Altman's behavior, she asked to take over as Zoe's
probation officer.

On February 20, after sixteen years of practice as a
psychiatrist and two months as a patient, Dr. Sidney
Altman hanged himself. He climbed the footbridge by his
river, attached surgical suture wire to the railing, tied the
other end around his neck, and jumped. He did an excel-
lent job. The suture sank an inch into his flesh. It took
four police officers to cut him down.

Zoe heard about Altman's death from Dr. Chasen.

■

**MOTHER ZOE (the Tunnel of Light and Purity):** *He didn't
have to say a word. I said "Sidney is dead. Did he take his
own life?"*

*Dr. Chasen looked stunned. "How did you know?"*

■

"The question," says Zoe, "is how could I not know?"

■

**ZOE [the Patient] (the Tunnel of Dreams):** *From his grave,
Sidney calls out to me. "Look what you've done! How could
you kill me, after I saved you?"*

*You know, I was so sick, at that time. What if I made him
sick? He seemed so strong. I am sure this is not the case, but I
feel guilty.*

Barry Bertrand says that Altman never found out about
Zoe's lawsuit. He stresses this. Altman never knew. The
only person who knew, other than Zoe, Sister Johanna,
and himself, Barry Bertrand, was Earl Chasen. Every
year on August 6, until August 6, 1991, Mother Zoe
baked a birthday cake for Dr. Altman. And every year,
until April 30, 1992, Selina went up to his office and laid
flowers by his door.

## Zoe Parry: Inner Structure

*August 1992*
*Discussing Dr. Wald, mothers, early childhood.*
*Approximately 100 personalities.*

**SECRETS**
Angel Child

Body of an
Expression

ZOE

Enter "Passed-
Away" Angel
Child and Suffer

Protected by
Angel Child

Isolation of a
Soul = Empty
Tunnels

**SILENCE OF
THE HOLY INNOCENTS**

Holding Cell

Boom!   Pow!                    Bang!   Bang!

# Zoe Parry: Inner Structure

### August 1992

When mothers and Zoe's therapy with Pat Wald are discussed, Zoe's inner geography twists and involutes. Her personality map of August 1992 shows one hundred alters in five areas. She scatters drawings over the page: blood, knives, piles of cash, Jewish stars, crosses. Stick figures stagger from one side of the page to the other, labeled "Passed Away and Suffer": Sidney Altman, Pa Pa, Luke. Grandpa and Grandma are tidily dead in a little coffin.

This month, the name of Zoe's core is "Isolation of a Soul equals Empty Tunnels." Zoe feels completely alone. She's discussing events that she believes are sinful and secret, events that, to this day, pull her apart.

# 4

# Mommy Pat

It was a sunny morning one week after Sidney Altman's death. Winter had turned to spring. A riot of sparrows swooped into the purple lantana hedge by the Parrys' house and began quarreling over food trash.

Inside, Zoe was deaf to the birds' cries, to the breezes rattling her screen. She was on her bed, dolls heaped around, a music box lullabying in an endless loop. Davey was at school; Janet, at mass; Carmine, out hunting for a C'zy Eff'cy Ap't, Ch'p. Today Barry and Suzi Bertrand were to meet with Zoe to evaluate *Parry vs. Altman*. In the midst of dressing, she had lain down to soothe herself.

Wrapped in her mother's old lace quilt, she sniffed the corner, curled into a fetal position, put her thumb in her mouth, and began to suck.

The phone rang. Her message machine flicked on. *Beep*. Zoe May's voice whispered, "Zoe? Are you there?"

Pushing away the dolls, Zoe picked up. "Hello, Mother," she said in a normal voice.

"Well, Zoe, I've, uh, done it," Zoe May quavered. "I've finally cut the cord."

Zoe, silent, twirled the phone cord in her hand. The

dolls lay helter-skelter near her, eyes wide. Jesus stared at her from a 3-D postcard on the wall.

"I've sold my things and— moved."

The phone cord bobbled. "What?"

"Moved, Zoe. To Manordale. To, um, a lovely town house. With all new fixings. Even a, um, a dishwasher." As Zoe gasped, she added, "It's only twenty miles away. You had three weeks to say whatever you desired! You approved this, you know—over Sunday dinner."

Mrs. Bryant had a consort—Harry McEwen, who had been Dave Bryant's boss. Gallant and authoritarian, "Rhett" had since Bryant's death squired Mrs. Bryant to Zoe's house each and every Sunday. Often they'd brought dinner; Zoe, unable to cook or to eat, had sat and listened. She'd heard enough of Rhett's jokes, Zoe thought now, for a lifetime.

"I approved nothing of the kind," she said.

"I know you like Rhett. He's a nice, nice man."

"Rhett's an asshole." It just popped out. "And you're not even married!" Outside, in a beat of wings, the sparrows started away.

"Well, don't take on so. I feel quite badly enough—"

Betrayed! Zoe yanked the phone from the wall. Instantly she plugged it in again. The line was dead. She didn't have her mother's number.

One hand reached for the other wrist and slashed. The fingernails raked the soft skin, three, four times, till red blood dripped onto her mother's quilt. The dolls stared, smiling painted smiles. Still, the telephone did not ring.

"Ready?" came Janet's voice from downstairs.

Clad in white silk and houndstooth-check wool, jeweled, perfumed, wigged, and painted, Zoe sobbed as Janet drove her to the Bertrands'. Janet had taped Zoe's wrist and dressed her; their friendship was based on lifting each other over the humps. This year, as Zoe had come to dread leaving home for any reason, Janet drove her everywhere.

"Calm down, or you'll blow your meeting."

Bertrand and Bertrand was—still is—one of the top five medical malpractice law firms in Florida. Handling two to three hundred cases at any given time, Barry and Suzi Bertrand, brother and sister, were enormously busy. Their time was money, Janet reminded Zoe.

"Let's focus on what you're going to ask Mr. Bertrand."

"I can't think about anything but Mother."

"Settle down. This is important. And you're smearing your mascara." Janet pulled over. "There are tissues in the glove compartment."

Twenty minutes later the Bertrands' secretary ushered them into Barry Bertrand's office—a cool bath of leather-upholstered wealth. Carmine was already there, perched on a chamois sofa. "I found a place," he said. "Cheap."

*"Shh,"* said Janet, holding up a finger.

Carmine grimaced tightly and hunkered down.

Behind his desk, Bertrand narrowed fleshy eyelids. Malpractice lawyers must have a bit of family therapist in them, or they don't last in their business. He noted the silent spat, the friend playing monkey in the middle, the way Zoe quietly grabbed attention: a good chemistry for a lawsuit. He'd already decided to take the case and this was encouraging. Now Bertrand half-stood and held out his hand. Zoe lifted hers. The bandaged part did not show. They shook.

"Hello, Mrs. Parry, Ms. Moore." Bertrand's voice is like chocolate. "Have a seat. I'm accepting your case."

"Why?" Zoe chose the chair farthest from Carmine.

Bertrand blinked. Articulate, worldly, thirty-eight, he'd formed a favorable impression of Zoe's toughness. In their two previous meetings, he'd met only the feisty alter Donna. He had no idea how dissociated Zoe was, or how depressed.

He answered literally. "Reason One, frankly, is Judge Wood's opinion of you. He stuck his neck out for you and he's the finest jurist in the county.

"Two, I believe your story. Three, it's fascinating.

"Four, my sister and I can break ground with this case. Several of our current negligence suits dovetail with yours.

"Five, and most important, is how we work together.

Lawyer and client have got to get along—and I think we can.''

He hitched his chair. Three pairs of eyes tracked him. ''Altman's confusion of roles—serving both as your therapist and probation officer, initiating sexual relations, then reversing the patient-therapist dynamic and having you advise him—should not happen. Ever. We have a chance to make that assertion law, and that is professionally exciting. Plus we may win a considerable sum from the estate. Now, Suzi and I have drawn up an agreement—''

''I'm suing Elyse Altman?'' Zoe grabbed her purse. Carmine sighed explosively.

''Do you have a problem with that?'' inquired Bertrand.

''Oh, gosh.'' His client had the look of someone who's been socked in the gut. ''Gosh, yes. I don't want a cent of Elyse's money. You gotta make sure it comes out of insurance.''

Bertrand scrawled a note on his phone pad.

''I couldn't face them in court,'' sighed Zoe.

''Whaddya mean, court?'' Carmine's face turned red.

''If we go to trial—'' started Bertrand.

''No way,'' hissed Carmine.

''We might have to,'' Zoe whispered. ''I feel so—I can't say. I have to make things right—''

Her husband rose and started pacing. ''Yeah. I can just see the headlines. 'Former self-rapist gets screwed again!' ''

Zoe closed her eyes.

''Forget it,'' insisted Carmine. He put his face up to Zoe's. ''You are not dragging our good name through the mud. Not mine, not Davey's. Not anymore.''

His wife sighed. ''I'd want to kill myself if I didn't—''

''Yeah, that's great, dear. That solves everything.'' Carmine lifted his hands. Janet's foot began to jiggle.

''Calm down, folks,'' said Bertrand. ''Nobody's saying we've got to go to trial. We might settle.''

''Couldn't she get more in court?'' suggested Janet.

''What if I lose?'' Zoe asked her dismissively. Now both her hands were on the purse.

Bertrand nodded. "This case will hinge on why Zoe kept going back to Altman. Juries don't understand the concept of transference. They won't see why it turned sexual, or once it did, why she continued therapy. How could a jury understand in two weeks what takes years to develop? Chances are, they'd think, 'The guy was a doctor! He knew what he was doing!' "

Zoe's eyes welled as she concluded, "We can't win?"

Carmine looked up to God, then out the window.

Bertrand held up his hand. "I didn't say that. After discovery, if the evidence is good—and it will be—there's the mandatory settlement conference. We could come out fine. The guy suicided, remember? I don't think they'll insist on a trial."

" 'Discovery'?"

"The process by which a lawyer obtains information," said Bertrand. "Getting records and so forth. And my personal favorite—depositions. You can ask witnesses a very wide range of questions indeed. The only test is, 'Can this question lead to discoverable evidence?' Which means we can ask almost anything, Zoe."

*Anything,* Zoe mused. *There's a lot I need to ask Sidney.* The tears rolled out; mascara blackened her cheeks as she signed the papers.

■

After the meeting at the Bertrands', Carmine had rushed off, while Zoe rode to her next appointment.

"But Pat understands me," Zoe pleaded.

Janet despised Wald. "She's so unprofessional! The way she bounces in and giggles, 'Next! Tee-hee!' And the way she asks you to come in at night! Meanwhile, I sit in the car, till ten, eleven, midnight, freezing and waiting, waiting and freezing—"

"So she can give me more time," whispered Zoe.

Janet's hands whitened on the steering wheel; she fell silent. Later she'd tell me, "Zoe needed all the therapy she could get. She trusted this dip-head. And at the time I thought trust was the most important thing. God forgive me."

Trust wasn't the most important thing to Zoe. Nor were skills. She saw doctors through her own unmet needs.

Dr. Wald's gaze in pictures is uncertain. Her voice on tape sounds nervous, then overassertive; her handwriting in documents wavers; her values shift with the winds.

The Board of Medical Quality Assurance maintains files on Wald. The attorney general is in the process of assessing the legal admissibility of evidence against Wald. This evidence thoroughly suggests, through Wald's own words, that at least with Zoe, she was a manipulative cheat. Her analyses were self-serving and predictably unhealthy for Zoe.

Another therapist in Wald's community describes her in a hushed voice, shuddering, "She isn't listed anymore—*is* she?" The therapist adds that several of Wald's ex-patients have bitterly complained—not just Zoe.

When two therapists unacquainted with Wald examined Zoe's material on her, they urged her to sue. Another therapist tells me that Wald should be removed from practice.

The consensus: Wald can't enforce limits. Her love is worse than none—it's using and disrespectful. Plus she has one bloody hell of a history.

Wald has been a member of the American Psychiatric Association, the American Medical Association, and the Association of Medical Women. On paper she's qualified to practice. She passed medical school and a rigorous training program. However, she's a shadowy presence. I could find no articles on or by Wald, for example. After 1983, she removed her phone number, address, and vita—everything but her name—from the rosters. It's a rare member of a professional organization who does that—who runs from recognition.

That day, one week after Altman's death, Janet pulled up to Wald's office, a green condo on the coast, with forebodings but no hard facts. She watched Zoe all but skip up the path toward her session. Janet's foot jiggled on the clutch.

Inside Zoe, an alter who'd slept for years, had already

begun to make her presence known. A rebel "just because," Serena had about as much in common with Janet as James Dean would with Mother Teresa. With her yellow hair, blue eyes, and lust for hot dresses, hot sex, and hot food, Serena, eighteen, now craved Wald. As a child she'd defied Zoe May and run off to hunt women. Today after Zoe May's call, she'd cheered. Now she felt she was free to love Wald—and free to make Wald love her back.

■

**SERENA (the Tunnel Protected by the Golden Child):** *From the moment I'd met Pat in 1969, at the Richfield Center, I'd adored her. Her hair was gray. She had violet eyes, a very pretty face, and a beautiful smile. Around her neck she wore our gift—a gold locket with a picture of big Zoe on one side and Zoe at age five on the other.*

*In Pat I'd finally found my older woman, the mother who would fill my empty spaces. I always wanted her, always. In 1974 I told her I loved her. She couldn't handle it. Suddenly, without saying good-bye, she turned me over to Dr. Frederick Small. There was no closure. I was devastated.*

*In 1978, when Sidney contacted Pat, I knew I must call her. When things started going so wrong, I did. When I found her again in 1981, I gasped. Pat had platinum blonde hair! She looked young! Her office was exactly the same. Pink walls and a rose-colored couch, prints on the walls, of girls and mothers. And her smile, her touch, these hadn't changed. And the love. Oh, God, the love.*

■

Wald had gone straight from life as a debutante into college and her training. Licensed in 1966, three years before Zoe first limped in, Wald was by 1982 about fifty, divorced and menopausal, carrying the load of two kids, a huge debt, a taste for primal escape, and unfulfilled desires.

Zoe remembers, she and Wald spent little time on Davey, Carmine, and Janet or on Zoe's work as a geriatric nurse's aide or on how she could mark out a bearable territory as a homemaker. They spent hours on ideal parents, Altman as Satan and other men as ball-less jerks, being in touch with feeling and caring, and the ultimate leap from a final Peak out into Universal Oneness. A less adoring patient might have requested some mundane, practical advice. Zoe didn't. To her Wald seemed sympathetic and safely sexual—a balm after the dogmatic, bossy Sid.

■

**MOTHER ZOE (the Tunnel of Secrets):** *It was my fault, I sobbed, that Sidney had died.*

*Pat held me, kissed me, and wiped away my tears. "None of this was your fault," she said. "Someone should have sat down with Sidney. I used to do it all the time. One case, the shrink was a full-blown paranoid schizophrenic, running a camp for wayward girls. What got me onto this?" Pat giggled. "Merde!"*

*"Thank you for taking me on," I cried. She nodded, looking oh, so sympathetic. Then I asked, "Remember our little locket?" She smiled and opened her hand—and there it was. She had kept it all these years!*

■

Zoe says Wald was terrible about limits, including when sessions would start and end. She then describes some strange interactions between Wald's patients. Usually a therapist's patients do not even see each other. Individual therapy is usually, by choice, an exclusive relationship.

According to Zoe, the patient who had the appointment after hers, an enormous brunette whom we'll call Adrienne Eames, soon became her rival and her tormentor. Adrienne apparently thought nothing of interrupting Zoe's session, even walking in. Today, at the session following Zoe's meeting with Barry Bertrand, she knocked when she wanted Zoe's session to end, followed Zoe down the hall from Wald's waiting room into the bathroom, and stood by the stall door, dropping intermittent insults and threats.

*I'd better change my appointment time,* Mother Zoe

thought. She got up without finishing her business and went to gather her belongings. Adrienne followed her back. "Yes, Patsy and I have so much to say to each other. Our sessions go on for hours."

*She's mine, bitch,* thought Serena.

■

From Wald's, Janet drove Zoe to St. Ann's, to her weekly session with Sister Johanna. In June, Sister planned to retire to her order's mother convent in upstate New York. Today she reminded Zoe of this.

In 1993, Sister Johanna is in retreat; she will only speak for three minutes, to Zoe, not me. She refuses to corroborate facts about 1981 and 1982 or to reestablish any connection. "At the time I did God's work. But now I do not wish to be more involved. God tells me my work lies elsewhere now." Reminded of her letters on Zoe's behalf, the notes the Bertrands kept regarding her testimony, and the statements she gave to the Board of Medical Quality Assurance and asked if she has anything to add, the Sister replies, "Whatever you wish to write about me, you may. Zoe Parry will always be in my prayers."

As for Father Kirkland, he can hardly remember any details, his memory is so sketchy and it happened so long ago; such a terrible case—wasn't it? Is Zoe still a Catholic? How is Zoe faring—in her new church?

But Zoe had forgotten Sister would soon be leaving, Sister, who was so dear to her. Sister's glasses were smudged, her eyes weary after a lifetime of hard work and harder prayer, her cheeks lined but serene, her hands folded calmly. Zoe ached with pain and love and the flooding fear that without Sister, she would die.

Sister bowed her head. Zoe joined her; they prayed. After, Zoe smiled at Sister, pleading tacitly for more.

Sister sighed. "We've made terrific headway. You are fighting the good fight with your lawsuit. You will make a good life for yourself, Zoe."

Zoe did not believe she could make a good life for herself, without Sister. So Zoe's inner system busily began to incubate an internal convent—the "Poor Johannas." To this day, the twelve Johannas sublimate painful feelings and suppress knowledge of Zoe's painful actions, through trying to please God in thought and deed. Originally they awoke to strengthen the Catholic alter Zoe Ann, whose faith had been shaken by the Altman ordeal, and to find a venue in which she could do saintly deeds.

Sister Johanna began to speak about a certain mission in downtown Tampa, called Haven. This mission houses a lay order of Franciscans, called tertiaries.

If she herself were living in the world, Sister enthused, she would work at Haven. The order helped the poor and the sick, teenage mothers and their infants: "Holy Innocents of God," Sister called them. This was Zoe's most secret name for herself. Sister's sanction of Haven, she felt, was an omen.

Early the next day, Zoe had Janet drive her. Forty minutes down the highway, the outside world changed from green and blue to brown and gray as they whipped past suburbs into a burned-out district shadowed by abandoned factory buildings. Haven occupied the one clean block. It included a church and five tenements decorated in Early Graffiti.

As Janet waited in the car, Zoe—lugging a bulging thirty-gallon trash bag—entered Haven, hunted and found Father Tigris. Sister had not mentioned the looks of the man. Tall, his fine hair cropped short, he resembled a young Frank Sinatra. As Zoe, confused and pleased, set down the bag, it spilled out clothes and toys. Father smiled. "What's this, Santa?"

"An offering." She lifted a cross-eyed stuffed panda.

"Did anyone tell you we're doing a Christmas party for the poor in ten months?"

Zoe shook her head.

"Now, correct me if I'm wrong," he said, smiling, "but I think you're about to say more. What's your name, dear?"

"Zoe Ann."

"God bless, Zoe Ann. What's up?"

"I need . . ." she whispered. "Not just to pray, but to redeem by concrete acts the salvation of this dear soul."

"Ah." Father frowned. "How, exactly?"

Zoe left an hour later, carrying a slim volume, *Hidden Power: The Rule of the Secular Franciscan Order*. Her head buzzed with ideas; her heart, with comfort. She'd met three of Haven's twenty tertiaries, who'd hugged her when they saw the offering. The Poor Johannas were elated. For starters, Zoe had promised Father to beef up the Christmas party for the poor.

Once home, Zoe memorized The Rule. Then she called Father. "Let me join your order."

"Whoa, Nelly. Not so fast. Initiates practice within the community for a year. Then the order decides on them."

"So I can join next spring?"

"Summer, perhaps. Let me mail you our schedule."

■

A few days later, Zoe sat in Sister Johanna's office crying. She'd just told Sister about Haven, and her secret hope that Sister would decide to stay had just been dashed. Sister had congratulated Zoe, patted her arm, and begun to talk about her own imminent departure. "You'll be in such good hands. I've been researching Sisters who practice, not just psychiatric social work, but actual professional psychology. A Sister Bernadette Alain's name came up. This woman seems to be one of the finest—"

"Thank you, Sister," said Zoe, thinking, *I want you— not this Bernadette!* After the session, she had Janet drive her straight to Haven, where she could try to immerse herself in more good deeds than were humanly possible. She quadrupled her already commendable effort.

Zoe was unconscious of the stress her unusually good behavior was causing her system. She balances equal and opposing forces. Generating a convent of twelve strict nuns, she would also generate a coven. By now they were already lighting candles, making anonymous telephone calls, and making secret plans to protect Zoe, in their own way, from the pain of Sister's departure.

While Zoe studied St. Francis, Serena studied Wald.

She decided: Wald hated men as much as she did. When Zoe had denigrated Carmine, Wald—doing what she called supportive therapy—had romanticized Zoe and ripped him to shreds, clucking, "You're a heroine. I don't know how you can stand him." She even asserted that it was Carmine who needed therapy—not Zoe. Serena found that kind of cute.

"Do you really think so?" It felt like the jolt of truth each time statements like these connected.

"Yes! Don't let them bring you down! You're the hero, not him!"

Serena loved it.

But on March 5, Wald revealed her true point of view. It wasn't a hatred of men, but a love of money that motivated her. Zoe was crying, "How can Carmine even consider a divorce? It's immoral! Irreligious!" She dropped the fact that if they divorced, Carmine's health insurance would no longer cover her. Wald blanched.

"You are so ill," she sympathized. "You don't deserve this stress, in addition to everything else. Zoe, you must become independent. We've got to get Social Security to pay for sessions—lots of them."

"But that's a public agency. I'm on probation." Zoe was ashen—thoroughly shamed. To this day, what society thinks of her is fearsomely important. "The kidnapping, Sidney—I'll have to tell SSI about all of it?"

"So what, if it pays for your care?"

■

**ZOE [the Patient] (the Tunnel and Body of an Expression):** *Pat scrawled a letter, folded it, and handed it to me. "No question, with this, they'll pay," she said.*

■

Alone in the elevator, Zoe opened Wald's note:

To Whom It May Concern:

The above patient carries a primary diagnosis of

schizophrenic reaction, chronic. . . . Recently she and her psychiatrist had a sexual relationship. During this time, she was served with a divorce and regressed considerably. She is infantile and hysterical. She has never reached a genital level of function. She has never held a job. She has never even functioned in her role as wife or mother . . .

Zoe sank to the floor of the elevator. "It was the kiss of death," she said later.

It certainly was a breach of standards. While sometimes, yes, a doctor may phrase her evaluation to a patient in one way and differently to an insurance carrier and to herself, the doctor simply does not just hand such shocking bad news to the patient. When the bell pinged downstairs, Janet had to scrape her regressed friend off the elevator floor.

"Later," says Zoe, "to make matters worse, yet another support crumbled."

The phone rang. Zoe, lying wrapped in her mother's quilt, slowly rolled out of bed and answered, "Parrys'."

"He don't want you, you used-up old bag—he wants me."

"Who is this?" Zoe's voice acquired energy.

"As if you don't know. This is Linda—Carmine's girlfriend. He's gonna leave you, no matter what you pull."

"What are you talking about?"

"Whadja do, bitch—disconnect his phone?"

■

**MOTHER ZOE (the Tunnel of Secrets):** *I realized that Carmine hadn't just rejected me—he'd chosen someone else! After I finally hung up, I called Carmine. The phone buzzed twenty, thirty times—no answer.*

■

The next morning, there was still no answer.

Wild with fear, Zoe had Janet take her to Carmine's. "The man might be seeing this Linda, but I loved him.

Maybe not as a husband, but surely as someone I cared for, who'd supported me for two decades," Zoe later said.

Janet sat in the locked car, with the windows rolled up.

After banging on Carmine's door, waiting, and banging again, Zoe heard a weak shuffling from within. The door clicked open. "Stubble covered Carmine's face," Zoe says. "He looked like he was about to keel over."

She forgot Linda. "Oh, Carmine! What's wrong?"

"I feel totally weird," said Carmine. Suddenly he clutched his gut and moaned, sliding down the doorjamb.

Carmine was not a whiner. Zoe hauled him inside. He'd never even unpacked. Cartons littered the floor; shirts spilled out, dragging in the dust. Naked light bulbs glared on bare board shelves, a sheetless bed. *Poor Carmine, to be ill in such a place,* thought an alter, the Bride.

She felt his forehead. "Did you call in sick?"

"You do it," moaned Carmine. "I feel real uptight. Tell them I'll be back Tuesday."

But he wasn't. His symptoms worsened. His arms became too weak to lift a toothbrush. Nobody connected this to the ruined marriage. Was it chance that when Zoe's affair with Altman ended in disaster, Carmine had an affair and a breakdown of his own?

After two weeks, Zoe moved Carmine back to their home so she could watch him between appointments. Between Lottie's, mass, counseling, Franciscan meetings, and visits to doctors, time was at a premium. And with Carmine sick, paying for his apartment had added an emotional burden to a financial one. Zoe lost even more weight. "I felt," she says, "like Daniel in the lion's den."

One rainy day, in the car (Janet was marketing), as she thought up ways to kill herself, Zoe saw her hand rise of its own volition. The index finger wrote on the misty glass: Danielle. And Zoe felt a surge of joy. She visualized a tall, thin woman with light brown hair and hazel eyes, who looked almost like herself, but who loved everyone.

Danielle lent Zoe power, lessened her overt symptoms. She sang around the house. Soon Carmine was begging Zoe to fend off his girlfriend. After ten phone calls, in which she spoke only to Carmine's wife, Carmine's lover became his ex.

Babying Carmine was strange for Zoe. All her father figures had vanished; where now could she find comfort?

The morning of March 12, three weeks after Altman's death, Zoe found out. She and Wald were discussing men.

Carmine and Zoe had made love only once this year—the night she'd tried to get him not to divorce her. "It was horrible. I could see him thinking about Sidney. It's so ironic—I never even liked sex with Sidney!"

"I'm too young for sex!" piped up a child's voice.

Wald's eyes teared, and she held out her arms.

The thirty-seven-year-old mentally ill woman awkwardly clambered into her psychiatrist's lap. "Daddy lost. Need Daddy. Daddy help Little ZP. Where Daddy?"

Dr. Wald held the clinging woman, whispering soft maternal words. She used this same strategy with her two most childlike patients—Adrienne and Zoe. Soon the woman started sobbing for Mommy instead of for Daddy.

Wald hugged her hard. "What a beautiful moment we've discovered together! Do you feel how centered you are, how connected—?"

■

**MOTHER ZOE (the Tunnel of Secrets):** *And then all of a sudden I was out in the hall. Pat was really upset. "If you ever do that again, we'll have our sessions outside!" I felt so bewildered. What had happened?*

■

**SERENA (the Tunnel Protected by the Golden Child):** *She'd been crying about Sidney. And one of the little ones was holding on to Pat's breast for a long time. Her hand was just there—innocently, you know—*

*But then I was out. I couldn't restrain myself. I started touching her like a woman would, a woman who has been in love for a very long time.*

■

**MOTHER ZOE (the Tunnel of Secrets):** *Well, though I didn't understand, I apologized. She took me back in, gave me a hug, and then she held my two hands in hers and said she really cared. And then she popped a Hershey's kiss in my mouth and off we went.*

■

Zoe had long equated goodness with perfection, acceptance with identification, limits or separation with death, and—dangerously—emotional connection with sex. Serena wanted to devour Wald. If Wald had now drawn the line on this side of healthy, her patient could have begun to heal.

Instead, Wald joined Zoe on her side of the line.

Two days later, Zoe returned to Wald.

Wald looked especially pretty that day, says Zoe. Neither of them mentioned the previous session. They took their places, Zoe on the rose couch and Wald on a floral chair. Zoe began to speak; her doctor joined her on the couch.

■

**ZOE 10 (the Tunnel of the Silence of the Holy Innocents):** *She cuddled us. The little hand came up again.*

*And now she unbuttoned her blouse and her bra, saying, "This is what you need, isn't it?"*

*The little ones took her in their mouth. So did Serena.*

*Pat went wild.*

*She smelled real good, like musk. She was breathing hard, and it scared me. Cause I thought something bad was gonna happen. But I couldn't stop. Don't you see? It took away the pain about Daddy Sid.*

■

Standards for therapists are stricter today than they were in 1982. But therapists have always been barred from actions that will likely harm their patients, including sexual intercourse.

Wald knew the standards. She must have been well aware of what was going on. Sexual feelings are common and often unavoidable. They must be dealt with honestly and promptly.

Yet, instead of encouraging mastery of sexual issues in training, the professional climate in 1982 encouraged women therapists to face these issues privately.

Cloaked in privacy, able to rationalize her own motivations until it was too late, Wald violated both her patient and herself.

■

**MAZIE [Zoe 5] (the Tunnel of Secrets):** *I got so scared! I would go in and out, and sometimes I would float into consciousness sucking on Mommy Pat. Serena would push me aside. She knew all the stuff to do, that would make Mommy Pat forget what they were doing. I would just watch, and then it didn't hurt so in my soul.*

■

No patient can make a therapist "forget what they were doing" for a year and more: it is the therapist's legal and moral responsibility to remember.

Even Mazie knows this. Still, she blames Serena—because obsessed with Wald, Serena stalked her.

Serena shared none of Zoe's fears. She could do many things that would mortify Zoe.

■

**SERENA (the Tunnel Protected by the Golden Child):** *I would feel so free. I would pass her house very slowly and know she was in there. The light would be on. She'd be getting undressed. And I would try as hard as I could to see as much as I could. And then I'd go home again. And nobody was any wiser.*

■

One person soon became the "wiser." Now sixteen, Davey had been having all-night dates with his girlfriend, a knockout fifteen-year-old named Alicia Vargas. At three A.M. on March 18, Davey had just tiptoed in through the back door; Zoe, through the front door. They collided in the hall.

Aside from dreading a run-in over Alicia, Davey had as a child seen too much of Serena. He snorted. "You were seeing someone—weren't you?"

"How about you? With 'her'?"

"Don't you call Alicia 'her.'"

Despite Serena, Zoe did not approve of sex outside marriage. "What should I call her—tramp?"

"How about calling her the mother of your grand-child?"

"What?" Zoe stared at her son's face. The mouth was drawn down. She flashed on Davey at age two, pouting.

This baby was going to have a baby?

She, Zoe, was going to be a grandmother?

She screamed. Doors started banging. Lights went on. The Parrys stayed up all night, talking.

Davey wanted to drop out of school. By the baby's birth in October, he'd marry and find a job. Zoe gave Davey an engagement ring—a filigree circlet studded with sapphires, brought over from Ireland by her great-great-grandmother.

At seven A.M., Davey called Alicia to propose. Alicia's father, a strict Catholic, reluctantly gave permission.

By ten, the wedding was off.

Father Kirkland refused to marry the children. "Very few of these kids end up happy. If they're together in two years," he said somberly, "I'll pay for the wedding."

By eleven, Zoe was hiding under her quilt, crying, "I just can't handle any more."

"Felicitations," said Dr. Wald at two P.M.—in an emergency session. "This new, precious baby must be born into health."

"Fat chance."

"Nonsense. Our work has just begun."

"Well, Carmine's divorcing me, I'm broke, and we need our cash to help Davey."

"I have an idea." Wald described another patient, a semiretarded "schizophrenic borderline psychotic" named Tip Pardee. "The man is a genius with his hands.

He can fix anything—my roof, the plumbing, tee-hee, my *own* plumbing. *Merde,* he's crazy, so what? I don't pay him a cent, and what Tip does is he gives me his state insurance stickers.'' She smiled.

Zoe sat, crushed. ''You make love with this Tip?''

''Oh, *ma petite.* You are my favorite patient. More than Adrienne—I even told her so!''

''You discussed me with other patients—?''

Wald sidestepped. ''I can't work for free, you know.''

By the end of the session, Zoe had notified her insurance company of Davey's fictional three sessions a week with Wald, their ''family therapist.'' According to Zoe's journal, hundreds of dollars would come pouring in.

■

ZOE'S JOURNAL, April 7, 1982: *Pat is becoming so loving! Today I touched her breasts, she rubbed my buttocks. We played on the couch. I wanted her so bad!*

*Oh, Lord, why must Sister Johanna go away? In June, Pat will be all I have left—and she is not spiritual.*

■

Zoe's time sense was playing tricks on her. One moment she'd be praying at St. Ann's. The next she would come to, her heart aflutter, on the cement sidewalk in front of Sears (where her father used to work), at the hospital (where Carmine and Altman had stayed), once in the very nave of St. Peter's (by Altman's office) with an usher holding her down.

''What is it?'' whispered the man.

''I just don't know!'' came her high, childlike voice.

Finally, the church organist started to play and drowned out the whispers of the congregation.

Though she didn't remember it, Zoe had lit a candle and noticed glittering eyes, glaring at her. Adrienne had followed her from Wald's office to mass.

■

In April, Barry Bertrand had begun ''discovery'' on the Altman case. His first interview subject had been

Altman's ex-supervisor. He says, "I had only two questions for Dr. Chasen. The first was, what had ailed Dr. Altman? Dr. Chasen wouldn't say. I then said that I don't pursue litigation unless someone within the case concurs with my client. I asked, 'Do you believe her? Was there abuse?' "

His reply was "yes."

Bertrand called Zoe and told her things were going well. She was just getting ready for her date with Wald.

■

**ZOE'S JOURNAL, April 29, 1982:** *I had bought tickets to the play* Sophisticated Ladies. *Pat picked me up. Barry had called. I couldn't stop talking about Sidney. Pat was upset. . . .*

*After the play, we were hungry. We found a cheap little bar. She had some drinks and talked and talked. She said her ex-husband was a sociopath. When we left, she insisted on driving. The poor thing was drunk out of her mind.*

■

**SHERRY and ROSE (the Tunnel of the Silence of the Holy Innocents):** *She ran all the red lights. Pat went too far and made a U-turn. The police came and shone light in our faces.*

■

**ELEANORA BROWN (the Tunnel of the Silence of the Holy Innocents):** *They were writing out a ticket. Zoe tried to appeal to the cop. "Dr. Wald is taking care of me. I'm her patient." Pat freaked. "Shut up. I'll pay the ticket."*

■

So-called therapy continued. Wald traced Zoe's panic about Sister Johanna's departure to early neglect by her mother. She linked to this Zoe's extreme jealousy of Adrienne. "Often your fellow patients are like the siblings you never had," analyzed Wald. This was not news to Zoe, whose childlike side threatened constantly to burst through the sexual, devil-may-care shell of Serena.

"But—you'll be happy to know—Adrienne won't be

around much longer,'' Wald reassured Zoe. "Her parents paid some guy to marry her. *Fini!*''

Giggling hysterically, Wald flopped on the couch next to her patient. "Zoe, you're a delight. You're deep and clean and sweet and lovely. I've always had hang-ups. And to be this uninhibited, with a woman! I've been so curious about what women do together.''

"Now you know," said alter Serena. She reached for Wald, and they kissed. Wald drew back, almost in horror.

"Why am I engaging in this behavior?''

The patient listened, her eyes big with sympathy.

"Could I be a lesbian?''

Serena thought *sure,* but refrained from telling Wald.

"No, of course not. It would be crazy to prefer women, in this society. No, this is counterphobic behavior. I'm scared of your destroying me, so it's precisely what I've invited. And it's playful behavior, too. That's what it is. We're playing, and it's fine, isn't it? Being mischievous?''

That hurt. "Being mischievous?'' Zoe's voice trembled weepily. "But, Pat—I love you!''

Wald gulped. "I know, my dear. I know.''

■

Since puberty, Zoe had hated her body; recently she'd despised it. She'd lost thirty pounds, lost her menses, and flattened her breasts. After she fainted one day, Janet drove her to the internist Zoe'd seen since age eleven, Dr. Hendricks. Her kidneys were malfunctioning. He put her in the hospital.

Seventeen tests later, Zoe called her therapist. She recorded the conversation.

"Dr. Wald speaking,'' said Wald cheerfully.

"I'm in the hospital, in the final stages of anorexia,'' Zoe intoned. She heard a man's voice behind Wald, who quickly muffled the receiver. "Just a minute, Zoe.''

"Is that Tip?''

"What if it is?''

*Is she giving me the shaft?* thought Serena. "Come on, Pat. He's horrible. Get rid of him.''

Wald sighed. "I quite like being with him, Zoe."

"You know, Tip could sue you, Patricia."

After a long silence, Wald spoke. Carefully. "Zoe, I wouldn't advise your taking this tack with me."

"What tack? There's no 'tack.' "

"All along, you've been pushing me toward something I don't want—"

*You were as eager as I was,* thought Serena. "You said you were experimenting." The alter Mazie panics when Mommy seems to hate her. "But it was me who got hurt. Cause I wasn't experimenting." Her voice grew high.

Wald sighed. "But you knew I was."

The little voice whispered, "I can't eat. I can't sleep. I might die because of you, and you don't care!"

"You want to threaten me into rushing straight down to get you. I won't have it, Zoe. You can't manipulate me this way. I'm a therapist—remember? Quite a smart one."

Against medical advice, Zoe signed herself out of the hospital.

Later, only slightly pulled together, she took Alicia Vargas shopping. They bought a layette set and skipped lunch, as they were both nauseous; the mother-to-be from heartburn, and the grandmother-to-be from stress. Zoe envied Alicia her belly. She had wanted many children and, at only thirty-eight, would likely never have another. Next to the layette store was a pet store—The Chez Chanel. On impulse, she dashed in and bought Wald a "baby." Zoe named the poodle Sidney.

Early the next morning, Adrienne called. "I'm back! And guess who I was out with all last night, in Daddy's limo? With the darling, wittle baby Siddie?"

"How did you get my number?" Zoe choked.

"Now, who in the world could have given me your private, personal number?" wondered Adrienne aloud, and hung up.

Half of Zoe was furious. She had Janet drive her to Lean and Luscious, the gym where she knew Wald worked out each morning, and stormed into the weight room.

"How dare you give Adrienne my number?"

"Zoe!" *Clang!* Wald dropped her weights.

"Why do you keep hurting me?"

Wald sighed. "This is hardly the place to talk. How about coffee?"

"Janet's with me."

"Bring her along." Wald knew Janet hated her and had interpreted this as the blame a patient's family heaps on any agent of change.

Later, driving home, Janet sighed, "Geez."

"Okay, Janet."

"I mean, the way she goes, 'Oh, maybe this is unethical, I just know this isn't professional—What's on the menu?' "

"Just come out and say it."

"Are you seeing her?"

"Yes. Three times a week."

"I knew it!"

"For therapy!" warned Zoe. Janet nodded.

That afternoon, Zoe had her last session with Sister Johanna. They spent the time in prayer. If you'd been there to see their gracious smiles, you wouldn't have noticed how weary the one was and how distraught the other.

Later, Janet drove Zoe half an hour south to meet her new pastoral counselor, down past Wald's condo and Brinton Beach. Sister Johanna had praised this Sister Bernadette to the skies.

The little Duster swung into the tree-shaded parking lot of a parochial school in Sand Springs: Sister's practice consisted mainly of wayward girls. The peach and green outdoor hallways, the compact bungalows, heightened Zoe's feelings of being a child—she wanted to hide in a bathroom.

Sister's white and peach bungalow was cheerful with geraniums. Inside, the waiting room literature consisted of religious tracts, *Reader's Digest,* and *American Girl.*

Sister Bernadette, foxlike and brown with quick, precise motions—completely unlike the calm pink-white-and-blueness of Sister Johanna—waved Zoe into the main room.

"Zoe!" Sister Bernadette rushed up and seized her new patient by the shoulders. In a strong Swiss accent, Sister demanded that God give them both courage and fire. "Then we find a good healing." The fierce Sister seemed to Zoe a great activist; it turned out that Sister saw herself that way, too.

Sister Johanna had arranged that before she left for New York, Zoe would see Sister Bernadette twice. In her second session, Zoe whispered that she'd never been mothered. Sister Bernadette impulsively leaned forward and clasped her client's hands. Her own hands were thin and strong. "Here I will be your mother, *hein?*"

Weeping gratefully, Zoe squeezed Sister's hands.

■

According to her journal, Zoe celebrated June 22, her birthday, by driving Sister Johanna to the airport. She and Janet picked up Sister and her small carry-on bag at St. Ann's. Sister accepted a bunch of roses and a book, though she did say, "Zoe, I'll have to leave these at the door."

Zoe smiled. For the first time in weeks, she drove; Sister sat in front with her. Janet sat in the back. They all prayed together at the gate.

The plane took off. Zoe kept smiling.

On June 28, 1982, Barry Bertrand formally filed suit against the estate of Sidney Altman.

Bertrand remembers advising Zoe, "We have to prove three things. One, that he did it—that he egregiously neglected you. Two, that it was not what doctors should do. Three, that it directly caused you significant problems."

"What are our chances?" asked Zoe.

She seemed composed, says Bertrand, even when he discussed his plans to subpoena potentially hostile witnesses—Elyse Altman, doctors, friends, and neighbors. "We'll surprise them. Then I'll tell you your chances."

After they hung up, Zoe called Sister Bernadette. Zoe was controlled, except for her voice, which trembled slightly.

But then she phoned Wald and was not controlled. "We're going out—like you did with Adrienne."

"Now, look," said Wald.

"I am!" Zoe sobbed. "Why me? Why is it always me? Don't tell me, 'look.' I'm not blind. I can see—"

"So can I," said Carmine, home early for Zoe's birthday. Racing in, he snatched the receiver. "Look, Doctor," he yelled, "you have no business dating my wife." He listened. The phone cord stretched tight as he evaded his wife, who was frantically trying to grab the phone.

"Doctor," he broke in, sidestepping Zoe, "I don't care if she strips stark naked, whistles 'Dixie,' and does the hootchie-kootchie, you're the one who's supposed to help! I'm gonna see a lawyer. Yeah, about you, whaddya think?" He slammed down the phone. "I'm going for a walk."

As soon as Carmine was gone, Zoe redialed Wald's number. "I'm so sorry," she began.

"But Carmine is right," Wald said. "We all know it."

"Does this mean no more dates?" asked Zoe.

"I'm sorry—it does. We have to go by the rules now."

"I don't understand."

"No contact outside our sessions."

Five minutes later, Zoe helped Wald to change her mind. They would meet that very night.

In openly confronting Zoe about Wald, Carmine had challenged her alter Serena—who loved a dare.

The next day, Zoe accompanied Carmine to a lawyer whom he'd hired to draw up papers against Wald. Zoe says she "became hysterical and refused to sign." The attorney and Carmine agreed to wait until "Zoe saw the light."

After, in session with Sister Bernadette, Zoe wept, mourning the loss of Sister Johanna. She did not mention Wald.

At the end of session, Sister hugged her. "My goodness, if you don't gain some weight, I won't have anything to hug!"

The next evening, Zoe told Wald that they were now on opposite ends of a lawsuit that she, herself, wanted no part of. "But Carmine insists. And so does Sister."

Stricken—she'd never expected this—Wald apologized. She felt so guilty; she should have known better.

Zoe interrupted. "Well, I don't see that you did anything wrong. And that's exactly what I told them. I said I fell in love with you, and pursued you."

The next day, July 15, the doctor got a present in the mail: two teddy bears sewn together into an embrace so tight that the fabric around the stitches was ripping.

When Wald left her building that evening, she was greeted by Zoe in a white, chauffeured stretch limo. They glided to Wald's favorite restaurant and, once there, ate expensively. The limo had been charged to the Parrys' household credit card. Since Zoe kept the books, there wasn't much chance Carmine would notice.

Zoe says Pat Wald paid for dinner.

Possibly, till Zoe, no one had desired Wald this much. She was seduced not just by the display but by the combination of adoration and lust with threats.

"You hit just the right note," she told Zoe, later. "The proof, it's there, and honestly, I can't deny it."

After dinner that night, Zoe had the chauffeur drop them at Wald's house on Blue Heron Drive.

▪

**SERENA (the Tunnel Protected by the Golden Child):** *She pulled a necklace from one of the drawers and handed it to me.*

*I handed back the pearls and asked, "What is happening to our relationship?"*

*And she answered, "Nothing. We don't have one."*

▪

Zoe skipped three appointments. Instead she met with Sister Bernadette, who'd decided Zoe needed reparenting. This is exactly what it sounds like, an attempt to retrain a patient from day one, and it can be noxious. The idea of rebirth, for example, may reach the patient as an invitation for what comes before birth—sex. The more hurt the patient, the more dangerous the reparenting may be. Still, reparenting was very popular for a year or two.

■

**RONNY (the Tunnel of Secrets):** *Well, the adults that had come in completely disappeared. Zoe 2 and Mazie liked the idea of the nice, pretty Sister saying, "Wouldn't you like to sit on my lap?" Sister was very muscular. She could easily move that little body around. So she would get her in the position she felt most comfortable. With her nice voice she sang beautiful Swiss lullabies. She'd say, "Picture little birds, and butterflies," and with her fingertips she'd go down the child's cheek. Up and down, saying, "Little Didi. You are very safe. Very warm and cared for. With Mommy Bernadette.*

*"Little Didi, do you want your baba?"*

*And some adult came out and looked at that baba and wasn't too sure. But Sister was very insistent, so little Didi took the baba. The rubber nipple tasted awful and she spat it out. But Sister liked doing this, giving the baba, so little Didi said she did not like the milk. Sister got up and poured the milk into the sink; she had a kitchen there. And she poured apple juice, and said, "Maybe you'll like this better." And they did. Sister liked doing this, and this was mainly for her, not the patient. So they played baba. They played rock the baby. And lullaby. That was fun. . . .*

*One time, she said, "Sister gets very mad if she doesn't have her drink at a certain time." She got up and made her special drink in the blender. And then she said, "After her drink Mommy has to do her jump-roping." This was to get the energy out. Ha, so adults do this, exercise, whatever, but in session? Watching this Sister jump rope, in her long gray skirts . . . I remember thinking Sister was a complete idiot.*

*But the children thought everything was fine. I thought it*

*was a crock, myself. Zoe needed intensive therapy, yes, but to
be rocked? I think this could add to the pathology.*

■

Between reparenting sessions, Zoe stayed in bed, studying The Rule of St. Francis.

Days after the date with Wald, the phone rang. The answering machine came on. Zoe's message. Then, "This is Pat."

Zoe shut her Rule and picked up the phone. "Hi!"

"You bitch, why'd you report me?" Wald's usually light voice was thick with anger.

"What?"

"Oh, Miss Innocent, it's chance that when you come to my house, the next day a social worker happens to drop by? Because a little birdie told her my home was not fit for children?"

"It wasn't me!" Zoe was shocked, hurt. "I would never do that!"

Psychiatry was ruined for her, Wald continued, all because of Zoe. If she pursued a lawsuit, Wald's only options were to go to jail—she had no money to pay fines—or to disappear. She was fantasizing about vanishing—for good.

Zoe had no answer. They both knew she could blow the whistle on Wald at any time.

For months to come, though, Zoe would assert that it wasn't she who wanted to drag Wald down. Carmine and Janet were the culprits. Zoe kept saying she couldn't see why everyone around her kept getting mad at Wald, "who'd done nothing wrong."

Still, Zoe continued to crave Wald.

Zoe kept thinking, *therapists are supposed to mother you. Unconditionally. Like Sister Bernadette! I'm not quitting till I get this love!*

Thwarted by Mommy, a child swings back to Daddy. "Why can't Carmine protect me?" reads a journal entry in 1982. A real man would send Pat a letter to scorch her eyeballs!

*Oh, no. Poor Pat,* Zoe thought. Midstream in her musing, she switched what his letter should say; why not let her continue as a lover? "Please do not leave her on account of your ethics about our marriage. We have been celibate for years. I consider you more her spouse than I am."

*A perfect Carmine,* thought Zoe, *would be six inches taller, fifty pounds heavier, and infinitely more aggressive. He'd protect me but would also let me do as I wished.*

This ideal Carmine was so clear to Zoe because he already existed inside her, as an introjected alter—Carmine 2. Carmine 2 was mentally six inches taller. And inside Zoe's personality system, he was laughing.

Both those letters, the scorching one and the permissive one, had in fact already been written and sent. Carmine 2 had taken over the body and composed them himself. He'd restored the body to the female alters only after he'd mailed the letters. More letters, many more, would follow.

On August 22, Zoe Ann became a novice in the Secular Order of St. Francis. Some of her alters were none too happy.

It had been a hard week. Zoe had moved in Lottie—she'd lost her money and couldn't afford a nursing home; and Davey had also moved back to the Parrys'—he'd lost his job.

Seven months pregnant, Alicia Vargas had taken one step into the noisy house and then run away.

Zoe had watched as Alicia screamed at Davey, "It's not even your kid! D'ja ever think of that?"

As Alicia drove away, Davey had just stood there.

From that time until her novitiate ceremony, Zoe had prayed to the Holy Mother of God. "Please don't let them take my child. That baby is everything to mc."

No, the other alters were not happy, and no amount of goodness was going to please them. The coming grand-child was leaving. The Holy Innocents were being hurt. *See, this is the way God punishes you,* thought Zoe.

*This is the way God rewards you,* thought Sister Zoe Ann. It was September 18. She was holding two letters, one from a genetics clinic, the other from Judge Wood. The first stated that it was ninety-eight percent probable that Davey was the coming baby's father. To Zoe, this meant that the baby and Alicia would have to stay in town.

The second letter also contained good news. Judge Wood had formally ended Zoe's probation. He had agreed with the Bertrands that as Zoe had met all conditions over the past four years and had certainly suffered more than her share, she had now paid her debt to the State. She was free.

Zoe threw herself into Franciscan activities. She turned over much of Lottie's care to Davey, Carmine, and Janet and—uncharacteristically—woke each dawn to pray. At Haven, six hours a day, three days a week, she made sandwiches for, and prayed with, the poor. "God had saved me," she says, "and I owed this service to His children."

Zoe also joined the Right to Life movement and started training as a counselor on their hot line.

■

**MOTHER ZOE and SISTER MICHAEL MARIE (the Tunnel of Secrets):** *We saw abortions on the training film. The suction, the saline, the scraping. The fetus feels scalding. It feels being torn apart its little legs and arms and head, just like we would feel our leg being torn off from us. Different ones were out, using Mother Zoe's voice. We told the girls who called the hot line, it is murder.*

*Why do some think of themselves as Holy Innocents? It is because their innocence was ripped away from them when they were babies. Mazie is a Holy Innocent. And the children inside who received sexual abuse all feel just like what is in the trash can at the abortion clinics.*

*I wish it could have been a normal childhood for Zoe's little boy with the big blue eyes, the curly hair.*

■

Zoe had not been to therapy with Wald for the entire summer of 1982 and was uncertain whether or not she'd quit. After a few skipped sessions and unreturned phone calls, Wald had returned the dog Sidney, with a note that she didn't want him back. Then she'd gone away on vacation.

Sister and Zoe were now limiting the reparenting to lullabies and lap sitting. They spent half their sessions talking about holy political activism. Zoe was thrilled when Sister told her, early in September, about all the protests she planned. Next month, Sister was to march in an antinuclear demonstration. Along with five others in her order, she would chain herself to a fence at a military base in Cedar City and then allow herself to be arrested.

Zoe's alter Donna called several newspapers in order to help publicize Sister's demonstration.

Meanwhile, the alter Zoe Ann continued to erase all of Pat Wald's phone messages.

On October 1, Serena came to with her hand on the button. She rewound the tape. "Zoe," went the message, "I don't know how to react to Carmine's letters." These were the notes, some permissive, some scorching, that the alter Carmine 2 had sent Wald for the past six weeks.

"I can't deal with my feelings," Wald was saying. "If you have time to talk, my evening is open."

It was eight P.M. The members of the household were in the living room, eating popcorn and watching TV. Without alerting them, Serena grabbed the dog Sidney, tiptoed out, and drove to Wald's office.

"Zoe!" Wald said, half delightedly, half guardedly, when she opened the door. "And Sidney! Hi, little guy." She bent. Sidney licked her hand.

Serena shrugged. "Let's rap." She uses sixties slang—"rap," "cool," "groovy."

"All right." Wald gestured Serena in. "Why'd you bring Sidney?"

"He's half yours."

"I thought we'd settled that. We're not going to co-own a dog—especially one that represents Dr. Altman! Co-owning gives you power to act out. It gives all kinds of things."

"This is a valuable dog."

"Speaking of valuable, you haven't paid my bill. You owe me for several sessions."

"Sessions?" Serena raised her eyebrow sardonically. "If that's what you call them. I don't have any money."

"So you brought the dog in payment," sighed Wald. "Zoe, I don't know what I can do with you."

"I have an idea." Wald looked up expectantly. "Let's breed your Sidney to my dog Chrissy."

Wald groaned. "Oh, no."

"These are valuable dogs. You'd get the pick of the litter," her patient promised.

"No, no, no. Why would you want to pull this?"

"Patients are not as dumb as you think."

"Zoe, what I did tortures me in my soul." Wald picked up the dog and held him out to her patient. "I don't expect you'll understand."

"Oh, I do."

"Don't forget Sidney." As Zoe took him, Wald shut the door.

Wald didn't seem very tortured in her soul the following morning. Zoe was at her desk, planning a baby shower for Alicia, when the doorbell rang. It was Wald—with Tip Pardee, the male patient who was also her lover.

■

**ZOE'S JOURNAL, October 7, 1982:** *I said, "Pat, you are a NUT—why'd you bring him here?"*

*"Maybe if he likes you, he'll leave me alone."*

*"Pat!" I was outraged. And part of me was very scared.*

■

As Zoe argued with Wald, Pardee barged in. Though not a large man, he rippled with muscle. Zoe turned from Wald. "What are you doing? Get out of my house!"

He pulled himself under her sink. "Checking your pipes." He had a lazy, sexual voice, and after he pulled himself out and up, he stared her up and down and scratched his crotch. "D'ja know how old jer plumbing is? I'll fix it for free." He pulled himself back under the sink.

"That has nothing to do with—Oh, no. Stop it!"

"Don't be silly." Tip yanked the pipe. It burst. Water sprayed out, soaking her, and him, and the wallpaper.

It was two hours before Wald and her patient left. The floor was clean, the wall ruined, and the pipe patched—for now—with tape. Zoe could not figure out why Wald had brought Pardee to her house, but she was now convinced he would return, and rape her.

A week passed. The day of Alicia's shower dawned sparkling clear. The Parry house was beautifully clean, full of the good aromas of baking cake and hot appetizers. Zoe had high hopes for the occasion. Alicia's mother, Eugenia Vargas, Janet, and Zoe May were putting the final touches on the buffet table. Alicia and Davey were locked in the bedroom; and Carmine was on his way home, having taken the afternoon off.

Until now Mrs. Vargas and Zoe had been cool with each other. Zoe's son had inadvertently impregnated Eugenia's daughter: not a happy beginning. But today, Eugenia was thawing. The baby was almost due. In spite of everything, the grandmothers found themselves happy.

The door opened and Pardee exploded in, like a bomb.

"Come to fix what I broke," he yelled. *"Whoo-ee!* Smells great. You look mighty sexy, for two old broads."

Zoe May said, "Well, I never."

Eugenia's mouth formed an O.

Pardee sat on the hall table and leered at Zoe, who backed away.

Janet came forward. She is tall and strong. "You are not wanted here," she said, "not for plumbing or anything else."

Pardee's eyes narrowed. Suddenly he got up, leaving an oily buttocks print on the polished wood. "That so?"

"Please leave, before we call the police."

There was a long silence. Janet opened the door.

"Up yours then," said Pardee, and walked out.

Eugenia Vargas went straight into the kitchen. Zoe followed her; white around the lips, Mrs. Vargas—Eugenia no more to the Parrys—tidied a tray of spinach puffs.

"He's a strange man," Zoe apologized. "I don't know him. He promised to fix the plumbing for free, and I—"

"No need to explain," said Mrs. Vargas coldly.

The doorbell rang. Janet opened it. Guests poured in.

The shower was a huge success, lots of fun, lots of gifts, great food; but the relationship between the two grandmothers had ended, almost before it had begun.

■

The Altman case was in full swing. Barry Bertrand had filed suit for two million dollars. The lawyer for Altman's estate, a David Walsh, had countercharged that the amount was ridiculous, that the Parrys had "unclean hands in the matter," having caused most of the problem, he claimed, by their own negligence. He'd asked for a dismissal of charges.

In the first of eleven lengthy depositions, taken over the next six months, Zoe revealed many of the humiliating details. The first session, on a Monday morning, had to end after an hour; Zoe became hysterical.

That night, Alicia went into labor.

■

Zoe had been up all night waiting. She was outside the nursery, staring in the window at the babies, when "Surprise!" called her son's tired voice. She turned.

In a bassinet being wheeled down the hall toward her by the maternity nurse, blanketed in pink, lay a tiny girl, her eyes shut tight. Zoe hugged Davey—"Gosh!"—then ran to her. She was so new she still hadn't been cleaned. Zoe reached for the infant. "My baby," she crooned.

"Don't touch," warned the maternity nurse.

"Not touch her?" This was her baby—her future. This perfect, smooth, new being, who hadn't been abused, this clean, promised better self. "Not hold my little girl?"

Davey had to pull her away.

■

ZOE'S JOURNAL, October 13, 1982: *Her name is Janna Lynne Vargas. She was going to be Parry but the Vargases got to her birth certificate first. She has light brown hair and blue eyes. I pray she has a better life than her grandmother.*

■

That night, Janna Lynne developed jaundice—a very common condition in infants, but one that caused panic in Zoe. Though Alicia was released the next day, without Janna Lynne, Zoe stayed by the window all day for the next three days, in a chair, except for breaks to phone Wald and to go to the bathroom.

When Mrs. Vargas came to get Alicia, she looked at Zoe strangely. "Hadn't you better get some rest?"

"Our baby might die. I have to stay."

The nurses finally convinced Zoe that she was more needed at home than here.

Once home, she telephoned Wald and demanded a meeting. "My granddaughter was just born. I want her not to grow up ashamed of her grandmother. I want her proud of me."

"What exactly do you want, Zoe?"

"I want my records."

After a short silence, Wald said, "No way."

"I don't know why you're so paranoid," Zoe said.

"I don't show my patients my private notes about them."

"They must be incriminating. Would you rather give them to me, or have Mr. Bertrand subpoena them?"

"I can't give him my notes."

"You could just give him part of them."

"Zoe, they call that 'fraud.' "

"I don't see why you're so bent out of shape. This isn't about you and me! I'm not even curious what you wrote about me in your notes. I'm just testifying about Sidney, and Mr. Bertrand needs to support my testimony."

"Okay," Wald said furiously. "I will send your Mr. Bertrand something. Of course, dear, I'm sure he will show you whatever it is. Okay?"

"Okay. But—" Maternal feeling overwhelmed Zoe. *Poor Pat.* "I'd like to make you more comfortable."

"Nothing you could do," Wald carefully enunciated, "would make me comfortable." And she hung up.

■

Sister Bernadette had intended her antinuclear demonstration to be a humble action; she'd told Zoe that the Lord and she needed no other witnesses. But that afternoon, Zoe found herself unable to bear the thought of Sister in need, in jail, Sister, who had held her on her lap. So Zoe went to the jail and bailed her out.

"And I never heard such language from a woman of God."

Janet says, "She screamed, 'Why did you do this? Why did you take me out?' She was ranting. Almost spitting. 'I don't ever want to see you again.' And that was that."

Two weeks later, after Zoe had called her over a hundred times, Sister Bernadette actually allowed her to return. Once. For a final session.

Janet did not go in, and Zoe has blocked all memory of that day. But after, Janet watched Zoe sitting on a stone bench for more than an hour, tears streaming down her cheeks. "She rejected me! Another one rejected me! Why do they always abandon me?"

Janet remembers, "I said let's leave, they're going to close the gates!" The yard was empty. There were no girls walking, giggling. In the window of Sister's bungalow, the curtains parted slightly, once, and then were shut.

■

Zoe's weight was down to ninety-six pounds, she moved into her mother's house, and Dr. Hendricks called Dr. Wald.

Wald promptly called Zoe. "Have I done this to you?" she asked, contritely.

"You and Sidney." Zoe sounded like a hurt child. She did not mention Sister Bernadette.

"What can I do to help?"

Soon Wald had promised to come over, to mate the dogs.

■

**SHERRY and ROSE (the Tunnel of the Silence of the Holy Innocents):** *Serena and Pat played bad dog games on Mrs. Bryant's bed. Sidney got big and long and red. And Pat was laughing, trying to stick it inside Chrissy. Pat liked it when the dog squirted its stuff all over Mrs. Bryant's bedroom.*

■

**ZOE II [*the Host*] (the Tunnel of Dreams and the Body of an Expression):** *Mother Zoe was baby-sitting Janna Lynne that day. The baby was there, lying on the bed! Nothing happened to the baby. Mother Zoe was extremely protective. But Pat had a bad cold that day and kept wanting to pick up the baby, and Mother Zoe said, "Don't you dare!"*

■

The alters were still unaware of each other. Mother Zoe could consider herself "extremely protective of Janna Lynne," even as Serena masturbated the dogs in front of the baby. There is no direct conflict where there is no awareness: only the body knew, and it suffered. Zoe felt she was on the verge of a cardiac arrest.

December arrived. With it came the Christmas party for the poor, to which Sister Zoe Ann had devoted six months of effort. All feelings were blocked from the puppet that attended. Handing out the toys that she'd collected, the mannequin made sure that everything went smoothly and perfectly, then went home and collapsed.

■

**ZOE'S JOURNAL, December 23, 1982:** *No sleep. Can't think. Pat and Sidney, my two parents, my lovers, are gone. I don't know who I am. I am alone—dead and in hell—foaming in my own decay.*

*I have lost the battle. God help me find my mind. I give up, God. Take your child home.*

■

During January and February 1983, in a constant dissociative panic, Zoe checked into and out of ten hospitals.

■

**MOTHER ZOE (the Tunnel of Secrets):** *The children would wake in emergency rooms, on gurneys, screaming as they were being wheeled to X-ray or wetting themselves while being given an EKG. They could not be consoled. The legs would not move right, the heart fluttered, the arms lay dead. No one was sleeping or eating.*

■

Zoe was threatening suicide. In one moment of clarity she called Sister Johanna at the New York convent and was allowed a brief chat. Both her therapy with Sister Bernadette and with Dr. Wald, she said, had ended with the therapists' abandoning her. She had no idea why.

"I'm so sorry," said Sister Johanna.

"Can you suggest someone who won't reject me?"

"Amelia Ellis," said Sister Johanna, after a pause. "She is extremely gentle. She won't lecture you; she'll just listen. And she practices in your neighborhood."

"How old is she?"

"Sixty-eight."

"Is she a Catholic?"

"No. A Jungian."

Zoe said good-bye, left a message on Ellis's machine, and blanked out.

■

Zoe's journal from this time is a pastiche of brief entries, each in a different handwriting. "They say I ate dinner at the Holiday Inn—I don't remember." Or, simply, "Someone, help me!" On February 4, someone shakily wrote, "Karen Carpenter died today. She couldn't eat either." Karen Carpenter had died of anorexic starvation.

Meanwhile, Carmine had kept busy. His complaint of February 11, 1983, about Pat Wald to the Board of Medical Quality Assurance reads in part:

> . . . This very unethical doctor has encouraged my wife to drink with her and has had sexual contact with her . . . in so-called sessions, as well as other places. . . . My wife has a lot of problems, but this so-called doctor is adding to the pathology. I believe she is much sicker than her patients.
>
> Do you know why I believe my wife? I called this doctor and she admitted it to me—on tape. I beg you to totally investigate this doctor.

It was with shocked disbelief that Zoe wrote in her journal that night—blocking perception of the entries in most of the other handwritings—"Donna called the Medical Board about Pat. And Carmine wrote a letter! I can't hurt Pat! I totally disagree with these actions!"

The many other entries on the page were meaningless scribbles to her. Zoe was a front for an increasing number of alters and fragments who used her in order to pretend to the world that they were one person.

Bold, backslanted writing (Serena): "Pat is so mean."

Looping adolescent script (Zoe May 10): "Sister Zoe Ann attended a meeting with the Secular Franciscans. I watch her from somewhere, half asleep. I am God's stupid servant, unworthy of everything."

Angular childish printing (Mazie): "I want Mommy Pat back. Everything was okay until Serena had sex with her."

Perfect, small script (Zoe Ann): "Today is Sister Johanna's birthday, Dear heart—how I miss her."

And in Zoe's round, looping script—Zoe had fixated on one small savior: "That baby is a part of ME. She is my reason to keep going. I may not know who I am, but I know I love Janna Lynne."

Such dissociation is almost inconceivable to average people. We don't normally realize how multiple we are until the morning, say, we drive all the way to our office without noticing how we got there. In fact, most of us are not only capable of dissociation, we use it daily. The difference is we can, with effort, remember the dissociated events and integrate them into our lives. Zoe can't.

On March 14, 1983, Lori Elazar, an investigator from the Board of Medical Quality Assurance, rang the Parry doorbell. After introducing herself, Elazar advised the astonished Zoe to sue Pat Wald. "You can't let her get away with this," she said, squinting in the bright March sun.

"I'm sorry, please excuse me. I'm feeling very ill."

Elazar was used to patients' second thoughts. "Why are you folks so loyal to these doctors?" she said softly.

Zoe pretended she didn't hear.

"Who called HER?" she wrote in her journal, as soon as Elazar was safely gone.

"Don't hurt Mommy!" wrote someone childish.

Donna slashed the pen so hard across the page, she ripped it. "What the fuck's wrong with you, Zoe?"

■

Zoe found herself at Amelia Ellis's office with no memory of having made an appointment, shaking hands with an elderly woman who had long gray hair, crinkly eyes, and a soft voice. Dozens of pictures crammed her desk: children of every color, many obviously poor.

Ellis barely spoke—she listened. This, she would do for the next two years. "I had already mostly retired," she says about this case, "so I wasn't a gung-ho psychiatrist. First, Zoe told me about her and Sister Bernadette. The Sister gave her many messages that Zoe interpreted as sexual, maybe without the Sister's realizing it. Later, when Zoe kept calling her, she apparently got frightened.

When Zoe went to the jail, the Sister was terrified. She went to a priest, her mentor, and he said, 'Drop her right now. Do not see her.' And that is what she did. It was abrupt. Zoe was quite hurt. We spent a year talking about it.''

She couldn't affect Zoe's disorder, but at least Amelia Ellis did no harm.

■

The Vargases were concerned. Davey and Alicia were becoming increasingly violent. Though the two loved Janna Lynne, they were neglectful, immature, and combative.

After the baby shower—the day Tip Pardee came in to fix Zoe's plumbing—Mrs. Vargas had checked around town. She'd heard rumors, terrible rumors, about Zoe. She'd searched the clippings file of her library, and what she'd found—sensational media coverage of the kidnapping—appalled her. Zoe's malign secrets, Mrs. Vargas decided, must ultimately overwhelm anything good the Parrys could bring to Janna Lynne. She felt she and her husband must assume custody, quickly, decisively, before the baby got hurt.

The Vargases considered themselves righteous, normal, and orderly. That their daughter Alicia had sassed them at age nine, kissed boys at ten, run away at thirteen, and dropped out of school at fifteen, they blamed on some wild throwback trait in her personality, perhaps because her great-grandfather had taken off for California in the Gold Rush. They could not understand why Alicia had been attracted to Davey or to that other even more dangerous boyfriend she had now, Leon. But of one thing they were sure—they did not want to see any black-and-blue marks on Janna Lynne.

They didn't care what it took—they'd get custody.

■

ZOE'S JOURNAL, May 17, 1983: *Davey and I went to the Vargases' for what we thought was a reconciliation. I walked into a kangaroo court. Mrs. Vargas sat us at her dining room* table. She was smiling, I was smiling. Then came the blow. Mrs. Vargas said quietly, "February 3, 1978."

The blood drained from my face. I couldn't think. Alicia put a folder on the table. Inside were not only all the public records of the kidnapping—but my psychiatric file! Apparently some clerk had placed my private records in the public file, for anyone to see.

Mrs. Vargas said politely, "Would you like me to use these—or would you prefer to back off about Janna Lynne?"

A booming voice I didn't recognize came out of my mouth. "This is my granddaughter, too, and if you've read the papers, you also know that I would never hurt a child; even Jennifer King's mother agrees."

"So I should use them?"

"Go ahead," said the booming voice. "The entire state has read all about the kidnapping, and seen it on TV. I'm surprised you missed it. I just hope that when Janna Lynne learns about the things her grandmother has done, that she's been brought up with enough compassion to realize that anyone who would do that must have already suffered enough. And I trust that Janna Lynne will still love her grandmother."

■

Zoe doesn't know how she got home that day. Both Donna—"the booming voice"—and Barry Bertrand immediately called Judge Wood, who deeply regretted the mistake made by court officials under his jurisdiction. The papers had indeed been misfiled, and this was an actionable breach of privacy.

"She's paid ten times over for that kidnapping," said Bertrand.

During the next weeks, the judge found and reprimanded the clerk responsible for the error, and then he and Bertrand sat down to negotiate exactly what the State of Florida owed Zoe Parry.

■

Zoe's prescribed-drug use had worsened; she was now addicted to four medications, including the Dalmane and Valium that Altman had originally prescribed. She was down to two hours of sleep a night; the incidence of her blackouts and measurable palpitations had increased dramatically, to several per hour. Whole days passed, lost. She would look at the top of the newspaper and one month would have jumped into the next. She found herself in Sears, laughing and crying, ripping a bra to shreds. She found herself dialing Elyse Altman's phone number.

⬛

**ZOE'S JOURNAL, September 7, 1983:** *I don't know how or who has been taking the instructions all this year to become a Sister. I know I've been quite ill. But somehow someone was able to learn it all. They say I am ready to be Professed. To be married to God . . .*

*Who cares if we are crazy—if craziness says yes to God?*

*Amelia and I discussed my having a party for Janna Lynne's first birthday. After she gave me courage, I bought invitations and sent them off. I had Davey drop the Vargas invitation in their mailbox. It's been six whole months since I've seen Janna Lynne.*

*Mrs. Vargas just called and said yes, they would come.*

*The rest of the day was a blank. I can't tell anyone, even Amelia. I'll be put away for sure, and then I would never again be able to see Janna Lynne. So the people, the secret people, must remain a secret.*

⬛

In mid-September and mid-October, Zoe Parry threw two parties, which marked milestones in her life. On September 24, Sister Zoe Ann took formal vows in the Third Order of Saint Francis, becoming instead of a novice, a fully fledged tertiary. These lay nuns may remain married and do not have to live in a convent. And on October 13, the Parrys and Vargases celebrated Janna Lynne's first birthday—together.

"Every action is a treasure," said Father Tigris. "Pile up your actions and present them to God. God bless you, Sister Zoe Ann."

It was the day of Zoe's Profession.

Zoe May wept in the front pew as Zoe took final vows. "The room was spinning," says Zoe. "I did not remember having studied enough to merit taking these vows. I felt naked in front of all these people, who could surely see right through me, into my profound lack of knowledge."

◼

**SISTER ZOE ANN (the Tunnel of Secrets):** *There was a big party waiting for me when I got home. All my Franciscan brothers and sisters. But as I went through the door, I saw a Plymouth at the curb, with a woman inside, watching. Adrienne. I tried to ignore it.*

*There were beautiful cakes and oodles of food. We were so tired, we were switching like crazy. But we still tried to enjoy it—this was our party, to sanctify what we'd been working on all year! Then the telephone rang. It was Mrs. Vargas. She said that Janna Lynne and she weren't coming—that Janna Lynne had been hurt.*

*"Hurt how?" I said. She answered, and I blanked out. Later we found out what Mrs. Vargas had said—that Janna Lynne had been beaten by Alicia's boyfriend, Leon.*

*Zoe and others came out—the ones I call the hysterics, shrieking at the top of their lungs. The guests fell silent. Two of them, women, accompanied the hysterics upstairs. Then the Slasher came out, her fingers curled into claws. She pulled apart Zoe's shirt and ripped her skin to bloody shreds. The guests put in a call to Dr. Hendricks, who told them to give Zoe two Valiums and put her to bed.*

*Slowly the guests came upstairs. They gathered around Zoe's bed, holding her, speaking. The Holy Spirit filled that room. Seeing the people all around, one with her in the body of God, the devil departed and Zoe felt at peace.*

◼

The next celebration was Janna Lynne's first birthday party. Zoe didn't remember having reconciled with the Vargases. But apparently she had. Going through her desk drawers and Carmine's, she'd found papers—bills and a canceled court date—to show that something legal had happened.

What had happened was that Judge Wood had called the judge at family court. They'd had a two-hour discussion about Zoe. Judge Wood had suggested a compromise. Janna Lynne was to remain in the Vargas house, Davey was allowed to visit two days a week, and Zoe, one. The judge had cautioned the Vargases about using any of the private material they'd inadvertently been shown. Zoe was a fit grandparent, he'd told them. What was past should remain past and not be brought forward to poison Janna Lynne.

So on Janna Lynne's birthday, bunches of carnations perfumed the Parry house; bunches of balloons made it festive. Zoe made lasagna and salad and baked a mountain of rolls. She'd ordered a special teddy bear–shaped cake decorated with pink roses—one for each child who'd been invited.

It was a special day. Alicia came over early, seemingly bent on reconciliation. Apparently Leon had been as bad for her as for Janna Lynne, because she and Davey hugged and went to the bedroom to talk. Mother Zoe prayed that the two kids could someday grow up and marry.

The guests arrived—the Vargases, parents and babies from Alicia's Lamaze class. Everyone settled right in. Zoe had bought toys for each child; the noise was deafening but cheerful. Zoe had just brought out the cake—Alicia, Janna Lynne, and Davey blew out the candles together—when the phone rang. Gaily, she answered it.

"Where the hell are you?" screeched Pat Wald.

"Right here," said Zoe. "Oh, Pat, it's wonderful! It's Janna Lynne's birthday! Why don't you come join—"

"What are you talking about?" asked Wald incredulously. "I clear out my entire schedule, I get all dressed up and make reservations for the best restaurant and the best room in the best hotel, and all because you call me for a date? You can hurt me and hurt me, while I strain to be nice? Go ahead, Zoe! Sue me! I don't care what you do!"

Even Serena, who'd been in touch with Wald all along, sending her flowers and gifts, knew it was over.

Wald returned all the gifts with a cold little note meant to indemnify her from any future accusation of having permanently accepted them:

"Here is YOUR ring. As I told you at the time, since it was your birthstone and from a relative, I could not accept such a valuable present. I have held it only for you."

▪

Throughout 1983 and 1984 Zoe was in one hospital after another for ovarian problems, palpitations, migraines, breathing problems, insomnia, and panic disorder. Eventually, Amelia Ellis suggested that Zoe see a psychiatrist who had more expertise with severely disturbed patients.

Says Ellis, "I was quite well aware of several states. I didn't want to hear any more complications." At her age, she told me later, she didn't wish to be involved. "I am sure I shut Zoe off when she'd say things about Dr. Wald. It was too much. I couldn't listen to everything. I was very glad when Dr. Fischer came into the picture.

"I took Zoe only with the idea that she needed someone to be there for her. There was no trying to solve her problems or cure her."

Did Zoe, I ask, ever do anything out of character?

"One night she called and begged me to tell Carmine she couldn't sleep with him anymore. It wasn't the demand—though I answered I couldn't do that—but her tone. So harshly demanding. I'd never seen that with her. She was a sweet little gal, you know? Maternal and childlike at once. Religious. There was never any other extreme behavior."

Zoe had retreated into politeness; Ellis couldn't help further with the nondirective listening—once she'd begun to direct her patient's ramblings away from Wald.

Often alters would see half a dozen doctors a week. The bills mounted into the thousands. If the flood of debt wasn't stemmed, the Parrys would soon go bankrupt.

In mid-1984 one gastroenterologist told Zoe that her

problem was hypochondria, which could best be resolved through intensive psychotherapy. She responded bitterly when he recommended first a male psychiatrist and then a female one. "I've had plenty of experience with psychiatrists of both sexes, thank you." Finally, at the doctor's urging, she took the name of the woman, a Dr. Sarah Freed.

In her late thirties, Jewish, and happily married, Sarah was a graduate of three Ivy League schools; her undergraduate degree was in comparative religion. This immediately appealed to Zoe. "At last," she says, "someone spiritual!" And even after listening to the whole outline of woe, Sarah Freed had hope for Zoe's future. But she was not taking any new patients right now. She could prescribe medications and recommend a primary therapist.

They had three sessions. Zoe was dead set against taking any new pills. She had a point; she was still addicted to several other psychotropic medications that were no longer of any benefit to her.

Though no one had yet tried monoamine-oxidase inhibitors on Zoe and Sarah Freed felt they would be a good bet, she wasn't about to press an unwilling patient who didn't seem dangerous and whom she didn't know. Zoe's symptoms likely sprang from deep roots. What would allow this patient to get some sleep and to feel less helpless?

"Maybe hypnosis," she suggested.

"Hypnosis?" Zoe asked dubiously.

"Is that bad?" Sarah's dark eyes were compassionate.

"Christian Scientists are against hypnosis. . . . 'Malicious Animal Magnetism,' my grandmother called it."

"Gwynn Fischer doesn't have a malicious bone in her body," Sarah assured her. "She's skilled and ethical."

"What will she do?"

"I don't exactly know, Zoe. That's for you to negotiate with her. Supportive hypnotherapy, most probably."

"What about later? What will she give me then?"

"What do you need?"

*You,* thought Mother Zoe. But what she meant was very close to unconditional love, forgetfulness—and death.

Answered Zoe, "I don't know what I need." She was crying so hard, says Sarah, she couldn't hear the words.

# Zoe Parry: Inner Structure

*September 1992*
*Discussing Dr. Gwynn Fischer, diagnosis, the use*
*of therapy in treating MPD.*
*Approximately 100 personalities.*
*The Angel Child personality is in every tunnel.*
*Selena is in most tunnels.*

Pictures of suns are sprinkled in each tunnel. Each tunnel is connected by an umbilical cord to the Core of the Angel Child at the center. The Angel Child baby at center is connected by an umbilical cord to Baby Frozen at the left.

My Observers

My Creations of
Power and My
Students

Those I Send to
Light

Eternal
Protection

**THE CENTER
OF THE WORLD**

Grief

*The Angel Child
Baby*

*Core of the
Angel Child*

Baby Frozen

Those Under My
Control to Keep
Secrets

Guides and
Friends Not in
This Zone

My Subjects
Resting in Limbo
but Always
Ready to Protect
Me

Hell

Pit of Death

# 5

# Diagnosis: Multiple

On a dusty summer's day in 1985, a dented car wheezed up to the Center for Clinical Psychology—the golden monolith that crowns the lush suburb of West Grove. The car looked as if it had been through hell. So did its driver and passenger, Janet Moore and Zoe Parry.

Dolled up in a pink silk pantsuit, matching high heels, and gold religious gewgaws, Zoe lay air-conditioned into pink ice, passively tangled in her seat belt. As the car braked, her powdered chin banged the dashboard, her eyes rolled back up in terror, and she began to whimper like a child.

Janet was pent and frazzled. Dressed haphazardly in an ancient skirt, a forgiving pullover, and scuffed pumps, she muttered, "Friends are forever. At least it seems like forever."

They'd never before been to West Grove, and Janet had gotten lost driving, while Zoe lay in a Münch-like nightmare with her face between her hands, stupefied with fear, immune to the tidal wave of honking horns.

Janet gritted her teeth. They'd waited three weeks to meet this doctor. Now they would be late. Janet feared they'd antagonize the doctor; the last thing Zoe needed was the hostility of yet another powerful authority.

Zoe couldn't speak to anyone these days without

bursting into a fit of terrified crying or screaming. She spent hours under her mother's quilt, and Mondays sobbing in the Bertrands' bathroom after giving depositions. Lately Amelia Ellis had accompanied her to the lawyers' office, but even this did little good. Zoe's Monday blues now stretched through the following Sundays.

Zoe's list of symptoms had lengthened even more in the two years post-Wald. She'd added ulcerative colitis, fatigue malaise, and hallucinations to her pounding heart, night terrors, malnutrition, migraines, mystery fevers, stomach aches, and hives. Her addictions had worsened. Monoamine-oxidase inhibitors might have cut her anxiety, but she'd refused them.

She kept up this big front of perfection, says Janet— while making those around her miserable. Not that anyone stuck around these days. Davey and Carmine were out all day and half the night. Lottie, enfeebled, was in a nursing home. Zoe May had moved away. Zoe and Janet were holding down the fort. So to speak.

When I ask Janet why she stayed, she replies, "One doesn't leave a friend." When Janet is ill, Zoe does not leave her, either. "I knew then, and know today, she's capable of so much good in this world," Janet continues. "Friends must help each other. Nobody else will." Janet suffers from a manic-depressive illness. She enjoys relative stability in her role as Zoe's friend.

They arrived. Unsnapping her seat belt, Zoe reviewed what she knew about hypnosis, which wasn't much.

Ironically, given Zoe's fear of hypnosis, dissociators— especially multiples—live in what may amount to a perpetual state of hypnosis. Those who render their inner worlds hyperreal, hypnotize themselves.

Multiple personality is (among other things) a hypnotic coping strategy. During childhood, the multiple intensifies her inner world in order to escape or transcend what's outside. As Colin Ross, author of *Multiple Personality Disorder: Diagnosis, Clinical Features, and Treatment,* says, "MPD is a little girl imagining the abuse is happening to someone else." Zoe's alters are more than moods; they are concentrated physical states that filter and thus distort external sense perceptions. Each alter's belief that she is externally real and superior to the others, who seem internal and inferior, encourages her to develop a seemingly separate history. The cure does not involve negating the histories. The selves must discover how they are joined at the roots, how each is already part of something greater.

Zoe interpreted hypnosis as control by an outsider who could harm her, who could find the secret people and end Zoe's contact with her granddaughter. The outsider could force integration by showing Zoe's secret people a new relationship between inner and outer reality.

In CCP's suite 17-120C, Gwynn Fischer, double Ph.D., waited for her new patient. A crack hypnotherapist and expert in doctor-patient sexual issues, Fischer had organized well for this meeting. After speaking with Sarah Freed and Amelia Ellis and with Zoe, she'd begun to design possible courses of brief therapy. Fischer's approach is a brave attempt to combine Milton Erickson's "utilization principle" (teaching, patients to use their unique inner mechanisms) with Ernest Hilgard's more standardized, external approach.

Fischer's one-two punch had worked with less disturbed patients, hundreds of them. With the more disturbed patient, Zoe, she planned to begin with cognitive-behavioral techniques; and she would encourage Zoe to notice and utilize her inner workings. Brief therapy would take about eight weeks, and then she could send the patient back to Ellis, or even straight to Sarah Freed. The details would have to wait for this first meeting.

"Comprehensive patient care" is Fischer's promise. But Zoe didn't want this; nor would most of us, if we had stood in her wobbly high-heeled shoes. What she needed, she felt, was to be saved by magic mommy.

Fischer had no idea what she was about to face. She'd never seen a Zoe. In the mid-eighties, despite the appearance in popular books of characters with multiple personality, such as "Sybil," few therapists recognized MPD, much less treated it. Multiplicity would soon become what hysteria had been a century before: a condition that could illuminate an entire culture. The issues of responsibility, sexuality, internal versus external perception and structure, relativity, identity, imagination, and uncertainty all must be confronted in MPD. The rational, progressive, stepwise theoretical stance that usually rendered Gwynn Fischer so effective, was about to become her greatest handicap.

■

The door to suite 17-120C creaked open. Sally Harris, Dr. Fischer's trim brunette assistant, looked up with a smile. The smile became a frown as two women all but fell inside. Sally helped the women into chairs and brought them mugs of water.

At 1:20 Fischer opened her door, smiled, introduced herself to both women, and greeted the patient. There was a little bustle at the door. The patient's companion wanted to come in, and that, of course, was impossible.

It is said that the first five minutes of therapy are the most important. All kinds of unconscious messages are exchanged, and contracts, both conscious and unconscious, are made—these will affect the entire future relationship.

As Zoe's body trembled, her Patient alter allowed herself to be pushed forward through the tunnels. Through a mist of fear she peered out at the newest agent of Therapy. She managed a sweet social smile.

Gwynn Fischer was a manicured, successfully aging woman with warm, knowing eyes. The corners of her mouth twitched pleasantly, as if she found it hard to repress a smile. "So, Zoe, what's going on with you?"

Not addressing Fischer's question, Zoe asked a polite question about the doctor's family. A shadow crossed the doctor's eyes. Fischer would avoid the personal. Though this made Zoe curious, she did not venture another question. "Excuse me, I'm in such a fog," she apologized.

Fischer noted the fancy ironing job, the light perfume, the edgy, ladylike manner. Laughing nervously, the patient unconsciously plucked her cross and launched into a detailed recital of a dozen long-term, crippling symptoms.

Fischer asked Zoe, "What do you most need?"

"A good night's sleep," said the patient. But the eyes flickered and begged, *"A secret understanding."*

Bingo. This patient, thought the doctor, was going to be supremely hypnotizable. Actions, cognitions, feelings, all seemed dissociated from each other. Zoe inhabited a fantasy world already, one she seemed to desire Fischer to join.

Without alerting the patient to what she was doing, Fischer probed for imagery that she might use. The patient had said she was in a fog. Fischer could reframe that.

Fischer began to muse aloud about the feeling of drifting on a cloud, high above the earth. Sensing the whiteness, softness, how comforting. How delightful, to ride on a cloud. The breeze on one's face, how relaxing.

Zoe's eyes fluttered shut. Fischer noted this. Such swift hypnotizability often went with a history of abuse or with high creativity, or both. But in this context of brief supportive therapy a detailed history wasn't crucial: what mattered was to find the gross outlines and then to stepwise desensitize the patient to her specific fears.

Fischer obtained the following information:

Halfway through her lawsuit against an abusive male therapist, Zoe had begun another, against an abusive female therapist. This was the immediate catalyst for her present anxiety: she felt the current lawsuit was a "dreadful betrayal of Pat." As to her relationship with Wald, curiously, she "could not remember a thing about it."

During the past few months, she had lost even more time, more money, more things, than usual. She kept finding candy boxes in her room that she had not emptied, weird clothes, makeup, tapes, and journals, some in code. When she noticed these things, she lost time; when she woke, the things would have disappeared. Even more mysteriously, although she didn't get out of bed at night, her shoes, like those of the twelve dancing princesses, were worn and dirty each morning. She was sure she didn't leave the house, because each evening with her cocoa she ingested one thousand milligrams of chloral hydrate, enough to fuel a jet to never-never land.

"The symptoms have all improved, Gwynn," Zoe gratefully said, at the end of her first phase of therapy, in May 1985. Fischer had used passive hypnotic relaxation to encourage stepwise changes in Zoe's routine. The most important effect had been to stop some panic attacks at the moment of inception. Using guided imagery, Fischer had made audiotapes for specific situations such as nighttime, driving, and going outdoors. Zoe played these tapes incessantly. She'd reduced her anxiety. She was now able to sleep better at night, to walk short distances, and even to drive a little.

"Though I could never remember therapy," says Zoe, "I felt so warm, so right, with Gwynn: like I could finally get better." It was so comfortable for Zoe not to have to explain or to recall painful, disgusting events during sessions—just to sink into blissful, passive hypnosis. "Could we continue therapy," she pleaded, "since we get along so well?"

Fischer said yes, if and when Ellis and she wrapped up therapy. She also recommended group sessions. A junior therapist, one of Fischer's ex-students, was running a group at a clinic for patients who'd been abused by therapists. Six months with this Dr. Chantal, Fischer said, could help Zoe, who hadn't begun to identify her abuse issues, much less to resolve them. And Zoe must meet Dr. Chantal's supervisor. Dr. Bryna Wizniewski was one of the nation's experts on psychiatrist-patient ethics.

Fischer reiterated her conditions for taking on Zoe. During the next half year, Zoe would wrap up therapy with Ellis. She would not call Fischer during this time. Long-term therapy with Fischer would be extremely different from the brief supportive therapy: much less passive and possibly more painful. Zoe should not expect an easy ride. . . .

*Mommy likes us. Mommy will nurture us. Gwynn is a good mommy,* thought the infant alters inside Zoe's tunnels. They'd heard neither the conditions for long-term therapy nor the very appropriate limits. They accepted the popular view of hypnosis: a weird situation in which you were controlled by a, hopefully wise, witch goddess. The infant alters still craved what they'd never yet gotten—mother love.

*Letter, July 28, 1986, Amelia Ellis to Gwynn Fischer:*

. . . Since last May, Zoe not only has worked through a lot but has experienced significant life changes. She attended the group and also gained self-acceptance as we explored her fantasies about me. Now once again I am wondering if this is the time for Zoe to move on. She is entering a new phase of her growth. We have discussed termination. I will suggest that Zoe call you for an appointment.

The first Tuesday in August 1986, Zoe sat in Fischer's brown reclining chair, joyously waiting. She was too excited even to read Fischer's book titles or to puzzle out upside-down files. She wondered what hypnosis would bring today. Peace? She'd float, maybe, to the Golden Beach World with the angelic presence, Mark. The body lost all sensation while Zoe was in the Beach World. Zoe did not realize her own system's rule—pain first, floating later. Floating had its cost, which she could never foresee.

"Let's start," said Fischer.

A thrill ran through the system. *I look into your eyes,* thought the alter Danielle, who till now had loved only God, *and I know you!* Two new child alters sprang alert—Rebecca Gwynn and Gwynnie Louise—who'd formed during the six-month separation. Gwynnie Louise, age seven, was about to leap out and kiss her new mommy, when Fischer delivered a kicker:

"Let me remind you that long-term therapy will be different from brief therapy. The aims change. Instead of simple reductions in anxiety and fighting insomnia, we'll now be doing exploratory work as well."

"What does that mean?" stammered the Patient.

"We're going to probe for details of your past. Get to the roots." Details plus roots are what constitute one's inner myth.

Zoe shuddered. Profoundly, she did not wish to get to the roots. The surface was bleak enough.

"Also," continued Fischer, "we'll continue to strengthen your behavior in the present."

"First I've got to feel better, don't I?"

"That's why you'll be in deep hypnosis—to facilitate memory and potentiate healing," Fischer pointed out. "There's no prescribed recipe for healing. We'll work with things as they arrive."

"I'm scared."

Fischer smiled. "I know you've been through some terrifying situations. Perhaps it would help you if first, you quantified your goals."

"What would you like me to do?"

"Will you please jot down your goals and bring them to our next session? What would you like to accomplish?"

*Feed me, Mommy. Hold me. Never let me go.*

"Sure," said Zoe. She'd just contracted to objectify the subjective, and this is because a part of Zoe wants to believe that Mommy knows best. Zoe's intestines began to churn. *Secrets are secret,* thought one protector, the Golden Child. And the alter Selina thought, *This Dr. Fischer try, but already she make vicious mistake.*

Continued Fischer, "For your own good we'll have to observe clear limits. Given your history—abuse by two doctors—I've decided there's going to be absolutely no physical contact."

"No hugging?"

"No, not even a handshake."

The alter Selina was getting furious. *She abuse my children. She put children in dream state and then when they wake up crying, she will not even hold them? Already this woman look away.*

"But how about transference?" continued the Patient.

"Emotional clinging will obviously be harder to control. We can all expect a certain amount of dependency," answered Fischer severely, "but we wish to encourage health, here, in your external world. Previously you have been too focused on your doctors. Isn't that so?"

"I guess," said the Patient.

"That's that, then. I also would like you to continue with group."

"But I would prefer just to see you."

"I am not going to be infinitely available," said Fischer firmly.

"How about emergencies?"

"In emergencies, yes, but not all your frequent crises can be considered emergencies. You have a tendency to call and call; we must observe appropriate limits."

Inside Zoe's system, Selina was giving a running commentary. *She not call as much as you say. She keep boundary as best she can. This is what patient buy, is few minute of therapist's time.*

Fischer opened Zoe's file, which had been sitting upside-down on the desk. "Dr. Chantal says you're doing fine in group. You don't talk much, but the other group members say you contribute significantly. I would like you to continue calling Dr. Chantal with nonemergency questions relating to the issues brought up by those sessions."

"Sure," automatically agreed the Patient.

*Mommy wants others to care for me*, thought Mazie 5.

"Finally, we're going to have to coordinate your doctors. You can't keep scatter-shotting therapies."

"What do you mean?" The Patient didn't realize how many conflicting doctors "the body" had recently seen, but the number had reached two hundred.

"Open your purse. How many medications are you carrying?"

She was carrying a dozen different kinds of pills.

"How many medications and therapeutic appliances do you have at home?"

Her medicine cabinet was full, plus her night table, plus one shelf in her kitchen. A lot of the pills were vitamins, though.

"What's the name of your internist?"

"Which one?" Five pages of her personal phone book were filled with the crossed-out and overwritten names of doctors.

"I rest my case. Let's set up bimonthly appointments with Sarah Freed for your psychotropic medications, and at some point we'll choose one internist, just one, for physical checkups. You will then have time for a life."

"Great," said Zoe. Therapy with Dr. Fischer was going to be great . . . wasn't it?

Back in the tunnels, far back from the well-groomed exterior, still unacknowledged and unwilling to show herself, as they all were, the alter Alice knew therapy was not going to be great. For starters, she hated Chantal's group.

■

**ALICE (the Tunnel of the Golden Child's Observers):** *All those po' ladies, swappin' stories. I sees a lot of pain, bad heartache. One woman got pregnant; the therapist pay for the baby-killin', then dump her. Several women try and kill theirselves.*

*Dr. Chantal fine, and Dr. Wiz too. . . . They try and help, but the pain be too deep.*

*Bottom line is they's just a bunch of rich folks. And Dr. Gwynn's a real ugly white lady. Mean as a snake. 'Stead of making us better, she give us mind and mouth beatin's.*

*What I felt, and I suspect the others did too, was that it was gonna be a cold day in hell before Dr. Gwynn could suck me outta my tunnel. There's ways, and ways, of holding on.*

■

No longer did Zoe feel entirely relaxed with Fischer. Bizarre voices pulled her this way and that. Because now when she floated on that cloud, Fischer tortured her with questions.

*I'm too sick for this,* Zoe felt. *And getting sicker.* Only after the horrible probing, which she resisted to the hilt while pretending utmost cooperation, and the falling into screaming blackness, was there a short period of the smooth, milky comfort she craved. The price of that comfort grew session by session; yet Zoe craved it, more than ever.

From Fischer's point of view, long-term therapy was working. In four sessions, look what they'd accomplished! They'd charted goals; set a course. Zoe's list included fear of driving, agoraphobia, insomnia, and dependency issues; they were taking each of these, step by step.

"I began," says Gwynn, "with cognitive-behavioral techniques. Driving phobia and agoraphobia were treated with desensitization using progressive relaxation and hypnosis, followed by graduated exercises. First I asked Zoe to drive out the driveway, then down the block. By the end of the first half-year, she could drive anywhere, so long as someone else was in the car.

"Insomnia was treated with hypnosis. Anxiety, also.

"In six months, Zoe reduced her chloral hydrate and only had to return to it once, in a low dose. She reduced Valium but was never able to discontinue it completely."

Yes, Zoe could drive. But she didn't know who was driving.

It was becoming harder and harder to suppress her voices in session. The voices did not believe the induction was aimed at them, and so Zoe the Patient kept her guard up more than ever. This was especially painful when Fischer urged her, as she usually did, to stop being Miss Goody Two-Shoes and to speak her entire mind. Zoe felt she didn't have an entire mind to speak.

The protective fog was lifting, and it covered hell. During her sessions, voices would scream out things that Zoe couldn't remember. At the end, Fischer would refuse to hug her. Trying to walk down the hall afterward, she felt worse than ever. *But still,* Zoe felt, *Gwynn's a good doctor. I'm going to be the very best patient she's ever had.*

■

A year into therapy, progress stalled. Zoe seemed increasingly resistant and dependent. Her case against Altman's estate was coming to a close, and she brought that lack of trust into therapy. Sessions became turbulent, filled with her virulent accusations and childlike demands, punctuated by frantic, polite apologies. Fischer decided to ask Zoe to keep a journal. This often broke an impasse and taught the patient the meaning of psychological work.

Zoe cooperated. The journal came back. Yes, it started

as a journal: *Dear Dairy, today I went to the movies.*
But as Gwynn glanced down each page, she saw that
sometimes the handwriting changed dramatically. Some
of the content was abusive; some was wishful fantasy.
Several letters, in unformed, childish print, begged
Fischer to let Zoe sit on her lap.

Messages began to appear on Fischer's answering
machine; sometimes several a night.

"Come to me, darling."

"I will destroy you."

"I found out all about you, at the CCP party. The
story about your marriage was especially interesting."

"As I drive past your house, I think of you undressed,
brushing your hair, getting ready for your bath . . ."

As she played back the messages, Gwynn realized the
contrast between this patient and other patients. Zoe
had no run-of-the-mill disorder. This was a very deeply
disturbed, possibly even dangerous patient with no sense
of privacy and with only the most fragile tolerance for
mutually agreed-on limits.

What was Zoe Parry—a borderline? A schizophrenic?
An anxiety disorder patient? A cyclothymic? A dissociative disorder?

All of these, and none of these.

"Uh-oh," Fischer thought facetiously. "What if she's
a multiple personality? I'm glad Zoe isn't anything like
that."

Over the weeks, Fischer realized this was not an
outrageous evaluation.

She checked the standard definition of multiplicity
against her experience of this patient: the quick changes
into mutually exclusive feeling states, some of whom had
assumed or revealed names. The compartmentalization
of affect; the extreme hypnotizability. The manipulation
of two weak, sick therapists into symbolic re-creations of
her own abusive parents. And reluctantly she became
convinced.

Fischer didn't want a patient with MPD. Multiples
were notoriously difficult to treat. Standard parameters
for therapy had hardly been set. Besides, Fischer wondered, was she qualified? Her first instinct was to refer

Zoe to one of the few specialists then in existence. There was a psychoanalyst at CCP who was doing marvelous work on how multiple personality developed in young children.

Then another impulse kicked in.

She had taken this patient on, had pledged to help and heal to the best of her ability. She was on the right track with Zoe, she decided, and had a responsibility to see her through this therapy.

Faithfully, Dr. Fischer studied up. She reread Ernest Hilgard's *Divided Consciousness* and Jack Watkins's *The Therapeutic Self*, two of her favorite books. Zoe's dissociations could possibly be therapeutically utilized. If Fischer could control which alters would speak at which times, she could possibly structure a series of therapeutic abreactions—re-creations of the original trauma—in which Zoe would relive and heal from the abuses that had split her.

But Fischer could already see that putting one foot in Zoe's world while keeping one foot in her own—maintaining what Watkins calls a therapeutic self—was going to be a huge challenge. Each facet of Zoe would claim his or her own world. This patient would come at her from every possible direction.

Fischer decided to be very cautious and observant. She would go slowly, not trying to break new ground. She would continue hypnosis, regressing the patient, find out the specific emotional states that in Zoe called themselves separate people and explore them—while trying not to encourage any new personalities to form.

What happened in hypnotic regression, she believed, would pattern itself on deep, old, childhood decisions about how to cope with stress, decisions that had caused Zoe to flee the vulnerability and responsibility of oneness.

But what if the abuses had happened so early that they had prevented the development of any self at all? Babies don't have a self to speak of—a self is made, not born. The earlier the abuse had happened, the likelier it would be that some primal core of self was deeply damaged.

Floating on her cloud high above the cares of the

world, Zoe regressed with her mommy-doctor. Past Wald, past Sidney Altman. Deep into the tunnels: back, back, back.

Material came pouring out, some so explosive that Fischer could not explore it with Zoe's conscious self. The personality structure was so fragile, it couldn't take much. After sessions, Zoe would go into crisis.

In session, Fischer told Zoe that she was creating too many emergencies; that if she was ill, she should go to the emergency room.

Zoe, though outraged, obeyed her. Then emergency room doctors began to call Fischer. They excoriated her for refusing to help her patient; on these occasions Zoe would be waiting on a gurney right down the hall.

Therapists are used to patients' projecting their own emotional states on them and can often utilize these projections in therapy. But Fischer found herself getting angry. She also found herself constantly defending her own level of involvement and preparation. Often she made little decisions she could not logically support. Zoe's attacks sometimes caught her off base and out of control.

That was only human, Fischer reminded herself. That was the part of the challenge of being a therapist— weaving your human failings and successes into a process that potentiated the patient's own healing.

One day the patient was pulling her chain, crying, threatening her, and picking apart Fischer's imperfections. "Stop it," Fischer snarled. "We're all imperfect," she added, more calmly.

The patient shrank into the comfortable brown recliner.

"Not me," an angelic little voice said prettily.

"Who are you? A child state?" Gwynn Fischer asked, more sweetly.

The angelic little voice began to chant.

"There was a little girl, who had a little curl. Right in the middle of her forehead. And when she was good, she was very, very good." Suddenly the manicured hands formed claws. Swiftly Fischer's good patient sprang at her.

In spite of herself, Gwynn Fischer pulled back.

"But when she was bad—"

As the patient froze, her nails hanging right in front of the doctor's eyes, a hoarse voice whispered—

"—SHE WAS HORRID!"

# Part Three

# HER
# BURIED
# GOLD

# Zoe Parry: Inner Structure

*November 1992*
*Discussing middle childhood.*
*Approximately 100 personalities.*
*9 Tunnels.*

The Tunnel of
Observers

The Tunnel of
Waiting

The Tunnel of
Sorrow

The Tunnel of
Power

The Tunnel of
Protectors

**GOD'S CHILD
BABY FROZEN**

The Tunnel of
Past Lives

The Tunnel of
Light

The Tunnel of
Limbo

The Tunnel of
Guides

The Tunnel of
Secrets

## Zoe Parry: Inner Structure

### November 1992

In November 1992, Zoe's map shows, at its core, "God's Child—Baby Frozen." To discuss her childhood, Zoe has returned to her childhood metaphor of tunnels. The Tunnel of Past Lives is now at center left, the talking position. The Tunnel of Hell has disappeared: its inhabitants have moved to the far right, a position, for Zoe, of extreme dissociation. In speaking about the past via autohypnosis, a skill Zoe learned from Gwynn Fischer, Zoe's Gwynn Fischer alters move into limbo with the alters who were once in hell. Many alters who were social in earlier months, now move to the right, to protect and keep their secrets.

# 6

# *Childhood: Taking It*

In 1944, the year they conceived Zoe, Dave and Zoe May Bryant were thirty-eight and twenty-nine. Good Americans, salt of the earth, they'd wed at twenty-four and fifteen. "From love," according to Zoe May. The marriage "had its ups and downs." "I was very young," says Zoe May. "My husband was like a father. He would just almost run my life! He was on the possessive side and a bit domineering. But I loved him so, I would overlook it. I never did like dissension."

Along with dissension, Zoe May also never did like physical contact. It hurt. Fragile and jumpy, she used what she called her nerves as an excuse to avoid sex; according to one of Zoe's alters, "she started getting nervous after the marriage and slept in the bed with her mother-in-law when she was real scared." "Nerves" was a euphemism for fear of anything outside her control. Which was everything. Especially burglars, fire, and Dave Bryant.

Dave Bryant was short—five feet three. Though Zoe's friend Diane Timothy recalls him as a "wimp," to Zoe May he was both emperor and judge. Chubby, Dave disguised this with well-cut suits and a brisk manner. He had thin red-blond hair, a winning smile, and an occasional lively sense of humor. He could shoot the head off a snake at forty paces, too—a skill he'd learned growing up on a farm. This terrified Zoe May.

Dave Bryant was a salesman. First he hawked typewriters and later, at Sears, Roebuck, TVs. At work he was hail-fellow-well-met, with a handshake and a grin for everyone, particularly for the young ladies. At church, he was considered a godly man, who could heal the sick with prayer. At home, Dave studied *Science and Health,* ate Zoe May's pecan pie, and eased out his belt. He loved TV, *You Bet Your Life, Zorro, Million Dollar Movie,* you name it.

Bryant's social life was a round of Wednesday meetings and Sunday dinners. His greatest love was not Zoe May but his annual brand-new Buick. Each year he'd have a family photo taken in front of that Buick. He loved waxing it and going for a spin; Zoe May would never learn to drive, and to this day Zoe is phobic about cars.

Though there were many pictures of Buicks, there were few of Dave Bryant's natal family ever displayed. He had eight siblings; in 1944 his parents were still alive. Zoe May says that Dave's father was an alcoholic; his mother, "a saint." The siblings had all gone on, become millionaires, bag ladies, thrift shop owners, lawyers, mechanics, and salesmen like Dave Bryant, who had only a sixth-grade formal education.

Zoe May says that her husband was "a naturally loving man." But he was starved for touch. She had a horror of touching him; he feared touching anyone. Bryant was mortified about his hands.

"His hands were permanently disabled. The bottoms of both bled. His sweat glands had dried up early in life. He thought he'd been infected by germs thriving on the Mississippi farmlands where he lived as a boy. He used a special salve and held his crippled hands downward showing only the tops, which were normal. He shook hands with his fingers. He would grasp the other person's hand with his thumb."

In deep hypnosis with Dr. Fischer, Zoe asserted that Bryant had not been infected by the farmland, but by illicit activities with the farm animals. She said that her father put on a good front, but . . . She couldn't remem-

ber, and broke off the reminiscence. And she repeated,
she hated his hands.

■

**ZOE 2 (the Tunnel of Light):** *Daddy's rough. It's scary. When
he touches us I'm scared I'm going to get it, too. Deep cracks
that open up and bleed. Lizard hands. No like to hurt his
feelings. No put your hands on me, Daddy!*

■

From the outside, the Bryants' lives seemed passably
normal. Concentrating on housework, Zoe May cooked
his favorite dinners, good old southern roasts and side
meat and black-eyed peas and cobblers drowned in
whipped cream. The best moment of her day was when
Bryant pushed his plate away and praised her.

The couple's most violent argument—"We didn't have
many," states Zoe May, "perhaps one a week?"—was
in 1944. After nine years of trying for a baby and two
miscarriages, Zoe May wanted to adopt. Bryant blew his
stack. He wouldn't hear of any child of alien blood
coming into his castle. Zoe May dropped the matter. Her
family pride had been stung by those words, "alien
blood."

"Mother wants me to mention," says Zoe, "that I
come from a very good family. There are seven attorneys
on her side, and one superior court judge."

A good southern family. Blood and fire and denial
and manners. Mostly white folk from England, Ireland,
France, and Germany, who farmed hard, worked hard
and fought hard during the Civil War—fought hard in
gray. Plus there might've been some (don't mention
them, hush now) in the clan. Zoe May's discourse on
family greatness segues to oratory about her grandfather,
Zoe's great-grandfather, "a wonderful man," putting a
black man "in his place." Denial runs big in this very
good family. A formal portrait shows that great-grandfather had dark skin himself, plus crinkly wiry hair, wide,
high cheekbones, and flashing black eyes. The fear may
have been linked to survival: when Anne Adams was a
child, she saw a black man in her town (suspected of

raping a white girl) lynched, his severed head put on a stick and paraded down Main Street.

The Adamses and Bryants feared anyone they considered different. Catholics, blacks, Italians, and Jews were particularly hated and would later turn up in crowds inside Zoe's inner family.

Racial and ethnic issues aside, a six-generation family history of the Adams and Bryant clans turns up the happy traits of fertility, saintliness, and hard work and the sad traits of depressive illness, suicide, alcoholism, gastrointestinal distress, alleged incest, and torticollis neck, an atrophic muscular syndrome in which the head trembles on its pinnings.

Zoe May had six sisters and one brother, Luke. She spent the years from age six to fifteen, between Luke Adams's birth (he was the youngest) and her marriage, traveling with her sisters in a vaudeville troupe called The Sunshine Kiddies. Luke stayed home and was adored.

Zoe May worshipped her mother, Anne, and passed her awe, adoration, and fearful respect on to her daughter. "The only happy times I ever spent were with my mother, playing paper dolls and making pretend families."

One strong family pattern continues to this day. The clan rule is if a mother is unstable, she moves her children to the home of a sister. She then raises somebody else's children. Most of the children feel rejected and turn on their mothers later on. In the 1940s one of Zoe's maternal aunts had a baby with an African-American and, when the child was ten years old, in one of Zoe's alter's words, "shipped her off to her own kind." In the 1950s Zoe would move in with her cousin Virginie; Virginie's own children had previously been shunted off to other aunts. In the 1980s Zoe's son and mother would move in with her. Compared with other families, the Adamses went through an uncommon number of such splits and recombinations.

Almost as soon as they had coupled, Zoe May and Dave Bryant were reabsorbed into the previous generation. At first they moved to Jackson and lived with Dave's parents. Then they moved to Chicago and lived with Zoe

May's parents. They never did establish a completely separate household; neither would Zoe.

The Adamses gave the Bryants the upstairs floor of the enormous, quirky clapboard house that Lukē Adams had built himself in 1908. "We had a bedroom, huge kitchen, living room, and bath," says Zoe May. "My mother had a kitchen downstairs, living room, dining room, and two bedrooms, and a basement and an attic.

"My kitchen was my favorite room. It had been converted from a sleeping porch, so there were plenty of windows. I could look out to a big oak tree in the backyard and squirrels running across the roof. I used to enjoy baking, and whatever I baked, I would take some down to my mother."

This is a pretty domestic picture. But by 1944 all the erstwhile Kiddies were anxious and depressed. Luke Junior was off fighting World War II. One Adams girl had died in childbirth; four, including Zoe May, suffered from chronic colitis. Two married alcoholics. Three were religious fanatics. Of the five who would have children, four would either abuse them or marry someone who did. The fifteen Kiddie offspring—Zoe's cousins—today include eleven identified patients (of whom four repeatedly attempted suicide and one succeeded), two saints, two sexpots, a physicist, a psychologist, a nightclub singer, several business people, and of course, those seven attorneys.

What Zoe May's feelings were upon missing her period in late 1944—after two miscarriages—can only be surmised. I doubt that Bryant knew early that a child was on the way.

During her pregnancy, goes the family lore, "Poor Zoe May had a nervous breakdown. She didn't consult a doctor until the seventh month, and the one she chose was a sadistic alarmist who told her that at thirty she was too old to have a baby and would probably die."

Zoe May was even terrified of the room and bed she and Dave Bryant slept in. There her sister Julia had died in childbirth. There her grandmother Juliette had been miraculously healed of a fatal disease.

"This goes back to the time Mary Baker Eddy was

alive," says Zoe. "Mrs. Eddy's pupil, a gentleman, was summoned to the home; my grandmother Anne at the time was seven years old and had a severe earache. Great-Grandmother Juliette was dying of an ulcerated bone cancer in her leg. First the gentleman came over to my little grandmother, who was crying hard, and he gave her what they call a treatment in Christian Science. He told her, her ear was perfect and that God had made it so. She believed this. Her ear was healed. Then he went upstairs. My little grandmother looked up to heaven and prayed to God that he would spare her mother. Well, you can call it a miracle. I do. That cancer went into remission. A small white scar formed, and that was that. This miracle, I think, would persuade anyone. The whole family joined up. Juliette became a practitioner, and so did my grandmother. She was summoned to Mary Pickford's home in a chauffeured limousine once to give a treatment. This faith continued on, from that day.

"In the Adams household, no doctors were ever called. My grandparents would go into silent prayer. As a child my mother was treated by my grandmother or great-grandmother. Once a car ran over my mother's sister Rae and knocked her out. The police picked her up and took her to a hospital. Grandmother took her out and gave her treatments, and Aunt Rae miraculously recovered. There were many incidents like this that I heard all my life."

Juliette went on to die in that bed; Juliette's husband (Zoe's maternal great-grandfather) was chained to that selfsame bed during the last five years of his life, when he went mad. So each day and night that Zoe May would get into that bed or rise or enter her bedroom, she would ruminate about death. This coming child, feared Zoe May, would be the death of her.

Zoe May dissociated her fears, as she would teach her child to—"Put it up on a shelf in the back of the mind."

With Anne Adams's help, Zoe May got through.

Strange portents preceded her birth, says Zoe. "Just before Mother went into labor, an owl hooted in the oak tree outside her window, seven times. And one day, an Italian man came rushing into the house, saying he'd heard Mrs. Bryant was the seventh daughter of a seventh daughter. Her child, he foretold, would be special, psychic."

The tension built until Zoe May's big day. June 22, 1945, dawned humid and miserable, "toward the end of the war," says Zoe. She has told this story many times. "Mother labored long and hard. She said I 'made a very reluctant entrance into the world.' For over twenty-four hours I would come a certain way down in the womb and then go back up again. Later, she'd say I did not want to be born.

"Mother Nature took its course, and out I came, right into the sadistic hands of Dr. Foster."

"Right after you were born," agrees Zoe May, "the doctor injured you in the lower extremity, and you had like a period. It bled and bled. He said that would go away, and finally it did. But I believe he injured you and did not want to admit it. Your dad and I were terribly concerned. We kept you clean, and we kept changing you. And my mother, being a practitioner, of course we told HER. I think what finally stopped the bleeding was the prayer."

It is not rare for girl infants to absorb maternal hormones in the womb and to bleed or even to lactate at birth; this usually subsides in a week. Dr. Foster has long since passed on, so I cannot verify his supposed sadism.

What matters is that from the moment of Zoe's birth, her mother and grandmother had set a pattern of sadistic doctors sexually abusing a holy innocent. The constant cleansing and "changing" by Zoe's parents soon became the substitute for intimacy with the surviving child. The tiny martyr's ruination and healing became spiritual demonstrations. Nobody could restore the deflowered infant to virginity, cure original sin, except for Anne Adams, whom the family agreed was the local holy woman.

Zoe lived in the bedroom of death and birth and miracles and madness, from birth to age five. She rapidly became (except for food and God) her parents' sole source of stimulation. "They forgot about each other and concentrated on me." Aunts, cousins, and friends agree this is true. Instead of working out their problems, Zoe May and Dave Bryant triangulated them through their infant.

Paradoxically the attention they poured onto Zoe was a form of neglect. The parents never bonded with the real child, only with their vision of a perfect child.

Parental attachments are the foundation of self and the basis of all future relationships. An article by Dr. Peter Barach, in the September 1991 issue of *Dissociation*, discusses the issue. Intimacy affects development. A new mother's problems can rapidly spiral into disaster for her infant. Normally, when you take a child from its mother, the baby cries to bring her back. If crying doesn't work, the baby despairs and then becomes listless. Soon the child will respond to any loss by believing it deserves nothing better. Thus cold parents actually teach children how to become victims. When abused, the child will emotionally drift away.

Zoe May refused to feed her infant at night. "Mother claimed she was too sickly to wake up all the time."

Soon, "Mother got so depressed, she thought she was going to die. She sank to the floor in a fetal position, her finger in her mouth. And she wouldn't come out of her coma until my father arrived after work. I would go hungry until he fed me supper."

Today, Zoe's alters agree that the original baby self froze at about this time and split off Zoe II.

■

**ZOE II (the Tunnel of Patients):** *I took over so the body wouldn't die. I am so afraid. I start to perform as soon as I take over. I do everything like a robot. I never feel free. I cry a lot, but nobody hears me. I am now ten. As a baby I had blonde hair and green eyes. My hair turned brown. When mother would change into the depressed one, I would vanish into thin air. Baby Frozen would lie there, as still as death, until the father came home.*

■

"Back then they didn't know about postpartum blues, nor would my mother have had it medically treated even if she did know, because of her faith. So after three months she wrapped me up in a blanket, came downstairs, and gave me to my grandmother."

Anne, the spiritual heir of Juliette, was by 1945 the clan matriarch. During those three months, says Zoe May, "Mother told me to get ahold of myself. God had given me this little girl and it was my job to take care of her."

**ZOE II (the Tunnel of Patients):** *I was dressed in little silk and lace organdy creations. I wasn't ever allowed to get dirty.*

A 1946 photo of the Chicago house shows a normal-looking home of white clapboard; there's a lawn mower on the walk. A plump blond man in a white short-sleeved shirt and dark pants, his thinning hair raked to the right in a merciless part, squats holding up a wide-eyed baby. In her white ruffled bonnet and matching puff-sleeved dimity dress, her lace-topped socks and her pristine, buttoned leatherette booties, the baby looks stunned. Even her knees are clean—as though she isn't allowed to use them for criminal activities, such as crawling.

"She wasn't allowed," agrees Zoe's cousin Virginie in a 1987 interview. "Everything was, 'Oh, my! She'll get hurt!' If they could have kept her in a bubble, they would.

"She was pretty. But unnaturally spotless."

"She had trouble with digesting the formula. We had to change it again and again to get it right," says Zoe May. "She wasn't healthy. She was fragile. When she was just a few months old, why, she had a breaking out. It wasn't chicken pox; it might have been measles. We would call in a practitioner for these fevers, because that was the way we were raised, to work it out in prayer."

Many infants have trouble digesting formula. Also, when their sweat glands develop, most babies harmlessly break out. Anne, who had nursed eight children, might have reassured Zoe May; but perhaps she enjoyed asserting her own spiritual and maternal superiority. In any case, the foundations for struggling over who was more ill and for badness alternating with perfection had now been set in both mother and child.

Says Zoe, "I existed already terrified of every minute that ticked off the day. It was normal to feel the touch of death, and to freeze.

Continues Zoe, "Even when we're not frozen, we're always nauseated. Except when Mary Cora's out. She eats a whole lot of stuff and doesn't get sick. But many of us have to eat baby food, if anything."

Why didn't Zoe May call in outside help? She answers, "If a person uses his correctment, they could overcome many things. Jesus healed the sick without any drugs. God knits the broken bone. God-Nature.

"You can't serve two masters, God and man. You have to choose, God or the doctor, says Mary Baker Eddy. Put your trust in God. Pray for the outcome of whatever bothers her. Then she would be healed.

"The Scientific Statement of Being, which we try to live by, along with the Lord's Prayer, reads, 'There is no life, truth, intelligence, nor substance in matter. . . . Spirit is immortal Truth; matter is mortal error. Spirit is the real and eternal; matter is the unreal and temporal. Spirit is God, and man is His image and likeness. Therefore man is not material, he is spiritual.' "

Zoe's alters Carol Seemore and Virginia Zion today assert that Zoe May could never live up to the words of Mary Baker Eddy. But her mother, Zoe's grandmother? She was perfect. "Mrs. Anne Adams was the most dignified, spiritual person one could ever hope to meet. Strong in every way, and so loving. I never saw her act unkind."

Unkind, no. Intimidating, yes. For those first three months Anne Adams was an example impossible to surmount for the pitiable Zoe May. Then suddenly, brutally, she was neutralized.

"It was a warm September morning," says Zoe. "A soldier came knocking on Grandmother's door. Her son Luke was dead. My grandparents crumpled to the floor. The once happy house was filled with all the daughters, wailing for their beloved brother.

"As soon as I was old enough to listen, my mother told me how, in tragedy, Grandmother then turned to me. She came and picked me up out of the crib and told my mother that this little baby had come to take Luke's place.

"From this time on, Grandpa wanted me to be like Luke.

"In profound grief, Grandmother would come and get me out of the crib, sit and rock me close to her heart. Grandmother would scream and cry while holding me. It is scary to think of her doing that.

"Well, they found out that Luke had jumped or fallen from a window when he was hospitalized in the Philippines. He had shell shock. I guess he would see the enemy and hear gunfire, and he'd lost twenty-five pounds. My grandmother didn't want to believe that her son would take his life."

After Luke Junior's death, Zoe May reclaimed Zoe. She donned a housedress, dabbed on White Shoulders perfume, and sang as she worked. She put her "doll" Zoe in the playpen in the spotless kitchen, and cooked for two families.

Day and night, Zoe was told by parents and grandparents both that she was God's Perfect Child, that God did not make a child to be bad or sick or demanding or dirty or have limp hair or bad manners. "I was Mother's 'doll in a box,' taught perfect manners at an early age."

Zoe May was afraid to change diapers. Diapers were the dirtiest thing about having a baby. So—and this was practically unheard of in 1945—Dave Bryant took over, with his rough, bleeding hands.

■

**BLANCHE STEEL (the Tunnel of Observers, Guides, and Past Life):** *Her father diapered her. His hands on her vagina. I believe something happened to those little orifices by the time the child was six months old.*

■

Zoe May is still proud of Zoe's quickness as a child. "I took her off the bottle at seven months. She wanted it, but I thought, well, I would do like the neighbor across the street did with her children. Zoe cried, but so does every child. Occasionally I would give in to her to stop the screaming. I never did get angry with her. I knew she was having a problem to give it up, she loved it so. She loved the pacifier as well, which I took away at the same time." Zoe May sounds loving, but why did she remove both bottle and pacifier at seven months?

Zoe's version does not quite match her mother's.

∎

**ZOE 2 (the Tunnel of Light):** *Nite-nite. I scared. Bad mommy makes little baby go in dark room—by herself. Baby cries. Can't we have just a little light? She says no. Crib, with sides up.*

*No, don't wanna go in there! I do poopie in bed. Mommy has to clean it up! I glad. Not the baby, but I was. Down the leg, all over the sheets. Baby is crying. She had to go real bad. Mommy slapped her on the leg.*

∎

Shuddering, Zoe May bundled up the whole package—sheets, baby, and all—and brought everything into the bathroom. After putting on rubber gloves, she stuck the flailing baby into the sink and hosed her off, holding and shoving and scrubbing until the screams faded into cries, then whimpers. She dried and powdered and diapered the now passive child. When Zoe May was done, her daughter, sniffling, wanted her bottle. She knew where it was kept—on a shelf high above the fridge. She pointed.

The mother said "No."

"Ba-ba!"

"NO!" Zoe May tripped on a huge pile of laundry and caught herself a nasty smack on the counter.

The baby sniffled. "Ba-ba!"

"You want the ba-ba?"

"Ba-ba!"

"I'll GIVE you the bottle," came a harsh mutter. The mother took the bottle off the refrigerator shelf and threw it in the trash. She turned, her sweet face distorted with fury. The baby became silent. Zoe's memory ends.

Virginie says, "They expected too much. Zoe wasn't

allowed to express herself. She was watched all the time.''

Zoe's grandparents, as well as her parents, expected wonders. They'd be doing a disservice to such a smart, pretty child, they agreed, if they allowed her to be less than perfect. Says Zoe May, ''Zoe's grandmother loved her so, she taught her little verses she'd learned when she was a child. It gave her a lot of pleasure. It did me, too. Her father and I taught Zoe how to write her own name at age two and sing hymns. She read at three and spoke beautifully. I would have liked her to be more independent, though.''

Independence was treated as inexcusable rudeness, though. Zoe May recalls, ''When Zoe was a year old or two, I'd take her to the grocery store. And if anybody so much as looked at her, she'd hide. Mr. Snow, he owned the store, and he'd give her a cookie. She'd take the cookie, but didn't want any part of him. Of no one, as far as that goes!'' Zoe May punished Zoe for any rude exercise of judgment, such as refusing Snow's kisses. Today Zoe has an alter named Mr. Snow; he doesn't say no. The Bad Girl does say no—by hitting.

■

**MARIE-MARIE (the Tunnel of Light):** *Bad Girl bites and hits and pushes. She is seven now. She has dark brown hair and brown eyes. God loves you, Bad Girl.*

■

Zoe's photograph of Bad Girl shows a pugnacious-looking toughie in a snowsuit, boots, and fur-trimmed hat. She looks ready to pound your face into an ice drift.

■

**DEMON CHILD (the Tunnel of Secrets):** *I came out in 1947. I was two. And I have reasons why I'm bad, so fuck you.*

■

Bad Girl did not come out often. Zoe was too much her grandmother's child for that.

''Zoe had,'' says Zoe May, ''a pretty good understanding of Christian Science. I thought she would be a practitioner someday, follow in her grandmother's footsteps.'' Zoe May would have died to be as favored by her mother as Zoe was. She couldn't admit to resentment, but her subterranean jealousy erupted on more than one occasion. And so did her own self-hatred. She simply could not control herself around Zoe.

One occasion in 1947 illuminates the triangle; it also shows why Zoe so hated and feared Mr. Snow.

Zoe May, her mother, and Zoe were at Mr. Snow's store, choosing food for the evening meal. Apparently both women left the toddler alone in the shopping cart while they compared lettuces. Mr. Snow approached, holding a cookie. He was tall and fat and, as he had been cutting meat, he wore a bloody apron.

"How's my sweetheart?" he said, zooming in for a kiss.

In deep hypnosis, Zoe recalls what happened then.

■

**ZOE 2 (the Tunnel of Light):** *I felled out of the shopping cart on my head and hurted myself. Size of an egg. Nanny picked me off the floor.*

■

The toddler hung from her grandmother's arms, limp with shock. Her forehead swelled with blood from a deep, nasty cut. Then she screamed for her mother. So did Anne Adams. "Zoe May! Your daughter's been hurt!"

Mr. Snow came closer. "Is she all right? I feel so bad."

Zoe shrieked at the top of her lungs, twisted free, and ran up the aisle, sobbing, "Mama!"

Says Zoe, "I finally saw Mother and ran to her. She turned from me—and ran out of the store."

"She started running," the alter Donna says belligerently. "The child remembers. She was up the street and the grandmother was holding the baby, saying prayers."

"Yes," admits Zoe May. "She was *denying* the fall."

"She was denying the child had fallen?"
"Yes."

■

**MAZIE 5 (the Tunnel of Light):** *When you're bleeding, are they suppose to say you're not hurt, that's a false belief? That's scary!*

■

**GRANDMA NETTIE (the Tunnel of Observers, Guides, and Past Life):** *The grandmother was merely addressing to the child that matter has no sensation. She was teaching the child correctly that the lump was not real. And the mother runs away, hysteric. Without that mother, the child would have had a perfect demonstration!*

*Mrs. Adams could see this child was under the bad effects of a bad mother. This mother was laboring under a state of false belief—that so-called "depression"—and transporting this onto her child.*

■

**SISTER MARY (the Tunnel of Power):** *That is so unreasonable. Yes, you can pray for a child. But if she's lying on a concrete floor screaming, you take her to a doctor!*

■

From that day on, Zoe got headaches.

■

**ELEANOR (the Tunnel of Secrets):** *She had a headache after she fell. And what the mother did for it was tie a bandanna tightly around the child's head. Probably the worst thing. Didn't have it looked at. The body still has the scar.*

■

The headaches were a mystery to the Bryants, and they blamed the child for error. Zoe also remembers the adults sometimes blaming her for their own errors.

■

**ZOE 2 (the Tunnel of Light):** *I see my Nanny with a baby on her lap—me! Grandma eating corn. She make funny sounds and turn red. A piece of corn go-ed down the wrong way. Nanny can't breathe. Drops baby. I falled. Momma scream. Bad baby! I on the floor. Head hurts. I pray. God, help Nanny! Momma say I bad!*

■

When she mulled things over, Zoe May thought she was just being a good southern mother. Anne Adams, after all, had been far stricter.

"Her word was law. I didn't voice my feelings or show I was crying. I held my feelings in. Which sometimes is good. If voicing your feelings will make yourself and others miserable, why then, I say it's better to be silent."

When asked if this made her ready to explode later in life, perhaps at her daughter, Zoe May answers, "I can't recall. In fact, I was very overprotective."

And, too, she was embarrassed to stand before her mother with a daughter who seemed to be so sinfully sickly. This daughter reflected poorly on herself.

■

**ELEANOR (the Tunnel of Secrets):** *Zoe was holding her head one day. A friend of the family was over, another Christian Scientist, and she says, "What's the matter with you?"*

*Zoe says, "My head hurts so bad!"*

*The lady says, "You're too young to have a headache." That makes the child feel she's not having a real headache, no matter how bad it be. When the woman leaves, the mother is telling her how embarrassed she made her feel. Then they deny the headache together.*

*The headache continued to the present day. Now, I think that some of the headaches be migraines and some be caused by switching. I think people was already fighting for the body, to gain control, that these was switchin' headaches.*

■

"That child did a lot of affirming and denying," says Zoe May. "She was one that wanted to affirm the Truth. In all things about God. We sent her to Sunday school early, and we hoped she would go on after and be class-taught. Just not anyone can be a teacher. That is what we hoped for Zoe, with her native abilities and talents.

"We are taught in our religion that God made us perfect. So if bad things do come up, we deny that, and put God there.

"Zoe loved being God's Perfect Child. Because if you said she WASN'T perfect or she was a bad child, why, she wouldn't like anything like that! She tried to be perfect, and in some respects, yes, she succeeded! She was like a little angel."

Though dividing the world into rigid good and bad this way is harmful, what more deeply hurts a child is when a parent admits to seeing or doing only the good. This structure, in which a child learns to habitually wipe away memory of a parent's bad actions, sets up internal dissociations, mental blocks, and amnesias. The child learns to distrust his or her own perceptions, to reject and ignore his or her own experience. If this child is to keep a core of self, the child must split into a multiple personality, go crazy, or die. The child's inner life gets farther and farther away from external facts. As the emotional illness takes over, it begins to feel more normal than health.

■

ZOE 2, (the Tunnel of Light): *I go to Aunt Rae's house on Seven Mile Road. She says, "Here comes the little angel," and that is me. I a good girl. I know all my Sunday school stuff. Aunt Rae gets the family and says, "Come in here, Zoe." And I do. I say all my prayers. I sing my hymns. I say my rhymes. And then she takes me out, and to everybody we pretend I am her daughter. And she says, like my mother and all my aunts say, "Oooh, you little angel child—you are too good to live!"*

■

A baby in the extended family had just died and had also been described as too good to live. According to Dr. Fischer, "Part of Zoe unconsciously decided right then and there that she didn't want to be too good to live."

"Another part of me wasn't such an angel child," says

Zoe. She recollects a memory from hypnosis. "I was two or three years old. I watched the mother go down the stairs. There was a little closet in my bedroom, which had a window. And I could see the mother hanging out clothes.

"I got my beloved dolls off the bed. I mean, I really loved those little dolls and was quite the mommy with them. Well, I started beating them up, kicking, punching, hating them, picked them up by the legs and bashed their heads in."

■

**SERENA (the Tunnel of Power):** *The assholes put up the child as a perfect being to their perfect standards and didn't follow their own rules.*

■

Zoe May would not allow herself to see Zoe's bad behavior until the child was ten. "And then she RESENTED what she was told." Zoe May quickly adds, "Like any other child."

But from the time the child was born until 1955, Zoe May would keep the myth of perfection going. That meant she could neither notice the bad behavior, nor let it by. So she punished unconsciously. The one who hit became *not Zoe May*. The one who behaved poorly became *not Zoe*. When badness came out, it was extreme—and promptly forgotten.

■

**ZOE 2 (the Tunnel of Light):** *She gets spanked a lot, the Bad Girl. Then she goes into the closet. She wants to fall out the window so the mommy will feel bad then. There's lots of different levels to this house my grandpa built. Out this little window there's a roof. You can see right down into the big yard, with lots of leaves on the ground. And you can see the mommy hanging up the clothes. The Bad Girl climbs out on the roof. I don't know what happens then.*

■

Usually after these events, the child would pray in the closet, then go downstairs to be with her grandparents— and to avoid her mother.

"I loved to live in Grandfather's house. He would hold my hand and walk around with me, and I would think, golly gee, my grandpa built all this!

"Grandpa wanted me to be Luke."

Zoe, the Adamses agreed, had come to this world to replace the boys who had been too good to live—their son who'd jumped and died, Luke Adams, and the twin who had died at birth, Luke Bryant.

**ZOE 2 (the Tunnel of Light):** *They dress me in boys' clothes. She is fascinated with weenies. Daddy's and Cousin Lon's and Lon's brother.*

Zoe hands me a photo. At first I think it's of a boy in chaps, fringe, and spurs, but then I see the bow in the hair, behind the cowboy hat. Straight out of a spaghetti Western, riding a cardboard bucking bronco against a cyclorama of sky, the little creature grins from ear to ear.

"Grandpa was dark. His crinkly black hair had turned salt-and-pepper. He would have been handsome if he didn't have a twisting neck and twisting arm. That made him scary. And old-looking. He was always rubbing his neck. Grandma would rub it, too. All his life he smelled of liniment. He hated to shave, and Grandma would say, 'John, it's time!' And he would say, 'Miz Annie, I don't want to. I wish I lived in a log cabin with a dirt flo' and never have to.'"

Zoe's safe place was rampant with superstition.

"Grandfather always talked about witches and omens. If a sparrow flew into the house, it was a sure sign of death. If you rocked a rocking chair and no one was in it, something bad would happen to you or to the person who owned the chair.

"The grandmother hated the grandfather's superstitions. She would dress the little girl in a white sheet. The grandfather would be lying on his bed. The ghost would be given a candle and sent outside to tap the window. The grandfather would start up in extreme panic and run screaming out the door. The grandmother would laugh herself silly.

"Though she scoffed at the grandfather's fears, as an ardent Christian Scientist the grandmother strongly believed in the use of mind power for good or ill. This was another of those unexplained contradictions."

By the time the child was two, her grandmother had her perfectly catechized.

■

**DEBBIE ROBERTA (the Tunnel of Secrets):** *We would play practitioner and heal the sick and raise the dead. The doll would be dead. I would lay her down in Grandpa's toolshed and pray over her. Grandma was teaching us to give real treatments, but we practiced with the doll.*

*I would say, "This little girl is perfectly well!"*

*When it was dead, I would say, "Rise, in the name of Jesus!" And I would pull the doll up, and it would be alive.*

■

**ZOE 2 (the Tunnel of Light):** *I'd sing hymns for Grandma's friends and recite the poetry Grandma wrote. "There is no fear. God is here. His loving care is everywhere. . . ."*

■

Recalling the proud early recordings of precocious Zoe lisping nursery rhymes, the proud compliments about her perfect singing voice, Zoe says, "All this 'perfect little' stuff! You know, it gets a little sickening.

"I wanted to please Mother, so I performed."

■

The Bryants also raised Zoe southern-style.

■

**BLANCHE STEEL (the Tunnel of Secrets):** *The children inside of Miz Zoe would hear fights. "You took me away from my mother, and my home, and the South. I did all this for you, and look how you repay me!"*

*I don't know what Miz Bryant did to make him so angry. He was just angry because he never wanted to leave the South. He wanted his child to be born there. It was like she was. Even though the baby was born in Chicago, he taught her all the ways. The accent, the cookin', the respect. . . .*

Says Zoe May, "A true southerner raises her children to have respect for your fellow man and for each other. To be good citizens, starting in the home."

When asked the exact nature of that respect, she says, "If we caused trouble in our family group, we were made to get a little switch. But my mother was a dear friend. I was so proud of my mother." Anne Adams used to beat Zoe May hard on the legs for infractions.

"I tried to raise Zoe as I was raised. I wanted it to be so people would want to have her back. So I taught her not to bother anyone's belongings."

**DONNIE/DONNA WHITE (the Tunnel of Power):** *I came out with rage beyond rage. I would take the hitting without tears and even laugh at the mean old mother.*

"Everybody liked her," gushes Zoe May. "Wherever she would go, I was real proud of the way she conducted herself. Other parents didn't have control over their children. But Zoe was polite. Unusually so. Maybe my husband and I were too strict with her."

"My husband did the toilet training. He'd get up with her during the night and put her on a potty seat. My mother approved, because she never did like a wet bed." When was Zoe trained? "Before age one." Early training was not unusual in the 1950s—but Zoe May and Dave Bryant's training was.

**ZOE 2 (the Tunnel of Light):** *Sometimes my peepee hurts. I don't know why. My daddy, he wipes me. I good girl. God loves me. I say prayers. I no wet bed.*

■

**ANONYMOUS ALTER (the Tunnel of Secrets):** *Nine months old. The father is like a soldier. Every two hours he sets the alarm clock. He wakes up the baby. Sets her on the toilet. She is too little, and it is too big. She is half asleep.*

He did it on purpose. He let her fall in. Her backside went straight into the peepee water. Scared her.

He orders her to wipe away from the vagina. Nine months old! Doesn't understand. "The other way will get you infected." Baby feels dirty, germs down there. The father stands there, holding himself firmly upright so he doesn't fall asleep. He looks mad, like he wants to kill the child.

The father wipes the child with wet toilet paper. He says he wants her "clean enough to eat off."

By age one the baby goes to potty herself during the day. At night she screams.

Me, I'm older. Every morning I was told to have a bowel movement before the father went to work. This was so he would be there to clean me properly, so I would then spend the day clean. Later he told me that as a boy, each morning he cleaned up after the animals. Cow pats, hog slops, horse manure. If he didn't do this right, he got a whipping.

I still feel terror when I walk into a bathroom.

■

**ZOE II (the Tunnel of Patients):** *Mazie worries about it. The grown-ups too.*

As a child I would be in the bathroom brushing my teeth. My father would walk in, pull down his trousers, and urinate in front of me. I would stand there transfixed, staring at his penis. He would also step out of the shower, towel himself dry, and walk naked down the hall.

I was fascinated. My father's touch was welcome anywhere, any time. At least he wanted to be tender, feel my flesh openly, listen to the first words I spoke. My father's love was the only love shown to me!

■

"He was always overly protective," says Zoe May, "and more partial toward little girls than little boys. Maybe to the point that he was, um, abnormal." But sometimes, Bryant did not seem so partial to Zoe.

"My father would take me to services," says Zoe. "One Sunday he put me in the front seat and started the car. Then he realized he'd forgotten his Bible. Ordering me not to touch anything, he jumped out and ran inside."

■

**ZOE 2 (the Tunnel of Light):** *I did a bad thing! I pulled the stick. The car started moving! I screamed. The car go-ed down to the street. Daddy hear-ed me and ran out. He pushed the car as hard as he could. The car stopped. Then he came to me. I scared. But he just ask if I all right.*

■

Nobody could blame Zoe for being left in a car. And nobody could blame her for her bathroom education.

■

**ZOE 2 (the Tunnel of Light):** *I am a boy sometimes. I shake off the pee one, two, three. Is this my weenie or is it Dad's?*

■

Actually, it was Dad's. Bryant would have Zoe hold him while he peed. Later, events progressed.

■

**BLANCHE STEEL (the Tunnel of Observers, Guides, and Past Life):** *One year old, a hazy memory of the father sitting on the toilet. His penis is erect. The little child's legs are around the penis, and the father is bobbing her up and down.*
   *"You devil's child."*
   *Did the mother know?*

■

It was her fault, Zoe felt, that her mother was so strange and isolated. "At times she stared past me, almost catatonic. I'd find her lying on the floor trembling, sweating, curled up like a fetus. She lay on her bed for days in a row, crying and refusing food."

And then the mother would explode.

■

**MAZIE 5 (the Tunnel of Light):** *She would scream, ''I wish I'd never had you!''*

■

When asked whether she loved her daughter, Zoe May says, "Yes. But, no, that biblical whatever you call it, embracing, I didn't do much of that. I would give her a little pat on the head. It's just not my nature. . . . I wasn't a gushy type, but . . . Of course, I didn't have much love from my daughter either!"

Zoe May's unease with her daughter was so profound and painful, it seems to have sparked Zoe's first personality shifts.

"Once my mother and I took Zoe to a church tea at a lady's house," Zoe May relates. "When she answered the door, the hostess said, 'Such a sweet little girl.' "

Zoe continues. "A shy two-and-a-half-year-old girl accompanies her mother and grandmother, she is crying and clinging, afraid to look at the people. She is out of control. Her mother puts her in her friend's bedroom—alone." Beside herself with social fear, Zoe May wanted to end the situation quickly.

Zoe May adds, "She was screaming. My mother, she didn't know what to do, so she just went back to her friends. So I, of course, was left with my daughter. I must have left her just a little bit. And she then went into the kitchen, and they had some little cupcakes set out to serve. And so Zoe—I don't know if she was getting back at her mother and grandmother—she took the cupcakes and licked them every one! So embarrassing!"

Zoe says, "Another little girl emerges. She is smiling, self-assured, bold, and naughty. The orange icing is delicious. She has no fear of her ill-mannered deed."

"The lady found her doing that," says Zoe May. "So she comes out and tells me and my mother. And some of the ladies, they thought it was funny!

"And Zoe laughed! To think that she had upset her mother and her grandmother and the hostess. I didn't punish her, but I myself thought, 'What in the world ever happened to her, when she was in such a state, crying her heart out, and then she'd suddenly do such a thing and get pleasure out of the doing?"

The little girl did not have much to soothe her, aside from these occasional petty revenges and aside from God. Zoe May, who had taken herself from Zoe at birth and Zoe's bottle and pacifier at seven months, and who faded away in times of trouble, found most of Zoe's objects of affection equally embarrassing. So she'd take them away, too.

**DORA 6 (the Tunnel of Secrets):** *She threw away my precious Brownie Bear. "He's old and dirty. You'll get a nice new bear from Santa." At Christmas there was a giant panda, which I hated the second I saw it.*

*To me Brownie Bear was a person. I talked to him. I gave him presents. And he did the same for me. That bear loved me as much as I loved him. And my mother murdered him.*

Zoe searched for love objects her mother could not destroy. Her father's favorite sister—Zoe's aunt Mo—lived close-by. They hardly ever saw each other; Mo's second husband was black, and her younger daughter, ten, was the color of coffee ice cream. Says one of Zoe's alters, "When this gal came a-visitin' once, she wasn't the most welcome sight. A neighbor came up and said, 'Did you hire some help?' Mo's elder daughter, Marnie, though, was welcome. She was a pink-skinned blonde, close to Zoe May's age, who could act and sing."

After Mo's second husband died, the Bryants invited Marnie and Mo to Sunday dinner. The family exclaimed at the stunning resemblance between Marnie and Zoe, even lining up the cousins and comparing them point by point. Zoe's hair was not as curly and of course she was not developed, but the family agreed that she would grow up to be Marnie's twin. Zoe elaborated this into a glorious fantasy that eventually became the foundation for her future relationships with older women.

**ZOE 2 (the Tunnel of Light):** *She was so pretty. We wanted her to be our mommy. We thought maybe she really was our mommy.*

**ELEANORA BROWN (the Tunnel of Light):** *There had been a lot of talk about how hard it had been for Mrs. Bryant to get pregnant and how an adoption had been set up for the Bryants with this Christian Science girl that found herself in the family way, just before Zoe's birth. Zoe concluded that Marnie must have been that girl.*

Zoe May did not appreciate Zoe's preference. She was glad when Marnie and Mo announced one Sunday that they were leaving for Florida. Marnie had met an agent who'd gotten her work in a nightclub. He'd even promised her a bit part in a B movie, and he changed her name to Marnie Blue.

Before she moved, Marnie came over one last time.

**ZOE 2 (the Tunnel of Light):** *Marnie Blue loved us. She gived us an evening bag. It was gold and sparkly, and we loved it. We put our special things in Marnie Blue's evening bag.*

*My mom had a coin collection from great-grandfather. Indian-head nickels and a 1900 dime and pirate gold. Well, the mother took our evening bag. She put her collection in it and said it was her bag now, and don't you touch it.*

Consulted that evening to settle the ensuing fight about the bag, Bryant took Zoe's side. Zoe May huffed, "Well, if you're going to favor the child over your own wife, I'll just be on my way." And she withdrew—with the bag. It was an instance, she said, of the child's being constantly spoiled; she wasn't going to put up with it.

Zoe May was not entirely wrong about the spoiling.

Like her mother, Zoe was terrified of the dark. Her

fears increased after Marnie and Mo went away—not just because she missed Marnie, but because Mo had sent her younger daughter "off to live with her own kind." Zoe hazily linked this with her fantasy that she was Marnie's daughter or younger sister. Louisa had been sent away; therefore sometimes she too had dark skin. And a dark man was going to come and get her, Zoe, and take her away.

Says Zoe May, "After the seven-thirty bath, it was bedtime. She required that her father sit in the hall with the light on and read until she fell asleep."

Zoe adds, "I would have nightmares of scary men trying to get me, and evil witches coming out of the closet. Daddy would lay down next to me. Sometimes I would wake up in the night, and he would be there. Naked.

"Mother would say, 'Dave, put your pajamas on when you're sleeping with Zoe!' He'd answer, 'Oh, it's all right!' "

Zoe would shut her eyes and stay out of the argument. It wasn't nice. No, Zoe was a good little girl. If she said anything, perhaps her father wouldn't protect her anymore. Besides, she had to take the place of the bad mother who couldn't bring herself to be with her own husband at night.

Zoe May passively allowed the girl to take her place. Soon Zoe started to masturbate in front of her father. Young children often explore their bodies. But Zoe continued to show herself to Bryant until middle childhood. And many times, he became visibly aroused.

∎

**SERENA (the Tunnel of Power):** *He liked to watch. He never stopped me. I used to think as I was looking at him, "Let your prick get hard and your eyes glaze over. You're never going to have me."*

*Anyway, I was born age four. I am eighteen years old now. I am blonde with hazel eyes. I experience no anxiety. I don't let Zoe's scared stuff rub off on me.*

∎

In 1949, when Zoe was four, Luke Adams's torticollis—the shakiness of his neck and arm muscles—abruptly worsened. He was no longer able to work and sank into depression. When a rich relative died and left the Adamses an inheritance, they decided to retire to Florida. There they would find a house fairly near to Marnie and Mo's.

The Saturday Luke and Anne Adams left Chicago, while Zoe and her father waved good-bye outside, Mrs. Bryant came downstairs and wandered through the empty rooms. This was the first time in her life that she'd been separated from her mother. The shades were drawn, each bisected by a brown line halfway down that marked their customary position. The floors, shiny around the edges, were dull where the Turkey rugs had lain. Ovals and rectangles on the wall marked where the family portraits had hung. A tray of cupcakes, colorful with icing faces, sat temptingly on the kitchen counter. Leaning against them was a note in crabbed script: "For Angel Child."

When they came in—"Honey?" "Mother?"—Zoe and Dave found Zoe May lying on the kitchen floor, her mouth open in a wordless scream. Next to her sat a clown cupcake, smashed, with one gumdrop eye and a red licorice tongue.

The next year was an unceasing round of visits by practitioners: Zoe May seemed to have lost her faith.

Zoe remembers feeling Marnie and Mo and her grandmother and mother had all died. Suddenly there was no back-up mother. Since Dave was working longer hours, and Zoe May was catatonic, there was no one to take care of her at all. She learned what she felt was a neat trick: blanking out and going to a safe place—a better world.

The dolls on her bed accompanied her; they came alive.

■

**MAZIE 5 (the Tunnel of Light):** *We had the best times. They were my friends. Their names were Doreen, Elizabeth, Marcie, and Bobby.*

**RUTH (the Tunnel of Power):** *I love my doll the best. She's better than all the rest. We play and play the whole day through. She's my friend, through and through. My doll is good to me. My doll is named Marie. Marie is happy as can be. I'm so happy with Marie. At night, she stays by me so I won't get frightened. Marie is my best friend!*

At night, Zoe felt protected by the dolls.

Zoe kept her new world secret from her parents. But soon it had to be kept a secret from even herself. Her father tended to burst in on her, shocking her fantasy world further and further within.

She says, "Father would search under the mattress and in the drawers, hunting for heaven knows what." He would pull her hands out from under the covers if she was sleeping and lie down with her. Those were the times she felt safest—with her father lying down outside and her dolls within. She had company at every level.

**ZOE 2 (the Tunnel of Light):** *Mary has blonde hair and blue eyes, painted on. Barbara doesn't have hair, but the top of her head is painted brown. She's a baby. I'm a big girl. Sometimes the bad little girl comes out, and I stand in the corner and watch her. I can't stop her. What she's doing is a secret.*

According to MPD expert Colin Ross, "Dissociation is the basic defense mechanism that precedes and underlies the other defense mechanisms."

Zoe's anxiety mounted. So did Zoe May's so-called nervousness. Zoe May's sisters could not bear the separation from their mother, either; Aunt Lucie, Aunt Rae, and Cousin Virginie soon followed their parents to St. Petersburg. Zoe May pleaded with Dave Bryant to move and finally prevailed.

"Just before my fifth birthday," recalls Zoe, "in 1950, Father quit his job. They had some savings, and he thought he'd be the big pioneer. He had a vagabond personality and didn't mind exploring. So south we went, in a brand new green Buick. It was exciting. All I thought about was the alligators. I kept asking my parents on the way, 'When am I going to see the alligators?'

"When we arrived, we stayed with Grandmother in a beautiful Spanish-style home with a red tile roof, on a street lined with palm trees. It was exotic, for a little girl from Chicago."

Zoe's alter Mazie remembers the reunion.

■

**MAZIE 5 (the Tunnel of Light):** *Grandpa had gotten the neighbors to help him build a carpentry workshop. When we arrived, Grandpa shows me the shed. He says, "Here's a present for you, 'Luke' "—and hands me a paper sack.*

*Inside was a little green box with a saw, a hammer and nails, a screwdriver, a ruler, and a T-square.*

*The first thing Grandpa teached me was to saw real good, so I wouldn't cut my finger off. Then he asks me what I want to make. "A boat." So I got my wood and sawed pieces off to make a point. I hammered a piece of wood in, for a chimney. And then I painted it blue. Grandpa liked it.*

■

Despite this anecdote, the two generations did not get along as well as they had before, staying together in the Adamses' new house. Part of the problem was Zoe.

"Grandfather's neck shook and so did his arm. He looked so scary that when I saw him coming, I would run to Grandma.

"Grandpa smelled of liniment. His skin had shriveled into nothing but wrinkles. He was real sad. He stopped talking and would just sit there puffing his pipe. When anyone came over, he just faded into the background.

"He kept saying to my grandma, 'Annie, if anything happens to you, when I die the girls are only going to get one dollar. Because I don't like my sons-in-law, no sirree, and they're not gonna get a penny. Nope, the only one that likes me is Smokey.' It seemed like he didn't see me at all.

"Smokey was his cat. He was huge and gray. Grandpa would sneak him inside. Smokey would spray the furniture, and then there would be fights.

"Grandpa wasn't a kissy person. He didn't even like to kiss my mother. When I'd kiss him, he'd wipe it off. Mother would tell me to go kiss Po Po. I'd wrinkle my nose. I knew he didn't care. So I did kiss him, but not every time.

"There was always a scary feeling with Grandma, too. I loved her a lot, but when I was there, I'd get depressed. Everybody got on everyone else's nerves."

When she'd moved, Zoe's cousin Virginie had left her own daughter, Mindy, in Chicago with her own mother. She invited Zoe over often, as a fill-in for Mindy, and everybody was grateful. Zoe now knew that if she had a problem, she only had to run away to avoid it.

Within two months, Dave Bryant managed to find a job. The week he began work at Sears, in the typewriter department, his family moved into the new house he'd found.

With its white clapboards and slate roof, 731 Ashton Avenue looked more midwestern than even the Chicago house. It had two stories, plus an attic, and, weirdly for swampy Florida, a basement. With large windows and a gray-painted front porch, shaded by trees, 731 was an anomaly here, like Auntie Em's farmhouse planted awkwardly in Oz. The oak leaves hung limp and dusty all summer; then they'd turn half brown and give up the ghost.

For the Bryants, 731 was an enormous accomplishment, a whole new start. The Bryants worked diligently to make a home in this alien land. For the first time in years, they moved the spousal pillows, toiletries, and clothes into one room.

The happiest times at 731 Ashton, like the bad times to come, were tinged with sexual overtones.

"Father would come home," says Zoe, "and take off his good clothes and slip into slacks and a sweater. Then he'd sit on the couch, hand me a comb, and order me to comb his hair. Every so often he'd flinch and scream as if the comb was red-hot. Then we'd scream with laughter. I loved this game. I felt close to him."

After Steaming Hot Comb, Bryant would ask Zoe to search his pockets. She burrowed into one after another, and he'd shriek. Sometimes Zoe May would watch from a distance. Finally, when she reached the right pocket, which took some time because she didn't want the game to end, together they'd draw forth the gift of the day— candy, a toy.

Zoe May says bitterly, "Nothing was too good for you. Your father catered to you. 'This for Zoe.' 'That for Zoe.' He'd bring you a little something every day. Which shows me," she adds guiltily, "how he loved you."

Cousin Virginie disapproves. "Every whim was given in to. No matter what the child really needed. What she needed was a strong personality to say no and make it stick."

Zoe sighs, "I so wanted my parents to love me! Especially my mother. I wanted that special relationship which a mother and daughter should have. She never told me she loved me."

But Dave did. So even today, she protects him.

■

**SHERRY (the Tunnel of Secrets):** *We will never tell his secrets.*

■

**DEBBIE ROBERTA (the Tunnel of Secrets):** *Nothing my daddy says or does is wrong. What me and Daddy do in private is none of your business.*

■

Accustomed to defining themselves in a community through church activities, Zoe May and Dave Bryant joined the Second Church of Christ, Scientist. As Anne and Luke Adams were already members in good standing (she was a practitioner), the Bryants had instant entry and prestige.

"Every Sunday, Father drove us to church, all dressed up. He taught Sunday school. I couldn't go in with them, as I was too young, but I could watch my father lead the group into a special room. They all looked up to Mr.

Bryant. He was a *first reader*—the equivalent of a pastor."

Zoe would have to be dragged by her mother to the preschool group.

Zoe May had first brought Zoe to Sunday school at age three, as had been the rule in the Adams household when she was growing up.

"My daughter was shy. She held on to me and, uh, but I told her everything would be all right and everyone would be, uh, kind to her, and she'd learn about, uh, God. But still she cried. I felt real bad to leave her. I went on down, and I could hear her crying even in the church service. When I went up there to pick her up, why, I felt real sorry. After that experience and all, I really wasn't that insistent. It was just once in a while. Not every Sunday. Cause I knew what she was going through."

Here, in the new home, Zoe was always expected to go to Sunday school.

Zoe started adding stupidity about perfect health to her other stupidities. Suddenly she came down with childhood diseases. Complaining about these was beyond impolite in the Bryant household—it was heathen. Zoe would complain hardest on Sundays.

This defiance seemed strange to the Bryants, in light of what they saw as Zoe's miraculous ability to heal through prayer treatments.

■

**MAZIE 5 (the Tunnel of Light and the Little Flower, the Tunnel of Power):** *Aunt Rae's hands were full of arthritis. Nobody had been able to help her. I gave her a treatment, and she was perfectly healed. All the grown-ups agreed I had the power.*

*Nobody could help Cousin Virginie with her migraines. Except me. I would rub her temples, and she'd be healed.*

■

**CAROL SEEMORE (the Tunnel of Power):** *From then on, when you walked into a room with your aunts and grandmother, they would stand. In respect.*

■

Such a saint should not be getting measles and mumps and whooping cough. Zoe's parents brought her to Paul Barnaby, a senior practitioner, for strengthening in faith.

■

**MAZIE 5 (the Tunnel of Light):** *I was always scared, though they weren't mean. It was spooky, Mr. Barnaby's office. I would have a fever or be coughing. He would say, "Little girl, you're not sick. This is just a false belief. You cannot be sick, because you're the image and likeness of God." But I still felt sick.*

■

**CAROL SEEMORE (the Tunnel of Power):** *But you know, dear child, you had some miraculous healings, because we could see clearly, to unsee your false belief. We were able to put these thoughts into your mind.*

■

I believe Zoe May's vacillation was harmful to her daughter. First forced into going to Sunday school, then never knowing when she'd again be forced, Zoe must have been in a constant state of dread. If she went, she felt stupid, and if she didn't, she was taking advantage of her mother's weakness. Her successful attempts at supernavigating the school through miraculous healing resulted in increased expectations that she do well in Sunday school. She began to feel more and more stupid and sick, until one day she found herself unable to read.

■

**ROSE (the Tunnel of Light):** *I couldn't be perfect, even though they said I was. I was far from perfect. Because I was stupid.*
   *The teacher handed out homework. For two times she had been looking at me, and she saw I did not understand. So this time she gave out handwritten homework to the five other girls and a typed piece of paper to me. I wouldn't take it; I felt so ashamed.*

■

One of the things Zoe was stupidest about was anger. She threw tantrums (not unknown in five-year-olds); these her family thought were evil. Dr. Fischer would later say, "Any expression of rage was 'off the wall.' Feelings of rebellion had to be totally repressed. Zoe learned she must never say or do anything to offend or alienate either parent. To this day, she is afraid of anger."

Zoe was also stupid around strangers.

Four months after the Bryants moved to Florida, another couple, old friends from Jackson, joined them.

Says Zoe, "John Perret was from a good, prominent family. He was a college graduate and was my father's oldest and closest boyhood friend. He was six feet tall and weighed two hundred fifty pounds. Though only thirty-two, he looked old. Once a linebacker, now he was going to fat. I couldn't like him as much as my parents did." Perret and Bryant—neither supposedly drank—teased each other about having beer bellies.

Fleur Perret was a bit of a thing, polite and effusive; she and Zoe May had gotten along fine in the old days.

The Perrets moved into a cute bungalow a couple of miles down Ashton. Dave Bryant invited them for Sunday dinner.

"Whey, hey! Who's that big girl there?" John Perret squatted and held out his arms.

Zoe took one look at the heaving belly, the red tongue, the goggle eyes, and, inexplicably to the Bryants, ran upstairs and hid. Zoe May followed her, scolding, "Look how hurt you made your father's friend!" She ordered Zoe to be good to the Perrets. Or else.

Bryant introduced the Perrets to his church community and told them his home was theirs. Says Zoe, he told her she'd better be friendly. John Perret, he said, was very sad because he and his wife couldn't have a child of their own. "He's not lucky like me," he said, giving Zoe a big hug. "He doesn't have a perfect, smart, beautiful little girl like you, so can't you just give him a peck on the cheek, when they drop by?"

"Yes, Daddy," said Dave Bryant's good little girl.

From then on, when the Perrets came to dinner each Sunday, Angel Child would dutifully kiss John Perret.

When she came forward—prompted by her parents—he'd put his wet gloppy mouth on her cheek and go smack. "Hi, sugar!"

"It was always 'sugar' this and 'sugar' that, with John Perret, and the older women seemed to like it. We'd go in to dinner, and I would watch him shovel in the food as though there was no tomorrow." Perret's goggle eyes darted where they weren't supposed to. He'd catch Zoe staring when he'd belch into his napkin, and she'd catch him goggling when she leaned forward to grab the salt. He'd wink. It was a horrible game that they played under the Bryants' noses.

After dinner, they would all go out for a drive. Up and down Flagg Highway and home in an hour; these weren't so bad.

A few Sundays passed; then the drives changed. Zoe usually sat in the backseat between Fleur and her mother. One day Perret turned around in his seat and said, "Zoe sugar? Can you see okay?"

"Yeah," she muttered.

"Zoe!" warned her mother. "Really, John, I don't know what gets into that child."

"Aw, maybe she's bored," he murmured. "I know what that's like. Hey, c'mon up front and sit with me."

"No thanks."

"Why, Zoe!" With two fingers, Zoe May gave her a sharp little smack on the leg, which nobody else could see.

Zoe whispered, "Mommy, no! I don't want to sit in his lap!"

"You be a good girl," said Zoe May. "You just came from Sunday school. Now, you mind your manners." And she shoved Zoe over the front seat, into Perret's arms, with a very aggravated kind of push.

"I felt like my mommy didn't love me. She gave me to him. Tears in my throat, and the horrible taste of dinner." As Zoe sat rigid on Perret's lap, her bottom bumping his belly, she could hear Zoe May and Fleur carrying on in the backseat about recipes and home decoration and church until the girl thought she would scream.

"I would sit there as my father pointed out sights. The

sparkling ocean. The clouds. The restaurants and houses developers were building, more and more of them each week." John Perret had fat thighs and bony knees. "He carried on animated conversations with my father, whose eyes were glued to the road—he was a very careful driver.

"And one afternoon, while my father and John were speaking of John's upcoming job as a math teacher, and my father was betting him he'd be principal in ten years, John Perret carefully reached up under my perfect, pretty organdy dress and found my secret place with his fingers."

Zoe sat rigid, too afraid to move.

"As he continued talking to my father, his fat finger moved slowly up and down. Part of me wanted to scream. But another, more powerful part dared not utter a sound."

This was the moment, says alter Serena, when she split off.

▪

**LITTLE SERENA AGE 5 (the Tunnel of Power) and the DEMON CHILD (the Tunnel of Secrets):** *I helped take some of the pain away. Cause I, like, got so angry I would have killed him if I had a knife. From that day on I hated men with a passion.*

▪

Zoe May comments, "I never will be able to understand that man. He was so well thought of in church! And I thought she wanted to be up there, close to her father. You seem to think I thought an awful lot of John Perret! Well, I didn't. I didn't care that much about him. The thought never occurred to me, that's all. . . . I trusted people."

▪

**MAZIE 5 (the Tunnel of Light):** *And when we got home, my parents would make me go up with him to my bedroom. He would say, "Let's play school." We'd play dolls or model little people out of clay. And then he would say, "Go to the chalkboard and show me your ABCs."*

*He's standing behind me. I'm writing my letters like he's telling me to. He's got his hand up under my panties. This isn't a very good room. It's a terrible room. He says if I ever tell Mommy or Daddy, they would die!*

▩

After the Perrets left, Dave Bryant would hug Zoe, call her Angel Child, and give her a toy or a piece of candy.

If she hadn't been what Bryant called good, he'd push her away and call her Devil's Child. "In a religious family," says Zoe, "this is worse than obscene. He used the expression often. He was dictatorial, critical, and unpredictable. I had to guess what would please him. If I crossed him in the slightest, he would yell out that name. I could never express my fear and anger, and thus developed the habit of swiftly blanking these out of my mind."

She does not mention the awful loneliness, the imposed silence that led to her craving a friend just like herself, who would understand. A true friend could defend her against John Perret—could control the horrible power of sex.

▩

**CARRIE LANETTE (the Tunnel of Observers, Guides, and Past Life):** *When Donnie came out, everybody saw Zoe had fallen from her state of grace. The father would punish her. And the mother was extra rejecting. "I wish I'd never had such an ugly, disobedient child. I am so sorry for you."*

▩

In a snapshot the little blonde girl stands alone, with no particular expression. She wears a plaid cotton dress with a full skirt, puff sleeves, and a white Peter Pan collar. "Happy to pose alone," comments Zoe. In the next shot, Dave Bryant has his arms around her. Now the girl scowls fiercely. Her entire body is rigid. The father is the picture of well-fed respectability, his cleft chin dimpling as he smiles. In a third photo, the child stands legs apart, arms hanging on to some old wood-and-metal structure, mindless of how it is dirtying the plaid dress. Her careful ringlets have come undone and straggle around her miserable, tense face. Zoe says this is the alter Donnie. She must have rescued the third photo from the rejects pile—or perhaps the Bryants saved it as an object lesson of how unhappy bad little girls can be.

**BLANCHE STEEL (the Tunnel of Observers, Guides, and Past Life):** *Dave Bryant was obsessed with his pretty daughter. He would hold her close, cuddle her.*

*Zoe felt guilty. The mother would catch her and say, "Daddy loves you more than he ever loved me." She felt bad, but at night, her fears were so strong. She kept dreaming of John Perret, but he didn't have a head.*

*Zoe kept her father in her bed to chase away the monsters.*

When asked why her husband moved out of the master bedroom into Zoe's room, Zoe May says, "I was frigid, I guess. Not cold in other ways. But this other part [sex] was repulsive. . . . I guess Mr. Bryant was like any other man. Highly sexed. But I didn't like to sleep with anyone."

Zoe asks her, "What if you'd had to sleep with your own father, Luke Adams?"

Zoe May shudders. "Oh, I couldn't have stood it! No, *mmm-mm.* The thought just never occurred to me! Never ever. To sleep with my father? I never saw my father—only with his clothes on.

"But at the time, I never gave it a thought. Because you had so much dependency to be with someone at night. I just never thought anything about it."

Zoe asks her, "Did you trust your husband?"

"Of course! I had perfect trust!"

"Why?"

"Because he was my husband—and I just did!"

In September 1951, Zoe suddenly got stupid about kindergarten. The Bryants could not understand why Zoe shivered whenever they tried to prepare her for school. They'd praise her letters and ask her to show them her ABCs on the chalkboard in her room, and she'd go blank. They'd enthuse about the schoolyard, about the great swings and sandbox and the beautiful grass and trees, how cozy the school looked and how friendly—and she would have a fit.

■

**MAZIE 5 (the Tunnel of Light):** *John Perret was taking me out on drives alone. He'd say, ''Zoe promised to show me her school.'' I wouldn't want to go, but my mother would insist that I be polite and remind me how terrible it was to be rude to a guest.*

■

"I thought he just wanted to take her on the swings," says Zoe May. "The thought never occurred to me, that anything was going on. Because I trusted people. But I don't, anymore."

■

**MAZIE 5 (the Tunnel of Light):** *He'd park on the side where the auditorium was. There were big shady trees and nobody around because it was Sunday. I would beg, ''Can we go home now?'' And he'd laugh. He made me lie down on the seat. And he put his two big, fat fingers in my little, tiny opening. It's h-h-hard for me to t-t-talk about these things. I-I, it h-h-hurt me bad!*

*I want my mommy! Somebody, help me! But nobody does!*

*(Crying, very scared.) He's putting his big hand over my face! He says he's going to kill me. And (high, panicky) my mommy and daddy! I won't tell! No, I won't! I promise! He keeps pushing! And he won't stop with his tongue. And with his fingers. And he is, like, tearing me . . . to pieces . . . and I can't breathe . . . and he's pinning me down.*

*I can't see his face. I've never been able to see his face. I see his big stomach. And his brown suit. But for me, he—has—no—head.*

■

**SERENA (the Tunnel of Power):** *Mazie would just lie there and take it while he put his tongue all over her, like a Popsicle. He put his hand over her mouth and nose. That's why Zoe 10 can't breathe.*

*I have some very diabolical ideas about killing men; they started then. In fantasy I plunged a sharp knife into his fat belly. Then into his back. Ripped his penis off. Tore out his hair in bloody chunks.*

Mazie can't describe her own arousal and her terrified compliance and her dissociation, because she's been well taught that ladies never talk about *down there*. Besides, she can't remember. She can't describe the sound of his breath. How he lets himself go with her, and grunts, and how she cries under his hand, in silence. She does not remember getting dressed again in the backseat, alone, nor the sound of his zipper ratcheting up his fly. She cannot describe going back into the house to conceal this from her parents. Or how he'd come in saying, "What a good girl she's been."

After punishing her for six months for her dreadful screaming and night terrors, and her deadness around John and Fleur Perret at Sunday dinner before the drives, Zoe's parents suddenly became concerned. Bryant became even more strict—pulling her dress down if it rode up her legs, telling her to keep her legs shut tight. Never be alone, if she could help it, with boy or man. On some level, Dave Bryant knew about John Perret. The alters who saw this felt supernaturally vengeful. Certainly the natural kinds of vengeance—telling, avoiding, killing— were not possible.

**The GOLDEN CHILD (the Tunnel of Observers from Darkness):** *Born in the age of Pericles, about 429 B.C. Well educated, unlike other Athenian girls. Taught in secret by a friend of her father's, a Sophist. But there was another influence in her life. Her aunt taught her the evilness of the mind. She soon realized she did indeed possess powers of darkness. She could cause a person to go insane, become ill and kill themselves.*

While the Golden Child was mulling over a way to retaliate, Zoe's fear alters continued normal life.

Her first day of kindergarten was torture. "The teacher jerked me by the arm because she thought I was talking. The kids laughed because I couldn't read the word 'carrot.'

"The next days were no better. Mother walked me every morning and picked me up each afternoon. I would beg her to stay, as I was terrified of being alone; she would force me inside the fence. I would stand inside, watching her walk away. Never knowing whether she would come back to pick me up. I would wail, and my teacher would drag me inside."

The horrible good-byes left both mother and daughter feeling abandoned. They would desperately cling to each other at odd moments. Other times, they'd compete for the status of littlest girl.

**MAZIE 5 (the Tunnel of Light):** *We would color together sometimes. She'd have one side of the page, and I, the other. And we'd see who did the very best at staying in the lines.*

*Sometimes she would be a little girl! We'd go under the dining room table and play paper dolls. She used to cut them out of the Sears, Roebuck catalogue. Real good ones, she made sure of that, so she could play with them too! When she was the little girl mother, she was funner, like a sister.*

*We would play "Chopsticks" on the piano and go up and play with my dolls.*

*We didn't play together very often. In memories, I can't see her face. I can see the father's face, I mean, how you really look. The mother, I have to look at a picture.*

*Mostly she was depressed and didn't have time for me. There was this lady that stared off into space. The vacant lady. I didn't feel there was a mother there.*

*A lot of times she was the witch mother.*

*The mother says to Zoe to this day, "I wish I hadn't been your mother. I would have been a better aunt."*

The alter Cynthia split off now. Today when we discuss Mrs. Bryant, Cynthia does not speak—she chants. In a secret language. Ironically perhaps for a multiple, the substance is a lament that Cynthia is all alone.

At the end of the tape Cynthia slows to her customary robotic deadness. "Until now nobody has been allowed to hear the secret words. You cannot write this, what you have just heard. It cries out the pain of the system."

The pain of the system was so great that the alters decided one lifetime was not enough to encompass it all. This pain, they began to feel, must be accumulated karma from many lifetimes: spans in which they'd sinned. The pain was God's special test for them, His purgatory, before He could admit them to the world of light and joy. The witch mother and secret father were truly agents of God.

■

**MAZIE 5 (the Tunnel of Light):** *I would write. And Father would watch. One time, we were sitting in the living room and he was reading and I was writing, he asked what it was, and I said, "My book." He read it, and said gravely, "You're the second Mrs. Eddy!" He told me that when Mrs. Eddy was my age she'd been called three times by the Lord. On the third time she answered, like Samuel, "Yes, Lord, your servant is listening."*

*I would hear my name called, too. I'm not fibbing!*

■

Feeling this private channel to God, Zoe became convinced that her specialness and sexual power went beyond anything Perret, or any human, could reach. Her continued survival—unensurable on the earthly plane—reflexively snapped into the world beyond. The lay of a leaf on the sidewalk, the slice of pie dished out to her, were secret messages from God or from saints down through the ages—those who had been martyred and misunderstood. Sexual impulses, of course, came from Satan: God and Satan were duking it out in her own body. Supernatural godliness, hypersexuality, and channeling of the dead were Zoe's magic charm, whose continued power could only be ensured by secrecy.

Zoe began to hide her secret writings in inaccessible holes. This way she felt she could grant herself the power to control her own sexuality. She also hid the writings in Marnie Blue's evening bag and in her jewel box, giving Marnie Blue the power to control her, both as a fantasy mother and as a sex goddess. Later, after Zoe developed breasts, she would hide her writings in her bra.

■

**MAZIE 5 (the Tunnel of Light):** *In the closet, wadded up in the tips of shoes, I would hide them. Under the pile of dirty laundry. In a little ripped part in our rocking chair. Sometimes I would borrow the mother's coins and hide them in my spots. Sometimes I would write code messages on little teeny pieces of paper. Even though nobody could read them, they had to be secret.*

*I had a magic ballerina jewel box, a gift from Marnie Blue. It had a secret drawer that you could pull out. Only Marnie and me knew how to open it. I would hide things from the mother there.*

■

These hiding places were refuges in which one could fertilize the self. By age five, Zoe had crawled into a womb in which she could protect her private faith, in which she could fulfill her forbidden desires.

The secret places, however, were not inviolable. The mother would gather the dirty laundry, would shake out the shoes. She scolded Zoe about ripping the upholstery on the rocking chair. It was puzzling how that little hole kept reappearing, no matter how often Zoe May "stetched it."

The five-year-old can also cope with secrets and violations by encoding them within her body. To herself Zoe became the phoenix who cyclically burns, then rises from the ashes.

Too many events, though, were beyond even the most optimistic unifying legend. These Zoe blocked. Her kindergarten year, 1951–1952, passed in a blur that to this day she cannot remember. Occasionally she goes through violent abreactions: replays of repressed events. To stay a holy innocent, a multiple personality, Zoe must compulsively re-create a split-off past. She has previously abreacted this story with several therapists: now her alters put the whole tale together.

●

**MAZIE 5 (the Tunnel of Light):** *Please, please stop. Please stop. He's rough. He puts his hand over my mouth. I can't breathe. Please, he looks like he's going to kill me. He's holding my hands tight. I can't move. Serena can't hit. A-a-and he makes us take our pants down. And he pees, right in our . . . in our peepee hole. And, he's pulling my hair. I'm l-l-limp. I, I c-c-can't talk very good about it. My teeth ch-ch-chatter. Finally he gets disgusted and takes me home.*

●

How did the abuse by John Perret end?

Waking up with an excruciating headache, clenched jaw, a pounding heart, and tears on her face, the five-year-old alter abruptly abreacts an awful fuss one day, after which she cannot see any Perrets around the house, even when we go over this time Sunday by Sunday.

●

**MAZIE 5 (the Tunnel of Light):** *Finally, I can't pee. The whole area is on fire. I'm hiding behind the sofa crying and laughing with pain.*

*Mommy comes in. She says, ''Well, what's wrong? What's happening to you?'' I can't tell her for the longest time.*

●

Zoe May says of her daughter, "She started acting rather strange. She'd kind of go off in a corner. She wasn't herself at all. She talked to herself, was withdrawn-like, and wasn't a happy person.

"One day she hid behind the couch. And I thought, 'That's odd! You're not playing games with me!' And I told her, 'What are you doing?' She cried a bit, and then said, 'That man did something to me.' And then she told me all about this person that I had put on a pinnacle. She said he made advances toward her. That he made her—I don't like to say the word. Uh, fondle. Him. And he also, uh, fondled—her. But he never actually did put, uh, the, um, in her. I guess he knew better than to do THAT. But he wanted her to, oh, my heavens! I just couldn't hardly bear to listen to the things she was telling me. And I thought, well! I wonder if she's making this up!''

Later, Zoe May cannot recollect ever suspecting that Zoe had made up the whole thing.

Zoe cannot remember her mother's initial reaction. She abreacts someone yelling at her, at first calling her a little liar and then blaming her.

▨

**MAZIE 5 (the Tunnel of Light):** *I blanked out while Mommy made the phone calls. And Daddy came home. I don't know how much time went by. But his face was bright red. In a faraway dream I heard them talking. He said, ''I'm going to kill him.'' And Mother was trying to deny everything, she said, ''Well, no no no, it's not that serious!''*

▨

"Of course I thought it was serious," responds Zoe May. "I, uh, told my husband about it, and he just really flipped his lid. Said he'd like to just kill him. And I said, no no. Don't do that. What good would that do? To be put in jail for the rest of your life? No. Don't let's go to violence. But we will cut off the relationship of this man coming to the house, and also his wife."

Everybody in the family reiterates: Zoe May never did like dissension.

▨

**MAZIE 5 (the Tunnel of Light):** *(Crying.) So I think, ''Maybe it WAS my fault!'' I was a bad girl, and just look at all the heartache I caused!*

▨

Zoe May continues, "I called this friend and told her, and she said, 'Oh—did he do that to her?' and that he'd done that to several other girls! She never had believed it, but now she did, now that he'd done that to Zoe as well! And I said, 'And you KNEW—?' And I said, 'Well, why didn't you TELL ME?' I just couldn't forgive her! She said she hadn't believed it, that she just couldn't, and I told her, 'This is the end of our relationship.'

"That was it. I could have pressed charges. But I didn't want to put Zoe through that, and bring it out, because I thought if it was brought out, if my husband had any contact with John Perret, then some terrible thing could happen. I just couldn't do it." Zoe May feared that Bryant actually would murder Perret and be put in jail; she did not and still does not realize that the terrible thing, the rape of her daughter, had already happened. In Mrs. Bryant's polite society, terrible private events are not as terrible as terrible public events. As long as you can keep things going on the surface, life can be said to be normal.

After the abreaction, the alter Mazie feels better. Now she evaluates being abused by John Perret as an instance in which a depressed mother could not protect her child.

■

**MAZIE 5 (the Tunnel of Light):** *The abuse isn't a secret anymore. My secret is that sometimes it gets very hard being the Little Mama. I have to take care of grown-ups, because they don't do a very good job. What I wish is that someday I could just play and not have to worry about taking care of Mama and always being perfect and never being angry. I wish I could be a real little girl.*

■

Zoe will not recall her parents' subsequent fights: who did they blame for the ruination of their child?

Zoe says, "I'd blank out while they were discussing something. Once I snapped awake. My father had grabbed my mother's favorite vase from the end table. He stood yelling, his veins bulging, with the vase raised high to throw it. My mother and I froze. Then Father yelled, 'Go to hell!' and smashed the vase to bits."

Each parent seems to have tacitly blamed the child.

"Once I thought Father was going to kill us. He came at us like he was going to choke us. His hands were two inches from our neck when they stopped. I remember them shaking."

Zoe remembers only one actual beating. Just after the Perrets apparently vanished, Zoe's parents took her to an amusement park. After going on every ride, she didn't want to leave. She had a tantrum and, according to Zoe May, "caused a lot of trouble. The way she acted, and kicked up her heels, and then lay down on the sidewalk—and, um, we were trying to pull her up, and she wasn't about to. So on the way home my husband told her she'd be punished, even though my parents were on their way over.

"He took his house slipper, and it wasn't a hard one, it was just a slipper. But it could hit hard enough, if you hit really good. And he gave her a spanking. On the rear end.

"My mother and father were there. They didn't want to hear that! So they said that they were going home. They couldn't hear crying and yelling like that. They started walking home down the street, and it wasn't a short distance either. And all the time he was just giving her a, you know!"

Both parents dashed out after Zoe's grandparents, leaving the child hysterical on her bed. That's when Zoe 6, also known as Bathroom Girl, split off.

After the slipper beating, another alter, Dennis, burst forth from deep inside Zoe.

■

**DENNIS (the Tunnel of Power):** *I was six. A lot of bad things happened. That's when I developed my games. They're not pretty. The little girls in the system won't like it. But I'll tell it like it is.*

*Mazie and the other girls used to catch butterflies and let them go. I didn't let them go. I would hold them. After the little girls saw how pretty the butterflies were, I would pull off their legs. I couldn't stop yanking off their body parts. Different ones each time.*

*Then I would hold them in my hand and watch them. Cause I knew they were suffering.*

*After a while, I would want a change. So I would let them go. They would fly off, all crooked. I used to get a delight out of seeing that.*

*It's better, man, to pull the legs off some butterfly, than to chop up some woman—isn't it?*

■

Zoe May decided that what Zoe needed was to take her mind off recent events. Together, they decided to redecorate her room. It had been white. Now it became a perfect fantasy in pink and gold. Zoe chose moiré wallpaper, pink with gold flecks. Zoe May found a pink and gold French provincial desk, wardrobe, dresser, bookcase, and night stand. Dave Bryant had Sears ship out an enormous double bed in which Zoe could have her friends sleep over—once she made friends. Zoe May covered the bed with a pink and gold bedspread and backed it with a costly pink and gold headboard.

The gold-shot curtains were drawn tight, so as not to fade the fluffy new pink rugs. On the silky pillow shams and on the trunk at the foot of the bed, Zoe carefully arranged her beloved dolls and stuffed animals. A large radio stood on the storage chest. A mirror on the dresser seemed to double the number of dolls. Zoe sat before the mirror each morning, brushing her hair a hundred strokes. She'd watch the dolls opening their eyes—smiling at her. Telling her she could do anything.

Part of Zoe decided to become a star and told everybody. Eagerly her family seized on her star quality as the reason for her difference.

■

**MAZIE 5 (the Tunnel of Light):** *Every Saturday we'd go to Aunt Rae's. She'd make chips and dips and chocolate caramel cake, and Uncle Si would crank up homemade ice cream. Rae would take me in the bedroom and put lipstick on me and eyebrow pencil, and say, ''You're gonna be a movie star, cause you've got the talent!'' And she'd take me out to the company and I would perform.*

*Grandpa's mind was going. When I sang, he went in front of the whole company butt-naked except for his underwear.*

■

Once home, the girl would dance again to her records. Over and over she turned and twisted, kicked and tapped and twirled and bowed. When she was done—and she was the best dancer in the world—her dolls would applaud her. She'd flop down on the bed, regardless of her sweat, chest heaving, and drift off into a hazy pink sensual dream.

■

**SERENA (the Tunnel of Power):** *There was this doll. I guess I started getting really turned on. That was some doll. Bobby was a beautiful boy. And later, Marcie and Elizabeth. Marcie had beautiful long blonde hair and blue eyes. Elizabeth was named after Elizabeth Taylor, in National Velvet.*

*I would turn into a little boy and kiss them passionately. Already, at age five, I knew how to use my tongue. I would take the doll and rub it all over, up and down, back and forth. I could feel the sparks, the heat between us. They were alive, and they adored me. I fell madly in love with these dolls, at age five and six.*

*Sometimes I'd kiss Bobby. Sometimes I'd beat him up. If he looked like the baby, I'd hold him and soothe him. But if he looked like the man, I would bash in his head. He didn't have a penis, he was just plain, like the girls. I knew what penises looked like, and didn't like them, so I told him I had cut his off.*

■

Zoe May was still nervous about her daughter. She'd perform in front of the family, but at school she was shy.

"Zoe went withdrawn-like from other children," sighs Zoe May. "It sort of blighted her. She didn't want to go to school, even worse than before.

"So I went down to see the teacher and told her to, uh, to be aware of someone who would say they were, uh, a member of the family, and they might take Zoe off. I didn't feel real good about her safety. And so therefore I would walk her to school up until the fourth grade.

Other little children didn't have their mothers do that. But they didn't have that experience. I didn't trust any man. Or any woman, either."

In class Zoe caught the teacher staring at her. This made her even more shy. Even more fearful. Would the teacher do something to her?

■

**ZOE 6 [Bathroom Girl] (the Tunnel of Secrets):** *I would wake up in one of the bathroom stalls, standing on the seat. My sack lunch in my hands. Not knowing how or why I got there. I would eat my lunch there. I didn't want to be seen. I was afraid to stand in the milk line, so I would go without and choke down the sandwiches dry.*

■

Today, Zoe May regrets that she didn't console her daughter about Perret; she feels guilty she downplayed what she calls "things." "I tried to talk with my daughter about these things somewhat," she rationalizes, "but I was not schooled in any psychology. I didn't quite understand why; I know where the trouble started, but didn't know it could make such a dent in somebody's mind! I thought she would get over it. I, uh, tried to minimize it, to lessen what she went through, to make as little out of it as possible, that the man that did it to her was very ill, and so he was. Though I might have gone too far and told her not to trust men, when I was so resentful. I wanted her to beware, so it would never happen again. I tried to keep her from brooding over the past and try to live today."

Nobody mentioned Perret to Zoe, nor told her they'd done anything concrete to prevent him from finding her again. Word only leaked out at Christmas, 1951, when he killed himself. Shut up in a psychiatric hospital, he hoarded pills, took them all at once, and suffered massive irreversible damage. That's when Angel Child—the perfect little girl—became The Golden Child—the perfect little revenge.

■

**MAZIE 5 (the Tunnel of Light):** *The Golden Child killed him. He's really, really dead. She told me that she made him suffer. What happened was, Mrs. Perret called up and told Mother, and Mother repeated it to father, and I heard. I was not glad.*

■

**SERENA (the Tunnel of Power) and the DEMON CHILD (the Tunnel of Secrets):** *I felt sorry I wasn't there to finish him off in person.*

■

There was trouble in Zoe's paradisiacal pink room. Now, after Perret, there was a new twist to bedtime with Father.

"I was half terrorized," says Zoe in a low voice, "half yearning, that my father would place himself in me." She says she does not know if her father and she ever had actual intercourse. Dr. Fischer suspects that they did.

For this, Zoe blames her mother.

"But you see," responds Zoe May, "I had a problem myself! You had a problem where you had to be with somebody. I had a problem where being with somebody disturbed my REST. And so therefore, as sorry as I felt for your father—I wasn't being the wife I should have been—and no matter what way I did feel for the child— and of course, some of the time you DID sleep with me. And when you get two people together that has different problems, it creates, really, SOMETHING!

"And, well, yet, sometimes, I WOULD SLEEP WITH YOU! Which was hard for me! I would let you come in there, again and again, and each time that was hard for me to do!

"About the man, I couldn't forgive him. Though it goes against what I'd been taught."

Dave Bryant couldn't forgive either, though he was not as certain about who was the unforgivable party—he acted as if it were Zoe. Bryant's treatment of her was wildly inconsistent. According to Zoe, when she'd run to him, calling "Daddy!" sometimes he'd hug her. Other times, he'd push her away. "I'm not your father," he'd say. "Your father is in heaven." And then he'd bury himself in his books.

■

**BLANCHE STEEL (the Tunnel of Observers, Guides, and Past Life):** *He felt guilty. Mr. Bryant was placed by God to be a caretaker to this child. And he failed. He realized this, though he wouldn't admit it.*

■

**MAZIE 5 (the Tunnel of Light):** *I would cry, ''But you ARE my father!'' And run upstairs. I'd go in my closet and shut the door. Jesus said you have to do that—go into your closet. Sister Michael Marie says that means go inside yourself, but I would really go in and say the ''Our Father'' in the dark. I wanted my father, the one that was sitting in the living room reading his Bible. I gradually got convinced he was not my father. But I didn't know what God looked like. So I never knew my real father.*

■

**DONNIE/DONNA WHITE (the Tunnel of Power):** *When Mr. Bryant said that to me, I would get real mad and agree with him. ''It's true! You aren't my father!'' I'd say that another mommy and daddy were our real parents. ''We're all just waiting for you to die so they can adopt us.''*

■

The alter Donnie's threat was part of a wide repertoire of taunts directed at Bryant.

Since age two the child had been masturbating in front of him. Now Zoe May caught them.

■

**ZOE II (the Tunnel of Patients):** *I'd go on the couch as he read his Bible and pull up my cute little dress and be masturbating in front of my father. And he didn't stop me. In fact, he seemed to enjoy it. He'd get this look on his face and wouldn't say a word.*

*My mother came in. She was horrified.*

■

**SERENA (the Tunnel of Power):** *. . . Mazie's mother . . .* Patients: *My mother just said, ''Dave, what are you doing letting her sit there and do that?''*

■

The couple may have had a violent discussion; Zoe cannot remember. In fact, all her conscious memories get very thin at this point. School and home life from ages seven through ten are a blank, as is almost everything except for playing with Diane Timothy or with the neighbors' children, Allison and Addison Stone.

With Diane Timothy, Zoe acted as normal as she could. They played with Barbies and did each other's hair and went together to Brownies.

Her other friends were different. Despite being twins, Allie and Ad looked nothing alike. Allie was short, quick, and dark; Ad was tall, with red hair that stuck straight up and freckles. Their favorite game was Wild West.

■

**BOBBI JO (the Tunnel of Secrets):** *I loved to play cowboys. Ad was Zoe's friend and also mine. Sometimes Zoe would get to choose the game and they'd play house, but then Ad and I would play guy games. We made forts in his sandbox and played shoot-em-up.*

*Ad had a crush on Zoe. They would kiss. I HATED that. Zoe didn't know I was there. I guess she just thought I was her boy doll, Bobby, but NOPE I am real.*

■

**BOBBY (the Tunnel of Secrets):** *Ad and Allie and I would play in the playhouse for hours. We had a secret club. To get in you had to show what you got. Once you're in, it's great. Everything's magic. We're magic. Nothing can hurt us. We can step in front of a train. We're powerful. Especially our eyes. We don't have to use guns; we just use our eyes to kill.*

*We have secrets. Ad's penis is bigger, but I told him mine was growing. He believed me because I believed it, too.*

*I've learned a secret. You use the third eye. Right in the middle of your forehead. You can do anything, see things that other people can't. I started using my third eye, and my penis grew. It's huge. You probably don't believe me.*

■

**NOTES ON ZOE'S HYPNOTIC SESSION, Dr. Fischer, April 1987:** *Inserted pencil a little bit into friend's butt. When asked how she learned about things going in the butt, she said she didn't know. Another time, she tried to use a hot dog to penetrate a girlfriend.*

*"And it ain't a good idea for boys to sleep with their daddies either!" It ain't? (Startle response.)*

*Bobby was going to come out. He wonders where his weenie is. He wants one like Dad.*

*(Different voice, lower, rougher.) Mine ain't grown yet. My Dad has a long one. So I can stick it to the girl next door. Allie's a real good kisser. Have to wear Zoe's tan cowboy hat. I come out often, with Allie.*

*I went to the refrigerator, got a hot dog. Was so mad when I looked down and there wasn't anything down there. He was sleeping with my mommy for once. I put a hot dog between our legs—cold. Bad things don't happen to boys. Boys can do more stuff than girls, do more stuff TO girls. My daddy has a long penis with hair in back and on the sides. That's what I wish I had. It hasn't grown very much yet.*

*I don't get scared. I'm a boy. I'm never going to get those bee bites. (Bee bites?) You know, the marks on the neck and chest and arms. The bee bites, silly!*

■

Now, in 1952, it was Zoe's teacher who called Mrs. Bryant in for conferences. Zoe had become visibly strange. In the schoolyard, both boys and girls were picking on her. In class she drifted off, muttering, into daydreams. Sometimes she'd bang her desk as if to make some private point. The other kids would stare and laugh.

When other children lined up in pairs, Zoe would walk alone, her head down and her shoulders slumped, not acknowledging the spitballs that hit her back. She must have felt the little stings, though. Once, the teacher saw Zoe turn on a child next to the drinking fountain and try to rip her arm off.

■

**SELINA (the Tunnel of Power):** *Zoe was drinking, and so was this other little girl. I came out at that fountain, and that girl had done nothing to Zoe. I punched her in the stomach with all* *my might. Then I grabbed her by the arm. The anger had built, after Zoe was treated so cruelly by her teacher and classmates. I am not proud of this. I am ashamed.*

■

Mrs. Bryant was frightened of what she interpreted as the teacher's power over her child. She assured the teacher that her daughter was just going through a phase.

While Zoe went through her phase, Dave Bryant went through a phase of his own. In 1952, after Perret's suicide and after some of the unnamed events that made Dennis rip off body parts and Zoe lose time, Bryant suddenly became infatuated with his wife's third-oldest sister.

Zoe's Aunt Lucie, a petite recent divorcée, was the only one of the Adams girls to inherit Mr. Adams's appearance. She had what the family calls "olive skin and Mediterranean hair"; the others were all light-eyed blondes. That was why she was attractive to Dave. He equated what they called "black blood" with primal sexuality.

■

**ELEANORA BROWN (the Tunnel of Light):** *Maybe I come when Zoe be seven. Her Aunt Rae, she gather all the children roun' and say they's got black blood. And Zoe, she believe her.*

*I'm a real black person. And I'm proud of my race.*

*I use to be thirty-five, I now be in my fifties. I am five foot eight and I use to weigh about one hundred thirty-three. Now I eats more, so I weigh one hundred fifty-two. God don't care what you look like.*

*I still have my black hair. I pull it back in a bun. I am dark and has real dark eyes. I use to wear makeup, but no more of that for me. The Lord found me and I am saved.*

*These Adams and Bryant families, they put us down, honey, like you would not believe. All this "nigger" this and "nigger" that, it make me laugh, because of their heritage, one side of which they do not care to admit.*

*Zoe had been taught that all people who were not blonde and blue-eyed were the lowest of the low. The spirit guides directed that aunt to put the child straight, so that even in that family, she would not hate her people. Zoe had fantasies both about her people from England and from Africa. Later, when she went to a nonwhite high school, her dreams helped her make friends with people she could see as people, not as she'd been taught.*

■

**GRANDMOTHER MATTIE (the Tunnel of Observers, Guides, and Past Life):** *In past lives I had babies who was taken away from me, babies I had by Zoe's white grandfathers having their fun. My two little girls were taken by the slave master. My boy, I buried, down there in Mississippi. It's a good thing. He didn't have to go through what I went through.*

■

For their part, none of the Bryants admitted Aunt Mo's guilt at sending away her younger daughter. Neither Mo's older daughter, Marnie Blue, nor Mo herself ever saw this girl again. She grew up "among her own kind," found a job cooking in a boardinghouse, eventually opened a catering business, and is now in her sixties, a wealthy, successful businesswoman.

Aunt Rae told Zoe about "black blood"—at a time when Aunt Lucie and Aunt Mo were well within earshot.

Lucie was thrice forbidden to Dave Bryant—because of her genes, his unacknowledged niece, and his marriage to Zoe May—and hence thrice as tempting.

Their relationship was hardly wild. Bryant never got to consummate it. But he hurt his family deeply. "He was totally obsessed," says Zoe. "He'd follow her from the bus stop. She worked as executive secretary at a department store, alongside Aunt Mo. Father started leaving work early, showing up at Aunt Lucie's office so he could ferry her home. She'd moved back in with Grandma and Grandpa Adams."

Zoe May says, "I was disappointed as time went on in my life, and Dave's life, that he had a, a sort of attachment—or, uh, um, can't think of the word—for, uh, my sister. I couldn't hardly believe it! Mo was the one that brought it to my attention. So I confronted him. And he says there wasn't a word of truth in it. And I said 'I can see it for myself!' Still he denied it, right up to the point where he said that she was just as much a part of it as he was.

"And then I mistrusted my own sister. I thought she was leading him on. And this started a coldness toward her."

It also sparked more fear in Zoe: Would her parents split? Would her home break up?

■

**ELEANORA BROWN (the Tunnel of Light):** *Soon Zoe and her mother went together to visit Marnie Blue and Mo. To their apartment. They talked about it and Zoe, who the family called Big Ears, listened.*

*Mo didn't take her brother's side. Mo told Marnie to march Zoe May right down to an attorney's office and to file papers against Dave Bryant.*

*So Zoe May did as Dave's sister told her. She had Marnie drive her down and filed the papers. Later on when they came back, they were all talking about how bad this was going to be for little Zoe.*

*Well, Big Ears of course hid and listened. Everyone inside formed a secret plan, right then and there. They decided the Bryants should go right ahead and get that divorce. Then they could live with Marnie and Mo.*

■

Mo was especially vehement about Lucie's badness. And Marnie (who, after all, had lost her little half-sister to the Bryants' bigotry) kept saying, "Don't talk like that in front of the child."

■

**ZOE 7 (the Tunnel of Secrets):** *I dreamed I would go on the road with Marnie. And even though she had so much to do, she had special time for me.*

*In real life, later on, I'd visit her, and we'd walk her big dogs on the beach. I could get my feet wet without any mother to tell me I would get swept away by the tide. Then we'd come back and she would light a pretty fire, and she would hold me. She would put me to bed and tell me to come in to her if I got scared. And I would.*

*That week Mom was going to get a divorce, I stayed with Aunt Mo, and Marnie went off with Mommy. The Bad Girl came out as soon as they were out the door. She could hardly wait. She took all the little things off the shelves and put them every which way and jumped on the sofa.*

*I can't think about Aunt Lucie and my dad. It makes my tummy ache. I called Daddy that week and asked why he had to be with Aunt Lucie. And he said Mommy was a liar.*

■

The next week, when Zoe and her mother returned home, there was no discussion about the divorce. Gradually—as usual for the Bryants—the affair seemed to be forgotten.

■

**ZOE 7 (the Tunnel of Secrets):** *My father's gold watch disappeared. He'd inherited the watch from his grandfather, whom he worshipped. The parents turned the house upside-down, looking. The watch was found in one of Zoe's shoes in her closet, four days later.*

*"Zoe Bryant, why did you take that watch?"*

*"I didn't, Daddy, I swear it on the Bible!"*

*Sorrowfully, the father said, "We cannot have a thief around the house. And I will not have a liar share my bed." I was crying so hard. I knew I hadn't done anything, though in a dream I saw a little black-haired girl take the watch. I didn't want to tell on the girl, who I thought was a neighbor child. But I was so ashamed. I would have done anything Daddy wanted to make it all right.*

*Daddy moved out of the pink bedroom and slept on the living room couch for the next few days.*

■

Coupled with Zoe's unhappiness, Zoe May's unhappiness was dreadful to behold.

She'd broken down once again. Virginie says that Zoe May had never had her own identity; she'd relied on Bryant for everything. "He ruled her with a will of iron."

■

**ZOE 7 (the Tunnel of Secrets):** *Mommy seemed not to want to live. I would come in from playing. It would be dusk, and the house was clothed in darkness. I'd find her on the bed. It was so sad all the time. Her crying filled the house. I kept asking why she didn't feel well, and she'd say she didn't know. She would hiss, "I wish I'd never had any children."*

*I would say, "Me?"*

*And she would say, "I don't mean you."*

*And I would think, "Well, I'm the only one you had."*

■

If she hadn't had a child, Zoe May might have been able to divorce. Again, she could blame Zoe.

Mornings, Zoe May would stay in bed. A friend would come over to fix meals; or Bryant would buy Zoe breakfast in a coffee shop before driving her to school. Evenings, Grandmother Adams would bring over dinner. Today, Zoe May shudders when asked why she didn't speak. "I couldn't!"

Dave would spend half an hour at his mirror, preening and prinking for Aunt Lucie.

Like her mother, Zoe didn't admit to feeling jealous. Instead, she became extra specially sweet to her father, and she learned how to blackmail him.

■

**ZOE 7 (the Tunnel of Secrets):** *Me and Debbie Roberta, we'd want a toy or some candy. We'd say, "Dad, Aunt Lucie would want us to have this."*

■

Zoe May developed some ghastly unconscious rituals.

At night, if Zoe was reluctant to get out of the bathtub, Zoe May would beat her.

■

**CYNTHIA (the Tunnel of Observers, Guides, and Past Life):** *The girl wanted to play with the diver man her father had bought. She was making bubbles. The mother said stand up; the girl says no. She stiffened her body so the mother couldn't drag her out. The mother hit her and hit her.*

■

Both mother and daughter remember screaming. Zoe May says her daughter drove her to it. "I just don't know; I don't know what I DID. I don't REMEMBER. But at that time it seemed like she was going to stay in the tub and play.

"I'd wash her on her neck and behind her ears. But I never did want to wash the lower part of her. We were brought up to be modest people. I didn't feel I needed to wash that. She was perfectly capable. I had to see her ears were clean, and her neck and things like that, but no.

"It was time to get out. And if she didn't MIND me, then I gave her a spanking on her, uh, uh, on her backside.

"And my daughter would LAUGH at me. The more I would spank her, the more she would laugh! At the end, why, she'd get out of the tub. I don't think she cried. Not once."

■

ZOE 7 (the Tunnel of Secrets): *I don't remember. But I remember other things.*

*If I was playing in the yard and was a second later than the time she'd set to come in, she would race out and beat me on the legs. She showed a deadly fear of my being late.*

*I was sure Mother wanted to poison me. She kept the ant poison under the sink. Every day, unless I watched her make lunch, I would throw the food out at school.*

*The beating game usually happened in the bathtub, but sometimes it was in the living room, and she would use the vacuum cleaner hose. Beating and beating . . .*

■

Aunt Lucie met another man. Andy Brasero was six feet tall, of Cheyenne and Mexican descent. He painted houses during the week and murals during the weekend. He lived inland, near Glass Lake. Lucie talked constantly about Brasero, and at home, Bryant became very quiet.

At night, after dinner—Zoe May was still cooking her husband's favorite foods, even through the Lucie episode—father and daughter would be reading religious books in the living room. Zoe May would come in, wipe her hands on her apron, and crook her finger at her daughter. Silently Zoe would rise and follow her out.

Her mother would walk swiftly toward the kitchen. They'd go to the stove. The kitchen would be spotless—all the dishes and pans washed till they sparkled and put away. The mother would turn to the little girl and say, "You don't want to burn up, do you?"

"No."

"This is a gas stove. We have to make sure it's off."

The little girl would nod. Like her mother, she was deathly afraid of fire.

"It could burn us up. At night, when we're sleeping."

Says Zoe, "She would go to each knob, turn it, and say, "Off, off! Off, off, off!" And go around all four knobs. And then she would do the whole thing nine more times. Twenty times ten times five, one thousand times . . ."

The disturbed woman would silently pull her child out of the kitchen; they'd set off down the hall. Their next destination was the front door. After checking the lock, Zoe May would bolt and chain each and every window and door. "Closed, closed, closed. Locked, locked, locked."

"Safe, safe, safe," Zoe would chant.

Says Zoe, "Then she would put TV trays in front of each door. Three trays underneath each doorknob. "We don't want to be robbed, do we?"

"No, Mama."

"A robber would tip these trays over."

"They'd crash."

"At least then we'll have some warning." They'd walk back through the living room, where Dave was still trying to concentrate on *Science and Health;* he would ignore them.

With Zoe in tow, Zoe May would gather five more TV trays. She'd lock the chain on the hall door and put more TV trays in front of it. "You're clean," she would say. "And the house is clean. We're not going to burn up, and if a robber comes, we'll hear him." And then she would go to her bedroom. She would turn at her door. "Good night."

It was eight-thirty. Zoe would look at the chains, the window locks, and the TV trays. She would hear a rattling noise coming from the kitchen or start to imagine smoke. She'd feel the breath of a robber. "Daddy!" she'd scream.

Sometimes Dave Bryant would then go out. Being a staunch Christian Scientist, he did not allow liquor in the house. He did hide beer in the garage and would sneak out during the evening rituals. If he came in and crashed the TV trays, if Zoe then lay in her bed anticipating being raped by robbers, she does not remember.

▪

**BLANCHE STEEL (the Tunnel of Observers, Guides, and Past Life):** *The father liked to stay up late. But when the child would scream, he would lay down with her. She wouldn't dangle her hand from the bed because she knew somebody was underneath, ready to grab her, so she would sleep in a little, curled-up, sweating ball. She still has these terrors. The children hold stuffed animals, and there's a rocking motion the body goes through to help the body relax.*

*But then she had her father. He would put a chair in the hall and sit there, reading. She'd call, "Daddy, come to bed!" And he'd say, "In just a few minutes." When the child fell asleep, he'd remove the trays and go watch TV. He'd watch movie after movie even though he had to get up and go to work. At midnight he'd climb into the pretty pink double bed, with the stuffed animals and with his daughter.*

*Later, sometimes, she'd wake. She would feel this warmth against her body. And her pink flannel nightgown would be pulled up. She wore no panties. Mother had not told her she had to wear them. And there were no pants on the father. He was naked.*

▪

Zoe would lie awake, stimulated beyond endurance.

The rituals changed abruptly the night Zoe May told her father, Luke Adams, about Dave Bryant's crush on Lucie.

Zoe May had felt well enough to attend dinner at the Adamses'. Her mother had cooked for the entire family, every sister who lived in town, plus spouses and children. Everybody had just sat down—Lucie across from Zoe and next to Bryant, and Grandfather Adams at the head of the table, with Zoe May by his side.

When Grandmother Adams served the turkey, Bryant served Aunt Lucie, giving her the first cut of breast meat, ladling on extra gravy. In the middle of this, Zoe May leaned over and whispered to her father. His face got purple; his neck twisted and began to jerk rhythmically.

■

**ZOE 7 (the Tunnel of Secrets):** *Suddenly Grandfather stood, grabbed his chair, and raised it over my father's head. "Get out! If you ever dare to show your face here again, I'm going to kill you!"*

*Slowly, my father got up. "Come on, Zoe. Zoe May," he said, beckoning. "We are not welcome here."*

*I was so embarrassed. As we left, the entire family stared and whispered. They'd obviously been gossiping for weeks about how this would end.*

*That Christmas, Aunt Lucie married Mr. Brasero. They moved out to Glass Lake and invited us to spend a vacation with them from time to time.*

*God had answered my prayers.*

■

In 1952, Zoe developed a seemingly inexplicable fear of her grandfather. She'd shy away when he spoke to her. The poor man, agreed the Adamses, did not deserve to be treated like this during his dying years. They confronted Zoe. Zoe May told her daughter that her rudeness was embarrassing. Dave Bryant—who'd recently been reinstated in the Adamses' home—said she was the Devil's Child and not his. Anne Adams shook her head in sorrow.

■

**ZOE 7 (the Tunnel of Secrets):** *A little girl, who had dark hair and eyes and a pretty face, came forth from the shadows. She* *talked right back to them, the mother and grandmother both. She said she hated Grandpa, that he was evil, and that she never would hug or kiss him again. I was thinking myself, "Oh, my goodness! Nobody talks that way to them and gets away with it!" But she stood up for what she thought was right.*

■

There was a reason that the seven-year-old girl avoided her grandfather.

■

**ZOE 7 (the Tunnel of Secrets):** *I was already scared of Grandfather. His neck shook and the claw came up, and he looked like a scary Martian.*

*One Saturday my mommy and grandmother went shopping, and my grandfather said he would baby-sit. As they drove off, my grandfather said, "Come on, let's play!"*

*The backyard was magical. He'd planted a lovely rose garden. He had apricot and lemon trees. He encouraged me to climb the trees and feast on the sweet, ripe fruit.*

*We walked into the shade and into the farthest section, hidden from the view of the neighbors.*

*"Let's play!" I said excitedly.*

*His face wrinkled into a strange grin. He unzipped his pants. He picked up an old Maxwell House can that was lying on the ground, and with his claw he pulled out his penis.*

*It had brown freckles on it and was even larger than my father's. Long and hard and dark. His hand was shaking, so the penis was shaking.*

*"Touch it. It wants to be touched." He stared at me intensely, and his neck was shaking. I just stood there frozen. He peed right into the can. And he sighed.*

*I backed away slowly. Once I was in sight of the neighbors, I turned and ran into the house and slammed the door, scared all the time that he was chasing me.*

■

**DONNIE/DONNA WHITE (the Tunnel of Power):** *She didn't tell. But when he came in, I glared and made him wonder. "That's for me to know and you to find out!"*

■

**ZOE 7 (the Tunnel of Secrets):** *After, he'd follow me, with an apologetic look on his face. And one time, when I asked my mother if she was afraid of Grandpa, she looked blank, and said, "I hardly know him." I wondered if when she was a child he'd attacked her too.*

■

Though there is no evidence of any previous perversion by Luke Adams, in one of Zoe May's memories, when her parents were fighting, her father brandished a butcher knife at her mother. She'd run off to a neighbor, screaming that her father was trying to kill her mother.

Zoe began to have a recurring nightmare. She'd fry a man's penis in hot oil; when it was done, she'd throw it to the cats. Sometimes the penis belonged to her grandfather. But more often the severed organ belonged to her father.

One day at age seven Zoe woke from this dream, bleeding from her belly. The wound went so deep she could see exposed muscle. She screamed for her mother.

Zoe May practically fainted. She dropped her polishing rag, clutched herself, and moaned, "Why would you do such a thing?"

Zoe had no reason; she couldn't remember having done this. She didn't want to cause her mother trouble.

Blood was dripping on the floor.

Zoe May said, "I don't know why other people think you're pretty. You're not. You're ugly." Then she ran out of the room and locked herself into her bedroom.

Zoe knocked; no answer. She didn't dare to open the door. She could've heard the sounds of her mother's crying, if she hadn't been crying so hard herself. An alter came out to clean the wound and bandaged it.

At five-thirty that evening Dave came home to a dark house, to a sleeping wife, and to a sleeping daughter, and blood spots on the beige hall carpet.

"What's going on? Where's dinner?" That night Diane Timothy was going to sleep over, Bryant reminded Zoe. She jumped up and dressed. Then she had her father move all his things out of the pink bedroom so that everything would look normal. By seven, when Zoe opened the door to the Timothys, her blonde curls had been brushed a hundred strokes and her eyes bathed in ice water till they were no longer puffy. She'd even cleaned the hall carpet.

Even though Zoe had a secret wound in her belly, Zoe May had a serious headache, and the carpet still smelled faintly of cleaning fluid, 731 Ashton was warm with light, cozy with the aroma of baking cookies, and full of canned laughter from the TV. Dave Bryant was in the living room reading the Bible. As he put down his spectacles and said hello, Zoe brought in a tray piled high with homemade goodies. Zoe remembers feeling embarrassed—she didn't want Diane to know about the self-wounding or about her night terrors. She was also scared she'd have the penis dream.

The Timothys remember the Bryants as one of the most charming families of their acquaintance. A bit nervous, true, but full of southern hospitality.

The daughters were such good friends. On Saturday morning the girls took ballet and tap together. They also still attended Brownie Scouts. Mrs. Bryant was the assistant den mother. Diane remembers being jealous: Mrs. Bryant had brought Zoe to a models and actors' agency, to explore the possibility of movie auditions. She wanted her child to have all the advantages. Diane wished her parents could spoil her, like Zoe's.

■

**MAZIE 5 (the Tunnel of Light) and DORA (the Tunnel of Secrets):** *In Brownies, Diane and I sat together. We'd make things for our mothers. We'd go on nature hikes. We kept cracking up—Diane made the best jokes. She was the most outgoing, popular girl in the school—and she wanted to be our friend!*

■

Zoe made another friend—a Catholic girl named Eileen Dougherty.

**ZOE 7 (the Tunnel of Secrets):** *Eileen took me to a convent, to deliver a book to a Sister. When I saw the nuns, I fell in love. They invited us in. They were dressed in black and white, and the top part of their habit came way down. I could just see their eyes, nose, mouth, and chin. I asked Sister Luke whether she was uncomfortable and how she could talk with that cloth on her face. Eileen looked at me like she was going to kill me. But Sister laughed, told me she was comfortable, and asked if I was Catholic. I said "No." But a serious little girl came from the shadows and said, "Not yet." The Sister asked the serious little girl her name, and she said, "Zoe Ann."*

*Zoe Ann and I went to Eileen's church after that. As we prayed, the statues seemed to come alive and came down to us. I loved talking to the saints.*

Zoe May says, "It seems Zoe was searching for something better than what she'd been taught. I would find the Roman literature up under the bed. Maybe I was too strict with her. And she resented it." Asked what form the strictness took, Zoe May cannot remember.

It is possible that Zoe May beat her daughter, burned the literature, and forbade the friendship. Zoe does not mention Eileen again.

During this time Zoe May made even more of a point of healing Zoe exclusively through Christian Science.

In dance class, Zoe broke a rib falling out of a backbend. Her mother refused to take her to a doctor.

When Zoe started to cough, Zoe May told her to stop it, to stop all of this continuing, ungodly obstinacy.

**ZOE 7 (the Tunnel of Secrets):** *I had raging fevers. Blinding headaches. I was denied even aspirin. I lost weight. I suffered from night sweats. I was so weak I couldn't walk. My daddy would sit on the floor near my couch and hold my hand, all night. It's a wonder he didn't catch it, because I would cough* *in his face. I couldn't help it. I don't remember Mother ever holding me.*

*He tried to treat the illness with prayer. When he failed, my grandmother was summoned to treat it. I got into one of these coughing spells. She said, "Stop barking like a dog right this minute. Or are you a dog?"*

*She said "Know the truth, and the truth will set you free." But I was very sick, and didn't know what the truth was! I tried to be truthful, but I wasn't set free from pain. And she said I didn't have enough faith and that's why I was barking like a dog.*

*I remember drifting in and out of awareness, watching the others. Beyond that and the pain, I don't remember.*

*Later I discovered I'd had tuberculosis.*

■

Today there are still shadows on Zoe's X-rays and a positive test for TB (it's dormant). Her doctor says that her claim of having had TB is probably true. It must have been a fairly mild case; she must have been a fairly strong child; otherwise, the untreated TB might have killed her.

She was very ill for several months. Marnie Blue came over and brought Zoe gifts—realistic-looking figurines of horses. A white mare with a silver-gray mane—Zoe named her Mist. A golden stallion—Gold Dust. A roan with an amber mane—Honey. For an hour they played. "I wish you were my mommy," the child told her glamorous cousin.

Marnie hugged her tight. "Oh, honey," she said. "I'm going away."

"You are?"

"Yes. To South America." She'd been hired to sing at one of the most expensive resorts in the world.

For a year, Zoe slept with the horses and rode them into her dreams. Mist became an alter. Sometimes a magic horse, sometimes a girl, she was the key to a secret land.

■

**MIST (the Tunnel of Secrets):** *When the girls were very upset, I'd create a beautiful land for them. You can't venture too far* *into Mist Land—you can get hurt. Sometimes the girls slip away from my protection. Once they do, they don't slip through again. If they can get back at all, that is.*

*It's easy to give thought impressions to another. To make them see what you want them to see. It's especially useful if you are anxious. These little girls were very anxious—they had reason to be.*

■

**DEBBIE ROBERTA (the Tunnel of Secrets):** We'd go on our horses. My white horse, Mist, was faster than anything. I would get on her back, and Mist would come tumbling down, and the earth would get closer and closer till we thought we would crash.

Suddenly we'd land on a beautiful beach, all gold and white. The sands would open. Mist would go zooming through. We'd travel down into a world of blues and pinks and golds.

■

**MAZIE 5 (the Tunnel of Light):** Out of all the houses in Mist Land, mothers would come running. Beautiful mothers with different-colored hair, wearing calico dresses. They'd pick us up and hug us.

■

**BOBBI JO (the Tunnel of Secrets):** I got to go to Mist Land when I split off from Bobby. He stayed a boy; I became a girl.

Mazie and Debbie Roberta didn't tell you the bad part. Beyond a certain part of town, there's a jungle. If you go too far, then you see MEN, with spears and big black eyes. They can't come out. But if you go in, they surround you.

They grab you. They start eating you alive. They start with your feet. Then they eat your legs.

Then comes this big fat man, the biggest one of all. He's got a real scary face. After your legs are gone, but while you're still alive, you're tortured forever.

They tie you to a rock. Because you don't have legs, you can't get off. And every hour on the hour the big man comes and licks you. He's got a big fat tongue. Pretty soon you're tingling in spite of yourself—then you go crazy. All the little girls that go in the jungle end up crazy on a rock. So you gotta *be careful not to go too far. You gotta stay in Mist Land, where it's safe.*

■

Zoe still maintains secret lands. Dena, her hell, contains ten levels. The deeper levels become progressively more painful to those alters who find themselves there. A complex system of rules, rewards, and punishments controls who gets sent to what level of Dena and when.

■

**ZOE 7 (the Tunnel of Secrets):** *Lana and Zoe are the keepers. Zoe, the highest, has long red hair. Her skin is transparent; she wears a white robe. Zoe says we will never die.*

■

**The KEEPER LANA (the Land of Dena and the Tunnel of Waiting):** *In Dena, there are waiting stations. It is difficult to describe in your language. Dena has its own language.*

*Some people in the lower levels have never been out. They have to be sent to the tenth level because they would be harmful to those on the earth plane, were they free. On the tenth level, there is total darkness.*

*We would never permit the children to visit the tenth level. Bad people can be sent there. Some bad people are necessary to be out in the world, to interact. These bad people carry a strength that the body needs.*

*The important alters in this body have alters of their own. Some wait on the second level, which contains the nameless. People of all ages, who have met untimely deaths. The Nameless Ones are given tasks. Supervised by myself, by the High Priest, by Zoe, and by other Watchers.*

*Say Donna is out and gets tired. She is allowed to rest. Zoe or the High Priest or I pick someone from the second level to temporarily take her place. This person can imitate Donna down to the very last letter. So it is with Mother Zoe and with all. The only ones excepted are past life impressions, who remain themselves.*

*Who is the real person, you ask? All.*

■

**ALTA (the Fifth Level of Dena and the Tunnel of Waiting):** *I have been permitted to tell you about the fifth level. The souls here have not found peace. They have had many lifetimes on this earth but can't make their final transition. So they are stuck in Dena.*

*It's a sad place. Because they cannot let go.*

■

Zoe May was distressed. Her daughter was not perfect. By now, she was not even close to perfect.

In June 1953, when Zoe May pulled out baking supplies to fix Zoe a birthday cake, Zoe insisted on baking the cake herself. The cake came out lopsided. "She was very upset," says Zoe May, with distress still edging her voice. "I told her how she could even it out, by cutting it off here and there. And so she did. But then she put the icing on. And the icing didn't do like it should have done. She was sort of like a perfectionist. And seeing that, she became FURIOUS. She took that cake and threw it, and all the cake and icing went all over the floor. Such a mess! I was very upset. I just said, 'Well, you'll have to clean that up! I'm not going to!' But she never did! And I was the one that had to clean it up! And I was so resentful!

"And then she went into the bathroom and slammed the door. The mirror shattered and glass went all over. It's a wonder it didn't CUT her. I guess the Lord was right there to keep her from cutting her face. Oh! I just couldn't BELIEVE it. I didn't do ANYTHING to her. I thought, I don't— The way she looked, I was afraid she would turn on me. Her eyes were FURIOUS. Penetrating-like. And I thought this was not the time to say anything. Then I said for her to help me get up that glass. And she stood there. She would not help me. I had to pick up that glass piece by piece from her face and hair, and from the floor."

Puzzled at her daughter's fury, Zoe May continued to try hard—often too hard.

■

**ROSE (the Tunnel of Light):** *There was a Halloween carnival each year. The mother decided to work in one of the booths. To* sell cookies. All the mothers were told to dress up. They dressed as witches and gypsies. But this mother wore a gingham yellow-check skirt and blouse, saddle shoes, and makeup—big freckles—on her face. She made herself a yarn wig with braids.

Donnie was embarrassed even to walk to school. She ran ahead. The mother trudged behind in her happy-looking doll costume, lugging the basket of homemade cookies. The mother walked fast, but she couldn't catch up. She said, "Zoe, you're embarrassing me!" And Donnie yelled back, "How about me? I can't even look at you, dressed like that!"

■

Zoe May couldn't win that year. Zoe tells her it was her own fault—not Zoe's.

Says Zoe, "The Golden Child was your creation. Your perfect child. She had intense anger and a feeling that she could completely control everything around her."

Zoe May comments acerbically, "Not control—manipulate."

"Manipulate!" says the high, calm voice. "You can say so, but there is a reason that the Golden Child acted that way, at age eight. Were you afraid?" she continues sweetly.

"Afraid? Well, yes! I was very careful. Because I didn't know the outcome. She dumped tables, and she threw drinking glasses wherever, and it would hit! I was always afraid she'd throw one at me!"

"Did she?"

"No."

"She was saying, 'Stay away, because you may get hurt.' "

On September 22, 1955, Zoe, now ten, was over at Ad and Allie's, playing Davy Crockett.

■

**ZOE 10 (the Tunnel of Light):** I was Ad's wife and Allie was our little girl. We fought off enemies, staked out food, and went exploring. Then we went out to Ad's sandpile and built the Alamo. I was totally absorbed. Suddenly Mother called. Reluctantly I went home to see what she wanted. She told me Grandfather Adams was dead.

# Zoe Parry: Inner Structure

*November 1992 (Thanksgiving)*
*Discussing childhood.*
*Approximately 130 personalities.*
*9 Tunnels.*
*The Angel Child connects directly to Baby Frozen.*

The Tunnel of
Waiting

Selina

Three Protectors

The Tunnel of
Observers,
Guides, and
Past Life

The Tunnel of
Secrets

THE ANGEL
CHILD

The Tunnel of
Patients

**BABY FROZEN**

The Tunnel of
Observers from
Darkness

Friends of
System

The Tunnel of
Limbo

The Tunnel of
Light

The Tunnel of
Power

# Zoe Parry: Inner Structure

### November 1992 (Thanksgiving)

Zoe's personality map now shows over one hundred thirty alters, including No Names, Convent Members, Coven Members, and Friends of the System—outside people whom Zoe has internalized. Now Zoe claims as many alters as there are grains of sand on the beach. She labels an area at the top of the map, "The golden beach of alters. No one will know them"; and fills a desert area with twenty layers of alters.

The core now is the Baby Frozen. The Angel Child proceeds to center left, and two tunnels' worth of observers and guides stand flanking her. Past-life observers drift up, above the Angel Child. While Zoe's demons and devils remain below, they now have a new, portentous name: Observers from Darkness. Most distant from the leftmost, social position now are the patients and those alters who carry secrets.

*I felt nothing. I didn't understand death. As a little Christian Scientist, I had been taught it didn't exist.*

*Dave Bryant had been at the Adamses' house all day, giving constant Christian Science treatments. The seventy-one-year-old man had been frail for some time. Now he'd had a stroke.*

*Zoe felt responsible for her grandfather's death.*

■

**ZOE 10 (the Tunnel of Light):** *We went to Grandmother's home. All of Mother's sisters were there with their husbands. Grandmother seemed calm. I watched my aunts cry and neighbors bustle around with food.*

*For some reason, I hid on the service porch behind the washing machine. It got dark. Grandmother and one of my aunts came in and started talking. Grandmother described the agony Grandfather had suffered. How he gasped and struggled for his last breath. I started feeling unreal. I walked back into the living room and blanked out.*

*My next memory is lying in bed with Mother. Shaking. Sweating. My brain exploding.*

*And then for the first time in my life I felt my own heart beating. It was loud and fast. The whole bed felt like it was shaking because of my heart. I got closer to my mother. I knew I was dying, just like Grandfather.*

■

The next day, the Bryants drove Anne Adams and Aunt Rae to arrange the funeral. They brought Zoe, whose habit it was to cross the street rather than walk in front of a funeral parlor. Zoe turned white. "I can't go in."

Zoe May patted her hand. "I don't think you should either." In the front seat, Anne let out a huff.

Aunt Rae pointed her index finger at the Bryants. "Nonsense. She's a big strong girl, and it's perfectly all right. At her age she should know about these things."

Zoe looked back like a deer that has been caught in headlights. "I should?"

"Aren't you the least bit curious?"

Zoe was, though she hated to admit it.

■

**ZOE 10 (the Tunnel of Light):** *At the door, we were greeted by a man in a nice suit. It was silent. The sweet smell of flowers filled the air.*

We were led up a winding staircase. I couldn't breathe. Aunt Rae looked at me. Most inappropriate to my feelings, I smiled and took her hand.

The man led us into a room filled with shiny boxes. I saw a small white one. "That's for a child," Aunt Rae said.

Inside, I burst into a million pieces.

Grandmother picked out a gray box. She turned to me. "Po Po would like that one."

Still we didn't leave. We looked at suits in a showcase. Next to that was a light green dress. To this day green scares me. Grandmother finally picked the blue suit and signed some papers.

Downstairs once again, we went.

When the door closed behind us, it sounded like thunder.

■

Aunt Rae and the family smiled at the Angel Child. I was silent stone, with a smile to make them happy.

Next thing I remember, it was night. I was all dressed up and riding with Grandmother, Uncle Si, and Aunt Rae. Aunt Rae said, "Soon you'll be seeing Grandfather."

Back at the mansion, the quiet man led us in, where we met Father and Mother. Grandmother walked ahead. The quiet man opened a door and turned on the light.

Grandmother walked to the coffin and picked up a hand that was inside. I was pushed close to Grandfather's body.

There wasn't enough air in the room. A loud sound jarred me—my name. "Zoe! Go kiss your grandfather."

Uncle Si pushed me. I wanted to run, but my legs moved forward. I was standing by the side of the gray box.

Grandfather's chest was still. He didn't look scary. In fact, he looked handsome, better than he did before he died. The new suit was nice, and it fit him well. His neck and arm were straight, and his face in rest had lost that leer. Any moment he would ask to go home.

"Zoe, take his hand!" said Uncle Charlie. I couldn't. But

*suddenly the other little girl was there, and she did. The room was full of people, church friends and family. Aunt Rae gave a small white book to the brave girl. "Now we'd like you to greet the guests. And hand them the book, and make sure they sign it." And, oh! She was so poised, smiling and giving everyone kisses.*

■

Everybody in Zoe's family remarked how she must have loved her grandfather, to mourn him so. After school each day, the fifth-grader would go into her room and cry. At school she was doing C and D work. Each night she'd get insomnia. She lost weight and shot up like a scarecrow. The grown-ups tut-tutted: you never knew how precious a family member was to you until you lost them.

Aunt Rae would come over each afternoon to commiserate with Zoe May. Zoe—who rejected the mug of cream of celery soup, her favorite, which they'd try to feed her—would wait till she heard the low murmur of the women's voices. Then she'd go to her closet and pull out a box of candy, a bag of chips, a can of dip, a bottle of soda. She'd open the window to dispel food odors and wolf down everything as fast as she could. Then she'd stuff the trash in her schoolbag, where it became another alter's responsibility. Looking in the mirror, she'd say, "I hate you, you fat sack of shit. You're nothing but a blimp, Mary Cora." Then she would run into the bathroom and throw up. By the time Rae checked her again, she'd be asleep on the pink silk bed, surrounded by wide-eyed dolls and finished homework papers.

Eating disorders can be seen not just as an individual's disturbance in body image, but as expressions of a family problem. Though Mary Cora saw herself as weighing three hundred pounds and blamed only herself, the ten-year-old body was actually waiflike and anorexic. The child's home was intolerable, she was growing breasts that attracted her father, she had no control over growing up and dying, and she had nowhere else but food to turn to for comfort.

■

**MARY CORA (the Tunnel of Secrets):** *All I do is eat, eat, eat, and all I think about is food. At Christmas I take the two-pound sampler that Mrs. Bryant's family sends her, and I eat the whole box!*

*Everything I could find in the house, I mashed together. Anything salty or greasy or sweet. Cheese and olives, and potato chips on top, I loved that. Cream cheese and a can of cream of chicken soup and mix it together into a dip. You just keep eating it faster and faster. And pretty soon someone makes you throw up. You don't want to. Because the food makes you feel good and you want to keep it inside.*

*I'm fat and ugly and bad, and I should never have been born. That's why I eat. I can't help myself. Mother Zoe buys brownie mix, and I eat the batter. All of it. Not just a lick, the whole thing. I can't stop. I'm miserable and nobody likes me. Because all I do is eat.*

*I just ate a pound of peanut brittle. She's gonna get a stomachache. When I stop eating, I go rest. In a western town from the old days. I have a big pile of books right by my bed. And I devour the books, just like I devour food.*

■

Most susceptible to eating disorders are perfectionist girls, girls who don't want to mature, girls who struggle with their parents for control of their bodies. Zoe was all of these.

In his book *Families and Family Therapy*, a family therapist Salvador Minuchin describes the "psychosomatogenic family"—a family that implicitly encourages body image distortions in a child.

The development of psychosomatic illness in a child is related to three factors. They include a special type of family organization and functioning, involvement of the child in parental conflict, and physiological vulnerability.

The kind of family functioning involved is characterized by enmeshment, overprotectiveness, rigidity, and a lack of conflict resolution. . . .

Conflicts are submerged, and the child feels responsible for protecting the family. . . .

The psychosomatically ill child plays a vital part in his family's avoidance of conflict.

If a family can accept its disagreements and openly resolve them, if a father can accept his child without sexually threatening her, the child may break out of the anorexia/bulimia trap. But the Bryants were not that type of family. Especially, Dave Bryant was not that type of father.

■

**ZOE 10 (the Tunnel of Light):** *He'd follow me to the bathroom and grab my genital area from behind. He referred to this as "goosing" and thought it was very funny.*

■

Zoe blanked out three months, until Christmas.

The Bryants went shopping together for a tree. Zoe May sat in the car—even in the warm Florida winters she felt "freezing"—while hand in hand, Dave and Zoe ran up and down the fragrant rows, searching for perfection in pine. When they brought the tree home, Zoe May popped corn and strung cranberries. The ornaments were precious—the Bryants bought one expensive new bauble each year. Because of her deathly fear of fire, Zoe May would never allow candles or Yule logs; the strings of lights Zoe loved could be switched on for only an hour.

On Christmas Eve, in the cozy living room—the relatives who had been invited for cocoa and gifts had not yet arrived—Zoe suddenly screamed and collapsed against the wall. Her parents ran to her.

The girl's legs stuck out at a ninety-degree angle. Her hands lay passive in her lap. Rigid and silent, she stared.

"They're all coming over. What will happen, with Zoe like that? It certainly won't be very festive. You'll embarrass everyone. Get up. Do you hear me? She doesn't hear me. What could be the matter with the girl?"

The matter was that Zoe had discovered the maddening value of passive resistance. Used as a method of torture, as a hard-edged weapon, this powerful strategy can backfire.

The Bryants could not see Zoe's dissociations through their own. They called Paul Barnaby, the Christian Science practitioner, who arrived just as the relatives did. It must have been quite a show, the festive tree, the gifts, and the constant merry bing-bong of the doorbell. The guests, who were all adults, hushed as they came in and saw the child sitting staring in the corner. Bing Crosby was singing "White Christmas" on the radio. Mr. Barnaby stood above the corpselike girl, lifting her hands and chafing them. The lenses of his wire-rim glasses reflected red and green lights, blinking on and off. He patiently repeated over and over, "You are perfect, Zoe, because God made you so. Stop listening to fear. Get up and join the party." Meanwhile, the party shivered on the couch, opening gifts with the tiniest rustles, merely sipping the cocoa, and murmuring gentle phrases about Mary Baker Eddy.

Occasionally a sharp look would escape from a grown-up. For a child with all the advantages—look at that mountain of gifts!—wasn't the girl just a tad ungrateful?

Christmas morn dawned. Dave Bryant had ushered everyone out early, tidied up (Zoe May had felt faint), and tucked Zoe into bed, hoping that a good night's sleep would cheer her. He'd stayed up till midnight transforming 731 Ashton into a winter wonderland. There were artificial snow, sleigh bells, and Christmas carols, cutouts of Rudolph the Red-Nosed Reindeer and ribbon candy and hot cider with cinnamon and enormous glitter-spangled stockings stuffed to the brim. For breakfast there were homemade waffles.

Dave was up by six. He dressed his limp daughter in her Christmas best—fancy panties, a starched French petticoat, a red plaid frock shot with gold thread and edged in lace, red stockings, black patent-leather Mary Janes, an antique gold and garnet ring. He saw that her hips were still narrow, but her breasts were starting to form. He washed Zoe's face, brushed out her curls, and topped them with a huge plaid bow. Then he carried her to the living room. Zoe May came in.

# Zoe Parry: Inner Structure

*December 1992 (Christmas)*
*Discussing annual Christmas nervous breakdown.*
*21 personalities plus Jesus and the Poor Johannas.*

"Trees are enclosed in Christmas tree shapes; "Fear" is rooted in "Protection."
Protectors are enclosed in an "ichthys" fish shape.
Hope tree is topped by a five-pointed star.

Fear Tree                                    Isolation Tree




**PROTECTION**




Waiting Tree                                 Panic Tree



Hope Tree

# Zoe Parry: Inner Structure

## December 1992 (Christmas)

Zoe's Christmas 1992 personality map shows that at Christmas, she transforms. Instead of her usual one hundred fifty alters, only twenty-one are out: a hyperreligious, dejected, anesthetized minority.

Instead of the usual tunnels, there are six crude drawings of trees, with alters hanging as ornaments of doubtful festivity, from each.

On the Fear Tree hang seven child Zoes. From the Isolation Tree dangles Baby Frozen. On the Protection Tree hang Zoe's saints and sisters, enwombed in an ichthys—a symbol for Jesus, in the shape of a fish. On the Tree of Waiting hangs Zoe Host. On the Tree of Panic, hangs Mother Zoe. On the Hope Tree, beneath all, rests Baby Jesus.

"She's still like that. Should I try Mr. Barnaby?"

"Let's try the waffles."

"This isn't like Christmas at all. Should I call?"

"What will he think of us? Of her obstinacy?"

The girl lay rigidly on the couch, a Christmas napkin tied around her neck, to keep her dress clean. The waffles she did not touch. The gifts fell unopened from her hands.

"Should I open them? This isn't what I call Christmas."

"Read from *Christ and Christmas*."

"You do it, Dave."

He opened the slim blue book carefully. It was three-generations old—the original edition. "Angel Child, listen. 'Fast circling on, from zone to zone . . .' "

"Your favorite poem, dear."

"Listen to Mrs. Eddy's words. 'O'er the grim night of chaos shone one lone, brave star.' You play the star, dear."

It didn't work.

The Bryants had run out of ideas.

■

**ZOE 10 (the Tunnel of Light):** *The next memory is Mother crying. I was bundled into Father's car and driven to Cousin Virginie's. I loved Virge. She was full of fun.*

■

Virginie recalls what happened next. "Zoe came in, all dressed up like a little doll. But she was the unhappiest doll I have ever seen. Her mouth turned down, her eyes downcast. I asked her what was wrong and she didn't say a word. Dave said, 'She won't move. She has no interest in anything.'

"Zoe May beckoned me into the kitchen. She said, 'I don't know what we're going to do. There's something terribly wrong. She won't even open her presents.'

"She asked if Zoe could stay with me. I said I'd be glad to have her."

■

**ZOE 10 (the Tunnel of Light):** *I sat on the couch. Virge rocked me gently in her arms. Mother hadn't thought to do that. Then* her son came in. Artie was two and had bright red hair. He handed me a toy Santa had brought him. I had to smile. A little sense of hope rose in my heart, and it started to feel like Christmas.

Virge put on music and scrambled me eggs. I ate heartily—the first meal I had enjoyed in three long months.

I stayed there for a whole week. Virge mothered me.

Her house was the center of the neighborhood. The door was always open; friends would drop by. The smell of coffee was always in the air and baking cookies. My cousin had a weight problem. Mornings we would do our exercises to Jack La Lanne, and then we would both eat cookies.

Sometimes the memory of the past months would overwhelm me. I would find myself sobbing in Virge's closet.

The day came when Mother and Father were to pick me up. I did not want to go.

For the next seven years, I lived with Virge on and off. She was more of a mother to me than Zoe May ever was.

■

Each Christmas from then till now—for almost forty years—Zoe has had a nervous breakdown. Each year it's a total surprise.

Paradoxically, even though she became much more disturbed in 1955, Zoe also became more of a caretaker to her family. Her mother says, "I'd taught her the basics. She could make a full meal at age ten. Meat loaf, baked potatoes, vegetables, dessert." In fact, Zoe May now began to pay Zoe five dollars a week to make meals and keep house. She reasoned that she was far too ill to constantly do such tasks and that everyone would benefit from this arrangement.

After school, Zoe would clean house and fix dinner, while her mother lay in bed too depressed to move. By the time her father drove up, the house would be shining.

Very occasionally Zoe would play with a friend.

■

**SHERRY (the Tunnel of Secrets):** Th-the g-girl was older, in ninth or tenth grade. P-p-playing doctor. St-stuck-k a c-c-coat hanger up, up our . . .

■

Sherry is half blind, half mute, and half deaf. The other
alters say she can't get away from danger. She was often
out in 1956.

Soon after the coat hanger incident, Zoe began to
menstruate. Her mother didn't notice—but her father
did.

■

**ZOE 10 (the Tunnel of Light):** *He didn't just goose me
anymore. Now he followed me into the bathroom to see if I
had my Kotex on properly. . . .*

■

Virginie corroborates this. "Your mother and you were
like sisters. Your father dominated two instead of one.
You couldn't have any secrets, either of you. He had to
hear everything that was going on. I remember him going
in with you, wanting you to show him your napkin. Now
that is the truth. And Anne would say, 'My gosh, here
she's a big girl and it's a wonder he don't even want to
burp her!'

"The family no way wanted to go along with this. But,
though we knew there was something definitely wrong,
we couldn't do a thing about it. Her mother was very
fearful, and I didn't know it at the time, but so was he.
There was something very sinister about him—something
I felt, too. It must have been hard for Zoe all along. And
that is why she had problems, I think."

■

**BLANCHE STEEL (the Tunnel of Observers, Guides, and
Past Life):** *Goosing and tickling the little girl, that's seductive
and sick. Pinning the Kotex on the sensitive, developing adolescent, that was abnormal and embarrassing. Telling her he didn't
want her to smell like the mother. He forced himself into the
bathroom when she was having a BM, to see how she washed
herself, until he was satisfied.*

■

In an agony of embarrassment, Zoe finally stammered, "Daddy, I don't want you to come in anymore."

He turned beet red. "Ingrate. Wretched girl. So you don't want your father's guidance!"

■

**ZOE 10 (the Tunnel of Light):** *Once he couldn't totally manipulate me, he rejected me. "Now that you've got a mind of your own!" That really hurt. I used to sit in the bathtub and cry my heart out—my whole body just shook—saying, "Daddy doesn't love me anymore."*

■

**SERENA (the Tunnel of Power):** *And the dreams came back, about frying the father's penis in hot oil and throwing it away.*

*And about that damn father. Every single night the child would look for him. Deliberately. To have sex.*

*There he would be, in one room or another of the old house in Chicago. He'd be sitting or standing. His pants would be unzipped. His penis would be sticking out, hard. Instead of running away, the child would go to that daddy and have a horsey ride. And the child would climax in her sleep.*

*Now, nothing happened with the mother like that. But in the dream, then a child goes looking for her. . . .*

*Mother is laying in the bed. And the child goes and lies down on top of her. The child has a penis. Sometimes the child penetrates the mother; sometimes she masturbates her. And they climax. Then the little girl falls into the mother's arms, and they sleep.*

■

Once a week Zoe had time to go to the library. She read about the goddess Athena and Queen Hatshepsut and Nancy Drew; about the great saints of medieval times who lie buried in vaults under Gothic cathedrals, but who through their faith never die. She read about the queen who was exhumed after seven centuries, her hair still golden and her face unlined. She read how the Mother of God appeared to St. Bernadette in the grotto at Lourdes, where the holy waters carved a wonder in the earth.

The book would drop from her hand. She would see a

tiny opening in the ground, which at first seemed an animal's scratch. Entering, she would feel it widen out into a mysterious subterranean cathedral. A scent of spices filtered down from on high; the sweet voice of Mother Mary . . .

Once, giggles woke her. Her fellow fifth-graders, and their mothers perhaps, had followed her in. The mothers nudged their children—"Who is that weird girl?" Zoe got up—leaving the Catholic books in the library—ran home, scoured the bathroom, cooked meat loaf.

Five dollars a week soon added up to quite a sum in the secret niche in Marnie's jewel box. Overtly Zoe was proud of her ability to run the household, and she enjoyed counting her cash. But late in September, 1956, she got very ill. She had started again to cough.

■

**ZOE II and the LITTLE FLOWER (the Tunnel of Patients):** *I would lose my breath, cough uncontrollably, and vomit all my food. I looked like some poor child living in an underprivileged country. Big green eyes sunken in a little face, staring hopelessly. I was taken out of school.*

■

Zoe May pities her daughter's plight. "Oh, she had a terrible siege. It went on for months. And even after the terrible part was over, why then, she had coughing spells."

Asked if she took Zoe to a doctor, "No, of course she had no medical treatment. I don't even know what they do for whooping cough. She found out because, why, you have to visit a doctor to get back into school, and so therefore she was diagnosed in school, by that doctor."

Asked what the illness was exactly, Zoe May describes Zoe in coughing spasms, refusing to leave the living room wall. Asked how she treated it, Zoe May says she asked her mother over to pray. Asked what Anne did, Zoe May says she commanded Zoe to quit barking. Zoe turned red from effort, rose, and got some water. She started coughing again; the drink splattered all over the kitchen. Then the prayers began anew.

With dismay, Zoe May speaks about how long the poor child had to stay home to recover her strength. The period of recovery? "Six months. She missed sixth grade."

Anne Adams was not the only helper summoned. Virginie came over many times. She would visit and hear Zoe in the closet, sobbing as she tried to hold back the coughs. After months of this, Virginie sat down Zoe May and said she was worried about Zoe's health.

"We're doing all we can," said Zoe May defensively.

"I want you to take her to see my doctor."

"That is against the family belief."

"It's your right not to get care for yourself, but you mustn't penalize your child."

In July, when sixth grade was out, Virginie coerced the Bryants. "You'd better call a doctor," she said sternly, "or I will."

In the Buick, Zoe May and Dave Bryant cautioned their daughter about the den of error. "Don't let that doctor undress you."

"Don't let him talk you into anything."

"You're going against your father."

"Doctors don't know what they're doing."

They sat in the lobby. Zoe was terrified to sit down in the waiting room and appalled at the medical history form, which—as no one in her family had ever admitted to illness—she had to leave almost blank.

"Well, come in, young lady!" Dr. Hendricks seemed a nice enough man; plump, with a tidy mustache and a neat white coat. The room smelled strange, of bizarre antiseptics, and mysterious machines lurked in every corner. He ordered her to strip. Zoe did not summon her parents. Instead, she undressed and lay trembling, white as the paper gown that inadequately covered her. When Hendricks put on the blood-pressure cuff, she fainted.

After the exam, Hendricks bluntly informed the Bryants that Zoe's spells and nervousness were abnormal. Her heartbeat was irregular, she still had whooping cough, and she seemed abnormally frightened. He recommended that the child see a psychiatrist he knew, a Dr. Jack Hirschberg.

Surprisingly, Dave Bryant took Hirschberg's phone number.

■

**ZOE II and the LITTLE FLOWER (the Tunnel of Patients):** *They reluctantly brought me. On two occasions.*

*Dr. Hirschberg was oddly maternal and reassuring. My parents waited while he took me aside and asked personal questions. I said I loved my parents and felt I would die without them, though they scared me. I told him how sick I'd been. I mentioned John Perret and my grandfather, that they'd both died. And then I told him I slept with my father. His eyes widened when we said that.*

*He said I had to get away from my parents and might benefit from visiting the community hospital for a few weeks. I could continue my studies because they had a school there. And that he and my parents would visit me daily.*

*I cried with relief to think I might cure my depression.*

*Then he told me to wait while he called in my parents.*

*I could hear my father shout angrily, "She's not crazy."*

*The doctor was saying, "Is it normal for a child to be this scared? If she had pneumonia, would you let her die?"*

*Nobody answered for a minute. And he said, "What your daughter has wrong with her is just as serious."*

*My mother was crying. "What does she have?" she asked.*

*"Anxiety neurosis and hyperventilation."*

*"What do they do for that?"*

*"Talk therapy."*

*"Talk about it? Talk?" My father dragged me home.*

■

Virginie tells Zoe, "Your father would not believe you were sick; neither would the rest of the family. But you truly needed help. I had realized this before, and later, when you were thirteen, I realized again there was something wrong. But we could not make your father listen. And your mother went along with what he said."

The Bryants can't check their behavior against that of others in the world, because they see this world as erroneous and false. Thus their habits and perceptions turn in on themselves and become ever stronger. Their problems, they come to think, are healthier than health.

When Zoe next visited her cousin in August 1956, Virginie had a plan. "First," she said, "I'll take you down to the clinic. We'll get a letter that says your school will admit only vaccinated children. Dave won't be able to say a word against that.

"Second," she continued, "you'll have to decide what's troubling you the most at home, and change it."

Zoe knew: it was sleeping with her father. None of her friends did that, and it was her most secret shame. She didn't tell, but she pressed Virginie's hand and thanked her.

That very afternoon, Zoe received her first polio vaccination. Then she returned home, trembling to fix what troubled her most, barely able to admit it to herself, let alone argue it out with those she saw as monsters.

# 7

# Adulthood:
# Dishing It Out

At home each night, before eleven-year-old Zoe put on her pajamas, the Bryants would ask her whom she wanted to sleep with today, her father or her mother. They'd agreed that Zoe was far too clingy to sleep alone, and they didn't know that learning to sleep alone was important. Her father would look most pleading, and she'd choose him. He would hold her until she slept; and in the morning when she woke, her nightgown would be up around her chest.

The night of the vaccination, an alter named Doreen chose Zoe May. Dave looked shocked. Doreen timidly explained, "None of my girlfriends sleep with their father." Bryant's face crumpled; he nodded and returned to his Bible.

How Zoe fit in with society concerned Zoe May, so much so that she'd occasionally try to overcome her own fear. For a reunion of Zoe's scout troup that month, she took six girls including her daughter on a canoe trip in one of the state parks. She describes absolute terror: "I have such a fear of water. And we were in this little canoe, and I could hardly handle it. I was thinking it would tip, and I'd go over." It did.

"I'll never forget that," says Zoe. "Donna laughed so

hard we almost fell out of our own boat. The girls joined in.''

"I thought, how could they laugh when I was so panicky?''

Eleven-year-olds are not easy to handle. Parents must accept their child's eventual freedom from them and their whole family system. They must be willing to admit that their child can be different from them. But the Bryants admitted nothing beyond their family and their church. All difference was either unadmitted or seen as Satan.

That afternoon Zoe had laughed because her mother looked so funny and afraid, and the other girls were there—but she'd also loved Zoe May for risking the ride.

When Zoe moved into her mother's bed, it was because she saw that "Zoe May didn't want to sleep with Father, either." Psychologically, Zoe's dilemma was that if she rejected her father, she would grow up to become her mother. How helpless she must have felt, under her momentary relief.

Zoe May's nighttime ritual was the exact opposite of her husband's. "When you would get into bed," she tells Zoe today, "I would tuck you in so that I would not come in contact with you, body-wise." She sounds as though contact would have been the worst thing in the world. But as she continues, her voice softens. She does love her daughter, within her enmeshed and rigid definition. "Before you went to sleep," she tells Zoe, "we had a crazy little thing we would say. I'd say 'Itchy-boo,' and you'd say back, 'Double itchy-boo.' But that would be the only contact."

Switching pronouns, Zoe May continues, "I would tuck her nightgown in around her legs, tight. And later, when I got into bed, I would have the cover there between us so I wouldn't—I'd feel like she wasn't in the bed with me!" Her voice trails away. Zoe comments, "She was afraid of me."

From then on, every night that she was home from age eleven until her marriage at age seventeen, Zoe slept with Zoe May, who couldn't even bear to go outside. Zoe's level of fear soared. Doreen loved Zoe May, made her gifts each day, wanted to make her proud, got As and Bs, prayed and cooked and cleaned—and trembled.

Doreen's presence, her adulation, seemed somehow to liberate Zoe May. Suddenly, she applied for and got a job: she would be wrapping presents in a department store. When she told Dave, he just grunted. Now Zoe May placed Zoe in full charge of the household during the week.

"She prepared all the meals," reminisces Zoe May. "She would clean house. She did this every weeknight from age twelve to age sixteen. I was proud. 'Cause some daughters are not interested enough to do that sort of thing.

"What she did with the money I gave her was, she started a hope chest for when she'd get married. Every weekend she would go down to Sears, Roebuck and buy towels, or pots and pans. I thought it was nice, but I'd say she was old for her age." Doreen would ask for her pay on Saturday morning and then spend it immediately, otherwise it would disappear.

Zoe May's voice is edged with disapproval. When asked how Zoe was old for her age, she says, "My daughter was very angelic until age eleven, when she seemed to branch out away from her mother's and father's way of thinking."

The mother-worshipping alters grew stronger and stronger, until the day Zoe and Doreen had come out during a church concert. Donna was at the piano, trying to perform her showiest recital piece, when suddenly she faded.

■

**MOTHER ZOE (the Tunnel of Light):** *I did not know how to play. My fingers went all over the keyboard, and horrible sounds emerged. The auditorium fell silent. The curtain came down. I got up and rushed out. The faces were blurs. I found the bathroom and stayed there for hours, my mother and friends trying to get me out.*

■

After two hours, the door opened and the girl, laughing and flirting, danced out.

That day was when the branching out started. The

flirting alter was Serena, who'd last been out during the John Perret years. She still hated men. During that church concert, as she'd looked out over the audience, she'd seen a lot of sympathetic female faces.

Soon, Zoe discovered yet another way in which she was unlike normal girls. "They were interested in boys. I wasn't."

Though her parents wouldn't notice this for two more years, the alter Serena had discovered women. Though her classmates called Zoe "the girl who lives at the library," in fact, Serena was, and is, the girl who longed for Mother—for any mother figure she could find.

■

**SERENA (the Tunnel of Power):** *Now started the days of my wild freedom! I used to love Brinton Beach Park. Zoe 10 didn't know how to have fun, but I did! I used to stuff my gut with chili dogs and onions and cheese. I adored blue cotton candy. And the roller coaster rides thrilled me down to my toes.*

*Okay, so like, the father took us to Brinton Beach one day, Diane and me and two other girls. I'd stuffed myself and gone on all the rides, and it was time to leave. We were going to the car. It was not the best of neighborhoods. So we pass this liquor store, and there are these cute girls out front, like, smiling at me. I toss my long blonde hair, and geez, I knew I had a nice shape. I was wearing black capris and mother's black sweater. Mother always used to say black was not a color—but I liked it!*

*So we pass these gals. I see them nudging each other saying I'm pretty young and cute, and I get a good vibration. I'd been reading my lesbian books right along. Diane and the other girls whisper, "Don't look!" and Mr. Bryant drags me back to his house—that hellhole.*

■

Unlike the time six-year-old Zoe had gotten dragged home and hit with a slipper, this time alter Serena was determined to have her way.

■

**SERENA (the Tunnel of Power):** *I couldn't get these girls out of my mind. Doreen and Zoe 10 were doing their girly stuff and* *homework crap, with their plain-Jane look and those glasses. It wasn't gonna get me anywhere. So I experiment with Mrs. Bryant's makeup. I thought I looked pretty good. I probably looked ready for Halloween. Anyway, I take, like, three buses down to Brinton Beach and get off right by that liquor store.*

*There's a group of real masculine women, ranging from twenty to forty, standing out in front. I walk past them and go into the coffee shop next door and order a burger and fries. This girl comes over to me. Her name is Katia. I tell her I'm Serena. She orders me a Coke and we share it. She's, like, eighteen. She asks if I'm a runaway, and I say yes. If I have a family? I say, none I want to talk about. She could identify with that. She offered me a cigarette and I took it. I told her I was thirteen—not eleven. She said, "That's old enough," and we arranged to meet right there, next week.*

*We talked for hours and took a walk. I'm thinking, "Hey, man, better get back." So we exchange phone numbers. And then I get back on the bus like a good girl, and before I know it, I've blanked out.*

*So Zoe 10, she's the one that gets home with all the makeup on her face. In a dream I kind of see Mr. Bryant standing right out front with a watch in his hand, sniffing the smoke and perfume on her, yelling, where the hell have you been? And she can't tell him. What I wouldn't have told him if I could!*

■

The alter Serena was a Wild Thing. Dr. Hirschberg's final and last report reads, "Patient transferred her anxiety to the question of her father's death, at age eleven. Sometimes she wished him dead." Serena didn't think anything of yelling out, "Die, asshole." There was always Zoe 10 to take the punishment. Or Doreen. Or mute little Sherry. Or one of the Catholic girls, who liked being martyrs.

With promiscuity and alcohol, cursing and running away, picking up women and dropping them, added to her repertoire, Zoe's system exploded from perhaps ten dissociated states, into perhaps thirty. The alters became more opaque to each other as their behavior became less permissible.

■

Serena could come out at almost any time. She was helped by Zoe May's reactions to the change in her daughter: utter, punishing coldness, alternating with abject terror. Zoe May recites with amazed grief her daughter's behavior at Christmas.

In 1957, "We was baking cookies. My daughter was helping me. Suddenly I wondered where she was. A minute later I looked up and thought, 'Oh, my goodness!' She was all dressed and painted like you wouldn't believe. Tight pants and a low-cut blouse, and she said she's going to Brinton Beach, and don't try to stop her.

"I told her that wasn't any place for a child to go alone. She said, she was going to, whether or not! The look which came up in her eyes—oh, my. I don't know what she would have done to me, to get her way! So I thought to myself, maybe this is just a phase she's going through."

■

**RONNY/LILLIAN (the Tunnel of Observers, Guides, and Past Life) and SERENA (the Tunnel of Power):** *Dora's wimpin' around with those cookies, and I feel myself buzzing around behind her, for like an hour! I couldn't take it anymore! I grabbed the body. I give the mother a look that could kill, and like zip, I'm outta there.*

*I was getting pretty well known down in Brinton Beach. Everybody liked Serena!*

*And that's when I left for, like, three days.*

■

"There was a time," Zoe May corroborates, "when she was missing for three whole days. I called the police. This was the first time I found out my daughter was drinking and going out with women. I just felt devastated. Oh, having a child gone is an awful thing to go through! The police don't even start investigating till after twenty-four hours.

"I called Mr. Barnaby, and we prayed the whole time for her safe return."

■

**SERENA and RONNY/LILLIAN (the Tunnel of Power):** *I was out, man. It was like a lightning bolt had struck me, but in a good way! Serena could drink an entire bottle of Cold Duck and not feel it. And Ronny liked dope.*

*So I'm, like, down there, and that's when I meet La Charamusca. That means candy cane, you know, the twisted sucker that lasts for hours.*

*Katia had asked to be my pimp. I said no. I wasn't gonna have any man touch me! I could've used some cash, sure, but what I used to do was take Dora's baby-sitting money. Yo, Dora, did you ever notice your money was gone?*

■

**DORA (the Tunnel of Secrets):** *Yes. I did. I thought something funny was going on, but not what. That's when I opened my own bank account.*

■

**SERENA (the Tunnel of Power):** *I'd take out the cash, and you always use to say, "Did I take it out?" And you couldn't remember. I used to steal more cash from the mother's purse and go buy a sexy black outfit and sexy earrings. And then I met La Charamusca—Charra—and decided to stay with her.*

■

At the Palms the jukebox had been playing Serena's song. She'd gone in, chosen a table, and sat, swinging her leg. She ordered a tuna fish sandwich and coffee. The waitress quirked her eyebrow at the coffee order, but brought it.

A Puerto Rican woman in her thirties came over. The child thought she was beautiful. Dressed in penny loafers, denims, and a crisp white shirt, the woman looked masculine and feminine and entirely sexy. Her black hair tumbled over her collar. "I may join you?"

"Sure!" They introduced themselves.

"Serena, that beautiful. I am La Charamusca, you know, the candy," the woman explained, "what you suck. Charra."

The child giggled. "That's so funny! I love that!"

Charra's mouth quirked; the tip of her tongue slid out. The music changed to the twist. She asked the girl to dance.

"Sure! Great!"

They twisted, their bodies close but not touching. "What age you, *querida*?"

"Eighteen!"

"*Sí*—so old!" Charra rolled her eyes.

The music changed again, to a slow dance. "I love you, honey," said Charra, pulling the girl into her arms.

"I didn't feel I loved her," said Zoe later, "but I had a lot of sexual feelings, and I wanted to live with her." They polished off the sandwich. Then Charra brought the child outside.

They walked arm in arm, giggling and bumping hips. Charra was thirty-four but seemed delighted to act like a child.

Though the lobby and hallway of Charra's building were dingy, to the child they seemed bright and magical. Every cracked tile, empty fixture, and cracked brick breathed history, mystery, and the fulfillment of a dream. Charra led the child to a third-floor apartment, unlocked it, and said, "Go, go," accompanying her words with little pushing motions.

The studio was nearly filled by a double bed without a cover, an old wooden bureau crammed with pictures, a pint-size refrigerator, and a chipped table cluttered with a one-burner hot plate, three black-spotted mangoes, and candles in many colors. Open French windows overlooked the ocean. The child ran to the windows, breathed the salt air, and rhapsodized, "It's perfect!"

Charra threw her arms around the child and inhaled her mixture of smells: baby shampoo, talcum powder, and White Shoulders perfume. "*Qué linda*—how beautiful," she said.

"You too," said the child huskily. They kissed.

They made love by the light of the setting sun. At first Charra was rough, but later she became very gentle. On the second day, Charra showed the child pictures. She'd left a daughter in Puerto Rico, with her own mother. She babbled in Spanish and cried, and the child patted her back, trying to comfort her. "I no good, I no good," the woman kept saying.

"You are good; you're good to me," the child answered, rubbing the woman on the back, on the neck. The woman turned and hugged her passionately; and again they were making love.

Charra taught the child. By evening of the third day, the little body had learned many variations of cravings and tastings and explorings, plus a deeper, stronger hunger that, focused now, would remain. Now, instead of just thinking she needed a woman, she knew it. "Stay with me."

"Yes, I stay."

"Forever."

"Forever? No understand."

Suddenly the child was dizzy. "Oh," she said faintly.

"What wrong?"

"Oh," said the child again.

"Wait. I buy medicine." The woman was out the door.

The child was nauseous now. She dressed, putting on the sad high heels, which were a little too large; the dirty white panties and the black tight pants; the black pullover and the dangling rhinestone earrings. She could hardly move. She felt as if she'd just run a hundred miles, not made love and slept and eaten and, for the first time, done exactly whatever she wanted. Minus makeup, she walked out of Charra's apartment and down the stairs.

Outside, she had to walk through an alley to reach the ocean boardwalk. Dizziness overpowered her. She stumbled, hit the wall, and felt her legs collapsing. "Oh," she said again, as voices exploded around her, her spirit rushed up through her solar plexus, and her body struck the ground.

Zoe 10 woke in a pile of stinking trash, surrounded by police and a ring of beach people. It was night. Red and blue lights were flashing, reflecting off the concrete walls. "She's coming to," said one police officer to another.

"What's your name? Where do you live?" Silhouetted against the flashing lights, it was a threatening voice.

Zoe was too scared to answer. What was she doing

here? In these strange clothes? As she started to fade into darkness again, she heard the far sound of a baby crying.

■

**ZOE 2 (the Tunnel of Light):** *I want my mommy, I told them. I peed my pants. They wrapped me in a blanket and taked me to the police station.*

■

"I'm sorry, Daddy," Zoe whimpered, when her two gray-looking parents came to bail her out.

When they arrived home, Zoe May undressed her daughter, sponged her, pulled on a clean nightgown, and tucked her into her own bed. Says Zoe May, "She was dazed. She couldn't tell anyone where she'd been."

Zoe slept for thirty-six hours and woke fresh as a daisy, with no recollection of having gone anywhere out of the ordinary. No one mentioned her disappearance to her.

Inexplicably to Zoe, her aunt Rae "turned on her" at this time. "I guess the mother was having some kind of nervous breakdown. And she went to stay at Aunt Rae's, so I called there, and Rae answers the phone. She says, 'You little murderer! You're a devil, that's what you are.'

" 'Your mother is dead. You want to see her, you can come to the funeral.' "

■

**DORA (the Tunnel of Secrets):** *I was trying to be so perfect, and all these things were happening to me. I never knew what to expect. I would wake up and my hair would be blonde. And then I'd have to sneak out and dye it brown. It kept going blonde, brown, blonde, brown. I was going crazy. I didn't understand why Rae turned on us, why the mother left, what we had done.*

■

Soon Zoe May returned, with half her daughter's alters unaware that she'd been away at all. The alter Serena blocked awareness of the mother's breakdown from Zoe.

Serena hated Zoe almost as much as she hated the

mother. She wanted to take over the body one day and did everything she could to hurt the others, who were constantly dyeing what she considered her hair and throwing out her clothes. She couldn't do much about the hair, except change its colors so many times it began to fall out; but the clothes she hid in the rafters of the garage, near Dave's contraband beer. Dave would bring the clothes in to Zoe and rip them up. He got furious when she'd deny the clothes were hers. Zoe May would hold her ears and scuttle off to bed.

Tensions erupted the next time Serena dressed up for a jaunt. It was not until 1993 that mother and daughter confronted each other about this event.

"When your daughter was twelve or thirteen," accuses the alter Selina, "you hurt your daughter."

"Well, that part . . . was very, uh, bad . . . I would like that, uh, to go, uh, out of my mind."

"Relax, Mrs. Bryant. Everything is all right. There are no hard feelings between myself as Selina, and you."

"All that I can say is that all this led up to, uh, feelings, the way that my daughter was carrying on."

"By the way," interrupts Selina, in the Indian accent that Mrs. Bryant politely ignores, "that was not your daughter; that was Serena." Mrs. Bryant does not question this. Today she is resigned to her daughter's unusual worldview. "Serena want to go out, and then what happen?"

Says Zoe May, "One thing led to another. When she just stood up there and defied me, and told me she was going to do it no matter what, and I thought I would never, uh, SEE her again, the anger just rose until I myself lost my temper.

"I think that there was a candle on the table. In a candleholder. And I just picked that up. In my mind I thought that a candle couldn't really HURT anyone—"

"Did you actually stop and think?" asks the accent.

"I felt the rage," quavers Zoe May miserably. "But then, uh, I never REALIZED what a thing like THAT could DO!"

"You could not stop yourself?"

"No, but I mean you, you didn't try to, uh, get AWAY!

To save yourself! You just stood there and laughed in my face!"

"Where was the hand, Mrs. Bryant?" prompts the voice.

"Well, the hand—I think you was trying to, uh, I don't know! You had it up here doing this or something."

"Covering her head?"

"Yes."

"Face?"

"Yes. And it was a good thing, or I would have hit your face. But I hit your hands." In great pain, she amends, "One hand. One hand."

"And then what did you do? You keep hitting, hitting?"

"No, maybe two times. No more. Then I realized—"

"No. There was a HAND, I see, on TABLE in the DINING ROOM. She put her hand on table. I see many blows."

"No!"

The voice drops, becomes threatening and confidential. "What happen to vein, Mrs. Bryant?"

"Well, uh, it came UP. But it was not many blows. I think the most blows that I ever gave you was two blows on that. That was enough. You know. So I stopped. And then you screamed. But you stood up there and defied me. And you laughed, to bring out the, uh, WRONG IN ME. It's true! So then I saw your vein sticking up. And I thought, oh, my gosh! Then you wanted to go to the doctor. And I was WILLING."

When Dave Bryant arrived, he rushed Zoe to the doctor. Whimpers Zoe May, "I don't remember the diagnosis."

"Does 'blood clot' sound like diagnosis?"

"I don't know."

"He took you out in the hall, Dr. Hendricks, and this was very serious, did he not say? In fact, he say it was a blood clot which had to be watched, and he gave daughter shots to thin the blood. And what did your husband say?"

"Well, I, you know—what did he say? I'm trying to think. Oh! I know! He said, 'If anything happens to my daughter, I'll put you in jail for the rest of your life.' But now, that was only one incident! And it was done in a fit of temper. Not realizing. Many years ago. So I don't feel that should be brought up. But you feel that it should. That shows you what a person, in a fit of temper, what they will do. Especially when someone is laughing at them.''

In 1993 Mrs. Bryant is in her eighties and a dependent of her daughters. She is frail, deaf, and arthritic. She has had too much time to think about the sum of her life. She still dreadfully fears that adolescent, even after thirty-seven years—as many of Zoe's alters still fear her.

"I didn't ever know when that other would come up. So I lived a life of blocking it out. I just didn't want to think about that part!" She means Serena.

"And also you block out things," Selina says, "about husband. Painful things."

"Yes," Mrs. Bryant whispers.

"I believe we have to face truth," says Selina gently.

"Well," says Mrs. Bryant, crying, "I don't want to."

■

**The LITTLE FLOWER (the Tunnel of Patients) and ZOE 12 (the Tunnel of Secrets):** *I woke in the middle of the night. I couldn't breathe. I couldn't talk. I lay on the floor, pounding my fist, helpless. They turned the light on. I was blue. They went looking through the Christian Science Journal to find a practitioner to call at that hour. I left my body.*

*Finally I felt an angel of the Lord. There was a great pressure on my chest, and I started coughing out the liquid.*

*The next day Virge took me to Dr. Hendricks. He said the right lung was very infected.*

*I was struggling for my life, and not to help me, not to call an ambulance, not to do anything except run around the living room and pray! I could have died. And Mr. Bryant puts on his horn-rim glasses and pulls out a magazine.*

■

In adolescence, martyrdom can feel transcendent, and powerful sexual urges can feel almost religious. One's agony can be transmuted into mad, unrequited love.

■

**MOTHER ZOE (the Tunnel of Light):** *Virge was thirty-three and I was twelve when she first stirred my sexual feelings. From that time until the year I was nineteen, I was totally obsessed by her. I thought she was the most special person in the world. I wanted to sleep with her, like a child would with her mother, but also to make love.*

*I kept this from her for a while, but then told her. She took it well. She always acted normal and healthy with me. It stirs me to tears to think about Virge.*

*I needed to talk to someone about these feelings. My parents were impossible; my friends would have thought I was a freak. I felt something must be terribly wrong with me. That's why I told her. There was nobody else I could go to.*

■

Virginie tells Zoe, "I started to realize you were extremely dependent on me. I never realized you were in love until you told me, at age thirteen.

"You had extreme mood changes. Sometimes you were sweet and gentle. Other times, you got into trouble and told me all kinds of lies. We had quite a go-round with those lies.

"But you crept into my heart, just like you were one of my own children. You had a wonderful way about you.

"Even with my husband. You knew how to manipulate him. You would have his coffee ready when he came in, a napkin, and a little green ashtray. You were quiet and easy to be around, and he couldn't stand noise. So you had an in to stay at my house for as long as you wanted.

"But each time you started doing okay, then your mother would come and take you home. And she'd put you back in school. You'd go for a day and then you'd get sick.

"You would do anything to get out of school, even lie."

Zoe answers, "I felt trapped."

Virginie touches Zoe's arm. They smile, in perfect harmony. "I had a lot of fun with Zoe. She had a side of her that was hilarious. We'd go shopping and do nothing but laugh and have the best time. And she was very brave. She wasn't afraid of anything."

Apparently Virginie and Zoe would go down to the local department store and yell at each other in the hillbilly accents of Virginie's youth. All the other customers would stare at them: but neither cared.

■

**MOTHER ZOE (the Tunnel of Light):** *She'd say, "Ara-belly? Ara-belly Garbageblossom! Where are yew?" I'd answer, "Over this way, Petyewnee!" We'd carry on for hours.*

■

The Beverly Hillbillies did not play every day. Virge, though healthy by Bryant and Adams standards, got sick a lot.

When Zoe was thirteen, Virginie and she developed complementary illnesses and took turns nursing each other. First, Zoe developed *globus hystericus*—the sensation of a lump or mass in the throat. Virginie says, "You'd be there with a mirror and flashlight, and we'd look down your throat."

Zoe continues, "It went on for a good six months. I'd eat baby food and milkshakes—I couldn't swallow. I went to throat specialists, which I'd get out of the phone book."

Virginie finishes the story. "A hysterical lump. I had it myself later on, so I knew exactly what it was."

Next, Virginie got her own competing hysterical lump. Virginie's husband would take turns with Dave Bryant, driving the ladies to Zoe's specialist of the week. Zoe would allow the doctor to violate her throat with the tubular instrument, but Virginie would gag and spit it out.

They did everything for each other. In 1958, when Virginie's son Artie started kindergarten, she was having a nervous breakdown, and Zoe took her place.

■

**DOREEN (the Tunnel of Limbo):** *Each morning I dressed little Artie and made sure he was sparkling clean. And we walked to school that very first day. I introduced myself to the teacher,* *and said I was in charge, because the mother was not feeling well. "And don't listen to anyone but me."*

■

**MOTHER ZOE (the Tunnel of Light):** *And then we'd go take care of Virge. She'd have six anxiety attacks each day. We'd giver her phenobarbital.*

■

**CONNIE (the Tunnel of Power):** *She got real bad migraines. I rubbed her shoulders. I rubbed her neck. I rubbed her back. I wanted her.*

■

Virginie says, "The child was right by my side for three months. She fixed me hot tea with brandy and honey. If I felt bad, she was right there to see what she could do. She has a lot of compassion. Other members of the family were not quite as patient. They told me it was all in my head."

Zoe continues, "Yes. Our family are good people, but they don't understand nervous illness. They've never experienced it." Though that statement makes no sense, it must feel true. Both Zoe and Virginie need to crawl under another's skin, to feel close enough.

To get Virginie's attention, Serena would play pranks, which both judged hilarious.

Virginie says, "One time my mother and grandmother were visiting. I thought I'd fix floats. Unbeknownst to me, my sweet Zoe poured wine into the root beer. Liquor was never supposed to cross the lips of a Christian Scientist. Grandmother had the glass in her hand. Mother went to take her own glass, smelled it, and said, 'My God, there is liquor in this root beer!'

"There was quite a little to-do. Grandmother had a fit. Zoe May kept saying, 'I know my daughter didn't do it, because she knew my mother would have just mopped the floor with her!' I found you on the porch, giggling with the empty bottle. I thought it was funny, myself, but I didn't want to let you know because it was such a bad thing to do."

Zoe giggles. "Poor Grandmother Adams."

They look lovingly at each other. Obviously each thinks Grandmother Adams could've used a tad more humanity.

To some alters, the only thing wrong with this perfect relationship was the lack of physical intimacy. Once it became clear that no matter how impressed she was with her cousin's independence, Virginie was never going to have sex with her, it was time to go. The alter Serena decided to take the host body out again to Brinton Beach.

Serena swung out of the bus onto the boardwalk. Home.

"Well, hi there," said a tall woman with copper hair, dressed in a bulging version of Audrey Hepburn's beatnik outfit. "How old are you, honey?"

Serena smiled. "Sixteen."

"You thirsty?"

"Yeah."

From that time on, Zoe kept finding papers pinned to the inside of her bra. Always a name and seven or ten symbols—a coded telephone number—written beneath. She'd get chills up her spine, and she'd burn the papers.

About dealing with her daughter, Zoe May says, "I got to where I learned to block it out. Then when I was cleaning up under her mattress, I found it." When asked *what,* Zoe May answers, "A book wrapped in brown paper, about women and women. Making love.

"And so therefore we followed her, Mr. Bryant and I. We went to the gay bar ourselves; he went in and tried to plead with Zoe to come out of there. She was wearing clothes that would draw attention to the body and a lot of makeup, trying to attract women. She was so angry at her father for even coming that she hit him in the face with her purse and cut him. And then she kicked him in the lower extremity—in the groan [groin]. I cannot understand this. When I asked her why she'd done such a thing, she wouldn't answer."

These days the alter Rose was often out.

■

**ROSE (the Tunnel of Light):** *Rose. That's me. Wanted to be pretty. I use Serena's makeup. Get the lipstick on crooked and* eyebrow pencil all over my forehead. Rose get mad because everybody at Brinton Beach liked Serena and not Rose. So Rose would hide Serena's makeup. And Serena would have to steal to buy more makeup.

∎

Also trying to fill Zoe's emptiness, the alter Rona was born at this time. Zoe's period had finally become regular. Rona was born age fourteen and pregnant. With the money she found in Zoe's rocking chair and in the jewel box, she'd go to the local dime store and buy layettes.

∎

**RONA (the Tunnel of Light):** *Little shirts and dresses and toys and baby bottles. I was still a virgin.*

*Yes, I did a lot of unusual things that year. It was because we all felt so empty inside. We needed something to fill that void. For me, it was having a child.*

*I truly thought I was pregnant. I told Virge that I was, that I'd had an affair with a man, and didn't tell her who, and drove her crazy.*

∎

Virginie says, "I was so shocked my hair stood right on end. She told me the biggest lie you ever heard. I couldn't understand who it could have been with. The girl was standing there with the most innocent look on her face, saying, 'I don't know how you're going to tell Mother.' I fretted and stewed, and wondered how to break the news to Zoe May, until I almost had a nervous breakdown."

∎

**RONA (the Tunnel of Light):** *I was going to have a virgin birth and name my child Virginia. I thought I was impregnated by God or had split off a cell in my womb. I bought maternity smocks and stuffed a little pillow up inside my capris. I looked six-months pregnant. A long-legged skinny thing with this pooched-out tummy. I would stand by the bus stop, hoping that an older woman would pity me and take me home. People stared.*

■

Zoe had no awareness of Rona. When Virginie called to ask her how her pregnancy was going, Zoe thought she was nuts. "You're kidding." She blushed. "I'm not pregnant."

Later, Zoe searched the trousseau chest and found a complete layette, just as Virginie had said. Seriously frightened—she had no idea where the things had come from—Zoe called back Virginie, begging for help.

■

**ZOE II (the Tunnel of Patients):** *I said it had all been a lie—though I had no idea what was happening. Later Virge called my mother.*

*There was a big discussion that night. My father went so far as to admit that Dr. Hirschberg may have been right to recommend the mental hospital. He looked frantic as he described things I didn't remember, about his daughter going off with women. And he said, "I would never be able to forgive myself if anything serious happened to you, Zoe."*

*My poor father. I forgot how possessive he was, how domineering, in a sudden rush of overwhelming love.*

■

Zoe May thinks that her daughter's false pregnancy was a way to draw the family's attention away from the sexual behavior. "Until that year my daughter was always one not to draw attention to herself, and now this. When Virginie called me, I went down to the street corner and saw for myself. And it was true. She was standing right there, looking pregnant! Maybe she felt if she had a child, she would be more complete within herself."

Alters gave birth to alters. The alter Ronny/Lillian split off to keep Serena company within the system.

■

**SERENA (the Tunnel of Power):** *With Ronny around, I was less lonely. She was a pal to hang with. She wrote poems and shot pool. We'd walk down the boardwalk, Ronny in her jeans and me in my wild outfits.*

*I was getting stronger. I needed sex. I had to have it. It was keeping me alive. Think of Count Dracula, and the blood that kept him going. Sex is what kept me going. That, and being with Ronny.*

■

**LONNY (the Tunnel of Secrets):** *Guess who else was there? Me, Lonny. I was only eight but really interested in those chicks. And this is going to sound weird, but the one I was most interested in was Serena. When she developed, I would stand in front of her and, like, touch her chest. I had a crush on Serena all that year.*

■

These alters didn't stick around to reap what they sowed. One night Serena turned on Zoe May. Screaming, "I want you dead!" she beat the mother savagely, kicked her in the stomach, and then stormed out.

Zoe May punished the girl on her return. But the alter who returned was Zoe, not Serena.

The alters had no idea how to get what they wanted without hurting someone.

The next time Zoe got ill, with quinsy (an infected sore throat), the Patient called Dr. Hendricks, set up an appointment for an examination, and then, by having Dr. Hendricks call the family, blackmailed them into taking her to the hospital for an elective tonsillectomy instead of treating her with prayer. The family did not appreciate Zoe's ghastly and blasphemous independence.

■

**ZOE-THE-HOST (the Tunnel of Patients):** *When I woke from the anesthesia, the entire family gathered around my hospital bed. The second I cracked my eyes open, Aunt Rae snarled, "You see what you did? You made your throat hurt even worse."*

*The mother stayed all night, lying on two chairs, while they kept giving us shots. At midnight we threw up blood.*

*The next day the whole family came to take us home. They were still mad. We'd just had this operation, and nobody was nice to us. Especially the grandmother. You could see her praying. Even Cousin Virge rejected us.*

*They put us in the mother's room. Cousin Virge brought up a quart of ice cream and a spoon. She told us to be still—we had caused Mother enough trouble.*

*I got up and went to my room. The mother was there, lying on the bed with the entire family around her. She looked dead. Someone noticed me and said it was my fault she was so ill, 'cause our surgery had made her faint. We cried the rest of the day. All alone. Our throat hurted real bad. And nobody even came in to see us.*

■

Now came Zoe's first suicide attempt. Zoe May does not connect Zoe's swallowing an entire bootleg bottle of aspirin with any of Zoe's previous cries for help.

"It was some embarrassment," she hypothesizes, "that Zoe was going through with a neighbor child. She wanted to impress her. Of course the neighbor girl told me. We took her to the doctor, and he put a tube down her throat. Pumped her stomach and sent her home. He was pretty old-fashioned, Dr. Hendricks. I asked my daughter how she could do such a thing. She said she didn't know." For Mrs. Bryant, that closed the matter.

■

At fifteen, the alter Doreen had the personality system's first extended affair, with the "neighbor child"—the eighteen-year-old girl who'd saved her life.

■

**DOREEN (the Tunnel of Limbo):** *We'd met in high school, Jessie Kassel and I. At first we had a normal healthy relationship. But I started feeling attracted. Jessie was beautiful, blonde with very blue eyes and a sensitive, warm personality.*

*I spent some nights with Jessie. She had three sisters and was quite motherly, with these little girls running around. That was attractive, as well as her being older.*

*When her parents would retire for the evening, we'd pet. The first time, she put her arm around me and said, "What's the difference, whether you're kissing a boy or a girl?" And I* agreed. Our faces were very close and she kissed me, and a tingling started throughout my body.

She had a spacious room with expensive furniture and a bedspread made of lilac silk. I felt I was sinking into a sea of flowers as we lay down and began taking off our clothes. Thus began our sexual relationship.

Jessie and I wrote love letters when we were apart. It was scary, yet very exciting.

We made plans to go to college, then to get fantastic jobs and buy a home. We became just like a married couple.

●

Doreen hid Jessie's love letters in Serena's and Zoe Ann's old hiding place, up under the mattress. There, of course, Zoe May found them, as she'd found the books in brown wrappers and the Roman Catholic tracts.

"I was suspicious," Zoe May says, "and then look what I found! That Kassel girl seemed so friendly and nice. But when I found out what was going on, why then, my thoughts about her changed." When asked what she did next, Zoe May purses her lips. "I thought I'd get rid of the letters. I just tore them up and burned them."

Remarkably, none of the alters ever said a word about this to Zoe May. There were no more letters under the mattress and no discussion of any anger Zoe felt at her mother's destructive intrusion. Did the relationship stop? "No," says Zoe May philosophically. "It kept on just the same, all the way up until Zoe got married."

●

**MOTHER ZOE (the Tunnel of Light):** But part of the system rebelled against the lesbianism. I started dating a body down the street from Jessie. He was tall and quiet. I liked him very much. His name was Stanley Knight and he was nineteen. We'd go for walks and to the movies, and hold hands. I was delighted to find myself normal. This hurt Jessie. She'd say, "I can't believe this! You're with me one moment, and then how could you go kiss Stanley?"

●

Stanley and Zoe attempted to elope, but Zoe's age prevented it. After, Stanley wanted to continue the relationship, but Zoe's parents forbade it. "The boy's background was no good," says Zoe May. "His parents were alcoholics. He was older. Nice looking, as far as that goes, but we didn't want her to see that type of fellow at all! Jessie was the one who told me about them eloping. I don't understand the relationship with Jessie and then run off with Stanley. Maybe she was trying to get back at her parents."

Actually, Zoe was dying to leave her parents and to ditch school. Though the alter Dora intended to go to college, a new alter kept writing in her diary that her mother had married at age fifteen and she wanted to do the same.

With Jessie furious and Stanley forbidden, Zoe needed a new friend. Virginie's daughter, Mindy, had recently left the various aunts' houses where she'd been stashed and returned to her mother.

On and off, Zoe still slept at Virginie's. At first Mindy was jealous—did her mother care more about a niece than her own daughter?—but then they became good, if wary, friends.

"You two," Virginie tells Zoe, "would get into some real stinkers together. You'd swear each other to eternal secrecy, and then you'd come and tell me. She'd get mad at you. But she'd tell me not to tell on you to your parents. There was a lot of jealousy. Mindy would say, 'You go everywhere with that girl, to the show, here and there.' And all I'd answer was that she was on dates all the time."

Zoe finishes her thought. "Mindy was a normal girl. You see I wanted to be with Virge, but Mindy wanted to have fun—so we did."

Actually, Mindy and Zoe did not reveal all their secrets to Virginie. One night that they were together Zoe got raped.

■

**DOREEN (the Tunnel of Secrets):** *Mindy and I were walking downtown. A man looks out a window and says, "Hi, babes. Why'n'cha come on up?" It was a nice summer evening, and stupid us, we trot upstairs.*

*His name was Ed, he was thirty-three and handsome. Mindy got sloshed on a couple of beers. I just had a half. She got real silly and passed out in the hall. And once Ed and I were alone, he yanked my jeans down and stuck his penis in. Just like that. He was thick and I was small, and he started grunting. He was riding me up and down, and I was crying no, get off. He groaned and the semen went, psiouuuu! Right in. I was so scared. I went running out. "Come ON, Mindy." He sticks his head out the window as we're running and says, "Next time will be better, Doreen."*

*When we got back to Virge's, I cried and Mindy gave me a vinegar douche. But I thought I needed help. So I told Zoe's father. He told Dr. Hendricks. And over the next six weeks I got three massive doses of penicillin and a lot of tests, to see if I'd contracted a disease.*

■

Zoe does not say how her father took Doreen's news.

In 1961, at age sixteen, just after her annual Christmas breakdown, Zoe picked a psychiatrist out of the phone book. "I was falling apart," she says. How long did she see this psychiatrist? "Six months." Did he help her? "No."

While Zoe was seeing the psychiatrist, the alter Serena was getting more and more outrageous.

■

**SERENA (the Tunnel of Power):** *I would go down to the waterfront, where the tough homosexuals hung out, and the male and female prostitutes and the dope peddlers. I had my hair bleached blonde and wore heavy eye makeup, and I would go down and sit on the beach. They thought I was a prostitute, too.*

*Now I could flirt openly with the older butches. I would say I was eighteen or twenty-one. The women would buy me drinks until I got a buzz. And then we'd stagger down the boardwalk to the various apartments these women had.*

*Some of the sex got quite violent.*

■

Many times, a child alter would wake up in bed with a strange woman, with no idea of how she'd got there.

"She found herself in the worst situations with the worst people," says Zoe. "Men also picked her up at the beach."

■

**SERENA (the Tunnel of Power):** *I conned my way out of sex with most of them. But a couple times I'd get in a car with men, and they'd want to take me to a motel. I would kiss them passionately, unzip their trousers, and play with them till they were satisfied. And then I'd smile and say, "Well, I have to go now, but I'll meet you later." And I'd name the place. "I can't wait to have sex with you." And run out of the car!*

■

In 1962, with one semester of high school to go, Zoe permanently dropped out. She felt she couldn't take all the pressure. Zoe May comments, "With all her daydreaming, I don't rightly know how she got as far as she did."

Zoe made a new friend, a red-haired dynamo named Carla, who drove a pink convertible with fins. Carla was boy crazy. On weekends they'd drive down the coast to Freeside, a small town by a naval base, and pick up sailors. That is where Zoe met her future husband.

Carmine Parry recollects their meeting in far more detail than does Zoe.

"It was late June 1962. Three P.M. I was off that day, walking around town with my buddy Bob, trying to see what trouble we could get into. Clowning around. All dressed up in summer whites. Little did I know what I was getting into.

"Anyway, we spy these girls. Walking down Pier Street without a care in the world. They pass us; my friend wolf whistles loudly. Then they turn around and smile. So we make our move. We walk up to them and start talking.

"Carla is not a bad looker, dressed up in a tight polka-dotted thing and spike heels. But it's the other one we can't stop looking at. She's young with long light brown hair and the prettiest green-blue eyes. Slim, with a petite, nice shape. I really liked this girl. They ask questions about navy life, and we tell them Bob is a deckhand and I cook for thirteen hundred people. Bob and I toss a coin to see who'll win this girl. I get heads.

"I wanted to know all about her. I asked if she wants to walk down and get something to eat, and she did. Both of us being on the shy side, we hesitated a lot in talking, but her being shy made me more comfortable. It was hard to get the conversation going. Zoe could tell by my accent I was from the Northeast, and she felt she'd lived in Greenwich Village in some past life. I thought that was nice, especially since, personally, I'd never been there.

"A couple hours later, Bob and Carla show up. I couldn't drive—felt kind of ashamed. So I tell this Zoe I've got a Cadillac back in New Jersey. She's impressed. We get in the car and drive up the road to Lights Out Point. Now that's a lover's lane. And we park. Bob and Carla get in the back, and we get in the front. They're fast workers. They're making out, and I haven't even got my arm around her. After an hour, I ask if she wants to go home, and she says yes. So Bob drives us. He and Carla had other plans.

"We talk about my brothers and sisters. I have three of each. She tells me she's an only child and it gets kind of lonely. She dances and plays piano and reads, and I only read sports magazines and dance with my sisters. I start feeling close to this girl, so I finally muster up the courage to put my arm around her. She looks at me with pure mistrust, but I go on. I leaned down, took her face in my hand, and gave her a little kiss on the lips."

The alter Dottie Mae—the Bride—opened her eyes and looked up at the shy young face hanging anxiously near hers. The system sees Dottie Mae as similar to Zoe May Bryant at age fifteen: southern, pretty. Dottie Mae felt she loved this sailor. To Carmine's surprise, the girl put her arms up around his neck and kissed him passionately. He says he fell in love right then and there.

"The next weekend I hitch twenty miles to her parents' house. Knocking on the door, this petite lady answers. She looks shocked to see this sailor on her porch. I say I'm there to see Zoe Bryant. She said, 'Well, I don't know about that. Wait here and I'll go talk to her.' She closed the door and opened it again. 'She's only sixteen, you know.'

"I'm getting more nervous by the second.

"Finally Mrs. Bryant let me in and invited me into the living room. We made polite conversation for an hour while she kind of stared at me. Then she got up and went down a long hall to Zoe's room. I later found out Zoe was hiding under the bed! Her mother had to tell her to come out and see this polite young man!

"I found out much later, Serena was furious for letting a man into the house. Zoe 2 was hiding under the bed. And Lonny and Bobby thought the whole thing was dumb. Finally Mrs. Bryant coaxed her out, and I took her out for burgers. When we came back, Mr. Bryant drove me to the base.

"He didn't like me. He was a short, stern man who didn't talk to me at all. And we drove for almost an hour.

"Zoe and I had made plans to meet the next day at Virginie's house. Zoe and I sat on the porch and held hands, and I kissed her as many times as I felt safe. That cousin watched her like a hawk. When I went back to the base, I couldn't get her out of my mind. It had only been a week, but I decided to marry this girl.

"She'd told me about this Stanley and about this man Fred. Fred was her math teacher in high school, twenty years older, and a Sunday school teacher with Mr. Bryant. Fred had proposed marriage, but she hadn't given him an answer. Her mother wanted her to marry him. But I thought it was strange of her parents to let her date her teacher. I told her Fred would have her over my dead body.

"Saturday came around again. I hitched down. Zoe was dressed in a pink sundress which showed off her golden tan. She looked all of thirteen. She was wearing light pink lipstick and no eye makeup, which she had the other times. She looked small, delicate, and innocent. I adored this child-woman. I was wondering when to pop the question.

"Mrs. Bryant fixed us lunch, and I was still wondering. Then Zoe and I got on a bus for Orange Grove, which still had a nice shopping area at that time. I was still wondering. We got there and walked over to the stores. We found ourselves in front of a jewelry store, and then I knew.

"I was standing there trying to figure out how I would like our life to be. My thoughts were racing. I had lost three mothers before I entered the service. At that time I thought my birth mother was dead. Later I discovered she'd been put into a state mental hospital when I was three. Everybody in my family, all six brothers and sisters, not to mention my father, had kept this a secret from me. I did not want my life with Zoe, or the life of any kid we would have, to be like mine had been till then. A father who called me 'stupid jerk,' hit me till I was so scared I couldn't talk, and sent me off to live with an aunt.

"Our home would be different. We'd live near the ocean, which we both loved. We'd have kids; I would prove my father wrong. I would show everybody I could be a good provider.

"So as Zoe and I stood in front of Forever, I invited her in to look. In the navy we didn't make too much. I asked the man to bring out a tray of the less expensive rings. Zoe tried on the prettiest, which had a microscopic diamond chip. Then she handed it back, said 'Thank you,' and was already out the door.

"I stayed behind for a second and told the man to hold the ring.

"We found ourselves at Sears, Roebuck, where Mr. Bryant managed the TV department. So we went up to visit. When he saw his daughter, he gave her a big salesman grin, and he shook my hand like I was a long-lost friend. He seemed like another Mr. Bryant!

"Slowly we made our way back to Forever. Zoe thought we were heading for the bus stop. But I took her small hand in mine and asked her to be my wife. To my surprise, she said yes.

"I can't tell you how happy I was. All my dreams had come true. She smiled and gave me a kiss. I took her in my arms and could hardly stop kissing her. And all the people on Market Street looked at us and smiled."

It was a scene right out of the Susan Hayward movies

that Zoe so loved. But in a movie, once it's happily ever after, they draw a curtain over the ensuing years.

Carmine says, "Little did I know at the time that I was marrying not only my beautiful childlike bride, but also women, men, and children of various religions, all rolled up in that one little body."

Carmine had his work cut out for him in his choice not just of a wife but of a father-in-law.

"That night, at the Bryant table, I was shaking in my shoes. I told Mr. Bryant I had asked his daughter to marry me, and she said, in the soft heavy southern voice she sometimes used, that it was true. I was going on tour, and we planned to marry when I got back, at the end of December.

"The room fell dead silent. Mr. Bryant looked at me like he wanted to kill me."

Dave Bryant asked Carmine with heavy contempt, "Jest how d'yew intend to s'poht mah dawtah?"

"On my navy salary."

"He snorted."

"All my friends and their wives are doing fine."

"And jest what is yo' ethnic background, Mr. Parry?"

"E-ethnic b-b—?" Carmine stuttered in times of stress.

Mr. Bryant continued sarcastically, "Jest wheah'd yo' daddy come from?" The way he said it left some doubt as to whether he thought Carmine had a daddy at all.

When Carmine said that his father was born in Boston and that his family was Catholic, Bryant's face turned purple.

"This is nevah gonna work out!" He rose. Zoe flinched. "I fo'bid yo' marriage." His hand slammed the table. Then he left the room.

By the next weekend, Mr. Bryant had come around—as far as he was ever going to. Zoe had called Virginie and Virginie had called Bryant. She'd reminded him about Jessie and Stanley and the whole beachful of older women. "Just what would you do, Dave," she'd asked, "if your daughter ran off with another woman? You might never see her again!"

Zoe had called Marnie Blue, who was shocked her

cousin would want to marry at sixteen. "Don't, don't, don't!" Marnie said. "Come live with my husband and me!"

Zoe had also called Jessie, who rushed over. She sobbed, "Don't marry that sailor! We can work things out!"

But it was Zoe May who had spoken up decisively for the marriage.

So that next Saturday, when Carmine once again sat kicking the legs of the dining room table and looking desperately down at his home-fried chicken, okra, and mashed yams, Bryant grinned—the cheerful salesman. "Well, son," he said, "looks like you're gonna have yew a civil ceremony."

"At the time," says Carmine, "I just thought the man loved his daughter. Later, I wondered. He tried to set the rules for both of us. Both Zoe and I wanted a Catholic wedding, and so did my brothers and sisters. I just knew Zoe would become a Catholic later, when she got older. But we found ourselves planning the civil ceremony—just like Mr. Bryant ordered.

"And later, when Mr. Bryant suggested we move in with him and Mrs. Bryant, we did—to save money. That's when I began to wonder, living with them."

■

**The BRIDE DOTTIE MAE (the Tunnel of Limbo):** *I was so in love, even after two weeks! He was so kind and sweet! I know Others didn't want to marry him, but I adored him. And I want it known that Carmine's bride is not, and has never been, a lesbian.*

■

In the summer, Carmine went on his tour of duty. Zoe planned the wedding and elaborated her trousseau. She asked Jessie to be her maid of honor; reluctantly, Jessie agreed. "The poor thing," says Zoe, "every time we spoke, it would end in tears. What could she do but accept the situation?"

In October, Zoe asked her father to call her former

math teacher, Fred, and tell him she was marrying Carmine.

At first, Zoe felt great—free of Fred and school, feeling loved. Each day Carmine sent a card.

A sample: "I received your letter yesterday and enjoyed hearing from you. I just hope I can hold on till the twenty-ninth of December. It will be the most important day of my life."

Zoe May would make lunch, then Zoe would visit the library. At least that's what she thought she did. Actually, Serena cruised Brinton Beach seven days a week.

The annual nervous breakdown was short this year. Christmas arrived, and with it, Carmine. The Bride opened the door to a tan, fit-looking stranger. They swept romantically into each other's arms and kissed, then she brought him and his suitcase inside. As she showed him the couch where he would sleep until they married, they babbled excitedly about their bright future.

Ding-dong, went the doorbell. It was Jessie Kassel. Graciously the Bride introduced her best friend—who'd sleep with her to calm her prenuptial jitters—to her fiancé.

**MOTHER ZOE (the Tunnel of Light):** *Jessie spent the last two days with me. She was still trying desperately to stop the wedding.*

*One day I left Jessie and Carmine alone. She came on to him. The next-door neighbor saw everything. When I got home, she came up and said, "Do you know what your girlfriend is doing with your fiancé?" This angered me. But Carmine didn't do anything.*

*Someone did make love to* her *the night before the wedding. And it was a very emotional experience. She tried to explain. She was trying to get me to see that he was not right for me, that the marriage was not going to work. And some of us said yes, it was. And Jessie cried. We spent the rest of that night, until dawn, saying good-bye. With Carmine just outside, on the couch.*

Compared to the wedding, the prenuptials were bliss. The alters switched at the rate of several per minute. Zoe remembers feeling extremely anxious and depressed, and hearing voices through a buzzing in her ears. Early on the twenty-ninth, she went to the beauty parlor. After the stylist finished, the anxiety took Zoe over. She ran into the bathroom and locked the door. Disregarding the used tunics and hair clippings littering the floor, she sank down, curled into her fetal position, and started to suck her thumb.

■

**ZOE II (the Tunnel of Patients):** *The wedding was held at an old Victorian mansion, now called Chapel Happiness. It was white with green trim and latticework and ivy and flowers everywhere.*

*I was escorted up to the bride's room. I sat. The room was charming, light pink with flowered wallpaper. Someone had sent me a dozen red roses. I did not dare open the card. I just sat, looking at the bride doll in the mirror.*

*Jessie rushed in. She clutched me and begged me not to do this. I put my finger on her lips. The guests arrived.*

*My old girlfriends came up. Diane Timothy and some others. I smiled falsely and tried to look happy. Finally they left me alone.*

*I realized I didn't know the man at all. He was a complete stranger! I had no idea now why I'd said yes.*

*The wedding march began. Jessie had gone down the steps. Everyone was in their places. I came out to the top of the steps. Someone inside screamed, ''Fall, Zoe!''*

*Of course, I didn't fall. I walked beautifully downstairs, took my father's arm, and walked over to my husband-to-be.*

■

**MOTHER ZOE (the Tunnel of Light):** *The wedding was all very clinical. It was a civil ceremony, as my father had ordered. Perhaps it was good that God wasn't mentioned, because this was not holy matrimony—it was a sham.*

■

Zoe was also feeling guilty. Though nobody suspected the existence of the secret people, she'd been hearing voices for as long as she could remember. She remembered waking up in enough strange beds to realize she was no prize for a man who wanted a childlike virgin.

■

Zoe had never looked beyond the wedding to the inevitable second act—the honeymoon. Carmine and she did not drive far—just to a large hotel in St. Petersburg. Zoe was frightened even to go into the lobby and certain that the bellhops and guests would laugh at her. Carmine carried her over the threshold of the bridal suite—and tripped. He put on a brave front, but he, also, was terrified.

Carmine ordered six champagne cocktails from room service. They sat sipping, making polite conversation. Suddenly Zoe bolted up, ran to the suitcases, took out every stitch of their clothing and obsessively began to order the drawers and the closets.

"Hey, you're making me dizzy," said Carmine. And suddenly Zoe realized she, too, was dizzy. The champagne hit with a bang, and she sat down on the bed.

Carmine sat down next to her and stroked her arm gently. She looked up, trying to respond, reached out a tentative hand, and missed his arm by a mile.

They began giggling hysterically. Still gently touching his new wife, Carmine undressed himself and her, and they lay there, seemingly enjoying each other for a moment. Then she clamped her legs together and began to cry. "I'm sorry, I'm sorry," she whimpered.

"Oh, honey, it's okay," said the gallant Carmine.

According to Zoe, the alter Doreen somehow managed that night to pleasure Carmine, and for the many subsequent nights that Zoe could not bear anyone's touch, Doreen often came out to save her.

According to Carmine, "I was very happy after the marriage. My dreams seemed to be coming true. Zoe was a good support, and we were the best of friends.

"I saw some changes in her personality but thought these were women problems. She had crying spells—not like a woman, but like a child of two or three. We had to order a night-light from room service, and she had to have it on the entire time we were there. She would crawl into my arms like a helpless child.

"But boy, once we got home, could she cook lasagna!

"Zoe wanted five children, but I said three were enough . . . if we ever had regular relations."

■

**ZOE II (the Tunnel of Patients):** *Carmine was stationed in Pensacola. He wanted me to join him there. I had never been away from my parents . . .*

■

According to Zoe, there were many fights right from the beginning. Carmine threw tantrums when he did not get his own way. "He wanted a lot of sex. Zoe was submissive, but Serena fought back."

■

**MOTHER ZOE (the Tunnel of Light):** *During our first weeks in Pensacola, I was still too frightened to permit penetration. But I yearned for a child, and this was the way to get one. I went to a gynecologist, who examined me and said there was no obstruction. That the failure was mine—a problem with my attitude.*

*Serena hated Carmine from Day One. There were knock-down-drag-out fights between the two of them. One time Zoe had made a big platter of lasagna. Carmine came in and started an argument, and Serena came out and threw the platter at him. It landed against the kitchen wall. It was quite a mess. It shocked Carmine—where was his submissive little wife?*

*Sometimes Serena stayed out for days. Poor man.*

■

**DENNIS (the Tunnel of Protectors):** *Oh, man, I had to stick around for all their marital relations. I hated this guy. Sometimes I would come out and Serena would come out. And the only thing we had in common was we both hated Carmine's guts.*

*So when I'd come out, maybe they would be playing a card game. And I would hit him in the face so hard he didn't know*

*what happened. He didn't know Dennis was around, man. And
Dennis hated everyone, but this geek in particular.*

■

**SERENA (the Tunnel of Power):** *Anyway. She moved up to
Pensacola with this dude and lived in a Quonset hut. Which
looks like a little tin can. When it rained it sounded like
hailstones the size of golf balls, coming down on this little tin
can. Zoe was alone most of the time. Carmine went out to sea.*

■

There was nothing to do. No TV, no phone, no radio. Zoe
stayed on her bed in the tin can, listening to the golf
balls, staring up at the light shimmying on the ceiling.
Whenever he was in port, Carmine made a point of
dragging his wife out to the naval functions and introducing her to the other navy wives. She would smile brittlely
and phase out during the introduction, and when they'd
get back, he would turn on her in fury. "No wonder you
don't have any friends!"

Zoe was so shy she was almost mute. The only creature whose company she enjoyed was a puppy, which
she found shivering on her doorstep in the rain. She had
lain on her bed with her eyes wide open, fearing the
scratching noises were a burglar trying to break in. And
then, "So what? Who cares if they find me dead and
everything gone?" came the thought, and she'd opened
the door.

They were supposed to stay on the base for six
months. The puppy got Zoe through twenty-five days,
and after that, she threw a few things in a suitcase and
took the bus back down to St. Petersburg.

Zoe May and Dave Bryant fetched Zoe from the
station. They didn't say they'd told her so; they just
drove home in silence. Bryant tossed Zoe's suitcase onto
her bed. Zoe set the dolls in their old positions.

The next day was Saturday, and with her old friend
Carla, Zoe went to the coast to pick up sailors. Zoe
forgot that she was married.

A letter from Carmine arrived each day. "Mom and
Dad, take care of your wonderful selfs and don't work

too hard. How's my Wink? Pensacola is lousy. I bet you know why."

Five months passed. Carmine ended his Pensacola tour and was stationed back in Freeside. When he came to get Zoe, the Bryants urged them to stay. For economy's sake, the young couple agreed. The Parrys took Zoe's bedroom, and the Bryants, the master bedroom. Though the Bryants bought twin beds, Zoe and Carmine kept Zoe's virginal French provincial suite. Pushed to the back of the shelves by Carmine's navy souvenirs, Zoe's dolls stared at the humans reproachfully with their big glass eyes.

Zoe began to let Carmine consummate sexual relations, though she tended to clench up and he, to break dolls; both feared being overheard by her parents. Halfway through the act the young folks would start rigid— not from ecstasy—as the hall door slowly creaked open and then shut.

■

**DORA (the Tunnel of Secrets):** *Mr. Bryant was cold to Dottie Mae. He didn't speak to us while we lived at the Bryant household.*

■

Soon, Carmine suggested they find an apartment out of the range of the Bryants' sensitive ears. Bryant stormed that they were making a big mistake, that they couldn't even afford the sixty-four dollars a month an apartment would cost. "It doesn't make sense to leave when you don't pay a dime here!"

Their new bungalow, twenty miles away, overlooked the boardwalk on which Zoe had first met Carmine. It was a beach house, all shutters and rattan, hard to keep clean—the sand blew in—but small and manageable.

Zoe played wife, but her distaste for men grew overwhelming. She is the first to admit, "I was far from being a woman. I was a little girl." She also has dim recollections of boiling hot pans of lasagna hitting the walls and oozing down to the accompaniment of male screams.

Just after Zoe's eighteenth birthday, Carmine contracted a mysterious fever. His head ached; his joints swelled to triple normal size. After his temperature soared to 104 and stayed there, Zoe had Bryant drive him to a hospital.

He had a severe case of rheumatoid arthritis.

Carmine was flat on his back for a month and lost forty pounds. The doctors said he would be in a wheelchair for the rest of his life, with very limited lower-body function, then transferred him to a naval hospital fifty miles away.

Zoe could not bear cooking for one in the empty cottage. The view of sailors and girls parading up the boardwalk, arm in arm, laughing, struck her each morning like a blow. Soon the cottage stood abandoned, and Zoe's old room creaked with the sound of a chair, rocking, rocking, and with a woman's muffled sobs.

■

**MOTHER ZOE (the Tunnel of Light):** *As depressed as she was, the Bride still pushed herself to see Carmine every weekend. Her parents drove her.*

*Somehow this pretty little gal would come out all fixed up. All the sailors at the hospital would whistle, "Hey, Parry, how'd'ya get someone like that?" This flattered her, but inside, she was crumbling.*

*During the entire three-hour drive home, she'd scream. She would lie on the floor of the car by the backseat, holding her hands over her ears, wailing that she was dying.*

■

Even if Dave Bryant had understood Zoe's shifts in personality, it would have been difficult to drive for three hours while trying to ignore a screaming daughter.

Carmine says that this was the first breakdown of Zoe's that he knew about. "She kept the others a secret. She had terrible spells, Mother would say. She'd just sit and stare off into space. She wouldn't eat, and she had terrible nightmares." He remembers immense frustration at being cooped up, crippled, while his wife spiraled down into madness. "But her family reassured me. They said suddenly she'd snap out of it and be her old self. She wouldn't remember. That was for the best, we all agreed."

The Bryants and Virginie all agreed that since Zoe was getting worse at Ashton Avenue, it would do her a lot of good to move in with Virginie once again.

Virginie's home, too, was unchanged from the old days. Zoe sank gratefully into her cousin's warmth.

But soon Virginie suggested a psychiatrist. And the psychiatrist suggested shock treatment.

▪

**DORA (the Tunnel of Secrets):** *She snapped out of it. I guess it was shock treatment to hear she might have to have shock.*

▪

Virginie said she was happy that Zoe was her old self and avoided any further mention of nerves.

"That gal wasn't afraid of anything," Virginie marvels, forgetting how afraid "that gal" had been just the week before. "We'd go to all the stores. Her little car had a problem, that the exhaust would go up into the car, and the windows rolled down, and I didn't know whether I was going to get home in one piece! She drove me places where I didn't know where I was going, and it scared me half to death."

▪

**SERENA (the Tunnel of Power):** *Virge acted like, omygawsh, omygooness! But she had a ball. The Palms, to my surprise, was unchanged. We ordered beers. Some of the gals that knew me from old times came up and started talking. And one took, as Virge would say, a hankerin' to her. She was a-flirtin' at this bawr. Virge goes, "I don't know how I litchew tawk me inter this, Zoe." It was real funny, 'cause this big stompin' butch, two hundred fifty pounds, comes up and commands Virge to dance. Virge doesn't know what to say!—"Oooh! I'm with HER!"*

*Drivin' her back, Virge is wonderful. She says she thinks the family is so prudish. "Honey, I cain't tawk to ANNNYbody but YEW! We cain really delve into spiritual matters." We talked about reincarnation. She promised me that one day we would "conjure up sperrits together."*

■

**CONNIE (the Tunnel of Power):** *Then I pulled the car over—and told her I loved her. She said she didn't love me that way . . . and I blanked out.*

■

Zoe took Virginie home, then drove away.

Four hours later, Virginie remembers, Zoe called. A little voice on the other end of the line said, "Help! I'm bleeding!" And then Zoe hung up.

"I knew it was your voice, Zoe. I walked the floor and didn't know where you were and was as panicky as could be. I didn't know what to do! I called your home, and your mother didn't know either. We were all frightened to death."

Zoe answers, "I have no memory of this."

"You'd be gone days at a time, everybody out looking."

Zoe says, "The wild girl must have been out, to satisfy her own pleasures. Where she went, I do not know."

This pattern continued for nine months, through Fall 1963. Then Carmine was transferred from the naval hospital to a VA hospital only fifteen miles away from 731 Ashton. Serena's behavior got even wilder. Though Zoe visited Carmine more frequently than before, after visits, Serena would take over. There was no stopping her, as she was the only one unafraid to drive. For months, while Carmine gained back weight and tried to rehabilitate his legs, Zoe's darker selves prowled the Florida night.

A psychiatric report summarizes that time. "The larger part of the patient's atypical sexual behavior occurred after marriage. She went out every night and stayed out. . . ."

"It was like Dr. Jekyll and Mr. Hyde," comments Zoe.

■

**DORA (the Tunnel of Secrets):** *She'd do chores during the day with her mother and Virge. At night, Serena would put on* black dresses, very low cut, tight and slit up the sides, and go off. She'd end up in somebody's bed and thought she was having a ball. Next morning Zoe would be home, wondering why she felt tired.

In Orange Grove, Zoe met a woman named Rhonda, a nice respectable thirty-four-year-old who worked at the jewelry store where Carmine had bought Zoe's engagement ring. Zoe had gone back, not realizing it was the same place, and they'd struck up a conversation. Rhonda had a nine-year-old daughter; she'd realized she liked women. Zoe decided Rhonda was the woman of her dreams.

Though Zoe felt shy and went home, the next morning she drove to Rhonda's house. She was greeted by her friend in a beautiful negligee. Rhonda fixed her tea and suddenly was all over this shy little girl, nuzzling, licking. Serena came out because she likes this sort of thing. And Rhonda seemed very pleased at what she had found at Forever. Their affair lasted until 1965. . . .

But Serena was not content with Rhonda. She kept going to bars. To this gay, Latin bar . . . She knew some of the gals from other bars, and they were drinking and talking.

One girl tried to talk Serena into letting her be her pimp. Serena said no. Suddenly she feels a burning in her arm, looks down, and sees a needle hanging. The girl injected her with some heavy drug, after all those drinks.

Serena became very drowsy and slumped in her chair. Some girl took her away. The girl's house was dark, and there was an altar set up with statues of saints and candles. The room was spinning so, it was like a merry-go-round.

The girl looked like a young Sal Mineo. Black curly hair, very attractive. She said, ''You need something to eat,'' went to the kitchen, and started scrambling eggs.

Serena felt trapped. She got up, grabbed the girl's jacket, and ran. She fell down the front steps and landed on the lawn. Nothing broken.

She got up and staggered down the street. The trees were swaying in a very unnatural way. The sidewalk looked like it was going to hit her in the face. She kept blanking, and when she'd wake, she'd have fallen on a different lawn.

It was a black-Cuban neighborhood. Men picked her up. Once she was in a car with this man; he had a hat on, his *fly was undone and his penis hanging out. He kept pushing her head down. "Suck it, baby." There was no fight left in her, and she blanked out.*

*Then she was in a house with men all around, and she blanked out again.*

*Now she's in a car with three men in back and two in front. She's half undressed, her dress is torn, and her shoes are gone. She starts coming up from the drug, and one man has his hands down her pants and his fingers groping. She's got to do something fast. She says, "My house is right down the street and I'm married to X [a neighborhood honcho] and he's gonna beat the holy shit out of you if you don't let me out." She starts kicking the guy, cussing up a storm.*

*Now she's outside, on Coral Way but way downtown, hailing down a car. She tells the driver that she's having a miscarriage and please get her to her sister. And she gives the address of a girl she's been attracted to, named Tara.*

*She's at Tara's house, pounding on the door. She's still intoxicated, with her ripped dress and Les's jacket falling off her shoulders. Tara's door opens and Tara's huge girlfriend comes outside. Tara isn't there.*

■

**SERENA (the Tunnel of Power):** *I was drunk out of my mind. And this gonzo bitch pushes me against the wall. I started screaming uncontrollably.*

*The neighbors, older people down the hall, peek out. And they slam their doors and call the police.*

■

**ZOE II (the Tunnel of Patients):** *I woke up in a hospital. It was three in the morning. Two police officers, one on each side, and a doctor examining me. She said, "You're going to have quite a hangover." Then she saw my arm. "What have you been shooting up with?"*

*Then the officers put me back in the car and headed for jail. And one of them, a young guy, made a puss at me. "If you give us some, we'll forget the whole thing."*

■

**SERENA (the Tunnel of Power):** *I had a fit. "Go fuck your-selves," I told them. And they replied, "You belong in jail, you bitch."*

*At the jail I get my one phone call. I called Mr. Bryant, and he said he'd be down to pick me up.*

■

**MAZIE 5 (the Tunnel of Light):** *Why am I in jail? I'm scared. The woman next to me just killed her husband. I throwing up. I pee myself.*

*Now I'm at the end of a long hallway, and the guard has let me out. At the other end of the hallway are Mommy and Daddy. Mommy is crying and Daddy looks mad.*

■

When she woke up two days later in her pink and gold room, Zoe was, according to Zoe May, "her own sweet self again." And that night, Serena went back to the bar. "She was trying to be Miss Detective," says Zoe. "To figure out what had happened. But it was no good. She couldn't remember anything, and she went home."

Carmine comments: "When I heard she'd been ar-rested I couldn't hardly believe it. That really hurt me." He signed himself out of the hospital, and he rushed to the Bryants'.

After almost a year of grueling physical therapy, he could walk with two canes. The navy had given him a medical discharge and a monthly disability check. He tried to take charge—to make life be normal. He refused to live with the Bryants—his handicap, he said diplomati-cally—and so Zoe and he rented half a duplex a few miles away. The apartment had a large backyard, two bedrooms, a living room. And Carmine, who'd been studying in the hospital, got a job as a junior accountant at a law firm.

Now that Carmine was home, he saw how the alter Serena was acting. "I couldn't believe my eyes when my Zoe walks out of the bedroom dressed like a hooker. 'You goin' out like that?' I ask, and she starts in on me! I couldn't believe the mouth on her! She pushes me and runs outside.

"She acted like she couldn't stand me, or any man. I see her beat-up car, swinging out the driveway to who knows where. So I walk out as fast as I can—not so fast, on those canes—and follow her in my little Chevy. Down to the worst part of Brinton Beach."

When Carmine saw his wife in action at the Palms, his temper flared. "One time, and I'm not proud of this. It only happened once. Not that I beat up on my wife, but I hit her. I was going nuts. I couldn't stand not knowing where she went, or if I would ever see her again." His words are the same as Zoe May's; apparently they've evaluated Zoe together. "After the beating I was so ashamed. I vowed I would never touch her again, and I haven't."

Carmine came home early that day to have it out with Zoe. She was in the bathroom, applying false eyelashes.

"What do you think you're doing?"

She looked up coolly. "That's my own damn business."

Enraged, he hit her. "You bitch! You whore! Not with me, you don't!" Again and again his hand descended.

Bleeding, she started cursing. Suddenly her eyes glazed over. With superhuman speed, she grabbed a bottle, smashed it in half on the sink, and held it, edges facing Carmine. "Touch me again and I'll rip your guts out."

A later psychiatric report comments: "She was homicidal, but feels a part of her prevented her from murder. She'd been feeling as healthy as she ever had in her life. The palpitations had subsided. She is quick to admit she enjoys the type of relationships she was seeking that night."

Zoe is amnesiac for the next few months. But Virginie states, "She turned on herself. She got hysterical. Self-mutilation. She used to scratch herself bad, bite herself, and then her face became contorted from, I don't know, fear or what."

Zoe asserts that she was actually having a reaction to the mild analgesic she'd taken for her headache.

Again, the family had tacitly agreed to shut their eyes. Zoe's big conflict at the time was she couldn't decide if she was going to stay with Carmine and get pregnant or to move in with Rhonda.

Was Zoe going to have a child—or be a child? As usual, the answer would be "both."

■

In early 1964 Zoe conceived; then she miscarried.

■

**DORA (the Tunnel of Secrets):** *Mr. Bryant had come to take her grocery shopping. She was six or seven weeks along. She really wanted this baby.*

*Suddenly she started cramping. Mr. Bryant had to do the shopping. She sat in the car praying to God to spare the child. When she got back to the apartment, Mr. Bryant never knew. We can be closed-mouth, no matter what. He put the groceries away and left. The minute the door shut she went into the bathroom. She lost the baby in the toilet.*

■

Zoe did not tell anyone about the miscarriage. Instead, she flushed. And in the next month, saw fifty doctors.

■

**ELEANOR (the Tunnel of Secrets):** *Zoe would get the phone book and, I'm not kidding, sometimes in one day she'd go see five. She'd say she had this wrong, and that wrong, she had stomach problems, she had fever. She'd get all kinds of prescriptions. Something for allergies, something for this, something for that, for the stomach, for the hair. They didn't help.*

■

In 1965, Zoe once again became pregnant. This time the fetus survived. "She had," says Zoe, referring to the alter Mother Zoe, "the most horrible pregnancy. Sick for the whole nine months. Morning sickness at first; then toxemia." She spent much of the pregnancy at her parents' house so that Zoe May could take care of her while Carmine was at work. Dave would come home, see her swollen belly, and run out to his garage, unable to accept Zoe's pregnancy.

■

**DORA (the Tunnel of Secrets):** *The drinking became worse and worse. I guess it was his way of numbing the pain of losing his daughter.*

■

That Zoe had life growing in her felt wondrous to her. "She talked to the baby in her tummy and called him iddy biddy. Iddy biddy would kick her. And she loved it."

■

**DANIELLE LA MOND (the Tunnel of Secrets):** *The Bride could feel the tiny baby in her womb. She could feel herself loving the baby. She anticipated holding the tiny hands and giving a lot of kisses. She was joyous, but so afraid—she remembered losing the last little one.*

■

"At four months," continues Zoe, "she developed appendicitis and almost lost iddy biddy. Her white count was sky high. They rushed her to the hospital. The doctors wanted to operate. She begged them to pack her in ice. Her parents called Paul Barnaby, and they prayed. Zoe turned to her mother, with a feeling of peace in body and mind. Her mother was crying by the bed. Zoe took her hand and said, 'Everything is going to be all right. I can feel it.'

"A miracle happened. The white count came down. The pain subsided. The doctors were just amazed."

The baby was born two weeks late and was delivered by C-section after a twenty-seven-hour labor, at 10:28 P.M. on November 2, 1965.

Zoe stayed in the hospital for ten days. She nursed Davey for a week, but when her incision became infected, she agreed to having an injection to dry up her milk.

So Zoe was going through her most major hormonal changes since puberty, when three weeks later Anne Adams suffered a stroke and died.

The timing of the funeral—just before Christmas—made this the third strike for Zoe, and out.

Her grandmother's death would spark not only the annual nervous breakdown, it would be a catalyst for twelve years of creating alters upon alters, each less in touch than the last, that would climax in the kidnapping of Jennifer King.

■

**The BRIDE [Dottie Mae] (the Tunnel of Limbo):** *I felt too devastated to go to the funeral.*

*After, I started getting very ill. I didn't mean to. I felt like a failure and coward. I had everything I wanted, husband and child, and still got sick.*

■

The death of their ruling queen sent shock waves through the Adams and Bryant clan. "Your grandmother," Virginie tells Zoe, "ruled her daughters with an iron hand. Your mother felt so much fear growing up in that house. A fear that she transferred, and still transfers, to you."

Zoe May had in 1945 handed Zoe to her mother. Following her mother's model, in 1965, Zoe would have done the same—handed Davey over to Zoe May until she felt stronger. But at her mother's death, Zoe May took to her bed.

No matter how sick she felt, Zoe had to keep her son. Trying to comfort her mother and nurture her son, Zoe crashed. Far worse than her mother's had been, Zoe's blues started indigo and turned black.

■

**The BRIDE [Dottie Mae] (the Tunnel of Limbo):** *Davey's first Christmas, I bought the largest tree and decorated it lavishly. The blinking lights seemed to fascinate him. When I'd take him away at night, he cried. At night I put his bassinet next to Carmine's and my bed.*

*My mother came over every day to help with Davey. But the day she didn't show up, Davey wouldn't stop crying. I went to pieces. I gave him a bottle and then blacked out.*

■

This was the day of Anne Adams's death.

■

**The BRIDE [Dottie Mae] (the Tunnel of Limbo):** *Several hours later I woke up under the dining room table. Davey was still crying. I had done to him what my mother had done to me when I was an infant.*

*I ran to Davey, picked him up, and held him close. He stopped crying and clung to me, hiccuping convulsively. I felt so ashamed.*

*This was the start of my nervous breakdown. For the next four years I was housebound.*

*I was afraid of everything—cars, crowds, even the air. Luckily, my mother came over to walk me and Davey. She would hold my arm as I pushed his carriage over the pavement, which heaved under my feet.*

*Davey was so active. His noise hurt me. He pulled himself up on the bookshelves at age ten months, and then, crash, everything came down, and he screamed. I would burrow under the covers. The room would be spinning. I would try to get away as far as I could, feeling guiltier by the moment. I missed my son's entire childhood.*

■

Having a son, like having a husband, could have helped Zoe to grow up. Instead, she became even more her parents' child.

One Sunday when the Bryants were over, she was awakened by a rumbling noise from outside. She sent her parents out to see what it was. The Parrys' neighbors in the duplex were moving. Dave Bryant shouted for joy, wrote out a check, and raced over to the landlord. He chucked 731 Ashton—the Bryants' home of fifteen years—without a bit of nostalgia. In January 1966, the Bryants became the Parrys' neighbors, moving into the vacant half of the Parrys' duplex.

"My father decided to retire and spend his days with Davey," says Zoe.

Adds Carmine angrily, "He had no concept that I was

the father. He was nice to my son. Too nice. Overprotective. He'd try to make me feel like I was not the father—he was. We had more than a few fights. And mostly over the child.

"I wanted to leave Zoe many times. Because of the frustrations in our marriage and because of the way the father acted. But then I would remember the lovely girl I had hung around with by the beach, and think, 'She's somehow still there, under all those layers.' I hoped she was there. I hoped it with all my heart. And I stayed."

Zoe cried just like her grandmother—in the very same chair. Zoe May hadn't fed Zoe; apparently Zoe would feed Davey again and again. Zoe May had weaned Zoe early; Zoe wouldn't wean Davey until he was four. She sat in the chair, crying and rocking, and feeding the little baby until he became a wide, large boy.

**ZOE II (the Tunnel of Patients):** *My mother, whose sisters had called her "The Lady Of Sorrows," seemed happier. Maybe because I needed her so. She accompanied Davey and me everywhere. To the bank, to the store. I could have an attack at any moment. My ears would buzz, my heart would thump, I would gasp for air. If my mother hadn't been there, I would have died. I was always in terror and clung to my mother even in the happiest moments.*

*Sometimes another side would come out. Then the house would fill with laughter. Davey didn't mind who was out. He seemed to simply love me, to adore all my many selves without question. When I could, I would play with him, bathe him, feed him. His grandparents brought him gifts almost every day. After they moved next door, they took him upstairs often. Their duplex was across the hall from ours.*

Here, Bryant's drinking got worse and worse.

**DORA (the Tunnel of Secrets):** *He still wouldn't acknowledge that he used it.*

*When Davey was two, I walked out the door and he was lying on the stairs. I yelled, "Dad, you're a damn hypocrite!" And Serena just stepped over the body and spit at him.*

*Mrs. Bryant came rushing out to see what the commotion was. She, too, called him a hypocrite. He stank. She said, "You're doing everything you tell other people not to!"*

*Finally, when Zoe was twenty-eight and Davey was nine, the father declared one day that he was healed. From then on he never drank a drop.*

Though her parents seemed resigned to the status quo—Zoe's being an invalid, her father an alcoholic, Carmine handicapped, and Zoe May fairly competent (for her)—Zoe finally decided to do something about herself. In 1969 Zoe was almost twenty-five and her son was four, unweaned and uncontrollable. She'd held out this long because she dreaded being locked up, like Carmine's mother. The night Zoe decided to seek help was the night she saw Satan.

She was lying in bed. Her father was in the garage, and Davey, in the guest room with Mrs. Bryant. Zoe saw a flicker out the bedroom window and glanced over.

**MAZIE 5 (the Tunnel of Light):** *He was staring at me. A horrible face, with black piercing eyes. Bearded. Grinning. I swear on Mother Mary, Jesus, and the Bible. He was staring straight at us. He was.*

Fearing she was about to lose her soul, she called Dr. Hendricks and asked him to refer her to a mental hospital.

"He recommended the Richfield Center, a very reputable institution three miles away. They ran an outpatient clinic. This appealed to me because I could spend my days there and yet be home at night to take care of Davey and Carmine. I begged my father for his consent. To my shock he agreed."

She did not ask Carmine to consent—just her father.

On December 15, 1969—ten days before Christmas—Dave drove Zoe to her first appointment with Dr. Mildred Silverstein.

The security guard cleared the Bryants' Buick and unlatched the gates. The car swung into what seemed an English country park. There was nobody outside. Down a rustic lane they went, past a dichondra meadow, through a forest, and out onto the campus—a huge white-stucco mansion, set like a diamond into a manicured, emerald-green lawn.

Dr. Silverstein was a short grandmotherly woman with twinkling eyes, a strong Yiddish accent, and a hearty laugh. She sounded like Sophie Tucker—always ready with a joke. Says Zoe, "I found myself telling her things. The first was that I was in constant pain."

Silverstein patted Zoe's hand. "We'll help you."

"What's wrong with me?"

"That's what we'll find out now, no?"

"No, I mean, I don't know." Zoe laughed, finding herself paradoxically attracted. The woman's eyes looked green in certain lights, and she had a big, nurturing bosom. Zoe wondered if that shelflike effect was natural or propped by some anachronistic corset.

As Zoe fantasized, Silverstein explained the patient's obligations. "I had to attend morning circle with patients, social workers, and a doctor. I dreaded group therapy, being so shy. I would also have daily individual therapy with Mildred and a psychiatric social worker. I was trembling with fear. Yet somehow I trusted them. It was their job to understand."

Silverstein's tests took three days. She reported:

The patient has a history of "ESP" in which a voice warns her of danger . . .

Patient related two repetitive dreams. 1) She can fly to get away from dangers. But she flies high, recognizing that this could be dangerous. 2) Patient stands on the porch. A beam of light comes down.

Angels' voices sing, and she feels that God wants her.

Patient states she historically had more fun in her make-believe world than in the real world. Recently she feels trapped in her make-believe world.

I believe that Silverstein interviewed Zoe's Christmas alters, the ones that appear each year during her annual breakdown—mostly the child and religious alters. Panicky, childlike, and obsessively good, these alters do not show the brilliant side of Zoe's illness. Zoe's deepest, sickest alters would never accept therapy at Richfield.

The admitting evaluation continued:

Even now, whenever the patient panics, she goes next door to sleep with her mother. Patient takes her child along, and he, in turn, sleeps with her father.

Patient is overdependent on her parents and never saw a normal male-female relationship . . .

Until recently the cardiac illness served to get her more attention. But now her parents are getting disgusted . . .

Not much in her life is genuine and deep-seated. Neither of her parents seems capable of real depth of feeling or understanding. Perhaps the patient's emphasis on her heart best reflects what she is missing.

In 1970 through 1983—the height of Zoe's illness—sixty-four percent of those who today would be diagnosed with MPD might have been diagnosed with affective disorder. Since overlapping diagnoses are not uncommon, fifty-seven percent would additionally have been diagnosed with personality disorder, forty-four percent with anxiety, and forty-one percent with schizophrenia. These diagnoses were sometimes completely inaccurate.

A patient's diagnosis is critical: treatment is different for each disorder; people as ill as Zoe often try to kill themselves. In one study of 236 poorly diagnosed MPD patients, seventy-two percent attempted suicide; two percent succeeded. They overdosed, burned themselves, slashed their wrists.

Multiples in this study either forgot they'd tried to kill themselves or felt so depersonalized that harming themselves hadn't seemed to matter. Most had tried psychotherapy, drug therapy, shock therapy. No wonder they were suicidal. Aside from feeling like failures, they couldn't even feel like the same failure two times running. Different alters respond differently to the same treatment.

Silverstein prescribed Valium to calm Zoe and scheduled talk sessions. These therapies would work for a little while, and then, bewilderingly, progress would stop.

In the first week Zoe adjusted to her new schedule. At seven-forty-five each weekday morning, she'd kiss Davey good-bye and hand him over to Zoe May. Her father would drive her to Richfield. Carmine had agreed to pick her up at three-thirty sometimes, but said that when traffic was bad, she'd have to take the hospital bus back to the Bryants'.

Since the center charged on a sliding scale, the Parrys paid five dollars a week for Zoe's thirty-five hours of care, which included two private sessions with Silverstein.

Zoe flung herself into day treatment. For her, it was primarily a social experience. Some new alters arrived to handle the social stress—to be older, smarter, or funnier than were the other clinic patients.

■

**AUNT SOPHIE (the Tunnel of Power):** *I'm fifty-five years old. I love to do impressions and make people feel good—make them laugh at themselves.*

*I am four feet ten and weigh eighty-nine pounds. I've had everything lifted. At my age everything falls. I have black hair from a bottle and dark brown eyes.*

■

Zoe loved starting fresh. She hauled Carmine in five days a week for family therapy, and Davey, three days, an hour and a half at a stretch. The center's policy was to train the family as well as the patient, to change the immediate environment, which could make or break a cure. Of course, in order to truly change Zoe's environment, the center would have had to ask the Bryants to come in as well.

The center evaluated Davey as "emotionally disturbed." It wasn't a tough call. He refused to go to preschool. If led there, he'd throw things and run away, according to Zoe, "through all the dangerous streets. I knew what he was feeling. I remembered feeling the same. He didn't want to separate from me and my mother."

At this age, Davey was skinny and scowling, a handsome child with high tense shoulders and white-blond, fiercely curly hair. The alter Sharon Weissman, who wears a Jewish star and sees herself as having light brown hair and blue eyes, emerged in 1970 to help Zoe raise her son.

Says Zoe, "Davey screamed a bit at the center, but then I persuaded him he could truly help Mommy and Daddy this way." Continuing the theme that Mommy and Daddy were the important ones, she tried to sit in on Davey's sessions, and then (when refused) sat in the hall outside, so they'd have contact at the beginning and end of every session.

The alters Aunt Sophie and Sharon Weissman reflected Mildred Silverstein's humor, her Jewishness, and her motherliness. In nontherapy hours, Zoe began to visit synagogues on Fridays and Saturdays, as well as her usual churches on Sundays and Wednesdays. She had an incredibly busy schedule.

Zoe, her doctors, and her family all worked hard. They were certainly at the center enough. "For three years, from 1971 to 1974—longer than any other family at the time—we all tried so hard to understand. Though we never talked much at home about the center, we felt comfortable that we were finally getting the help that we needed."

Zoe came to some painful realizations which she'd previously blocked. "I found that my mother and father, who I loved so dearly, were abnormal and disturbed."

▪

**ZOE II (the Tunnel of Patients):** *The first year was pure hell. I felt abandoned to strangers. The other patients seemed alien. I sat in back and cried. In occupational therapy I couldn't do anything, even lace up a simple wallet.*

*They kept testing me. IQ tests. Thematic apperception. Ink blots. I was amazed (and so were the therapists) that my IQ when I was in a certain mood was 170. In other moods my IQ was 110 or even 80.*

*I realized with horror how I'd failed my son. He'd wanted a bottle until age four, two and a half years after Carmine had wanted him to stop. Our family always fought about this. Sometimes Carmine would actually grab the bottle away, which made him in our eyes into a brute and a villain. I fed Davey in secret. It wasn't till he was five that Davey actually learned to eat regular food. He had to be taught. He used to gag on anything that needed chewing, and spit it up. . . .*

▪

First, the center tried to normalize Davey.

▪

**ZOE II (the Tunnel of Patients):** *After that year, the authorities decided I'd gotten too attached to Mildred and reassigned her. I shrank at the thought of having to reveal myself all over again to a stranger. I regressed. I had to be fed and couldn't lift a spoon.*

*They assigned me to a man, a Dr. Frederick Small. He was nice enough, young, intellectual, and probably quite open. I hated him. It wasn't personal. I just hated all men. Plus I wanted Dr. Silverstein.*

▪

Silverstein cannot now be located. And when asked to comment, Small says simply, "I don't want to do that."

Though Zoe doesn't speak about this and perhaps does not remember, according to psychiatrists' notes from the time, she'd fallen in love with Silverstein, who after some unreported conversations with her colleagues had promptly been reassigned. On the rebound, while theoretically adjusting to therapy with Dr. Small—a very proper gentleman who reminded Zoe of her father—Zoe fell into a sadomasochistic sexual relationship with one of the psychiatric technicians.

■

**RONA (the Tunnel of Light):** *Henry Owens was black, about five feet ten, stocky, with a little line mustache. He always wore glasses and a black sweater. Apparently he worked here and moonlighted next door, at the Richfield Research Center, taking care of the animals. He had a van. What he would do was, he'd follow Zoe and ask her to have sex with him. At first she refused. But soon she felt like this was her fate. She was catatonic. Anyone can lead a catatonic patient anywhere.*

*This man got the patient into the bathroom, this patient with a history of abuse by men. He made her open her legs wide, and he peed in her. When the little ones came out, he made them lick his penis. He would do a BM, spread his legs, and make her wipe his butt. They could not refuse his demands. They even gave him their phone number.*

■

Unacknowledged multiplicity can lead a person into the worst abuse situations. Where a normal person would shy away, a multiple often submits, merely creating another alter to take the pain. Since the new alters fall along the same fault lines as the old, they almost inevitably bring the system yet more abuse. Though individually alters can be intelligent and social, when taken together and lacking insight about each other, they are sheep ready for slaughter.

Bereft at the loss of Mildred Silverstein, Zoe created an internal Dr. Silverstein alter. She then got the name of a therapist from a schizophrenic patient named Linda. "She's the best therapist I've ever had," said Linda, "and I've had plenty. She's playful and caring, and she's a doctor, so you won't have to go to anyone else for your medications."

Without further research, Zoe decided that God had spoken through Linda. Immediately, she called the doctor. "Hello," she said into the machine. "My name is

Zoe Parry, and I'm a patient at the Richfield Center. Linda Hubley recommended that I—"

"Hello!" Someone had picked up. "I'm Dr. Wald."

Zoe thought Wald had a wonderful voice. High and lilting, it sank to deep resonance when asking sensitive questions. During Zoe's self-introduction, Dr. Wald chuckled ironically, giggled, and made several funny jokes. Zoe enjoyed this responsiveness.

They set their first appointment for December 6, 1971—two and a half weeks before Christmas. From that day, Zoe gratefully attached to this new doctor all her unresolved grief from Silverstein. She would see both Wald and the Richfield man, Dr. Small, for the next three years.

Curiously, considering her thirty-five hours per week of clinic, Zoe still felt psychically frozen. Though she'd acquired sophisticated arguments to use on Carmine, she was not progressing. She still spent most of her hours at home in her grandmother's rocking chair. At day treatment—apart from her unconscious hours with Henry Owens—she sat in the corner; in occupational therapy she wrote poems, jealously guarding them from anyone else's sight.

■

**MOTHER ZOE (the Tunnel of Light):** *I would sit by myself hunched over with my head in my lap, feeling the presence of a screaming child inside. Someone inside would bang my head against the wall or beat me up. The nurses would hold me down. I had been there for two years when I met someone who changed my life.*

■

One morning when she walked into occupational therapy, Zoe saw sitting in her accustomed spot an older woman with short white hair. Several other women stood around her, laughing. Zoe hesitated. The woman quivered, with that preternatural radar some psychiatric patients have, and looked up. Her eyes were bright blue and very wide. Zoe looked away from those too-bright eyes, walked to an empty corner, and stood facing the wall.

"Hey, is this yo' spot?" Her accent was as sweet and rich as pecan pie.

"No, that's all right; please don't move, I'm fine."

"Aw, c'mon, sit." One of the patients pulled up another chair, and Zoe, blushing, sat.

The woman leaned forward. "I'm Crystal Moon McGuire," she said. "And, honey, I sure am sorry for taking your spot."

"Zoe Parry."

"I am charmed to have the honor of making your acquaintance."

■

**MOTHER ZOE (the Tunnel of Light):** *Crystal had spent three months as an inpatient in the disturbed ward, labeled manic-depressive. She was slim, warm, and compassionate. She was fifty-one; I was twenty-four years younger.*

*Her hair was not combed. She apologized and asked if I had a comb. I gave her one and she thanked me. She felt much better after combing her hair.*

*I had not made friends with anyone. But I felt a warmth coming from this woman.*

*We made small talk. I was still agoraphobic. She decided to get me out. And she did, little by little. She got me to walk down the long hall to get a snack at the canteen. Then she got me to the library. And then she got me to the hospital park. The staff could not believe it.*

*Crystal was popular. She'd been elected president by the other patients. To run the morning circle was her job.*

*Soon we started to confide in each other.*

■

Christmas Eve 1993, Zoe received word that Crystal had recently died, of cancer. She says her own memories are as fresh as on the day they happened. . . .

■

**DONNA WHITE (the Tunnel of Power):** *I had written an essay, called "The Day Zoe Died," and—unusual for any of us at that time—signed it "Donna," not "Zoe." I handed it to Crystal. She read it silently, her lips moving with my thoughts.*

*"I guess I know Zoe better than anyone,"* it started. I'm reading it right now, it's on the orange construction paper which we used to cut out Halloween pumpkins. *"Mostly I stay hidden. You never know what that girl will do next!*

*"Zoe's been bent on self-destruction for many years. Her early death from the world of reality was inevitable. Only love could have brought her back; she did not get love.*

*"Zoe's death touched her friends and family. She communicated for them the emotions they couldn't admit. . . . Her inner pain was visible, throbbing contagion. In her last hopeless years she became an exercise in masochism. . . ."*

Crystal handed back the essay. "Aw, honey," she said. There were tears at the corners of those bright blue eyes. "Do y'all have more?" she asked.

In the bathroom, half an hour later, Zoe handed Crystal a poem.

> *I don't want to go to bed.*
> *I'm scared of the night.*
> *There's someone in my closet.*
> *Hear him breathe! Feel his eyes!*
> *He's lived in my closet*
> *Since I was three.*
> *When I shut my eyes, he lies with me.*
> *Can you guess what his name is?*
> *It rhymes with "breath."*
> *I can never get rid of the Closet Man—*
> *Death.*

Crystal reached over and clasped Zoe's hand.

As Zoe's alters tell it, at that moment the southern gentleman alter, Martin Caine, awoke inside Zoe's body. He felt he had rediscovered his true spouse. But he did not show himself, until later.

**MARTIN CAINE (the Tunnel of Observers, Guides, and Past Life):** *They read the Bible together. Crystal would take the* *body's hands in hers and pray. Gradually I felt myself drawn forth. Until we shared mind, body, and soul.*

*I am NOT from this time. I came through Zoe's body when she met Crystal—the reincarnation of my Elizabeth from another, more beautiful time. I knew it was her the very moment we met. She also knew me from the other lifetime.*

■

That week Crystal and Zoe spent their days together. On Friday evening, when the patients held their semiannual dinner dance, Crystal asked Zoe to waltz.

■

**MOTHER ZOE (the Tunnel of Light):** *I told her I never danced. This was a lie. But who wanted to waltz in hell?*

*"Come on, Zoe—I won't step on your feet." She extended her arm to me. The music changed. I found myself joining the others on the floor, doing the limbo.*

*I felt so at home with Crystal. She made my third and last year at the center bearable. I had been silent, but with her magical chemistry, Crystal drew me out.*

■

Dr. Wald, Zoe felt, was also her friend. She felt thoroughly mothered for the first time since Cousin Virginie.

However, Wald apparently acted strangely even during these halcyon days. Zoe speaks about leaping around on office couches with Wald, giggling. She alleges that at other times, she'd sit on Wald's lap while Wald sang lullabies, and she'd trace the seams of Wald's dress with her fingertips. And there was the gold locket with its pictures inside of five-year-old Zoe and adult Zoe, the valuable gift that she says Wald accepted and even wore to sessions.

At that time reparenting was the latest therapeutic fad. As Sister Bernadette would do a few years later, Wald tried to bring Zoe up, fresh.

Zoe had once again placed herself in the center of a parental triangle: Dr. Small/Richfield as Dad, and Wald/the outer world as Mom. But this time Crystal linked both worlds, with disastrous results. Because she was a member of both worlds, Crystal seemed to Zoe to be all-seeing.

Crystal introduced Zoe to white witchcraft, in which she'd dabbled since her divorce. In the early 1970s around a thousand Floridians became witches. They'd blended paganism, feminism, the occult, and sexuality, and eclectically combined rites from Ancient Egypt, medieval England, and Europe, with their own. By mid-1972, when Zoe first learned candle colors and pattern formations, the witchcraft movement had already politicized into many opposing fragments, each calling themselves white witches and calling their opponents black witches.

Zoe shared her new knowledge with Virginie. Her first use of witchcraft is interesting, given her illness.

"You tried to drum up grandmother's spirit," recollects Virginie. They were at Zoe's apartment, with Davey. "You told me," Virginie says to Zoe, "this little incantation you were supposed to say. Then we would think real strongly about Grandmother and see if we could bring her spirit. Because she hadn't been dead too long.

"On your stereo was a big old-fashioned lamp. That was on. You said your incantation and drew the circle and lit your white candle for purity, and we had other candles going with a glass of water beside them. Then we said, 'Grandmother—can you hear us?'

"Well, the lamp began to flicker. Nobody was home next door. Your mother had injured her back that night and was in the emergency room.

"All of a sudden, on the wall right by us, came three loud sharp knocks. That scared Zoe so bad, she ran out into the street. I'm sitting there in suspended animation.

"Davey was in the bedroom. He couldn't have knocked."

Zoe agrees. "No, it was not my son that knocked."

"And the knocks were distinct bangs," Virginie marvels. "If there is such a thing as the spirit world, I think Grandmother, who was a prankster in her day, was the one who knocked! And that was the end of our experimentation. It scared us half to death."

That may have been "the end" for Virginie; Zoe went on. She threw herself into witchcraft with the intensity she devotes to any endeavor she judges curative and religious. She ignored, she says, signs of danger. At first the herbs, candles and music, the past lives and thought vibrations, seemed as far from harmful as anything could be.

In fact, in March 1974, Zoe seemed well enough, judged Dr. Small, to be discharged from Richfield. She felt she was progressing smoothly with Wald and also thought she was deeply in love with Crystal. Finally, she thought, she could break away from the Bryants and find a life of her own.

■

**MOTHER ZOE (the Tunnel of Light):** *When I left, I continued to see Crystal, now also on her own. She lived with her grown daughter, her only child, who was about to move on to her own apartment.*

*After the daughter moved, Crystal invited me over. Her apartment was in a white stucco house with a red tile roof. She loved plants and dogs. To me her home was paradise.*

*I saw her every week, leaving my son with Mother.*

*We confessed things we'd never reveal to psychiatrists. She described how her drunk husband beat her. I told her about John Perret and about my father. She said my father was cruel, but I said no, remembering how he loved me.*

*She'd play records. We'd dance smooth and slow.*

*I first realized I wanted her when she told me she had to leave for Louisiana. Her father was dying. I was bereft.*

■

When Crystal left, Zoe fell apart. With Small she'd go into her favored fetal position and sob. Small went from gently suggesting that she give up Crystal, to strongly urging it. With Wald, Zoe didn't mention Crystal; she regressed and clung, desperately reeling off a long list of mysterious symptoms. She didn't want to jinx her rapport with Wald by mentioning any other specific woman. She found herself terribly attracted to Wald.

In 1974, Pat Wald had never before had a patient who

followed her home, who burst in on her husband and flirted with him (as did the alter Serena), who threatened to kill herself if Pat was a few minutes late, who regularly regressed and lost bladder control, who sent expensive gifts, and who twisted even the tiniest expression of sympathy into an implied invitation for sex. Zoe did all these things once Crystal left to tend her father. Wald must have regretted her reparenting strategy, which was out of control.

"Zoe is a complex individual," starts Wald's later summary of treatment, which lists fifteen distinct severe problems, raging from chronic schizophrenic reaction through severe dependency and regression. "She wanted all the help she could get," notes Wald. "She'd call old therapists, kept several going simultaneously." She remarked on Zoe's "high intelligence, which creates resistance to therapy—suggesting more symptoms for her to acquire," and evaluated her as "essentially a good person—perhaps because she hasn't reached a maturity level where true sociopathic behavior would occur."

Wald tried her mightiest to shift Zoe to the exclusive care of Dr. Small. She scrawled missives on Zoe's bills— "You need to see only one doctor." "Dr. Small is a very fine practitioner."

Zoe could not cope with this. In March 1974, she regressed completely.

■

**ZOE (the Tunnel of Patients):** *I wanted to kill myself.*

*When I would talk, Dr. Small would keep saying, "Put the baby to bed and then, grown-up, talk to me." But I couldn't.*

*When I'd lost a quarter of my body weight, Dr. Small and I discussed hospitalization in the disturbed ward.*

*I told my father. He looked at me with pain. I knew he was so ashamed of me for needing seclusion, for being in such a state of error.*

*The next day I set out for what we all called "It."*

■

That day Bryant drove Zoe, as usual, up the lane to the white mansion. But this time, Zoe was greeted by Dr.

Small and two orderlies wheeling a chair from which dangled restraints.

■

**ZOE (the Tunnel of Patients):** *I had developed, said Dr. Small, "a runaway heart." My heart was beating two hundred times per minute.*

*Dr. Small took me from my father and pushed me through the rain toward It. Babies were dying all around, screaming, coming at me in a crowd.*

■

**MOTHER ZOE (the Tunnel of Light):** *As we moved through the darkness, a beautiful golden man parted the crowd of dying children. "I am Mark," he said. He pointed at the building, with supplicants moaning at its root. "Those are the remains of the living dead thrown down from the eighth floor, which is about to become your home."*

*"Who are they?" I whispered, so Dr. Small wouldn't hear.*

*"They were once called people," said Mark. "Be careful, very careful, when they take you there."*

*I felt myself bursting into flames. I lifted my hands, pleading in desperation, "Help me!"*

*"I can't help you here," said Mark, "only in my world."*

*"Take me!"*

*Mark snatched me out of the wheelchair and carried me away. Flew with me to the Golden Beach World. There I spent the next few days.*

■

Some alters stayed to see what would happen.

■

**ZOE (the Tunnel of Patients):** *A black woman dressed in white opened the door. Small wheeled me in, both of us dripping rain. The walls hung at strange angles. The air was saturated with flowers, cloying as carrion. I heard someone scream. Was it me? Suddenly I was standing next to a nurse in an elevator. We shot up to the eighth floor, the death chamber.*

*The nurse led me to a room that contained only a mattress. I stood frozen as she stripped me, threw a gown over my head,* and left, locking the door. I sank to the mattress on the floor and wept.

A key clicked and a man walked in. He snapped rubber fingers in front of my face and weird rainbow colors seemed to flash from them. I screamed silently for help. "She's not with it," someone said.

He turned me over and held me down as a nurse injected a stream of fire into my bare rear end. Then the man turned me on my back and strapped me to the mattress. My heart raced out of control and I died.

I awakened the next morning. A nurse was standing by the mattress. "You'll feel better today after the Thorazine injection last night."

I looked at her in alarm. "I'm not supposed to take any phenothiazines."

She was amused by my vocabulary. "I have to give you another overdose to keep you quiet."

I got up, pushed past her, and staggered out into the hall, where I fell to the floor screaming for help.

Two nurses raced over and carried me back. They thought I was delusional from schizophrenia. They gave me the second shot, and I lay there, my heart beating wildly as I waited for death. While I waited I got angry. I had not been violent. I had attacked no one. No one had even thought to check my story against my medical records. This place was supposed to help you, not act like the abusers you were trying to escape.

When the nurses unlocked the room hours later, they found little Zoe hiding under the mattress. They pulled her out and discovered she had urinated all over herself, the mattress, and the floor. They took her to the examining room and washed her. Zoe came out and explained she was frightened of the phenothiazines. Her doctor had said it caused a severe circulatory reaction, and wouldn't they just check her records? They said, "Leave the medicine to us. We give this to all patients on seventy-two-hour hold."

"I want to call my father."

"Seventy-two-hour-hold patients may not use the phone."

Then they gave her another injection.

Next day my heartbeat was even faster. I had difficulty breathing. The medication affected my muscles. My tongue was stiff, my eyes wouldn't close, my face was contorted. In the *mirror I saw an ugly stranger. As I lay on the mattress, my arms and neck jerked constantly. I felt I was being murdered, not helped to recover my wits. They threatened to put a tube down her nose and throat to feed her.*

■

Zoe's bad experience must have been worse because of her memory of Grandfather Adams's torticollis neck. In her experience, after one's arms and neck jerked uncontrollably, one would lose mental function and ultimately die.

After seventy-two hours, Dave and Zoe May Bryant came to visit. They stared at the matted, contorted figure on the mattress and then, shocked, at each other. Bryant yelled at the nurses, "What have you done to my daughter?"

"Nothing. She's just been given the regular dose of Thorazine."

"Good God," thundered Bryant. "Didn't you check her records?"

■

**ZOE (the Tunnel of Patients):** *They listened to Mr. Bryant, if not to his crazy daughter. The medication was stopped.*

*I had not bathed nor showered in a week. I had lost control of my bowels. My father marched downstairs and insisted that I be released. The head doctor agreed—if I was conscious enough to sign my name to a required waiver.*

*A nurse dressed me and combed my filthy hair as my mother sat, crying helplessly, and my father stood and waited. Somehow Donna must have come out and signed the paper.*

■

**LYDIA (the Tunnel of Power):** *The nurses stood there laughing, because her hands were shaking so from drugs. They were surprised when she signed.*

■

**ZOE II (the Tunnel of Patients):** *I went home and held Davey and ate some food that my mother cooked me. And in a week,* *when I felt more human, I returned to the rational side of the hospital—the day clinic.*

She did not, however, return to Wald.

The May missive on Zoe's bill ran, "Dr. Small and I have talked, and as you must know the conclusion is that it is best you work with ONE therapist at a time. After all, this is what you paid me for, to have YOUR interest at heart."

The June missive ran, "Payment overdue. If no payment is received soon, I will proceed as if you intend not to pay."

In July 1974, Crystal returned from Louisiana. Her father had died, and she was in deep mourning. More in love than ever—and with no Wald to take the heat—Zoe went to Crystal's house as often as she could, to nurse her back to health.

**MOTHER ZOE (the Tunnel of Light):** *I felt a male presence, yearning, whom I later found out was Martin Caine. He enjoyed nursing Crystal.*

*For the first time I began to dress in men's clothes. Martin was so male! I cut my hair short and gave up makeup.*

*Martin was the perfect gentleman. He, unlike the men in my family, would never hurt a woman. Martin was in command. He persuaded Crystal to move to a ground-floor apartment only a few blocks away from Zoe's. Then he could visit whenever he wished and bring his lady love one red rose.*

**MARTIN CAINE (the Tunnel of Observers, Guides, and Past Life):** *S'far as manners in this twentieth century go, I find them appalling. They don't know how to treat a woman. I courted Crystal in the old-fashioned way. I brought her flowers every evening, and we'd eat dinner by candlelight.*

*I hated the body I was trapped in. But I felt she could see through this shell and remember me in our last lifetime.*

**MOTHER ZOE (the Tunnel of Light):** *What happened next was beyond bizarre. Why Carmine went along with it, I shall never know.*

For two years I'd lived as Zoe with Carmine and Davey. Now Martin wanted time with Crystal, time he could not get in a small apartment with the Parrys. Martin bought Crystal a small gold ring set with a tiny chip of diamond, and I asked her to marry me.

Crystal couldn't believe this. "I've been a heterosexual all my life!"

Martin bit his lip. "Age is only a state of mind," he said. "And so is gender." Then Crystal flung herself into our arms.

■

Once home, Zoe told Carmine she was moving out.

He sat back stunned. "Why? We're happy here!"

That night, as Zoe and Crystal lay together in Crystal's bed at the new apartment, outside, Carmine pounded on the doors and shook the windows. "You bitch! I don't care what you do to me, but you're hurting Davey."

Though Zoe didn't respond to him, in Crystal's arms, she started to cry.

■

**MOTHER ZOE (the Tunnel of Light):** *Crystal and I held tightly to one another, and Martin held on to us all.*

■

Once she and Crystal were living together, Zoe seemed to concede her other battles. She accepted parting from Wald and doing therapy with Small. Wald must have been grateful for the reprieve. In July, on Zoe's bill, Wald wrote:

Thank you for your last two cards. They were very pleasant to receive. . . . My thoughts and wishes will always be with you as a therapist—and no, not as a personal friend. I thoroughly believe Dr. Small is more qualified. I want you to dedicate yourself to working with him. . . . One can't have two therapists and have any therapy. Dr. Small and I both learned this the hard way with you. For heaven's sake, grow and be independent! Live to the hilt! Dr. Small will help show you how!

Zoe took her mentor's advice. She "lived to the hilt." Zoe May recollects this with horror and nostalgia.

"Your father never did go in for lesbianism, Zoe. He resented Crystal, and I did, too. As time went on, though, and she was around—he wasn't exactly fond of her, but he was always nice to her. Nicer than he was to Carmine.

"I myself couldn't help but like Crystal, because she was your dear friend. To me she became like one of the family. . . . She was from the South, and southerners are friendly people! There were some strange things, though. One time they rigged up something that looked like someone taking it out on them for spite. They broke windows in their own home!

"They also both sort of talked about witchcraft, which I thought was ridiculous. One time they told me about some ceremony, but I certainly wouldn't get involved in anything like that!"

Zoe says softly that she indeed involved her mother in witchcraft—without her knowledge.

"I can't recall it at all! Oh, when Crystal and a lot of women stood around? Those were witches?"

Zoe says that indeed they were.

"I didn't know. I tried to block it out of my mind. That and the Catholicism. But if I had my preference, I certainly would prefer the Catholicism."

Crystal and Zoe married on November 8, 1974. Apparently neither felt that Carmine was any impediment, as they were soul mates. A heavy-set female priest performed the ceremony, in one of the new gay churches. Zoe May sat in front, in a blue silk dress; Dave Bryant did not attend.

■

**MOTHER ZOE (the Tunnel of Light):** *As Martin, I wore navy blue slacks, a white shirt, a blue blazer, and shiny boots. I had bought a flowing light green silk dress for Crystal.*

■

Carmine was angry about the marriage and devastated by it. Still, in only a few weeks the trio had worked out a novel arrangement.

■

**MOTHER ZOE (the Tunnel of Light):** *You see, Carmine kept on coming around at night. He'd say, ''Your son needs you,'' and beg me to return. I talked it over, and Crystal said she'd be happy to move in with us. She and Mr. Parry had a long talk. They settled that she would help Mr. Parry pay half the rent.*

*It was like there were two separate married couples in our apartment. Occasionally I stayed with Carmine. We'd all agreed that he and I should sometimes be together.*

*Crystal got along with everybody. She was very kind to Davey. Mr. Parry and she would play cards while I cooked. Sometimes she would share kitchen chores. In the evening we'd watch TV, and Crystal helped Davey with homework. He had asthma; Crystal would sit up all night and rub him with Vicks. She insisted. She wanted to help.*

■

Now both ménages were complete: the Bryants, from November 1974 until June 1975, stayed in one half of the duplex, and the Parry-McGuire triangle in the other. Davey shuffled in between.

Davey says Crystal was "all right, I guess." He's a man of few words. Though he doesn't volunteer details, he says that Crystal and Zoe raised him together and brought him to voodoo ceremonies.

Wicca, the witchcraft they were involved in, is a form of nature worship—paganism based in early European forms. *Candomblé* is quite different, based in African and Catholic forms. A stern Catholic might label both "satanic." Zoe considers herself a stern Catholic.

Davey was very curious. "When I was young," he says, "I opened up Crystal's drawers and saw pot and naked pictures of her and my mother. Not together, but separately."

What did he think of the relationship?

"It didn't bother me that Crystal was there. I just thought she needed a place to stay. When she'd yell at me, I didn't think she had the right, so I didn't pay attention."

Zoe interjects, "Crystal loved you, Davey."

"Yeah? She had a thing for my mom."

"Did you love your mom?" asks Zoe, faintly.

Davey snorts. "I love everybody." It hangs there.

Yes, Crystal fit right in. Despite Zoe May's evaluation, Dave Bryant seemed to get along famously with Crystal, as he did with most southern ladies. They talked by the hour about southern food and southern manners. Zoe assembled albums full of photos of Crystal and the Bryants and Davey and herself with their arms around one another.

▪

**MOTHER ZOE (the Tunnel of Light):** *Now Crystal and I were together, we were happy. But after half a year, Serena started to come out.*

▪

And not only Serena. According to Zoe, the alters Eleanora and Eleanor ran a stable of half a dozen prostitute alters—the main ones being Chandra and Connie. Younger tough alters, often male, hung around the ones they called "the girls," to make sure that their abasement didn't go too far. It's impossible to know what happened in what combination of voodoo, witchcraft, Catholicism, sex, and candomblé. The alters who remember these months are still not speaking about their experiences. But nights certainly brought sex with strangers, occasional thievery, and unique rituals. They certainly included attempts to control and appease nature by hooking into unseen, unperceived, and often malevolent power.

▪

**WILLIAM GEORGE BROWN (the Tunnel of Observers, Guides, and Past Life):** *Serena not the only one out in 1975. My name be Willie. I died young—a white man broke my neck.*

*Somehow I come back. I still be ten. I learned some modern ways. I ain't got no folks and I don't want any. I use to smoke and drink wine with Serena. I use to steal stuff, records and little stuff. I hung out with Eleanora and Chandra, too. Sometimes I have to suck off some dude in the backseat of a car. . . . The womens inside get in some real stupid fucking messes.*

**SISTER ZOE ANN (the Tunnel of Power):** *These people were in the business of prostitution, I feel, because Zoe already felt so dirty.*

**ELEANORA BROWN (the Tunnel of Light):** *I was Chandra's pimp. We had some pretty good times. They called me the Shady Lady. Chandra wasn't bad neither. Course, nobody knew how to do it like me—at a young age I learn how to please men and women, too—but I try to teach her what I know, and that was plenty.*

**CHANDRA (the Tunnel of Limbo):** *I was easily led by some stronger folks that live inside. I didn't always want to do what they said, but I did. I am ashamed. I got myself involve in voodoo. The priestess she say it be white witchcraft, but she lie. It be hard to get yourself out of that mess. But eventually I did.*

*I like the Baptist church, and I listen to a lot of nice religious programs on the TV.*

*I have light brown skin and hazel eyes. I have white blood in me. I am tall and thin, and wear a natural.*

Zoe, as usual, dissociated all these activities.

**MOTHER ZOE (the Tunnel of Light):** *I'd walk in the house at two A.M. with no awareness of where I'd been. Crystal would seem so hurt.*

*Davey's phobia for school also got worse at this time. He was nine and had already seen as many psychologists as I had.*

*His school was terrible, and there were bad elements in the neighborhood. We all decided we should move.*

■

The ménage moved to a large, old house on a cul-de-sac in a better neighborhood—Gardenia Circle. Both Zoe and Crystal loved the large garden behind the house.

Now Davey went to St. Vincent's School on Oblicuo, right next to a Catholic church. He was taught by the nuns whom Zoe so loved. Dave Bryant would drive all the way to Huerta Vista twice each day: to pick Davey up each morning, and to get him back home each afternoon.

Zoe does not remember Davey's childhood. One day, she says, he was small, and the next, he was thirteen.

Apparently she sometimes knocked Davey around. These are the memories Zoe is most reluctant to admit.

■

**DENNIS (the Tunnel of Protectors):** *Her son bashed me on the head one time, with a vase. I took a phone and hit him on the head. I also slapped the kid when he wouldn't eat.*

*It doesn't make any difference, man, does it, if I'm proud of what I did or not! 'Ey, man, I was hit in the face a lot. I felt the blows to my body, too.*

*You girls (He shouts at child alters in the system.)—you think you felt all the pain, with your little vaginas! Well, I have a dick, and it was almost pulled off by that asshole John Perret. So I'm fucking angry. Nobody's gonna pull that shit on me again!*

■

The alter Cynthia participated in Dennis's rage. After the vase hit, Cynthia also turned on Davey and bashed him with the phone. Perhaps the two alters struck the blow together; perhaps they hit Davey more than once. Cynthia says, "Zoe woke, wondered what happened, and rushed him to the emergency room."

As Crystal and Zoe became more involved in witchcraft, their mental illness became worse. They amplified each other, each eliciting the most primitive parts of the other's personality. As they soothed each other's intense needs, they felt the sexualized pain as deep, divine relief rooted in past lifetimes and in the goddess. The womb is the mother of life; mother and child have the primary bond—they both tapped into and twisted that bond. The cycle became self-perpetuating; ever more pain and sex became necessary to bring relief from worse actions.

Since late spring of 1974, Zoe had visited Dr. Small twice a week. "He was totally against Crystal, though," she recollects, "and so I told him even less than usual." He continually warned Zoe that she and Crystal were doing each other no good. It was true, but unpalatable. According to Zoe, Small also threatened that when she got worse, which was inevitable, and had to go back into the hospital, he was out of her life. Forever.

Zoe once again shopped for doctors. Whenever she was stressed or threatened, her body automatically created a new physical illness. Each new doctor would see each illness as a separate medicable entity; Zoe's alters never gave any one doctor the entire picture. To the alters, it was the doctors' fault, not theirs: who would want to waste time filling in those of shallow understanding?

One of the shallowest, Zoe felt, was Dr. Small. She says that he'd threatened to drop her if she had to go to the psych ward as a result of her relationship with Crystal. So she went hunting for more congenial, preferably female therapists. At a retreat Zoe attended, one of the psychiatrists, Magda Hoff, had given a workshop called "Divine Intuitions." Zoe had felt a special bond with her. Hoff practiced in Huerta Vista. This seemed to bode success: Zoe set up an appointment with Dr. Hoff—just before Christmas 1975.

■

**MOTHER ZOE (the Tunnel of Patients):** *I loved Dr. Hoff! She was so spiritual. She was about forty, with brown eyes and hair.*

*At the retreat we'd spoken about my converting formally to Catholicism; she'd been enthusiastic. She was even considering being my godmother—I'd asked her.*

Huerta Vista was quite far from Zoe's old duplex. She could no longer pop over to her mother's house and bed when things got bad. Within two weeks, she went ballistic. In the ranch house on Gardenia Circle, Carmine and Crystal and Davey were as tense, as miserable, as she. They fought, particularly about money. Carmine would yell it was Zoe's fault they couldn't afford a proper home. Why couldn't she go out like a human being and get a job? She would scream and go into a panic attack. The fights became so fierce, the neighbors soon began to comment.

Zoe decided to check herself into the hospital. She did, just for two weeks, under Dr. Hoff's care. As he'd promised, Small promptly dropped her. "I felt bad," she says, "but later I began to wonder if he wrote me off just because his therapy was failing."

She congratulated herself on finding Hoff, a Catholic therapist who understood her. She started conversion instruction at St. Ann's.

**ZOE II (the Tunnel of Patients):** *But I sensed something brewing, deep down under. I tried to push it back. Apparently Serena was coming out more and more often. And so was Selina.*

In a photograph from Spring 1976, Zoe-Selina wears a black wig. Her skin is dark. In a turquoise ankle-length dress, she sits in her grandmother's rocking chair, petting a huge auburn hunting dog. Zoe is still amnesiac about the dress, about the dark skin, about much of Selina.

"I would wake up with my skin colored brown from a darkener and with my hair curled tightly. I kept finding wigs. I would find weird journals, in code. I was afraid to touch these things, because I kept glimpsing people and hearing voices. Sometimes they seemed to be inside; other times, I would see them in the mirror or on the street."

There was a reason for Selina's growing strength. Huerta Vista boasted not only a fine Catholic community, but also a fine *candomblé* community. On the outskirts of town lived a woman who billed herself as a spiritual healer.

Isis Bergeron was an occultist of some renown. She lived and worked on the whole third floor of a 1930s commercial building at the end of Cieno. Isis was not one to live on the beaten track, nor was she one to stray too far from potential customers.

Today, Zoe's system is still so frightened of Isis Bergeron that the alters will scarcely speak about her.

■

**SELINA (the Tunnel of Observers, Guides, and Past Life):** *Tonight my spirit animal is with me. Protecting. You ask about a woman who seem to be of light consciousness. How I meet this woman.*

*Zoe is told by friend there was a good psychic to go to—maybe it would help her problems. So Zoe and Crystal travel to a place on the edge of the city. Zoe nervous and shy, with Crystal by her side.*

*Isis is tall. Strong, with hair descending in waves to her knees. Pale. Her eyes are black as night. She is old. This woman spend eight hours reading Zoe's soul. She find me, and I find her.*

*She tell Zoe, ''There has been a curse put on you. If you do not get rid of that woman Crystal, then you will die.'' She say she was in white witchcraft. ''Good magic!'' Even ''Christian magic!'' But when I read into her thoughts, this is not what I see.*

*She wanted Zoe to come back, so she could perform a special ceremony to rid her of the curse. One summer evening, they went.*

*Zoe climb the steep steps. I was there with her, ready to strike—if I have to.*

*Isis have Zoe take her clothes off. She put big white sheet behind her. She light candles, black and white, she read aura. Lots of gray around Zoe. Yes, that is the color of her sickness.*

*Zoe, she go easily into trance. It is natural for her, as it is for me.*

*Every day for two weeks, Zoe go there and take her clothes off. Isis read the colors and talk to her.*

*She saw innocent person, sitting there, Christian, vulnerable. (Bitterly.) That is how I got them, many lifetimes ago. With tricks. You come in easy. Make good promises. And your prey is unaware you want their soul.*

Of this time, Zoe remembers only, "Finally I possessed the courage to defy my father. I carried through my conversion to Catholicism." But even here, there were difficulties.

**CYNTHIA (the Tunnel of Observers, Guides, and Past Life):** *April 1977, she was to be baptized at St. Vincent's. But letters suddenly appear at the rectory, written in a strange hand, alluding to strange things. The priest had second thoughts and told her to go into further training.*

That day when Zoe arrived, the priest did not bless her. Instead, he handed her a letter. "Is this yours?"

Zoe read it. "It was about black witchcraft, about spells. The Father was very curious and very concerned."

The letters were from Isis and from the alter Selina.

**CYNTHIA (the Tunnel of Observers, Guides, and Past Life):** *Zoe Ann did not understand. She knew nothing about me, about Selina or Isis. She was innocent, taking her instructions. It made me so sad, because once I too felt innocent . . . before this curse was laid on me, long ago.*

*Torture and isolation, such loneliness as no one will understand.*

*Zoe Ann had to go to another church. There she was baptized on April 15, 1977. Totally oblivious.*

"In my twenty-ninth year," says Zoe, "I became a Catholic. I felt cleansed. Except for moments of demonic possession.

"It was terrible. At those moments I would wake up with blood on my face, my arms, on my abdomen. Over the C-section. I was horrified. The wound refused to heal."

In May 1977, the Bryants gave up their half of the duplex and followed Zoe to a house five blocks away from Gardenia Circle.

"Father stepped up his fight with Carmine. He wanted to totally control his grandson and said, as Carmine didn't take care of Davey properly, he had no right to be his father." Which made Zoe and Dave Bryant the two parents. Zoe said she was glad the Bryants had moved so close by.

She kept on going to Isis every two weeks and found herself losing huge chunks of time.

■

**CYNTHIA (the Tunnel of Observers, Guides, and Past Life):** *In another lifetime I had been a witch.*

*I was three when my grandmother adopted me in that lifetime. The grandmother had me helping in the ritual, killing animals, preparing the raw flesh for the mysteries.*

*I was forty-eight when they burned me. I was trying to help people. The doctor in the village started rumors, saying I was Satan's child. The people came to my cottage and dragged me out. I was screaming. They dug their fingernails into my flesh, ripping my skin to pieces. I was tied to the stake. My hands and feet were bound, and the flames consumed me. I shouted that I would get even. My soul was filled with rage.*

*In this life I met Isis Bergeron. A part of me had not grown out of evil. Selina and I performed rituals. We were too powerful, it seems. Isis threatened that she was going to take us over body and mind.*

■

**SELINA (the Tunnel of Power):** *That September Zoe go to Isis to be cleansed.*

*I denounce Satan right now, with my power animal behind*

*me. Satan's followers are always ready, watching. I tell young people, beware! Do not play with losing your soul!*

*A weakness came over me. A cold, damp evil filled the air, and I was tempted. I joined forces with this woman. Because in past life this was my strong belief. I thought I had conquered it, but I had not!*

*It is the middle of September now. Zoe is pushed back into the Land of Dreams. And out of the Land of Dreams I come, more powerful now, wanting my power back. Isis and I perform many rituals now, rituals I will not speak of.*

*We talk about past lives. She tell me I was her daughter, and that I believe is true. We both came through with respiratory problems, to pay off karma from Egyptian lifetime. And we practiced black magic.*

■

Isis deliberately encouraged Zoe's fragmentation. She split Zoe off from Crystal and from many parts of herself.

Zoe's darkest alters—Selina, Serena, Cynthia, Chandra, Eleanora, the priestess Oya, and the Demon—trained thoroughly with Isis. They say the senior witch had searched for years for an apprentice. She wanted Zoe as a channel for her own power.

Isis demanded total control. She psychometrized (charged) Zoe's jewelry, theoretically to take off Crystal's curse. Now every time Zoe put on a religious symbol, she remembered one woman only—Isis. She had her apprentice assist at ceremonies that Zoe says she doesn't remember. However, the alter Selina says this is when she began to fight back.

The split engendered by Isis was still present in Zoe's system. Gwynn Fischer's notes of November 1990 mention Zoe's continuing upset about the kidnapping—an event that sprang from her involvement with Isis—even as she sent a Christmas card to Crystal McGuire. Fischer's notes of May 30, 1991, state that Zoe simply can't understand her involvement with a Satanic cult. Our tape of March 21, 1992, amply demonstrates the terror that Zoe still feels:

■

**The DEMON (the Tunnel of Observers from Darkness):** *I ran that cult, using Zoe's body. I entered it when she was a baby! It was a little tender innocent I wanted, that I want. . . . I possess that body! I am in control! It is ME you have to deal with!*

■

On the tape, the child alters come out screaming, one by one. A thin, asthmatic voice wails, "Oh, dear God, please make the devils go away!"

While Isis further hypnotized Zoe, encouraged her priestess alter to grow in power, and named her Oya, Selina decided to fight fire with fire. She performed rituals aimed at draining Isis. She speaks about cracking a dozen eggs in a perfect circle, so that they'd be there quivering, white and yellow, the next time Isis came outside. Why she did this, she does not say.

Other alters remember feeling murderous. They were too frightened of Isis, though, to try to physically harm her.

Tragically, the one who remembers the most about actions against Isis is Davey.

"Zoe and Crystal took me to somebody's house. They put rocks and papers around. They spray-painted a window, and they wanted me to throw a brick through Isis's window. I was eleven. I wouldn't throw the brick. My mom was driving—she was real anxious that night.

"I didn't know about MPD. I just thought they were trying to get back at somebody. No, I wasn't scared. I just thought it was weird.

"Another night, Crystal and me, we were waiting; the mother went out of the car. There she was, in Isis's garage, squatting and ice-picking all the tires. I thought she was playing a joke. I guess I was off in my own little world."

Zoe feels worse about her relationship with Davey than about almost any other development. She was completely dissociated and incapable of acting like the same person in any two consecutive moments. Her primitive anger erupted. In a dark mood, she even threatened neighborhood children.

Gwynn Fischer's 1988 note reads, "One time she observed Davey being teased by two girls. She went out and told one girl to come into her house. There she switched to Selina, shook the girl, and started choking her. 'Something popped out' and told the child to go. She and all the little ones were afraid the police would put her in jail. The neighbors talked the police out of doing that."

It's a mystery how Carmine avoided seeing this. True, he had a night job. The only thing he seemed to notice was the vast amount of cash leaving the house.

Carmine felt squeezed. Davey still saw a psychiatrist two times a week, and Zoe, three; Zoe's care had mounted to a debt of thousands of dollars.

Finally Zoe agreed to Carmine's demand that she go job-hunting. But she felt angry. Why must Carmine abuse her so, when she was under so much stress? Besides, what kind of job could she get? She had no credentials. She didn't even have a high school diploma.

Zoe scanned the ads daily, especially those in the Christian Science newsletter, and there she found the job with the Kings.

Crystal was very disturbed that Zoe had dared take this job. So was Isis. Both Isis and she focused through Zoe's weaknesses.

The job was too much. Lillian wanted more and more, perhaps feeling that if Zoe was busy she would not be ill. Zoe minded the kids and the home, and Lillian would send her out to get face cream. At night Lillian would closely inspect every surface, the floor, the counters. Zoe felt that her anger at this was her problem—she must work even harder to please Lillian King.

Zoe asked Lillian to allow her so-called aunt (Crystal) to accompany her. Two for the price of one. Lillian dubiously agreed. But even this did not alleviate Crystal's jealousy. She decided Zoe and Lillian must be having an affair.

Zoe was so fatigued that she was hardly ever out these days. Zoe and Crystal were now raising Chihuahuas, and some alters apparently trained the dogs to lap at parts of the human body. When she was out, Zoe tried to retrain the dogs—to sit, to lie down, to fetch. She could not understand their dirty behavior.

Apparently, now Isis completed training her apprentice Oya. The pair had become entwined, body and soul.

▪

**SELINA (the Tunnel of Power):** *She make love to me. Something that was so special. Ceremony end in much sex. I make love to many in the coven. But Isis say I was hers. She wanted me never to make love with any other. And I agreed.*

*This was the only woman I had loved in this lifetime.*

*We still do not understand what went on that night. I was vulnerable, sitting in car and driving, with headlights sweeping past. It felt like someone entered my body. I lost conscious awareness of myself as Selina.*

*Now, Brazilian voodooism is natural to me. Like Catholicism turned upside-down. But that night what happen do not feel natural.*

*I meet Isis Bergeron at a certain church. There I sign Zoe's name to paper. Go through ceremony of marriage. Then we come home and have ceremony at the home.*

▪

The photograph, says Zoe, shows Oya in a white gown and golden wig, looking haunted, standing next to a kind-looking, motherly-looking woman in a gray suit and navy shirt. A statuette of the Virgin Mary, a huge, lit white candle, and a soothing picture of ocean waves at sunset complete the deceptively peaceful scene.

▪

**SELINA (the Tunnel of Power):** *I was out of my mind to go with this woman. Now I see. Then I no see. She was cruel woman. Still, I stay.*

*Two days later I felt a force inside my body telling me no, this not right for me. So I dissolve the marriage.*

▪

"If you leave," threatened Isis, "I warn you—your life will drip away little by little, in torture."

The alter Selina laughed in Isis's face, and left. And that night, the alter Oya called Bergeron's coven and urged its members to flee. Five did. With these, Zoe formed a new coven.

The Temple of the St. Marys seems to have been even more extreme than was Isis's coven in its heyday. The priestess Oya presided, with Crystal as her helper. With the defectors, plus some friends of Zoe's from Richfield days, she had everyone she needed—except for a high priest. This man would symbolize both male energy and Satan.

Zoe shudders at the man Oya chose. But the choice makes sense, given the yawning gulf of Zoe's self-hatred.

■

**SELINA (the Tunnel of Power):** *We took Henry Owens. The psych technician from Richfield. The one who had forced Zoe into sex.*

*We had been seeing him on and off since 1971. And we were to see him all the way through 1978. The poor little ones, what they have to experience with him!*

*You see, Henry Owens became high priest. And he brought two of his friends with him.*

*There were twelve of us. And on major holidays, many covens would get together.*

*Today I am sorry. Today I have awareness of children. Then I no have awareness. They see much sex, the small children. And I feel so bad about this. Because then they experience again what they felt with John Perret and the father and the grandfather.*

*What they experienced? Henry Owens would get down on all fours like dog.*

*His personality—not the color of his skin—represent evil. He would have sex with each member of coven. First with high priestess. Then other members. Sometimes there would be brother and sister of the same blood, in a frenzy.*

*And after orgy—sometimes before—he have one lady spread his bottom open. And we kiss his anus one by one. This is what you do with Devil. I felt so degraded. But it was my custom to give reverence in this way.*

*Yes, I am very primitive!*

*But I am sorry, very sorry—because of the children.*

■

For years Zoe was unable to speak about her demonic
alters. They'd pop out in Gwynn Fischer's office and
stare malevolently at her. Fischer evaluated Zoe's paranormal sensations as sick superstitions. "Highly hypnotizable people," she said in a 1987 interview, "sometimes
believe they have special paranormal talent. Zoe's so-
called possessions, I believe, are what someone with this
psychology would do with naughty impulses. As far as
getting better goes, I don't think it's going to help her to
believe there's a demon inhabiting her. It will help her
more to know her own bad impulses. She must learn to
use her strength, not to fight against it.

"There was nothing in her life to push her to act
more normal, so these other impulses ran away with the
ball game."

Christmas 1977 was coming, and with it, not just
depression. Crystal was in a manic phase, in which
everything seems possible and exciting. This time she
would drag her suggestible friend with her.

Zoe was drowning in fear of Isis.

■

**SELINA (the Tunnel of Power):** *I could not bow down to her.
That is what she wanted, and I could not. She put red candle
on till it melt. She put my name on paper. I was bound to her,
she thought, forever! She took a part of my soul!*

*After breakup of the soul union, there was a vicious fight.*

*Isis called Satan forth in the circle, and he came. Our eyes
met. His are piercing black. His face chalk white. He has
demons all around him. Ready to enter innocent people. The
demon voices possessed us and walked in our bodies.*

*But then I feel Cynthia. I see piercing green eyes, in mirror,
looking at me, looking at Isis, wanting to kill. Isis look back,
and she see Cynthia about to leap!*

*Isis grab me by the throat. She grab me by the hair. She try
to gouge my eyes out. She pull my lip. She grab my breasts,
until they bleed. She was very strong! But I have more powerful
mind. Cynthia, she enraged! She pick up statue and try to
throw it at mirror. Break the glass. Free herself. But Isis prevent
her. And suddenly she find herself outside.*

Zoe felt herself disappearing. The demons had accompanied her out of Isis's circle, into her life. A rasping voice (the Demon) issued orders to Crystal and pushed her, Zoe, down into a red and black pit. Crystal spoke directly to the voice and ignored Zoe.

**MOTHER ZOE (the Tunnel of Patients):** *One day just before Christmas I was in a session with Dr. Hoff. I took my place on the couch. Suddenly I was pushed to one side and flung deep into a mist-filled tunnel. The Blonde—Cynthia—came out. I could hear a little. Her voice was deep. She seemed to be in torment. She made animallike sounds, growls and roars.*

Zoe woke crying with Dr. Hoff crossing herself next to her. The therapist called her priest, and the next day they went together to Hoff's church to have prayers of deliverance said over Zoe. The priest sprinkled holy water on the trembling woman and told her to kneel and read certain psalms he'd marked. After, Zoe felt cleansed—but only for one afternoon.

It was becoming impossible to keep control, even at the Kings'. Once, she fed Jennifer and put her in front of the TV and then she went into the library to dust. Crystal was on the couch, reading *Martin Chuzzlewit*. The rasping voice said . . . Zoe doesn't remember.

The next day, Zoe signed herself into a hospital psychiatric ward for three weeks.

**CAROL SEEMORE (the Tunnel of Power):** *Zoe did not keep the hospitalization a secret. Lillian knew and even gave Zoe a mantra to use on the ward so she could sleep. Lillian adored Zoe and was determined to hold on to her no matter what.*

*Zoe thought it was strange for Lillian to want her back after she had confessed the job was too hard, that she was hearing voices. Perhaps Zoe was Lillian's crusade.*

*Zoe was angry that when Jennifer took her first steps, they were to her—not to Lillian, her mother. She truly felt that mothers should not leave their children.*

■

Crystal brought Zoe back in the middle of January. At this point Zoe was still frantic, still hearing voices. She phoned Lillian, her mother, and Hoff several times a day.

She took to hanging around Hoff's office. Once, when Hoff was at lunch, she broke in to look for notes about the failed deliverance from Satan. She slid open the windows, shimmied in, and pulled out her file. Few papers were inside, and those were uninformative. After looking through the papers, she put everything back, and left.

■

**MARTIN CAINE (the Tunnel of Observers, Guides, and Past Life):** *I begged her to leave witchcraft, but Crystal insisted it was healing all of us. She went into a frenzy. I held her down on the bed. . . .*

*And then Crystal was acting like she was in a faraway dream. I just couldn't reach her. And soon there happened something I'll never get over, ma'am.*

■

In the last week of January, they formed their plan. Later, in Zoe's closet the police would find marijuana, pieces of rope, and notes in code, which proved to them that the plan was premeditated.

Zoe would not remember this time until 1993. In 1986, when she moved into a new house and started long-term therapy with Dr. Fischer (she hadn't yet been diagnosed as a multiple) Zoe found Selina's and Mrs. Patterson's magic writings. Today, in 1993, she says, "I wish I'd known in 1986 I was going to meet these alters. I wouldn't have done what I did with those journals."

In terror at her discovery, Zoe shredded all the papers—perhaps a hundred small notebooks—and threw them away. The task took days.

It was February. Zoe was about to steal Jennifer King. But she would wait until Virginie's birthday—February 3, 1978.

# Part Four

# JUDGMENT MORN

## Zoe Parry: Inner Structure

*May 1993*
*Discussing last therapy session with*
*Gwynn Fischer.*
*16 Personalities.*
*One tunnel going from left/up to right/down*
*in concentric circles.*

Woman with No
Name

Scream

Madness

Pain

Fear

Panic

Confusion

Tunnel of
Lost Souls

# 8

# One's a Crowd

In 1993, for the first time, Zoe used the word *I* to mean everyone inside her body. So how (in the seven years since diagnosis) did Zoe become one *I*? . . . Or did she?

Without *I*, we cannot function in society. Think of voting, making love, exercising, thinking, eating. We cannot delegate such acts. They are essential.

Until D day, the date of diagnosis, the weak surface Zoe simply suspended the idea of *I*. But being branded a multiple personality exploded her polite veneer of self. Now each alter was reminded of the empty *I* frozen at the core. Each newly felt his lacks, which to him meant he lacked all. Each discovered she was not everyone, which to her meant she was no one. Each touched, if only for a moment, central grief. Each rose from that depressing depth to a new feeling of being just a part and not the whole.

■

In March 1992, I had attended one of Zoe's sessions. I wanted to see why Zoe feared Fischer so, six years after D day.

Fischer is stunningly typical. The "witch" turns out to be fit, articulate, fifty—Susan Sontag via Jack La

Lanne. She smiles nicely, shakes hands swiftly, picks her words carefully.

Dressed to the nines, awkward, Zoe chose a buttery leather recliner. Listening to Fischer's soothing words, Zoe, trembling, shut her eyes. The cough-wheeze of an old air conditioner faded into the background.

Soon I heard and saw other alters. I could identify them by body language, voice, expression, and what they spoke about. But how they fit together as a whole, *if* they fit, was not obvious. Marie-Marie turned in her toes, clasped her hands, and sang hymns. Selina glared at Fischer and spat out a few demonstrative words in her thick accent. Mazie curled up, shrieking that Animal had materialized right there in the corner and was glaring at her with piercing green eyes. Animal seemed so real to her, I found myself looking. I saw a black shadow, but it belonged to a file cabinet, after all.

I had asked Zoe to remember the kidnapping. She showed me she was trying. Hard. I saw that alters used switching to deflect memory as well as to find it. I saw how the body's features shifted. Zoe's nose wrinkled when she became Mazie. Her color ebbed from pink to yellow. The shape of her jaw changed; so did her muscle tone and her breathing. If alters are roles, these were well-developed.

Still, there was something puppetlike about certain alters. Each time they'd launch a word balloon, and Fischer would sigh and go off into a well-oiled therapeutic routine.

After the session, though, I believed what I'd seen.

I've heard actors speak about the dangers of getting too much into a part—being unable to make sense of what they were doing or, ultimately, to leave. When the phone rang later that night and I picked it up, what took place on the other end, however you may define it, was nobody's plum role and was not voluntary. I said, "Hello," and was answered by breathing. Then a rusty voice spoke. "This—is—the—one—they—call—Animal," she began. "I—have—just—tried—to—speak—with—Doctor—Fischer." Her flat voice was jagged with hate—real, live, destructive, shattered, powerful, and forsaken.

This was the first time Cynthia (also known as Animal) had spoken, "as myself," in fifteen years. She told me, with some irony, that she thought this was a special occasion. But Fischer just refused her phone call. She'd called Fischer first. That's why Cynthia had chosen to call me.

For an hour Cynthia ranted, intimating dark and lonely secrets—an excruciating history of neglect and abuse, both in this lifetime and in lives long past. She threatened to kill Zoe, talked about a knife close-by, hung up, and, after five heart-stopping minutes, called again. Both she and I had used the time to call Sarah Freed.

"Let Fischer live with her dismissal," croaked Cynthia melodramatically. "She did not want to hear my voice tonight. So she never will." Appallingly hoarse, with screeches breaking through, she sounded completely out of control. But no, she was not out of control—she'd called Sarah Freed. Rather, she was walking the edge of control; in our conversation, she tipped over and fell. It was a heart-wrenching moment for all. That another alter then peeked up over the edge and symbolically waved at me shows a survival talent that many experts find obnoxious.

■

Fischer and Zoe spent their first year of therapy working on issues such as, could Zoe trust Fischer or any therapist? It was a good question, given Zoe's history with Altman and Wald. Later this question of trusting doctors became, for Zoe, the question of what was the worst thing she'd ever done. In turn, the question became (she didn't yet admit the Wald affair or the kidnapping), had one of her alters killed Altman with evil mind power?

Most of Zoe's alters assumed that yes, she had that power, that the Angel Child had hurled mental thunderbolts, forced the male alters to call Altman, generally driven the therapist crazy. Meanwhile, the world seemed to vindicate Zoe. On April 6, 1986, Zoe had received her settlement check from the estate of Dr. Altman.

Though Barry Bertrand says he was happy with the settlement—"After all, we could have lost!"—Zoe wilted. Even as some alters budgeted the money—it could pay for therapy and for a house—others mourned. The cash proved (as nothing else could) that the affair and Altman's death had actually happened and had consequences beyond the border of the Parrys' tiny world. Paradoxically, it also proved that punishment for Altman's death would have to be internal.

Zoe's extreme and varied reactions to the settlement may have catalyzed Fischer's diagnosis. Alters bubbled up from the tar pits, brooding, "I wish Sidney were alive so I could rip his head off." Perhaps it was the contrast of vengeful statements such as these, with Mother Zoe's helpless sobs—he'd stood by her; she'd betrayed him; she felt responsible for his death—that inspired Fischer.

Remembers Fischer, she had been very skeptical about MPD. The disorder was rare; it was sensational; it was dubious. Some of Fischer's colleagues had publicly debunked MPD as the fantasy of greedy therapists and overcompliant patients.

Fischer remembers diagnosis quite specifically, in terms of her own thinking. "Since hypnotherapists were reputed to create MPDs by encouraging patients (in hypnosis) to name and isolate different ego states, I continued evaluating her material for months before I decided I was seeing an MPD and not creating it. . . . Plus I thought if I said, 'You're a multiple personality,' then she'd have even more problems. So I waited and watched. . . . It became apparent that her dissociation was creating situations she truly wouldn't want. As I began to see that the splits were truly not to her advantage and her victimization wasn't going to prove anything, then it seemed clear she was a multiple personality, and I was comfortable with the diagnosis."

For their part, Zoe's alters remember this time as intensely confusing. They came out, many say, and babbled a few words or glared at Fischer a bit, only to find themselves pushed back by others, unable to speak, or, most galling of all, doubted by Fischer. Says the alter Serena, "Though we wanted to trust her, she kept putting us down, saying we were emotional states."

Zoe does not remember the actual date or circumstances surrounding diagnosis. Late in 1986, she did begin to sprinkle her journal entries with conscious references to alters, but these references are in different handwritings, and there is no evidence that any one alter registered the specific presence of any other. There is no one point at which Zoe's whole system said, "Yes, I'm a multiple personality," or even, "I agree for the first time that there are many of us sharing a body together."

Despite what Fischer says, Zoe was not comfortable with the diagnosis. "Gwynn thought I was acting," she whispers. "None of us is. MPD goes deeper than that. Disbelief and fear of us are devastating."

To a multiple personality, diagnosis is like a stone thrown into a pool: a splash, ripples, and as the stone sinks, the depths change forever. To Zoe the old unconscious switching had been upsetting, yes, but it was also familiar. The new semiconscious switching, the psychological work, absorbing the data about MPD, the threat of someday having to integrate, the shame of failure—these were unfamiliar, intimidating, and repulsive to Zoe's alters.

None of the alters specifically introduced themselves to Fischer. If they burst through the Patient's voice and demeanor, they tried to cover it up as soon as they recognized they'd compromised their separate selves. Donna immediately purchased every book and copied every article she could find on the subject of MPD, and Sister Zoe Ann remembers telling Fischer that she was wrong about the diagnosis—look how normal Zoe was acting. This normalcy soon passed. "I'm not even in therapy," Serena wrote in a letter the following week. "Zoe is so naive, to think she could be helped by a therapist."

Mother Zoe went into a blue funk, caught a cold, and took to her bed. While she whimpered, Donna got political. Says Donna, "Zoe's past had to have meaning. She couldn't just stay a victim."

Sex between psychotherapists and patients was in 1986 illegal in only four states. In Florida, a state senator now formed a task force to investigate the subject. The senator asked Dr. Wizniewski—the head of the clinic that sponsored Zoe's survivors' group—to chair.

Fischer, Wizniewski, and Dr. Tricia Chantal (Zoe's group leader) were colleagues, linked by a belief in patient activism. A patient might hasten recovery, they believed, by suing the abusive ex-therapist. Most members of Chantal's group were involved in such lawsuits.

Chantal told the group about the task force. Some patients, like Zoe, fell silent; others got excited. Two—Sonia Flavin and Andrea Moss—volunteered to testify.

Sonia, a gorgeous brunette dancer, had done bondage sex with her ex-therapist. Andrea, a childish redhead, had been drugged and raped by hers. Each had been in and out of psych wards; each had divorced. Andrea's three children had moved away with their father; their whereabouts were unknown.

Parts of Zoe envied Sonia and Andrea their courage, but felt she must not, could not, promise to testify. Most of the alters still dreaded the demons who they felt had frequently possessed Zoe without warning, forcing her into heinous crimes and promiscuous sex. All the alters initially rejected Fischer's theory that they'd arrived to defend the core self. Mother Zoe felt that even if she admitted having alters (a statement she wasn't willing to make), they would certainly be bad and would seize any available opportunity to take over and publicly ruin her.

She vehemently denied that she, too, was an alter.

When Chantal's group decided en masse to attend the hearings, Zoe was dismayed. But she voted yes anyway, so that she would not have to cast the only no vote.

On December 8, the patients assembled outside the imposing State Office Building. They included (besides Zoe) a lawyer, two housewives deep into local politics, two executives, and an entrepreneur—not the types we generally think of as natural victims.

Teetering in designer heels, supported at one elbow by Janet Moore, Zoe joined her fellow patients. Marching in, they were directed to a small auditorium, hot with lights. Zoe spotted the senator, made her way through the crowd, shook hands with her, and said assertively, "I'm so grateful for what you're doing."

The courage, temporarily and anonymously lent by Donna, faded; blushing, Zoe ran to her seat. "What possessed me," she stammered to Janet, "to go right up to a senator?"

Spotlights flicked on. Flashbulbs popped. The audience hushed. "In 1983," began the senator, "I introduced a bill criminalizing sexual involvement of psychotherapists and patients. . . . The measure was founded on some of the earliest research regarding the prevalence of this act and the great damage caused by it. . . ." The senator summarized twelve recent hours of public testimony. This day, she said, was for the victims.

Twenty ex-patients spoke: angrily, meekly, weepily. They'd all had affairs with their therapists and then, in trying to reveal the abuse, had been disbelieved, drugged, and jerked around. They'd lost families, businesses, and self-respect. Many had tried to kill themselves. Their stories were so powerful, the audience reaction so sympathetic, that even Zoe's meekest alters admit feeling angry at having been abused.

When the senator invited audience members to comment, Mother Zoe reports, a force seemed to carry her up through the crowd to the microphone, to make her blurt that she, too, had been abused—by both male and female therapists. This was the first time any alter had overtly admitted to having an affair with Pat Wald. She saw Janet gasp. Fear overwhelmed Mother Zoe; she blacked out.

At a break fifteen minutes later, the alter Donna found herself conscious and orating to a bunch of doctors. A dark, quick man in his thirties collared her and stuck out his hand. "Hi, I'm a producer," he said. "An acquaintance of Dr. Wizniewski's. My name is Bruce"—Donna faded—"Bruce Goldberg.

"Hey," he said. "This is an amazing story. You should tell it in public."

Zoe backed away. She agreed with activism, she said. But activism did not agree with her.

Shame ate at Zoe. She felt like a fraud, especially two days later when she received a thank-you letter. "I appreciate your courage," wrote the senator. "I realize how difficult it is to publicly discuss such intimate and personal experience. . . . Your effectiveness in the public eye will contribute significantly to any success this task force may achieve.'' By the time her eyes registered the words, "Sincerely yours," and scanned the signature, Zoe was no longer out. Donna was, vowing to keep going, despite the way "that wimp"—as she called Zoe—kept backing off.

The investigatory committee published its findings early in 1987. "Five to ten percent of Florida's 16,500 psychotherapists have had sex with their patients." That's 2,475 to 6,600 victims in one year in one state.

These findings did not comfort Zoe. What guarantee did she have that Gwynn Fischer was not one of the 1,650 annual abusers, no matter on how many ethics boards she sat? Besides, she felt (the shame hit Mother Zoe especially deeply) now the whole world knew every sordid detail about her and Altman. Everybody would throw it in her face. Many of the alters felt this, and their sense of a shadowy crowd, hanging its collective head under a barrage of public scorn, geometrically heightened their separate pain.

In 1990, Florida would illegalize psychotherapist-patient sex, but by then its incidence would grow—and reported cases are a tiny fraction of the true number.

Though it wasn't until 1993, after sitting tight for ten years, that Zoe attempted through the board to revoke Wald's license, in 1987 alter Donna sued Wald in civil court. She first broached the idea in a session. Fischer objected: "A lawsuit would inordinately stress you, Zoe.''

As the Patient nodded, Donna, within, looked at Fischer's strained face and concluded that there would be no support for her here. After the session she called Sarah Freed, and raged, "Fischer thinks I'm lying about Wald. I can tell she thinks I'm going to sue her too someday."

"Everybody's against me," continued Mother Zoe, sobbing, "even the Bertrands." They'd refused Zoe's second case; they thought there wasn't enough evidence against Pat Wald. The alters had amassed a huge file but kept most of it secret. Serena, especially, had mixed feelings about bringing the lawsuit. But on the strength of the few notes that Serena left on Zoe's bureau—the alters' common territory—Donna vowed to forge ahead. She telephoned all the members of Zoe's old support group and got a referral to another lawyer—a battle-scarred veteran named Francie Deakins.

Other alters made telephone calls, dozens of them, to every former therapist and current doctor.

Mazie vaguely remembers phoning Wald. Apparently, alters left (and still leave) hundreds of messages. "Why have you hurt me, Mommy?" "Come back, Mommy, I need you so much." And vengeful alters threaten Wald; how, Zoe does not say.

Consciously, the surface Zoe tried to forget Wald, to immerse herself in therapy. Unconsciously, she decided that Fischer was just like Wald. Someone should monitor her.

Zoe asked Sarah Freed and Fischer to call each other, to discuss her treatment, and they both agreed.

Freed called Fischer. They agreed on a chain of command. Zoe was Fischer's patient. Sarah would try to limit her advice to medication.

Fischer then did something that Zoe's child alters, especially, interpreted as a cosmically significant omen.

Zoe remembers coming out of hypnosis one day. Fischer smiled and held out to her patient a small hand-crocheted white afghan. "Here, I made this for you."

Zoe went blank. Then she felt the sun rise within her and pour light and trust through her dark universe. She felt the infant stirrings of her cramped and frozen soul.

"It looks little now," she remembers Fischer saying. "But it's going to grow and cover you all over, and make you safe." Zoe stammered her thanks and accepted the gift. She uses it to this day. The afghan, she saw as part of her promised new soul, with more—much more—to follow.

Fischer does not usually hand-crochet afghans for her patients. Zoe was Fischer's only case of MPD; the therapist was unusually uncertain and thus particularly methodical about treatment—particularly about maintaining the patient's wavering trust.

Apparently even to the therapist of wide experience,

one's first case of multiple personality is disconcerting. When the patient oversteps some boundary that had seemed rock-solid—and this will happen—the therapist may become overinvolved and angry. Gwynn Fischer was no exception.

It was an exciting time to be treating a multiple. The mid-eighties heralded the first conferences on MPD, the first journals, and dozens of new, dedicated experts. The number of cases boomed, as did the types and quantity of treatments.

But within Fischer's theoretical framework there were few precedents for successful treatment of someone like Zoe. "I found virtually no psychoanalytic writing on MPD. I was troubled, because I've found psychoanalytic approaches to be very helpful in understanding mental phenomena. A couple of analysts told me that MPDs 'weren't analyzable.' Later, though, some would say the opposite."

Fischer was by no means as dispassionate as her summary. Zoe's alters had argued vehemently amongst themselves in sessions. Now they broached Fischer's personal territory and began to quarrel there as well. Fischer's cool stance, which was based on keeping a certain distance, was undermined by an unfortunate incident that changed the balance of power in her and Zoe's relationship.

At a party celebrating the end of the task force, Zoe stood sipping punch with Sonia Flavin, when suddenly a deep voice called out her name. Turning, Zoe saw approaching Dr. Wizniewski's young producer friend, Bruce Goldberg.

"Interrupting?" he asked.

"Nope. Not really."

Sonia excused herself. After discussing Sonia and the support group, Bruce and Zoe chatted about therapist-patient sex. "Do you know that half the shrinks in our lovely state have a patient who's been a victim?"

"No."

"That's what my friend Bob says." Bruce shook his head. "He knows all about it. Plus Bob's wife works here, and she's written tons of articles about this stuff,"

Bruce said. "Maybe you've run into her? Gwynn Fischer."

Though Mother Zoe is certain she did not pump Goldberg for information and that she kept the encounter secret for the next six months, suddenly in session she hinted at some very juicy stuff, and other alters say that Bruce, ecstatic with inside knowledge and good wine, had (with their help) poured out everything he knew about the Fischers. These alters intimate that now whenever Fischer would probe too deep, they could forestall her by using this inside knowledge and throwing off her insights.

Matters came to a head six months later when Bob Fischer died suddenly. A week after the funeral, Gwynn Fischer returned to work. When Zoe expressed her condolences and Fischer deflected them by saying, "Let's talk about you," the alters dropped their bomb. Fischer sat silent as her patient poured out a hugely intimate set of condolences: consoled Fischer about financial woes Zoe couldn't possibly know about, commented on Fischer's political struggles in the therapeutic community, and rendered advice about Fischer's children. She even mentioned an intimate detail that Fischer knew she'd kept secret from everyone except Bob. All this was twisted and refracted through the lens of Zoe's strong unconscious desire that Fischer mother her . . . or else.

Fischer demands crystal-clear limits. She keeps her personal and professional lives quite separate. For six months she'd gotten odd glances from Zoe, intimating she knew not what. Now, after listening for fifteen very long minutes, Fischer responded quietly and fastidiously, "I'm sorry you had to carry the burden of this knowledge for so long."

A mild, soft voice with a strong southern accent replied with honeyed sympathy, "I'm the one who's sorry, because you've had such problems, sugar. Just like us." It was Chandra, an alter who sees herself as a former prostitute in her mid-twenties. Fischer was not comforted by this asserted likeness.

■

**CHANDRA (the One Tunnel's Circle of Screaming Lost Souls):** *You name it, she's gone through it. That's why I love Miss Gwynn—'cause she really do know what hell's all about.*

The alters carried this around, till one day in hypnosis it came out. After, while they and Gwynn sat there in shock, I said, "Mother Gwynn, it's all right. Let be." Lord, I don't like to get mixed up with therapists and patients.

■

". . . of course it hurts so much, lovin' and losin'. . . . I know exactly how you feel—"

"Zoe, it's time to stop."

Mother Zoe flinched. She had no idea what the body had just been saying but still felt Chandra's hurt at the abrupt dismissal. Obediently, she left. Later, Chandra left Fischer a phone message: she'd just been expressing innocent sympathy for someone grieving bravely and alone. Fischer had no call to treat her like scum.

Fischer began to lose her temper during sessions.

Zoe did not lose her own temper—much. She says she developed a "psychic fusion" with Fischer, a special sense that they were one—the exact same melding of minds she'd had with Wald. Zoe called Sarah Freed about the fusion. "It's only with Gwynn, not you." Sarah thought this was a danger signal. Zoe called Fischer and told her Sarah had said they were in danger. The two therapists promptly called each other.

After getting both therapists' attention, Zoe decided she felt comfortable with Fischer. The notion of psychic fusion is very motivating: if you and the goddess are one, you can say anything. You don't have to decide to trust. God has decided for you. Lying to or mistrusting the object of psychic fusion would be the same as lying to yourself. This Zoe does not want to do.

Still, they'd made headway. Many alters came out, using their separate voices.

The first to introduce themselves were the Zoes: Mother Zoe, the Patient, Zoe 10, Zoe 2, and Zoe 7. They didn't mind the thought of meeting each other someday. Though still feeling separate, the Zoes were beginning to believe themselves to be parts of the same consciousness, frozen at different moments in time. Soon Mazie 5 would join them. These were all good girls, anxious to please.

Marie-Marie and Sister Zoe Ann met Fischer, too. Then Donna came out to talk business.

And then it was Danielle's turn. At first Zoe felt greatly expanded by Danielle's joyful love of humanity.

■

**ZOE'S JOURNAL, March 22, 1987:** *Donna feels equality with Gwynn. Zoe has a schoolgirl crush. I, Danielle, am in love. How can I not love Gwynn when I tell her what is in my heart and soul?*

■

These alters felt hurt by Fischer's prohibiting contact. Other alters came out, said they were past-life impressions, and described how they'd been rejected over a period of eons.

An eight-year-old alter named Suzanna came out after one argument about touching and described her parents' death by fire in 1870. One of the young Zoes described lying on a bier, dead, in ancient Egypt, disemboweled and stuffed with fragrant spices. Alters spoke about martyrdom, about being burned at the stake and being possessed by the Devil. They dreamed about Lucifer falling in a rain of fire.

Serena, Selina, Cynthia (Animal), Oya, Eleanora, the Demon, and the male protectors, were all one to the good girls: they were Satan. And a mention of Mrs. Patterson could send them into a religious tizzy. Donna wrote to Fischer that Serena was a sexual, evil, magical threat from which she'd sworn to protect Zoe. "If she came out, she'd try to take over Zoe. If you conjure Serena, you will have much to prove to me."

Were it not for its sadness, the next period of therapy would have resembled a Neil Simon farce—slamming doors and huge stage reactions. Each alter dramatically materialized in response to some slur made by another. Some alters came out to revile Selina, to say that the evil witch deserved to die.

Selina is too proud to admit she felt insulted. That the

good girls saw her as the Devil and didn't accept her separateness as they did their own, she said was stupid. She recorded a tape, in an attempt to prove her right to live. She told Fischer she was there to protect the children.

■

**SELINA, Tape to Gwynn Fischer, early 1987:** *You want to speak to me. I have nothing to say to you. I do not trust you with my children. You do not understand them. And they need more help than I can give.*

*Gwynnie Louise tells me trust Mommy Gwynn. But I know she will not help. She will not even reach out her arms.*

*You must see the infant that sits in front of you. The two-year-old, three-, four-, five-, six-, seven-, ten-, and twelve-year-old. All are different. What you see is your own false reality. You see a forty-three-year-old patient and that is all.*

*The infant needs to be held. Not sexually. No. Zoe keeps obsessing, as do the children, why they are so untouchable.*

■

Like Selina, each dark alter came out with a reason to continue their existence. They reiterated, if Fischer wouldn't touch them, they'd die.

■

**SELINA (the One Tunnel's Circle of Screaming Lost Souls):** *Zoe would like to walk back into Mother Sea, slowly, into the cold sea and let it end. I could drive fast over a cliff. Painful for a second, but—No. It would gain more karma. The children still have a life they should live.*

*Can't you take the hand of the two-year-old?*

■

Zoe wouldn't review this tape or any other. If Fischer even mentioned Selina, she'd black out. She was scared Selina might commit a crime. She preferred to remain unconscious.

Both Fischer and Sarah advised Zoe that she could not forget unpleasant events, while hoping to become whole.

Zoe's alters wondered when the next axe would fall.

Would Fischer make the same old mistakes? She shared Wald's and Altman's pride, so perhaps she would also share their capacity for abuse. With the dark alters out, and the neediest alters, there was no telling what might happen.

■

**GWYNNIE LOUISE (the One Tunnel's Circle of Screaming Lost Souls):** *Can you hear me, Mommy? Whether you hold me or not, I know you love me. Could you hold the baby, though? She needs it more than me. She's real tiny, and she cries all the time. Little babies don't understand words, Mommy. You don't know all the things that are inside.*

*I love you, Mommy! When I grow up, I'll be you.*

■

To this pathos, Fischer remained cold. No way would she allow her patient to crawl into her lap. No hand-holding, no hugs. No similarity to Wald even in fantasy.

■

**DANIELLE (the One Tunnel's Circle of Screaming Lost Souls):** *In session our eyes met. Darling, I wanted to respond when you said I didn't care what happened to you. I do!*

*I don't desire to possess you; I want both of us to be free spirits serving mankind. Only in one way do I desire to belong to you, and that is to be your lover. Carl Jung, wasn't his patient also his lover? I admire Jung greatly. . . .*

■

"Your feeling is so out of touch with reality," spluttered Fischer.

"What feeling?" asked Zoe.

Fischer tapped the page, which Danielle had handed to her two minutes before. She'd already recovered from her anger. Still, she couldn't edit out a slight sarcasm. "You didn't read it?"

"No. It's private." Her tone was injured innocence.

"Private?" Fischer handed Zoe the letter, which went on from Carl Jung's mistress, to explicitly proposing that Danielle be Fischer's sex slave.

Zoe's eyes filled; without reading the letter, she handed it back. It's wrong to read someone else's intimate correspondence—even worse if you haven't been introduced. "How could Dr. Fischer betray Danielle's confidence like that?" she would later ask Sarah Freed.

Sighing, Fischer filed the letter.

If Zoe could get over Wald, Fischer reasoned, Danielle's invitations to herself might stop. She proposed that Wald and Zoe meet with a mediator. Meekly Zoe agreed, but then Donna yelled, "Don't you see that you're condoning this by saying, let's just nicely talk this out?"

Fischer replied she certainly did not condone the relationship, but she could see how even the prospect of a lawsuit had increased the severity and frequency of Zoe's dissociative episodes.

She suggested that Zoe's alters keep a daily record, which would be open to all of them. "Knowing what the others were doing, would diminish your fear." They'd identified only a few of those alters who considered themselves morally correct. But even these were daunting. Unlike those of Christine Beauchamp, Sybil, and Eve, Zoe's alters came tumbling out uncontrollably, fighting each other and Fischer, with no rhyme nor reason. There was no First Appearance, in which alters identified themselves one by one. They wouldn't give Gwynn their names. They wouldn't even release the mask of the Patient's empty symptoms and mannerisms, which they held in front of them like a protective shield as they bickered.

Zoe agreed to do what she called homework: to jot notes the night of a session and then to bring them in.

Cautious in person, Zoe overcooperated at home. Several alters let themselves loose on paper. The first week Zoe handed in fifteen pages; the next week, thirty. Fischer's willing patient or patients also brought in audiotapes, articles, gifts, and friendship cards. By the time Zoe quit therapy, her materials would fill one of Fischer's tall oak file cabinets.

On the first occasion, Fischer smiled and thanked her patient. By the third time, though polite, she was sighing.

■

**DONNA WHITE'S HOMEWORK PAPER, April 27, 1987:**
*Gwynn, I want you to write a book about our life. . . .*

■

"I can't write a book about you, Zoe!"

"Why?"

"I'm your therapist."

"So what? You can do it! You're a very talented woman. You don't give yourself enough credit, Gwynn."

Fischer laughed kindly. "That's not the point."

Zoe was at first puzzled, then hurt. Donna was furious. An ideal mother acts delighted with each of her child's gifts. Look what trust got her—rejection!

The rest of the session, Donna fumed. Zoe cried. Marie-Marie sang hymns. Whenever Fischer pressed an alter to discuss one point, any point, another came out and changed the subject.

Says Fischer, "I wanted to have Zoe anchor material from hypnosis in her awareness, by having her write about it after sessions. This did not work too well. Zoe tended to go off into fantasies rather than deal with the material. However, it did foster dialogues between various alters."

■

In projective identification, people ascribe their own feelings to another. Zoe was attracted to Fischer, not Fischer to her. When Fischer wouldn't touch her, Zoe felt unattractive, hopeless.

In August 1987, an alter called the Observer emerged to assist—and outflank—Fischer. Ancient, wise, like Tiresias at once male and female, the Observer stands to one side and comments on the action. The game is to identify what's going on, to control a therapist's reactions, and to get attention for child alters, without letting the system feel hurt.

■

**THE OBSERVER'S HOMEWORK PAPER, August 1987:** *You are facing resistance from all parts of the personality known on* *this earth plane as Zoe Parry. Perhaps there lies within this structure a lack of trust toward you, which to me seems reasonable.*

■

**ZOE II'S HOMEWORK PAPER, August 1, 1987:** *I must reject Gwynn before I'm rejected. I hate being dependent. I hate me. I hate my illness. I serve no useful purpose. I caused pain and sorrow to too many people. I am a freak. Bad daughter. Horrible mother and wife. Hateful to my neighbor. Bigamist. Kidnapper.*

*I confess my sins, but feel no better.*

■

When she read this paper, Fischer called Francie Deakins and counseled her to postpone interviews on the Wald case.

Now, at the nadir of self-hatred, Zoe's survival mechanism kicked in. Certain alters came out in hypnosis, and agreed finally to meet each other. Up until now Zoe had judged these alters unacceptably bad. Danielle had embarrassed her with her lust; Donna with her aggression.

Today, in her forest, in between the two tall trees, Zoe squirmed out from the tiny hole, stood, and brushed off her pink silk pantsuit. Then she watched Danielle come forth, then Donna. Donna's hair was darker than hers; Danielle's shorter. They stood blinking in the light, seeing each other for the first time clearly and simultaneously: the timid matron, the fighter, the yearning lover.

Zoe waited for Danielle to brush the pine needles from her yellow dress and for Donna to adjust her navy-and-white pinstripes. Then timidly, she said hello.

Donna abruptly stuck out one hand, wanting to shake.

Smiling, with tears in her eyes, Danielle extended both her arms. Her yellow dress seemed to brighten.

The three alters did not touch. Zoe was still frightened of Donna's abrasiveness and Danielle's longing. She was still frightened of any strong feeling.

Haltingly, Zoe told the two stronger alters that she

could no longer disown even the ones she considered bad. She must admit the bad parts with the good.

Said Danielle, "Is love bad? Is joy? Is strength?"

"Hey, babes." From between the two trees, sauntered Serena. Dressed in red, she flung back her long blonde hair. "I'll work with you," she said cautiously, "on one condition. What I say about Pat stays secret."

Zoe fled.

After this intense session, Zoe craved, as always, comfort. Though Fischer says she reassured Zoe within appropriate limits, Zoe cries to this day, "Gwynn kicked us out, merely because the hour was over!" She remembers the child alters on the floor, sobbing and holding up their arms.

After her introduction to Danielle, Zoe found herself more and more attentive to the details of Fischer's life. Every minute reaction, she remarked; every variation of what could happen in session or out of it, she fantasized.

■

**ZOE (the Tunnel of Hosts):** *Oh, Gwynn, I just saw a plane crash on the news. . . . I couldn't go on if anything happened to you. . . . If you ever take your life, please take mine first. I worry that you're not eating well, that you'll get ill. Please be all right! Please be safely in your home at 43 State Street, tucked securely into your bed, fast asleep. I know you get up at seven. You work too hard. . . .*

■

Fischer felt drained by Zoe. She says calmly, "I began to grasp what Zoe meant when she said she has no self, that her alters are attempts to create a self, when I read an article stating that MPDs may be born without or develop without the 'glue' that holds a self together.

"Taking a cue from my readings—there's a good article by a Dr. Seymour Halleck—I recognized the dilemma of requiring MPDs to be responsible for their behavior. Society is not ready to excuse what they do on the basis of mental illness. . . . When faced with the choice of becoming more responsible or being made a ward of the state, many MPDs rapidly develop coconsciousness."

Zoe heard that choice as another Altmanesque threat. Either do things my way, she heard Fischer saying, or I'll make you a prisoner of the state.

Getting Zoe to develop coconsciousness was two-steps-forward-one-step-back. Fischer let out acerbic comments about wimps, which the alter Mother Zoe agreed with, deeply resented, and never forgot.

"Good-bye, Zoe," Fischer would say firmly at the end of a session. "ZOE. It's time to GO. I have OTHER PEOPLE WAITING." After Zoe stumbled away, crying to Janet, Fischer would sigh at the huge amount of attention multiples took . . . while demanding more.

Complains Fischer, "It's been a constant setting of limits, in the most, the simplest—I mean, we've spent months this year on why she shouldn't leave long messages. I have at most ten minutes between patients; if she goes on for fifteen, I can't pick up a true emergency. We went over this and OVER this, and she was very angry. The issue has still not been resolved! And the same with the issue of sexuality. It's been years, and she does not let go!"

■

On September 1, 1987, Zoe finally met with Francie Deakins. Though Zoe'd dropped the board proceedings against Pat Wald, she'd decided to proceed with her civil suit. She deserved cash, she felt, to pay for therapy Wald had made necessary.

Recalls Zoe, "I showed Ms. Deakins many notes Dr. Wald had written to me. I played my message tapes. Her eyes widened and she whistled softly. As case-hardened as she was, Francie could not believe her ears.

"She warned me that the statute of limitations in a medical malpractice case was one year from the date of discovery of the wrongdoing. That though the evidence was strong, we might thus have only a slight chance of winning—it had been four years since we quit therapy."

They built an argument that Zoe had been incompetent between 1983 and 1987 and thus unable to file. *Parry vs. Wald* was still very much alive.

Some of Zoe's old feelings began to replay.

At home, Zoe started to call Janet "Mommy." They'd lived together for nine years and had tried to be adult with each other. Now that precarious balance toppled.

∎

**DANIELLE'S HOMEWORK PAPER, September 5, 1987:** *A strange secret game—Zoe acts like a baby, Janet encourages her. She climbs in Janet's lap. Though they don't do anything sexual, the thought of making love, which would be like incest to this child state, turns her on. After, she gets scared. I thought you should know, Gwynn. I guess it's harmless, but why is it coming out now?*

∎

The alters constantly competed with each other for Fischer's love. Danielle gushed, "Hypnosis is so sensuous! I have never shared with anyone this way, except with God." Each wanted Gwynn to see them, and no other alter, as the best, the most deserving patient. In their world, the less deserving are put to death.

The alter Mazie wrote a pathetic note, dated September 17, 1950, to Fischer. "Mommy, thank you for the afghan. I sleep with it under my pillow. Please for Christmas could we have a teddy bear?" If Mazie could be Most Deserving, she might not have to integrate—to die.

It is impossible to find one's humility, responsibility, sensuality, and power and simultaneously remain the good little, weak little, sweet little dying infant virgin.

As Fischer brought them face to face, Zoe's alters thought up ever better reasons why they shouldn't know each other. Among the most irrefutable was "past lifetimes." Zoe decided that all of it—the power struggles, the patterns, the violent emotions—came from events in her past lives, not this life. "In fact the more unreasonable, unexplainable, ingrained, intractable, chronic, or acute it is, the likelier it is to be from before my birth." If this body was just a way station, as the alters concluded, then they had about as much in common, as much reason for intimacy and integration, as people waiting at a bus stop.

Among the people at the bus stop might be a potential

mugger. One year after diagnosis, alters still had a problem with, do I accept the others or try to kill them? For the weak surface personality, who'd been such a good, polite victim, who sometimes couldn't tell the difference between masochism and altruism, it was Christian to accept them, like Jesus among the lepers. But she flinched at contact. Certain alters, she felt, were innately bad. And, in turn, those alters flinched from her; her passivity drained their energy.

Zoe prayed to God to protect Gwynn and herself from the beast who made Altman lose his mind and Wald lose her sense of right and wrong.

If Serena was Zoe, then it follows that Zoe was the one who drove Altman mad, who rutted with Wald, who flung pans of scalding hot lasagna at Carmine. If Zoe was Serena, then it follows that Serena is the wimp, that she's the Christian, that she's the one who despises sex. The collision is more than either can bear.

■

On October 13, 1987, after it became clear that mediation would never occur, Francie Deakins filed suit for Zoe against Patricia Wald.

In terror, Zoe called her pastor and begged him to let her off the hook. "God told us to forgive . . ."

But he disagreed. "Zoe, you've been chosen to help people. It was your duty to go through the first lawsuit, and now it is once again your duty."

"Why me?"

"Who else? You would be just as guilty as she if you let this go on."

Zoe despaired. "Why does everyone betray me?"

After the phone call, alters whispered to Zoe to run to the secret place and jump.

"No!" Zoe implored. "There are many projects Donna has started, which she must finish. Besides, Gwynn is the caretaker of my soul—not you."

Fischer did not want to be the caretaker of Zoe's soul. That job was loaded with sadomasochistic freight.

Zoe developed all-day migraines. She was sure she'd contracted a fatal disease—Alzheimer's, tumor, brain fever. A truer name for the headache would have been "switching."

Donna's activism would not let Zoe rest. Her latest intelligence indicated progress regarding patient-therapist sex: In 1988, a new law would obligate therapists to tell patients that these relationships were wrong. Donna was especially gleeful about one clause: a patient's previous sexual history would now not be admissible evidence in patient-therapist lawsuits. Zoe's alters could now tell Fischer all about Wald, without fear that the opposition lawyer would subpoena them and use this information against her.

Donna decided to forge ahead. The memos she now left all around the house—"No excuses, Wimp-O: Talk Up Now!"—had the Patient weeping and clinging when she found them.

Zoe's journal is blank from October 1987 through January 1988, when the law took effect. Zoe was in bed with what she thought was a fatal illness. But Donna was busily dialing the phone, stepping up Zoe's involvements.

Work, for example. Donna felt it was unconscionable for the system not to have a job. She was sick of slaving as a nurse's aide and as a baby-sitter; she judged these unhealthy for them anyway. Without a diploma, skills, or good health, Zoe was not qualified for much, despite high intelligence and aspirations.

Calling central casting for the alter Julie, Donna signed her on as a movie extra. Many agencies will try anyone with an interesting "look"; that, Zoe has.

Donna was not content just with finding part-time work. She yearned to prevent future patient-therapist sex, not just in Zoe's personality system, but in the world. Claiming to be an agent, she set up interviews on local news shows for Zoe, which tied in to the task force hearings and to the progress of patient-therapist initiatives through the state legislature. She told the producers to invite Dr. Wizniewski and the Bertrands as well. As in the lawsuit, most of Zoe was dreadfully unready even to go outside, let alone to appear on the evening news.

**MOTHER ZOE (the Tunnel of Light):** *Where was Stage 7? I was lost. No, there I was. Depersonalizing. Derealizing. Not here. Where is Donna? Finally a voice calls Zoe Parry. Oh, oh, down to hell we go. Terror beyond belief. Just as we get to the set Bruce Goldberg appears. He holds my hands and hugs me. And Dr. Wiz says, "Follow me."*

■

**JULIE (the One Tunnel's Circle of Screaming Lost Souls):** *At the end I was paralyzed. Then Donna shot through, and we were able to walk off. The switches were so quick the audience didn't notice.*

*Bruce Goldberg was backstage. He swung us around and gave us a big kiss. "You did a great job, Zoe!"*

*Zoe 10 said, "But we didn't answer the questions."*

*And Bruce said, "What are you talking about? Of course you did—every one!"*

■

Donna had even vindicated Zoe. In answer to the host's question, "Why did you keep going back to Altman?" she'd burst out, "Put yourself in the patient's place. If she said no, the doctor could have put her in jail for a decade."

"And if she said yes?" continued the host.

"If she said yes," said Donna harshly, "she was obeying her doctor's orders. And doctors," she continued, "are there for the patient's good." Looking at the red dot on the camera, straight into America's eyes, she finished sardonically, "We all know that."

After the show, at her session, Zoe cried, said she hated herself and Donna, raged at all therapists for making her hate herself still more.

■

Fischer began implosion therapy, an attempt to overload Zoe with her own unworkable strategies until they collapsed and she was forced to develop better ones. "It's used for the treatment of post-traumatic stress," explained Fischer. With the proper support, Zoe could in this way become less sensitive to pain.

However, since Zoe had no divisions in her day, no idea yet of how to separate flashbacks from the present, implosion therapy became implosion life. The way Carmine glared when she hadn't cleaned house was implosion. A friend's invitation to lunch was implosion. Even the hamburger at lunch was implosion, as it brought fears of colon cancer.

Implosion was tough on Zoe's household. Janet became acutely fearful after two weeks of listening to Zoe. Zoe, who must be the neediest victim in the group, couldn't see why. She interpreted Janet's reactive behavior as personal rejection; in turn Janet saw Zoe's redoubled screams as a mean-spirited attack.

Implosion therapy stressed Fischer as well as Zoe. There were constant crises. Reproaches. Calls. And roller-coaster sessions.

Fischer just tried to be a good therapist; Zoe, to be a good patient; alters, to stay out of it. But implosion took an L-turn to nowhere.

ZOE'S JOURNAL, February 16, 1988: *Another day in hell. I'm a parasite, a vampire feeding off psychic energy which does not belong to me. I called Gwynn from the market, where all the people scared me. She suggested I go home. But I am not more secure at home!*

Home was where the telephone was. Each time Zoe returned, the red blinking light on her machine signaled more implosion: lawyers, doctors, her family. Making demands. Discovering problems. Asking her to do things. It took weeks to do any one of these tasks. Zoe felt empty and leaden and kept taking to her bed. Even Franciscan meetings lost their savor. Even prayer didn't seem to work.

The result was her ever stronger wish to merge with Fischer, to escape implosion by crawling into the psychic womb of supportive hypnosis.

To a self-motivated individual, supportive hypnosis can be a servant of self. To Zoe, it was the only drug she'd found outside of church in which she could be dominated from head to toe for her own ultimate good.

Fischer wanted to use hypnosis not as a drug but as a teaching tool. She approved of the book Donna planned to write someday. She believed that if Zoe used hypnosis to split into past emotional states (alters) and write about them, she could develop healthy uses for her dissociation.

Says Fischer, "In the creative process, you dissociate for creation, and then you bring in your 'editor,' to find out whether what you wrote worked or not. The dissociated person usually does not bring in an 'editor.' He cannot do, what we call in cognitive psychology, 'reality checking.'

"Zoe had a pattern of destroying checkable products. For example, she shredded Mrs. Patterson's notes—said, 'This is evil!' and destroyed them. If she could write, I felt, she could develop a process of reality checking and a feeling that her peculiarities were not necessarily evil."

Encouraged by Fischer, Zoe tried to assemble and review materials.

Once, there was a red flash on Zoe's machine.

Francie Deakins said briefly, 'The judge will be hearing *Parry-Wald* six weeks from now."

Zoe's heart seemed to stop. She screamed.

Janet came running. Zoe was sprawled on her bed, clutching her chest and gasping. Two calls to 911. Twenty minutes later, Zoe lay strapped to another stretcher.

Heedless of the ambulance's careening, paramedics checked her heart. "Normal," one said cheerfully.

■

ZOE'S JOURNAL, May 24, 1988: *Called Sarah and told her how that so-called therapist left little Zoe crying outside, alone, afraid to move, with everyone staring. How Sally knocked on Gwynn's door and said, "Doctor, she's switched—she's still switching." Donna came out pissed. Oooh. "Fischer won't comfort the kids, but she told SALLY ABOUT US SWITCHING? Who is she to tell our secrets?" Donna yelled at Gwynn through the door. Finally Gwynn came out and said, "I don't blame you for being angry."*

■

The Patient said, "You're not my mommy any more. I want Sarah. She's the most wonderful mommy in the world." She began to cancel appointments with one doctor, to set them up with the other, then switch and reverse the process.

■

**SARRIE FREED, age 6 (the One Tunnel's Circle of Screaming Fear):** *I look just like Mommy must have when she was a girl. I have light brown curly hair and brown eyes, and smile a lot. I have the best mommy in the world; when I grow up I want to be just like her.*

■

Treating Zoe had not become easier for Gwynn Fischer.

In Fischer's long career, she'd only been courted and blamed this intensely once before: by a lesbian patient who'd lied to Fischer's supervisor about her when Fischer turned her down. Fischer warned Zoe, "I want no misunderstandings with you."

"Oh, I would never do something like that," Zoe assured her. "I would never go over your head."

In fact, when they terminated therapy in April 1993, Zoe would immediately go to Fischer's supervisor. The way multiples manage threat is unique.

Promises are also unique. "I won't call your supervisor" becomes, "Some of us will call. But I won't."

■

**MAZIE'S HOMEWORK PAPER, June 23, 1988:** *You are real mean, Mommy. You don't understand me anymore. I wish Mommy Pat would come back. She used to hold me.*

*I bet you'll be happy when I'm gone.*

■

Zoe's equation of Fischer with Wald had the paradoxical effect of making some alters trust Fischer. On July 5, 1988, in hypnosis, Zoe suddenly felt the presence of the core alter, Baby Frozen.

■

**ALICE (the One Tunnel's Circle of Sleeping Enclosure):** *The baby be in pain. Gwynn just see regression. But that's a real live baby, with a baby's needs.*

■

According to the alter Chandra, many personalities wanted to be in therapy but couldn't: a good therapist could have metamorphosed Cynthia's hostile stares at least to wary receptivity; Agnes couldn't talk, but Fischer should have seen how she needed therapy. "I myself thought that something bad was going to happen, like with Sidney and Pat. So I slept."

When she complains that therapy with Fischer didn't work, I ask Zoe why she thinks so.

■

**SISTER MICHAEL MARIE (the Tunnel of Light and Wisdom):** *The Golden Child wants to control. The tiny infant had no control, so now she must be in total control.*

*Zoe does not wish to look at the Golden Child. She must be willing to admit the tricks by which her own self leads her astray. But she must have a good guide to do this, and Dr. Fischer has not been that guide.*

*Zoe contacted an evil part of Dr. Fischer, who had thought she knew herself. The doctor was shocked to see this part. That is why the doctor is so tired. She carries an invisible weight on her shoulders. The weight of her own vision of success.*

■

Fischer says, "The psychodynamic work was slow because Zoe's self-esteem was so low, her defenses so strong, that she couldn't tolerate even very gentle interpretations. Attempting to draw some connection between present problems and her history or our relationship resulted in such strong anxiety that she felt disorganized—and that I was hypercritical. She viewed my efforts to understand as 'destroying our relationship.' In the early years, I would mistakenly gain confidence about offering an interpretation while working with a healthier ego-state, probably Donna, and then find that after, Zoe was in a rage about what I said. This still happens but I am no longer surprised.''

Fischer tried to get the fear alters to meet Mrs. Patterson in hypnosis; Zoe closed her eyes and rocked. Later she went to the emergency room for another series of tests. The analytic alters called Fischer, saying that Zoe must immediately get more therapy—far, far more.

■

**THE OBSERVER'S HOMEWORK PAPER, August 16, 1988:**
*Truly, the state of consciousness known on this earth plane as Zoe Parry would most greatly benefit from four or five sessions per week.*

*Perhaps you could reduce your rate.*

*Zoe Parry would pay the full rate if she could. She is extremely giving. She will pay you back every penny, if that is what you want. Money is not important when a human life is at stake.*

■

Fischer didn't want to see Zoe far, far more. She did want to reassure her patient. ''If you're angry with me,'' she said, ''it's not going to drive me away or destroy me. Today you can learn to trust yourself—any wild idea you have, you don't have to impulsively carry it out.''

''Don't abandon me like this,'' Zoe wept.

■

**ZOE'S JOURNAL, October 4, 1988:** *I feel someone is throwing me into the pit of insanity.*

*I called ''Sybil's'' therapist. She would be happy to consult with Gwynn.*

*Gwynn is so cruel. Makes me feel vile. If she'd meet my needs, I would grow.*

*I called Pat three times.*

*Called Sarah.*

■

Calling ''Sybil's'' doctor—the mother of MPD therapy— was yet another attempt to outflank Fischer. With the heavy capability of supernatural alters on one flank of her army, and intellectual analysts on the other, perhaps she'd be covered.

Wald didn't return Zoe's many calls, but quickly had her lawyers call Francie Deakins. According to Zoe, Deakins lost her temper with Zoe, said if the children did this they should be punished. That the children could ruin "her case."

Zoe asked Fischer if she would accept an antique diamond ring—an heirloom from Anne Adams—in lieu of further payment. "I believe it to be worth quite a bit. I have no need of diamonds when therapy is what will save me."

The alter Zoe 10 stopped the body from eating and asked a doctor to do a gastric probe, a procedure that involves the patient's swallowing a nasopharyngeal tube.

The alter Donna fumed, not at Fischer, but at how long the Wald case was taking.

That week, Zoe gave her deposition. An excerpt:

> Pat Wald caused such pain, such an increase in my symptoms. Many people, including yourself, Ms. Deakins, know that I'm telling the truth. I need financial compensation. My therapist can tell you, the money won't be for pleasure trips. I can't enjoy anything, after Pat.

Fischer and Sarah Freed conferred about the rapid deterioration in Zoe's physical health. She somatized every crisis, acquired new physical symptoms at every sign of stress. Depending on which alter they'd examined, each of dozens of doctors diagnosed symptoms differently and prescribed sometimes opposite treatments. Freed and Fischer set up a more viable routine.

Says Fischer, "We set up weekly appointments for Zoe with a psychologically oriented internist familiar with MPD—a Dr. Sandy Shenker. Gradually Zoe began to improve. Sandy Shenker became a good support to her."

Says Fischer, "The adjunctive visits with Dr. Freed and Dr. Shenker relieved some of the pressure within our therapy. Ordinarily one wishes to keep all the transference feelings in the therapy hour, but Zoe has a hard time containing her feelings between visits."

■

Zoe had no idea how the TV talk show host had gotten her name. But his producer had left several ecstatic messages on her machine. Zoe called him. "How did you find out about me?"

"From your publicist."

"Oh." Intimidated, Zoe felt she couldn't say she didn't have a publicist. "I should consult my doctor before making any appearances."

"Fair enough."

Zoe hung up, vomited. Sandy Shenker was out of town. Under her phone machine, Zoe had kept some old doctors' test request forms from the hospital; she filled one out. Janet took her to the emergency room for a complete scan of her digestive tract, as Dr. Zoe had ordered.

In her session, Fischer recommended, "Don't do the show."

"I called them back," says Zoe, "and told them I couldn't appear. Said that my doctor had forbidden it. And so had my lawyer."

Francie Deakins comments, "I had advised that Zoe not go on as it might complicate the case. The next thing I hear about this is a call from the host. He's livid! It's the day of the taping, and Zoe's canceled! I called Zoe and recommended that she go on."

■

**MAZIE 5 (the Tunnel of Light and Wisdom):** *A big limo came and took us to the studio—a teeny tiny room with no air. Unless you turn on the air conditioner, you can't breathe; sometimes they turn it off. The lights are hot. You can't see anybody, but you put these things in your ears so you can hear the host and the audience.*

*I got confused. I didn't think he understood anything at all. He didn't know a thing about MPD. That's so frustrating, when you've been hurt and nobody understands.*

■

**ZOE'S JOURNAL, October 2, 1988:** *Well, Gwynn was right about the talk show host. He is The Beast. We felt like trash. He said I was a high priestess in voodoo. Not true. They flashed the kidnapping clips. They did not warn me. They failed to say that Judge Wood expunged my record. He compared my case to the Son of Sam's. "Same defense," he said. I was so upset.*

*Called the producer. Told him in no uncertain terms I was never a high priestess. Said I would sue in spite of any paper I signed. He said he'd try to take that out. Liar.*

■

The producer did take out some embarrassing details, but Zoe was fuming. "All we wanted to do was to help others.

"We were offered money. We didn't want it. Francie took it and gave us half. We gave it to the church.

"After the show," adds Zoe, "I went out and bought a disguise: a wig and sunglasses.

"And that Sunday! The reactions at church! There were two ladies in back of me, gossiping nonstop. Finally they asked if I wasn't the woman on the show. When I said yes, they turned away. I felt like the worst freak in the world.

"After, one of the ladies came up to me. She was rude, caustic. Zoomed in on all the dirt. Missed the whole point, the misuse of power which causes personality change. . . . Well, with the grace of Our Father I made it through, with head (mostly) held high."

Says Zoe, "One good thing happened that week. I went to the vacuum repair store. The owner walked me out to the car. He asked if I was the one on the show. I started shaking. Not another one, please, God. Then he told me that he'd been abused as a child. And it was people like me who gave him hope. I felt I'd done something good in my life for once—even if just one person understood."

Fischer contacted Francie Deakins on November 18, 1988, and said Zoe was now ready to continue litigation.

■

**ZOE'S JOURNAL, December 19, 1988:** *I had a meeting scheduled with Francie Deakins for eight-thirty. Called at six A.M. to cancel. The heartless bitch said, "You'd better go. This will look bad." So I went. It was horrible. I felt so ill. Deakins feels I will lose the case. Not enough evidence. False. I brought proof, two pictures of me and Pat out socially. And there is more. . . .*

*The case is not over. Francie will talk to Pat's attorneys.*

■

This Christmas, with Donna out and the case progressing, Zoe was strong enough to avoid complete breakdown. Davey brought over a new girlfriend, a pretty twenty-year-old who ran a small boutique. They spent Christmas Eve decorating cookies with icing faces and funny sayings.

■

**ZOE'S JOURNAL, January 6, 1989:** *Saw Sarah. There are signs of danger between me and Gwynn. Therapy is the number one thing in my life. Beth told Sarah about the child on the floor wanting to be slapped. And Gwynn saying I have sexy eyes. "There's nothing like a good suck, chocolate is better than sex. Why don't you just jerk off." Sarah thinks she meant suck like a mother would. Oral needs. Wrong. I heard it right.*

*I felt so guilty I'd betrayed Gwynn to Sarah.*

*Session, Gwynn couldn't understand why I contact Pat. My poor answers of wanting to make things nice, come to a forgiveness, Gwynn wouldn't accept. I didn't like it when she said Pat didn't want to see me. . . .*

*I told Gwynn how high one gets making love to a therapist.*

■

Fischer had a cold. Phobic about disease, Zoe covered her face with tissues in order to filter out Fischer's malign viruses. The therapist guided her into trance, into an imaginary healing pool filled with golden fluid. "I pictured the white blood cells attacking the germs. Gwynn spiritual, helped me find my guide in the mystical temple. We have the power to heal ourselves."

Zoe's high faded after half an hour. Through flashbacks—February 3 was approaching—Zoe described the omens at her birth. The conversation drifted to Dave Bryant's having, she said, "liked little girls." "I feel so sad, talking about Father. I don't know if it was sexual. I'm not ready. I don't want to be probed."

■

**ZOE'S JOURNAL, February 3, 1989:** *Eleven years since the kidnapping. Her creativity is screaming. She must give the world her pain.*

*Acting out like CRAZY. Can't stop calling people. Lawyers are bastards. Therapists are nuts. Hold on to God. When personalities come out, just go with that particular person. Stop trying so hard to be Zoe.*

*It happened Thursday night. Palpitations. I was writing, and Selina came out. She is angry. She remembers everything. I could not stand it. I threw down the pad.*

*I did not kidnap Jennifer! I feel Selina's ghost. Go AWAY. I do not know Selina. I do not wish to find her.*

■

While Selina and Mother Zoe played tag, Francie Deakins settled Zoe's lawsuit against Wald, for a sum in the mid five figures. "Fifteen hundred dollars repaid the money Pat unlawfully took when she made me cash in and give her Carmine's savings bonds. The rest went into the bank—for therapy."

Zoe believes that what Wald did to her was child abuse. "There were two- and five- and ten-year-old children who depended on her, and she had sex with them."

To Zoe, a civil victory was nothing. She says, the child alters didn't understand lawsuits, nor the fact that Wald could still practice. "The money," she says, "cannot take away the pain."

Recently, with Sarah Freed's support, Zoe has met with a board investigator. Reviewing Zoe's material, he immediately forwarded her case to the attorney general. Zoe says she'll hire bodyguards and wear a bulletproof vest the day she goes to court. But she feels she's finally done the right thing—although she waited ten years to do it.

The day Wald settled the civil suit, Zoe fled; she went to the Osceola Springs Retreat on Lake Kinnara to pray.

Her return a week later paralleled her return after the kidnapping trial, when her father died. Once again she had to rush back: Carmine had suffered a cardiac arrest.

■

**ZOE'S JOURNAL, April 5, 1989:** *Carmine was exceptionally brave. They took him in at nine. Surgery ended at two A.M. He made it. Zoe feels she's Carmine. The ten-year-old is crying. Agnes tries to blank everyone out, and sometimes succeeds.*

■

Zoe felt too ill to visit Carmine again. She lay down with her mother's tattered quilt and Fischer's afghan.

■

**LYDIA (the Tunnel of Light and Wisdom):** *Hello, I'm Lydia. I'm seven. Zoe is asleep. I've come out to cook and clean and help. I feel sorry for Carmine but mostly for her.*

■

Zoe brooded for six months. Her journals are blank; she wrote few homework papers; she reports nothing.

The alter Dr. Silverstein analyzed those past traumas—especially the kidnapping—which she found most symbolic: *The primitive part thought only to get a new mother. Zoe was found naked in the fetal position, so that tells me what she wanted. She was saying, Lillian, the other baby was taken away. Here I am. Your new baby. Mother me.*

Even this mild self-examination sent Zoe into acute illness. In May 1989, she started bleeding profusely, shaking with chills, and hallucinating. The emergency room doctor diagnosed Zoe with campylobacter, a bacterial infection that can cause intestinal ulcerations.

After a week in the hospital, Zoe physically recovered. But though the campylobacter was gone, her alters were left even more obsessive about cleanliness. Between compulsive fits of bathing and scouring, Zoe lay corpselike on her bed, staring into the unknown.

■

**ZOE'S JOURNAL, July 11, 1989:** *Zoe is in a very bad way. Frozen. Somehow she must try to reach the Golden Beach World, Mildred Silverstein. . . . No, that was twenty years ago and I'm having a setback. Yes, I'm depressed but don't go all the way to the third level of complete isolation, trapped within a body that isn't even there.*

■

The week of July 28, 1989, Fischer told Zoe that the therapy homework was going nowhere—that the format had led to unfocused meandering and morbid rumination. "Let's stop handing in writings," she suggested in her best tone of empathic neutrality.

Zoe sat stunned. Her alters had strongly identified themselves on paper; she had invested so much energy. She felt Fischer had arbitrarily assigned the work, ignored it, and then cut her off.

■

On a bright, viciously hot day in August, Janet and Zoe drove to Francie Deakins's office for the last time. All the evidence from *Parry-Wald,* Deakins had boxed and left with her secretary. "It was such a cold, clinical feeling in Deakins's posh office. She didn't come out. She didn't even bother thanking me for the business."

"Good luck," said the secretary, nudging the heavy box with her toe.

"I felt angry and sad," recollects Zoe. "I wished Pat would have come to the mediation sessions. She owed me those sessions, the cowardly bitch."

The door banged Zoe's back as she lugged out the leaden box. *"Sheesh,"* said Janet.

"What a life," said Zoe ruefully, and they laughed.

That month, Florida illegalized patient-therapist sex.

Many politicians had joined the cause since the task force days. One senator acknowledged Zoe's activism with a letter. A handscrawled postscript reads, "May you find some peace for all the pain you have suffered."

Zoe did not find peace. In her sessions, she began to

yell at Fischer. What she needed, Zoe decided, was to love and to be loved. She called the Vargases. They arranged for six-year-old Janna Lynne to visit Zoe, for her first extended stay since 1985, when she'd been two.

Zoe blanked out the weeks before her granddaughter's arrival in October. The first days of the visit went well. She shopped with Janna Lynne, cooked her favorite foods, went to movies. The child alters loved these and the ice cream after.

The adult alters had their own agenda. Janna Lynne, Mrs. Vargas had told Zoe, had been seeing a therapist for two years. The child apparently had a dissociative problem, just like her father and her grandmother.

Zoe decided to speak to Janna Lynne about some aspects of multiple personality. The child took it well.

■

**MOTHER ZOE (the Tunnel of Light and Wisdom):** *Janna Lynne said, "Grandma! There are so many people inside of you? Really?" And that was a hard one. Dr. Kaplan explained that when you've been hurt in certain ways, some people go into a dreamworld to get away from pain, and create personalities. 'Course, we know we're people. . . . But how to explain that to a child, even one as smart as Janna Lynne?*

*Together, we must help this child into a better life. She's smart—if there's hope for anyone, we can hope for her.*

■

Janna Lynne seemed relieved that a grown-up understood her lapses in attention. Zoe was happy she'd helped her granddaughter feel less isolated than she'd been as a child. Also she felt so guilty about the way she'd raised Davey, she wanted to make sure that Janna Lynne got a better deal.

Late in the visit Mrs. Vargas called. She said she'd just been awarded custody of Janna Lynne.

The next few days passed in an unfocused blur while Zoe tried to wipe away tears, to paste on a smile. Janna Lynne, playing and prattling, would look at her sharply.

Some of Zoe's alters noticed Janna Lynne's noticing, and melted. How sensitive this child was—just like them.

These alters felt psychic fusion growing between them and the six-year-old girl. They felt the oneness locking into place.

Others felt a surge of pity and vindication: they believed Dave Bryant must have been reincarnated as Janna Lynne. Still others, perhaps the sickest, thought that it was Altman who had revived, inside the girl. In Zoe's theory of karma, an abuser reincarnates as a victim. This is only fair, reason the alters; ultimately, God is good: he manages such a fair deal for all. With effort, Zoe refrained from telling Janna Lynne about reincarnation.

Not recognizing this was progress, Zoe sank into her habitual Christmas depression as the holidays approached.

Feeling sad (and brave and fearful and grateful and destroyed), Zoe picked out a card and dashed off a message. She wanted now to accentuate the positive.

But when she received the card, Fischer freaked. Under holiday wishes was written, slanting upward: "Here's to six good years! And looking forward to a lifetime together."

At their next session, Fischer's voice had an edge. "You know, Zoe, I'm not going to be here forever."

It's hard to convey how upset Zoe got about Fischer's not-so-imminent departure. She was shocked. She protested. She cried. She acted understanding. "Could I call you after you retire?" she said faintly.

"I don't want any contact with you, Zoe, after I'm done with work."

Zoe could not move forward. The months came and went, as quickly as a calendar flipping pages in a movie. The pile of materials on Zoe's desk grew deeper.

Mired in an unnavigable impasse with Fischer, crying, complaining, Zoe despaired of ever being helped. Perhaps this gray existence was the best she could hope for. More alters were still coming out in session and outside, and abreacting what seemed like endless memories. They were frightening, but apparently Zoe couldn't hope for comfort and she couldn't seem to work out a self-perception that made sense to her. Why not just go on this way? Change doctors? What for? Working with someone else might be even harder.

Early in 1992, Zoe and I began to work together. The huge box of materials she dropped off contained many of the homework papers she claimed Fischer had ignored. On these papers many alters' most characteristic statements had been underlined, marked, cross-referenced, and annotated—by Fischer. Notes in Fischer's careful, even handwriting gave me many clues about the personality structure Zoe said Fischer had totally misunderstood.

The box also contained Zoe's tapes. Listening to them straight through, in chronological order, I would have a very different experience from Fischer's. I could listen to Zoe's hurt and demands without having to reap in-the-field consequences. I could rewind and listen again, without feeling I'd invested too much in one patient. I could even make mistakes, without having Zoe pour her whole being into my every word.

The facts of Zoe's biography—even the ones that have been checked with the Parrys and Bryants, with lawyers and therapists, with the records in the county courthouse—are not the central issue. What is, is the way these facts are placed in the time (1992–93), the place (St. Petersburg), and the special circumstance (the reinvention of one person's, or personality system's, life).

At first Zoe's MPD would flower remarkably under all of the attention, hers, mine, the therapists', the friends', the family's. It was the last hurrah. The process of examining something, in and of itself, brings change, both to the observer and to the observed.

In an August 1992 interview, Fischer and I discussed Zoe's progress since she began working with me. Fischer commented, "What she's been able to do recently is to accept parts that used to be so horrible to her. Finally, she's able to see that Donna's pragmatism is normal. And Donna seems kinder to Zoe. Donna is now a part of herself. She's aware of that, even if she doesn't always feel it.

"Another thing that's happened is she's now able to access personalities. Up until the time Zoe started working with you, it was very hard for her to voluntarily enter

an alter. Your condition for entering the project—that
alters had to work together—was good motivation. . . .
She's drawing on resources that may have been there
before, but which she didn't use. . . . It seems that some
alters have internalized some of the helping, my helping
and Sarah's and yours. And now she's able to help
herself.''

After speaking with Fischer, I asked Dr. Shenker
whether she thought Zoe's alters were distinct physiological—as well as mental and emotional—states.

They seemed to be. When we spoke about Dave
Bryant, Zoe got gastric and urinary tract pains; when we
spoke about Grandfather Adams's death and her mother's reaction to it, Zoe got heart pain. Dr. Shenker's
records show that her complaints come in waves. There's
a tantalizing but iffy correlation between the subjects of
our interviews, the names of the alters who pop out, and
her symptoms.

■

From the moment I had heard about Zoe's therapy with
Fischer, in which some alters would blat out everything
and others would then panic, I'd wondered about the
issue of privacy.

I had wondered: can hypnotic probing seem, to the
multiple, to be a reenactment of abuse? Was that one
source of Zoe's rage against Fischer? Did hypnosis seem
to combine Dave Bryant's rapes and Zoe May's neglects?

■

BETH (the Tunnel of the Golden Child's Observers): *The
alters had every right to present what they were feeling. If you
couldn't handle their reenactment of memory, it would have
been wise, long ago, to turn this patient over to someone
who could.*

*These were terrified infants and children with extreme death
fears, and all you saw was a manipulative woman in her
forties. Your own fear prevented a healthy touching. We are
just human beings. Why couldn't you act like one?*

■

Were our self-hypnotic tapes a way for Zoe to reclaim material from Fischer and make it her own?

After we discussed Wald, Zoe started to plan eventually leaving Fischer. Simultaneously, within Zoe's system, alters began to rebel against Angel Child.

■

**The GOLDEN CHILD (the Tunnel of my Creations of Power):** *I do appreciate what you're doing. All of you, inside. We're all working together. Don't listen to ANYONE who tells you we can be separated. And always remember: I'm in charge.*

■

Historically, Angel Child had indeed bullied the other alters into submission. But now suddenly, she could not.

■

**RONA (the Tunnel of Those I Send to Light):** *You have my respect, Angel Child. But I won't listen to you in the way you want me to. I'm not afraid of you anymore.*

■

The rebellion had repercussions. An alter, Woman with No Name, blocked so many of Zoe's conflicting feelings about Fischer that days passed without any conscious awareness. And on New Year's Day 1993 Zoe woke with her fist crashing into her face. She screamed and tried to hold her right hand with the left. But the alter in control was powerful and fully dissociated.

It took Janet, Carmine, and Davey to hold that fist. Even then they couldn't control the stream of invective that poured out. A harsh male voice called Zoe hateful names.

Zoe covered her bruises with makeup, but her face was puffy for weeks.

After two weeks of battering and a lot of cursing, the alter introduced himself. It was Dennis, recently freed from the Land of Dena, the alter who used to enjoy ripping the legs off butterflies. Zoe was a mess. In addition to her Christmas forebodings and the horror generated by memories of Wald and Dennis's bruises and her conflict about Fischer, the Slasher came out each night and ripped her skin.

Her breakdown had lasted three months when Zoe made the following tape:

■

**ZOE, Tape to Gwynn Fischer, March 25, 1993:** *I am grieving. I feel great pain.*

*Gwynn, I've learned about who and what I am, by your giving me the diagnosis of MPD. I've come to understand myself somewhat better.*

*What I've decided, Gwynn, is since you are so uncertain about your life, which affects me, I have to take the reins. I plan on going into weekly therapy with Sarah Freed starting the week of April twelfth. She makes me feel secure, not like a scumbag for having a setback. I would like you to have been that type of person, but you aren't.*

*I know you tried. I'm not saying you failed. You didn't. You diagnosed us, and we'll always be grateful.*

*(Crying.) I want you to know I'll always care about you.*

*I wish you could have not been afraid of reaching out.*

*But you held my mother's hands. And you never held mine.*

■

Despite this tape, made at Sarah's request, Zoe was not calm. At five P.M. on April 13, 1993, over the phone, a child alter sobbed to me that Zoe had a knife again and pills. . . .

On a pad I scribbled, "Call Sarah—NOW!" and tossed the note to my husband.

"What's wrong?" he mouthed.

"Suicide threat," I wrote. "Over Gwynn."

An hour earlier, Zoe had gone to her last session with Fischer. She taped it.

Alter Donna White sighs explosively. "Doctor Fischer." Her voice is hard and stern. "Why did you say that you would see other patients in your home, if you retire—and not this system?"

Demurs Fischer, "What you said was, do I have other long-term patients? I said, 'Many.' You said how many, and what was I going to do with them? And I said I may continue to see them."

"That's right. And how do you think that made Zoe feel?" Donna's voice frays.

Fischer barrels on, using facts as a trainer might use a chair with a lion. "You asked where would I see them. I said I may see them in my home." Fischer sighs. "And then you said you felt like shit."

"Do you really think," says Donna wearily, "that was appropriate, to tell her that?"

"I'd like to tell you the truth. . . ."

"All that the little ones can see is other patients going into your home and them being kicked out! This is negligence. She can't breathe. If anything happens, they're gonna know who to blame."

After leaving a brief phone message for Sarah Freed, using Fischer's telephone, she turns back to Fischer. "You never cared."

"Oh, but I did," says Fischer gently. "I do."

Then Selina's voice: "Bad thing you say to patient. This is a human being—" Mother Zoe: "—here. With human pain."

"I know you have pain," says Fischer.

"You caused more."

"I'm sorry."

Zoe says, "It's too late."

Mazie says, "It's too late—"

Beth says, "—all right. And that's all I have to say."

*July 1993*
*Discussing Zoe's future.*
*Approximately 130 personalities.*
*(The parts within the bird are italicized.)*
*(The parts within the flower are underlined.)*

"Time Does Not
Exist"

Fade Out                                    Yorker Circle

*Angel Child*
*Woman of Many*
*Flight*

*The New Baby*                          Seventh
                                                   Daughter

                              *Claw on Inner*
Owl Woman                    *Life*

Baby Frozen

The Gang                    *Convents 120*
                                *More Sisters*

No Entrance                                *Dena*
To ONE

"She Speaks In                          Eli Elijah Jesus
Dena"

# 9

# *Alone at Last?*

Late in July 1993, Zoe's alters are in a fever of ripeness, as they begin to absorb the system's single history. Each alone and all together, they're not having an easy time with the flood of new impressions.

Many of the alters who used to see themselves as purely good cannot now. Many of the bad alters, too, cannot be as pure because they see the consequences of their behavior immediately, in the child alters.

The alters equate accepting these flaws, this loss of pureness, with death. Those in the lighter tunnels are praying, as any religious person would pray on moving on into the next world. Rona—the waif who felt threatened by zombies during the kidnapping—is especially philosophical about letting go.

■

**RONA (the Bird's Wing):** *You have to die to be reborn into greater life. You have to die to the past. To old ways. And then you can rise again, to greater power.*

■

Some child alters are actually hopeful.

■

**ZOE 2 (the Bird's Breast):** *I want to be a big girl now. Mazie says the same thing. We wanna grow up and be big adults and good to children. We lived the past. And we survived it. I wanna be a woman someday.*

∎

Others are overwhelmed by the expectation of death.

In May 1993, the Patient had been calling Dr. Shenker several times a day, obsessing about her health. She felt that her palpitations were getting worse and that they would kill her. Shenker says Zoe will be fine.

With Shenker's permission, Zoe taped certain phone conversations, so that in the middle of the night, when her fears overcome her, she can replay the doctor's reassurances again and again.

Thus a cure is as elusive as ever. But there has been some progress. Though the alter Zoe 10 still drags "the body" to doctors more frequently than the alter Donna would like, at least now the alters can honestly discuss their symptoms.

∎

**MOTHER ZOE (the Bird's Wing):** *At the Digestive Disorders Clinic, we filled out a four-page questionnaire. At first I answered as my good old MPD self. And then suddenly I started to not censor. There was a range of 0 to 4, 0 not at all, and 4 extremely. "Do you often feel like other people are controlling your thoughts?" And I circled 4.*

*I looked at it, thinking "Oh, my God!"*

*And then I answered every question. All of us did. We wrote two whole pages, all about being MPD, in all our different handwritings.*

*This doctor comes out. I give him the questionnaire and actually explain my MPD.*

*He asked how many personalities I had, and I said, "Over one hundred." He looked a little faint, but said, "Perhaps we can help you."*

∎

"So can she move on from being a multiple personality?"
I ask Sarah Freed. "Is she ready?"

Without hesitation, Sarah answers, "Yes."

With help, Zoe has begun.

■

**DENNIS STEVENS (the Stem of Inner Life):** *When I came out of Dena, I had to fight like hell. That's why Mother Zoe got busted in the mouth. When I saw her in the mirror, I saw my face, Dennis. Strong and solid, with my black hair and beard. Here I was in this woman's body, and I hate women.*

*And then in January some of the others start reaching out to me. Beth draws this picture. And I come out and guide her hand. I realized I want people to know how I look. I have very dark eyes. Dark brown hair, mustache, and beard. I'm one hundred sixty pounds, five feet ten—stocky. Well built.*

*The guys inside invite me to join them. Forget it. Dennis stands alone. But Gino is trying to make friends, and William Brown, and Ronny/Lillian. For the first time in my life I'm testing out the notion.*

■

Change is slow, and the whole system must ensure that the body is not going to wake up one morning with a broken nose.

Sarah has helped the system to stop punishing the fragile core.

■

**CYNTHIA (the Tunnel of Hell):** *I am surrounded by demons, here in hell. They follow me, trying to take this body and this soul.*

*Some of the people have been created as defenses. Some are like myself. I am part of the temple, or soul, of Zoe Parry. You must believe me. I am She, and She is Me. She does not understand this. I need somebody to understand.*

*I grieve for the little baby. She was tortured by men, hurt by mothers. She had no choice but to be frozen. They hurt her body, and she felt the pain, the pain, the pain that burned . . . the pain . . . of choking . . . the pain . . . in the private parts . . . the pain . . . of knives being held at her throat. . . .*

*I do not come from this time. I have walked the earth many times before. I have not had any happiness. But now people have reached out to try to help me. I do not know how to accept kindness. No one has been kind before.*

■

Cynthia's rage is draining away. She's now seen by the rest of Zoe's system as a ghost who lies exhausted on the forest floor, awaiting release. Selina says she channels Cynthia's thought impressions. Selina, the voodoo witch of old, now sees herself as one of the system's healers.

■

**SELINA (the Bird's Wing):** *In meditation I work to help this lost spirit. So we can free Cynthia one day, and Mother Zoe can have peace.*

■

Time is on Zoe's side. A large percentage of the multiples who survive their chaotic teens, twenties, and thirties, spontaneously self-heal from ages forty to sixty. Whether they integrate or not, multiples can come to accept themselves.

The alters so promiscuous in the 1970s—Eleanor, Eleanora, Serena, and Chandra—have, in the age of AIDS, become chaste. Eleanor has left the Tunnel of Hell and entered the Tunnel of Watchers, where she monitors physical health. In the Baptist church to which she regularly hauls the alters, Eleanor/Zoe's face stands out pale among many shades of brown. Chandra mainly sleeps; on the rare occasion when she's out she watches religious TV. Serena has started a novel, the female protagonist of which is a serial killer of men.

Alters who see themselves as past-life impressions are gathering up their stories. The alter Suzanna says she died by fire in her parents' home. The alter William Brown says he died when his neck was broken by a white man in 1842. Sharon Weissman speaks about concentration camps and gas chambers.

Many of Zoe's alters who saw themselves as coven members are now transformed: either locked away in the internal punishment land of Dena or mutated into new personality structures. In March 1992, one unintroduced alter wrote Zoe a note that at the time seemed quite cryptic: "The Dark Ones Will Come to Shed Light." When later they came out on tape, one by one, the Dark Ones described themselves as an order of nuns who "still speak the old languages and wear the old habits." Seen through a glass, lightly, they are Zoe's old coven: a more self-mastered and socialized variation.

Some of Zoe's system has begun to live in the earth's time. Many alters have gotten subjectively older. The child alters are growing; the adults are inching toward Zoe's chronological age.

In the past two years, Serena developed from perceptual age sixteen to perceptual age twenty-five. Zoe 2 (the toddler alter) did not age, but did learn to speak fluently and abstractly. Beth matured from age nine to twenty-three, and now sees her function as teaching child alters and rage alters to become more socialized, both within and outside the system.

Instead of seeing themselves as acting-out fragments of childhood, many alters now see themselves as spirit guides and guardians, observers and interpreters. They keep track of events; they watch what all the alters do. They try to do what Zoe seems to want: to express and interpret the system as a whole.

※

What part did switching therapists play in all this?

Gwynn Fischer never wished to see the alters as separate people, preferring to think of them as emotional states. Sarah Freed tries to accept the alters on Zoe's terms—as people—without encouraging irresponsible, pluralistic multiplicity. Zoe and she walk a very fine line.

By May 3, 1993, a few of Zoe's alters were content with Sarah. "Therapy with Sarah feels different. Safe."

Dr. Shenker's note of May 19, 1993, reads, "Patient says she's thinking more clearly."

Sarah thinks that Zoe did not feel safe in her former therapy. "Most sexually abused people, including Zoe," she says, "have no sense of privacy. No sense of what they're allowed to protect, because their original boundaries were so invaded.

"Thus," continues Sarah, "multiples are uncomfortable with distance. In therapy they often prematurely describe some very personal experiences. They spill all before they develop trust, and then they snap back with some reaction. I try to encourage only the amount of trust that has been earned. That might seem slow, but perhaps feels more honest, to a person with that type of history.

"The hypnosis, particularly some of the very standard inductions, may have undermined Zoe's shaky boundaries even more. One example would be a directive to relax, to give it all out, to be completely open.

"Some of Zoe's memories," says Sarah, "came out far earlier than I think they should have. The hypnosis set up an artificial intimacy that Zoe jumped right into. This felt to Zoe, at once like Gwynn was her mother and as though she was being raped, for what is rape but unwanted, unchosen, and premature intimacy, imposed on one by another?"

On June 3, 1993, Zoe asked Sarah if she could ever be healed. Sarah leaned forward, took her hands, and said, "I'm counting on it."

▪

ZOE (Claw on Inner Life): *Losing your mind is a peak experience. What is reality—nothing but a speculative hunch! I don't say crazy is for everyone. Some people couldn't cope. But for us, honey—it works.*

▪

Zoe has not just met her alters, she has also re-met her family. She has made a new peace with Zoe May, Carmine, Janet Moore, her son Davey, and Janna Lynne. Not that this family is cured. It is not. That will take years, if it ever happens. But at least the family, which was so shattered and secretive, has made a fresh start.

Carmine has become philosophical about his wife's condition. "Over the past seven years," he says, "I learned that Zoe was many people, fighting. I hoped they would come to a better understanding. Living with a multiple is difficult and strange."

"Did you ever want to leave?" I ask.

"Many times," he says with a rueful grin.

"Why?"

"Behind the innocent eyes and sweet smile, I knew there was someone, many, watching. It is difficult to be yourself when you are watched."

"Do you want to leave now?"

"No."

"Why?"

Carmine sighs. "I have come to know and like or love many of the people in Zoe's system. She is my wife of thirty years, and I love her. All of her."

Janet Moore and Zoe Parry have long conversations about corruption in the field of mental health. They discuss their many grievances, which, given Zoe's history with therapists, sound quite justified.

"When you go into the hospital," says Janet, "they post your rights on the wall, but don't enforce them. Mental patients need compassion, understanding."

Zoe May and Zoe also have long conversations.

"If I had it to do over again," says Zoe May, talking about how she raised her daughter, "I possibly would do it different. I probably wouldn't be so overprotective. I just had the one and centered a great deal of my thoughts on her. Making fears that I shouldn't have had.

"I would tell other mothers, be very careful about who your child associates with. If the child says anything, it should be investigated. Don't trust men or women, or even the family. My daughter's problems were created by these monsters. Because in my depression I couldn't save her."

The old woman is less than five feet tall and deaf. She is not an enormous, powerful monster from whom anyone would run. Were he alive today, I imagine the same might be true of Mr. Bryant.

When asked about her present-day daughter, Zoe May softly says, "Sometimes I don't understand my daughter. She's a good person, and I love her very dearly—but she's surely different."

Davey has moved out of the Parry house, but he sees his mother frequently.

What was it like having a multiple mother? Davey is reluctant to speak about this. When asked, he doesn't want to talk right now, he has to do his laundry, he has to go to the store, to watch TV, he has to go meet some of the guys. On tape he blanks out, gives noncommittal answers, and runs out of steam. Davey has arguably been hurt the worst by Zoe's days of uncontrolled multiple personality. Nobody remembers exactly how he was hurt or, even if they did, knows how to fix the pain.

■

What would make Zoe's alters happy?

■

**DANIELLE LA MOND (the Open Air):** *To help people to look inside themselves and to realize that there is good and evil inside every human being.*

■

**SELINA (the Bird's Wing):** *To get message across. To make people understand about MPD. And also, to work out what remain Selina's secret.*

■

**BLANCHE STEEL (the Bird's Head):** *I would like for people to understand about past lives.*

■

**ZOE 2 (the Bird's Breast):** *To have a happy home. I like it now because we have birds. They're real pretty, and they make a lot of noise.*

■

**MAZIE 5 (the Bird's Wing):** *To be able to play with other children. To never be scared. I would like nice toys, and a nice mom and dad.*

■

**ZOE 7 (the Bird's Breast):** *For Marnie to be my mom; for Mrs. Bryant to be my aunt.*

■

**JULIE (the Bird's Wing):** *To make other people feel their own feelings, ones they're afraid to express. By seeing me perform onscreen, they would recognize themselves.*

■

**ROSE (the Bird's Leg):** *Talking. To you and everyone inside. And for teachers and caretakers not to make fun of retarded children like me. And to see other children happy and never get hurt again or get hurt in the first place. Because children never forget.*

■

**ZOE (the Claw on Inner Life):** *To find peace of mind and peace of body.*

*We've found a therapist; we seek a spiritual teacher.*

*Sarah is able to express human feelings, which so many therapists hide. You think, ''Finally, someone understands.''*

*Sarah believes that there will be a time that strength will come from within.*

*Sarah does not believe that our life has been wasted. She believes that we had strength to survive. She said that yesterday, and it touched us deeply.*

■

**DANIE LA MOND (the Tunnel of Hosts):** *We're happy living this life. As happy as we can be, put it that way. We do not intend to become integrated—as you, one, with many different sides to yourself. There will always be Selina, Danielle, Donna, Dennis.*

*Our goal is to function better as this group.*

■

**ZOE (the Claw on Inner Life):** *I want to be friends with each and every one. The doctors tell me that they are part and parcel of myself.*

# Key to Zoe's
# Personality Maps

## ZOE'S ALTERS

These are the alters listed on Zoe's personality maps. It is not a complete list: many others emerged during interviews.

Alters who make their first appearance in a given map are starred and are listed separately below the alters previously introduced. If Zoe has given a description of the alter, it's included.

The dates are estimates of when alters believe they first came aware in Zoe's system. The alters who never described or dated themselves are also noted.

Some alters introduced themselves to me before February 1992; they're not starred on the map.

Some alters who at first didn't use regular names assumed names in later interviews. The Blonde, Animal, and Eyes became Cynthia. Stupid One became Sherry. Zoe 5 became Mazie. The Bride became Dottie Mae. Bathroom Girl became Zoe 6, then Lilly. Bad Girl I became Roberta. Bad Girl II became Ronny/Lillian. Closet Girl became Shoney.

■

DATE: 2/92
DISCUSSING: The Kidnapping
PERSONALITIES: 57

## The Tunnel of Light and Wisdom

**Eleanora Brown** (1952) Age 35–55; 5'8", 152 pounds. Black skin, long black hair in a bun. Used to be the "Shady Lady." Now considers herself a protector of Zoe's system.

**\*Marie-Marie** (1952) Child alter, age 7, with strong feelings about the Virgin Mary. Blonde hair, brown eyes. Sings hymns. "In front of the crucifix, on my knees."

**\*Beth** (1955) Age 9–25. Brown hair, hazel eyes. Small and thin. Loves horses. "To make the little ones forget and to tell the truth."

427

*Donna White (1947) Also known as "Donnie." Age 2–48. Brown hair, brown eyes. "I speak up for the little ones."

*Dr. Mildred Silverstein (1969) Age 66; 140 pounds, short. Short black hair, dark brown eyes. Single. "I guide Zoe's therapists and correct their mistakes."

*Observer (Spirit Guide) (1952) Ageless. Hermaphroditic. "To think and reason without emotion."

*Cassandra (Spirit Guide) (1970) Looks 32. Not of this world. "To guide the Soul."

The Angel Child (The Innocent; God's Child) (1946) Looks 7. Can be any age. Blonde hair, deep green eyes. Wreaks supernatural vengeance on the enemies of Zoe Parry's personality system. "Her smile fools the world."

*Chandra (1977) Age 17–28. Light brown skin, hazel eyes, tall and thin. "I was born so the children wouldn't feel the sex."

*Ani (1981) Age 1½–2. Light brown hair, brown eyes. "Born during oral sex with Dr. Altman."

*Danie La Mond (1982) Age 20–30; 5'6", 110 pounds, thin. Short brown hair, hazel eyes, no makeup. "Danielle's butch sister."

*Danielle La Mond (1982) Age 25–29; 5'6", 115 lb. Brown hair, green eyes. "Born to bring joy."

Sister Zoe Ann (1952) Age 30; 5'4", 110 pounds. Sister in the Secular Franciscan Order. Brown hair, brown eyes, smooth complexion. "Since age 7 I've known the Catholic Church was for me."

Zoe 5 (1950) Age 5. Names herself Mazie in 1993. Blonde hair, green eyes, delicate, pretty. "My first memory is of John Perret, in the car."

Zoe II (September 1945) Age 3 months. Ash-blonde, hazel eyes. Has progressed in age to match Zoe's chronological age. "I exist because of the others. I have no clear identity. I am the empty shell."

*Bobbi Jo (1952) Age 10. Tomboy. "To save Zoe and take pain."

Zoe I (Mother Zoe) (1960) Age 15–35; 5'4", 110 pounds. "Carried Carmine's child. I am the Open Vessel and Gwynn's original patient."

*Aunt Sophie (1972) Age 55; 4'10", 89 pounds. Black-dyed hair, brown eyes. "Stand-up comic."

*Sharon Weissman I (1970) Age 25. Light brown hair, brown eyes. "Being isolated from my parents at the camps. I came to take care of Davey."

Sandra Christian (1986) Age 24. Brown hair and eyes, glasses. Plain. "I came to help Zoe fear the body less."

*Suzanna (1978) Age 7? Thin, black hair, blue eyes. "Spirit guide. My parents died in a fire."

## The Tunnel of Hosts

Zoe II (the Host)

Zoe (the Patient) (1956) Age 11–47. "I fear sickness and death."

## The Tunnel of Lost Souls

*Martin Caine (1972) Age 22. Tall, handsome, blue-gray eyes. "Fought in Civil War. Southern gentleman."

*Victoria La Mond (1978) "A southern woman from another time."

## The Tunnel of Limbo

*Willie Brown (1977) Age 10. Past-life impression, born 1832. Dark skin and eyes. Met his death by choking. "Gonna find that man who broke my neck."

*Becky Jo (1987) Age 5–20. Blonde hair, brown eyes. "I was born to be pleasing to my mother, Gwynn Fischer."

*Rebecca Gwynn (1987) Age 17–19. Blonde hair, brown eyes. "My purpose is to hypnotize and soothe the system."

*Sharon Weissman II (1970) Age 28. Big brown hair. "I had a silly crush on Dr. Frederick Small."

*Carmine Parry (1982) Age 38; 6'2", 235 lb. Black hair, brown eyes. "I am the perfect husband. I protect my wife."

Elizabeth (1978) Age 32. Brown hair, hazel eyes, gentle smile. "I am Janet Moore's friend."

*Doreen (1957) Age 13–18; 5'4", 105 pounds. Brown hair, blue eyes. Attractive and social. "My first memory is being raped in a hotel."

*Mary Cora (1956–66) Age 11–20. Bulimic, eats compulsively. "I am fat, plain, and ugly. I hate myself."

*Lydia (1986) Age 28. Tall, thin, blonde, light blue eyes. "I help Zoe take care of herself."

*Black Wolf (1952) Old Hopi woman. Shaman and healer. Alter Selina's teacher.

**\*The Bride** (1960) In later maps is **Dottie Mae**. Age 15–21; 5'5", 116 pounds. Long brown hair. Shy, unhappy. "My worst memories are of intercourse and losing my baby."

## The Tunnel of Hell

**\*Selina** (1952) Brown eyes, brown skin, golden curly hair. Heavy accent. "I come to reveal many truth. Memory is always now."

**\*The Blonde** In later maps, is **Cynthia Evans**. Blonde hair, green piercing eyes. Wears a black robe. "I speak the pain of the system."

**\*Serena** (1949) Age 3–30. Blonde hair, hazel eyes, slender. Wears sexy red or black clothing. "I feel no pain or anxiety. I was looking for the perfect woman, and thought I found her in Pat Wald."

**\*Mrs. Patterson** (1974) In one later map splits into **Mrs. Patterson (Good)** and **Mrs. Patterson (Bad)**. Age 50+. White hair, blue eyes, coarse voice. Can take any form.

**\*The Slasher** (1955) Age 3–30. Female. Long hands, sharp finger-nails. Is mute. Has not assumed a human name. Hates herself and hates Zoe's body.

**\*Animal** (1945–7?) Don't know age. Speaks in growls. In some later maps is combined with **Cynthia Evans**.

**\*The Demon** (1950) In some later maps is **Demon Girl**. Black hair, white face. Sometimes has a beard. "She has a horrible, hoarse voice. She is evil."

**\*Eyes** (1945–7?) In some later maps is combined with **Cynthia Evans**. Zoe's parent sometimes called Zoe "Bright Eyes."

**\*Connie** (1960) Age 18–43. Blonde, pretty. Hard jaw and eyes. "I was 14 when I came to the system. I love Cousin Virge."

**\*Eleanor** (1977) Age 54; 5'7", 125 pounds. Dark skin and eyes. Wears sexy makeup. "Her purpose is to sexually use men and women." In later years, she changed purpose; now she watches over Zoe's health.

## The Tunnel of Darkness and Death

**\*Zoe 3 months (Baby Frozen)** (September 1945) Age 3 months. Waxen skin, light brown hair, green eyes. "She just stares into space with dead eyes. Smells like a corpse or like the perfumes with which the priestess anoints her."

**\*Rajon** (1945) Age 33 and eternal. Olive skin, black hair, dark brown eyes. "She is a spirit guide who takes care of Baby Frozen."

*Two Male Guards (1945) Young, male; 5'6", light brown skin, black hair, dark eyes. Green body wraps. "They spirited away the dead baby and took her to Rajon, to be cared for."

## The Tunnel of Waiting and Secrets

*Bad Girl I (1948) Age 3–15. In later maps, she calls herself Roberta. Brown hair, brown eyes. "They called me the Devil's Child."

*Bad Girl II (1948) In later maps, she's Ronny/Lillian. Age 3–22. Black hair, brown eyes. Speaks with a Brooklyn accent. "I'm a fighter and never minded being told so."

*The High Priest (1970) "He does not choose to speak about himself."

*Bathroom Girl (1951) In later maps is Zoe 6 or Lilly. Age 6. Dark blonde hair, green eyes. Pretty. Hides in bathrooms when she gets scared. "Summer and sweat and beatings."

*Zoe 10 (1955) Age 10. Brown hair, green eyes. Thin. Coughs a lot. "I fear death."

*The Stupid One (1948) In later maps is Sherry. Age 3–12. Red hair, blue eyes. Stutters; is half-blind and deaf. "So afraid."

*Rona (the Waif) (1959) Age 14. Lanky brown hair, blue jeans, white shirt.

■

DATE: 4/92
DISCUSSING: Dr. Sidney Altman
PERSONALITIES: 72+

## The Tunnel of Watchers

Black Wolf; Connie; The High Priest; Lydia; The Observer; Rebecca Gwynn; Sharon Weissman I.

*Julie (1957) Age 34; 5'2", 103 pounds. Short brown hair, blue eyes. Bubbly, energetic. "I take over at social gatherings. I became aware of myself at a dance class. I'm the one that has found work as a movie extra."

*Priestess Oya (1976) Looks 26, but is ageless. Gold hair, glassy eyes, white robe. "She started the Temple. She was given this name by Isis Bergeron."

*Sister Michael Marie (Dark One #2) (See Convent, below. The Dark Ones came out over the course of several months.)

*Marie Martin** (1982) Observer. Spirit guide. "Marie Martin" was the name of St. Thérèse, before canonization.

## The Tunnel of Light and Wisdom

Ani age 2; Aunt Sophie; Cassandra; Chandra; Danielle La Mond; Donna White; Eleanora Brown; Elizabeth; Marie Marie; Mother Zoe; Sharon Weissman II; Sister Donna Pauline (Dark One #1); Sister Zoe Ann; the Angel Child; Zoe 5 (Little Mama).

*Rona** (1952) Age 14. She's also referred to as the Waif. Thin, brown hair, brown eyes. Wears jeans and a white shirt. "I came to take away pain and to have a child."

*Zoe 2** (1947) Blonde, looks sad. "She's their Doll in a Box."

## The Tunnel of Zoe of Dreams

The Patient (Zoe + Bobbi Jo + Danie La Mond); Zoe-the-Host (Empty Vessel).

## The Tunnel of Lost Souls

Cynthia (the Blonde); Martin Caine; Suzanna; Victoria La Mond.

*Agnes Caine** (1952) Age 36. Brown hair turning gray, brown eyes. "I made myself known in 1952. But I am a past-life spirit, of the most tortured level."

## The Tunnel of Limbo

Becky Jo; Carmine; Doreen; Dr. Mildred Silverstein; Mary Cora; Sandra Christian; Serena; the Bride; William Brown.

*Gwynnie Louise Fischer** (1986) Age 7. Feels she's Gwynn Fischer's daughter. "I exist to love and please Mommy."

## The Tunnel of Hell

The Demon (Mrs. Patterson + Animal); Slasher.

*Resuba** (1976) Coven member. Read backward, "abuser."

Two Black Men (see Sidney Altman and Dave Bryant, below. The Black Men, also called Dark Men, never came out. They were described by other alters, first just as dark men, and then later as internalized father figures.)

## The Tunnel of Darkness and Death

Infant Zoe (Baby Frozen); Rajon (High Priestess); Two Guards.

## The Tunnel of Waiting and Secrets

Beth; Eleanor; Roberta; Ronny; Selina; Sherry (the Stupid One); Zoe; Zoe 6; Zoe 10.

*Zoe 7 (1952) Age 7. Dark blonde hair, hazel eyes, extremely thin. Always coughing. "I fear Grandpa."

*Baby Robert (1950) Age 6 months. Can't talk. Cries all the time. "We think he exists to take pain."

The Dark Ones (Eight Remaining) (See Convent, below)

*Heather (1970) . . . to speak about herself.

*Markus (1970) Eternal, angelic, golden. A spirit guide. Flies Zoe off to the Golden Beach World.

*Paul (1970) Another spirit guide. Does not describe himself.

■

DATE: 6/92
DISCUSSING: Dr. Sidney Altman
PERSONALITIES: 92+

## The Tunnel of Watching and Secrets

Becky Jo; Beth; Carmine; Connie; Danie La Mond; Danielle La Mond; Julie; Lydia; Marie Martin; Observer; Rebecca Gwynn; Roberta; Ronny; Selina; Sharon Weissman I; Sister Michael Marie; the Angel Child; William Brown.

*Convent (the Dark Ones) (1981) Also called the Poor Johannas. They formed as a group when Sister Johanna retired to New York. In 1992, they wrote Zoe a cryptic note promising that "The Dark Ones Will Come to Shed Light." Over the course of interviews for this book, they emerged one by one to comment on Zoe's thought processes. They include Sr. Michael Marie, 42; Sr. Donna Pauline, 39; Sr. Bridget Mary Dunnigan, 63, Irish accent; Sr. Mary, 24; Sr. Zoe Paul, 27; Sr. John Robert, 67; Sr. Luke, 28; Sr. Thomas, 34; Sr. Josephine, 72. This is only one of four convents that Zoe says reside within her personality system, and which comprise 120 sisters.

*Rion (1976) Coven member. Read backward, "noir" (French for black).

*Giovanni Parry (1981) Older. A protector. Appeared to help Zoe defend herself against Sidney Altman.

*Gino Perrona (1981) Gina Perrona's twin brother. Protector.

*Alice (1977) Age 18–28. Dark skin and eyes. "I came to tell truth."

## The Tunnel of Light

Ani age 2; Aunt Sophie; Cassandra; Chandra; Donna White; Eleanora Brown; Elizabeth; Marie-Marie; Mother Zoe; Rona; Selina; Sister Donna Pauline; Sister Zoe Ann; Sister Zoe Paul; Zoe 2; Zoe 5.

## The Tunnel of Faraway Dreams

Black Wolf; Bobbi Jo; Oya; Selina; the Bride; Zoe Host; Zoe Patient.

*Virginia Zion (1951) Age 3–27. Red hair, blue eyes. "I exist to follow truth. I follow Religious Science."

*Carol Seemore (1951) Age 6–34. "I exist to break through the human delusion that man is not material but spiritual, and hope Zoe will turn away from error and realize she is God's Perfect Child."

## The Tunnel of Dreams

Doreen; Dr. Mildred Silverstein; Eleanor; Gwynnie Louise Fischer; Markus; Mary Cora; Paul; Sandra Christian; Selina; Serena.

## The Tunnel of Hell

Animal; Mrs. Patterson; Resuba; Selina; the Demon.

*The Coven (1976) Formed when Oya was named by Isis. Is also called the Conven—a mix of coven and convent.

## The Tunnel of Darkness

Infant Zoe (Baby Frozen); Rajon; Selina; Sharon Weissman II; Two Guards.

## The Tunnel of Walk-ins and Lost Souls

Cynthia; Heather; Martin Caine; Selina; Suzanna; Victoria La Mond.

## The Tunnel of the Lost and Blind

Agnes Caine; Robert; Selina; Sherry (the Stupid One); Zoe 10.

■

DATE: 7/92
DISCUSSING: Dr Altman, Sister Johanna, Dr. Wald
PERSONALITIES: 105+

## The Tunnel of Careful Observation

Alice; Beth; Cynthia; Donna White; Gino Perrona; Giovanni Parry; Lydia; Marie Martin; Martin Caine; Observer; Rebecca Gwynn; Ronny; Sister Michael Marie; the Angel Child; Victoria La Mond; William Brown.

*Ruthie (1950) Age 5–15. Brown hair and eyes, slender. Speaks only in rhyme. "She's a mystery to us."

## The Tunnel of Power

Black Wolf; Carmine; Carol Seemore; Donna White; Eleanor; Mary Cora; Oya; Selina; Sister Donna Pauline; Sister Zoe Ann; the Angel Child; Virginia Zion.

*Gina Perrona (1981) Gino Perrona's twin sister. Another protector.

## The Tunnel of Dreams

Bobbi Jo; Zoe I Patient; Zoe II Host.

## The Tunnel of Eternal Protection

God's Child (the Angel Child); Rajon; Selina; Sharon I + II; the Baby Frozen; Two Guards.

## The Tunnel of Guides

Cassandra; God's Child (the Angel Child); Heather; Luke; Marie-Marie; Markus; Paul; Selina; the Convent.

*Juliette Leigh (1955) Older southern woman. Holds some of Zoe's intergenerational family lore.

*Miss Beverly (1991) "Protects and watches."

*Miss Annie Lanette (1955) An older southern woman. Family history.

## The Tunnel of Hell

Dark Men; Demon; God's Child (the Angel Child); Patterson; Resuba; Rion; Slasher; the Coven.

*Desesop (1976) Coven member. Read backward, "possessed."

## The Tunnel of Limbo

Becky Jo; Chandra; Doreen; Dr. Mildred Silverstein; God's Child (the Angel Child); Lonnie; Sandra Christian; Serena.

## The Tunnel of Secrets

Agnes Caine; Chandra; Danie La Mond; Danielle La Mond; God's Child (the Angel Child); Mary Cora; Robert 6 months; Roberta; Selina; Sherry; Suzanna; Zoe 6; Zoe 10.

*Dr. Ashley (1963) Age 55. "He's Doctor Death. We have to obey what he says."

## The Tunnel of Light and Purity

Ani; Eleanora Brown; Elizabeth; Mary; Mother Zoe; Rona; Sophie; the Angel Child (God's Child); Zoe 2; Zoe 5.

∎

DATE: 8/92
DISCUSSING: Dr. Wald, mother, and early childhood
PERSONALITIES: 100+

## Secrets

Alice; Annie Lanette; Becky Jo; Beth; Black Wolf; Bob; Bobbi Jo; Carmine; Cassandra; Chandra; Connie; Convent; Coven; Cynthia; Danie La Mond; Danielle La Mond; Desesop; Donna White; Eleanor; Eyes; Gina; Gino; Guards; Gwynn Fischer; High Priest; Jackie A.; Julie; Lonnie; Luke; Lydia; Margaret; Markus; Martin Caine; Miss High Fashion; Mother Zoe; Mrs. Patterson; Observer; Oya; Paul; Rajon; Rebecca Gwynn; Resuba; Roberta; Ronny; Sandra; Sarah F.; Selina; Serena; Sister Donna Pauline; Sister Michael Marie; Sister Zoe Ann; Slasher; Sophie; Suzanna; the Angel Child; William Brown; Zoe.

## Body of an Expression

Zoe

## Protected by Angel Child

Agnes; Serena; "Bad Boy Die 2/82."

*Sidney Altman (1978) Introject of Dr. Altman. But Zoe says he has dark skin.

## Silence of the Holy Innocents

Ani; Baby Robert; Eleanora Brown; Elizabeth; Marie Martin; Marie-Marie; Mary Cora; Rona; Sharon I; Sharon II; Sherry; Zoe 2; Zoe 5; Zoe 10.

## Holding Cell

Mafia Women and Men; Mrs. Patterson; Ruth.

*George (See the Gang, below)
*Juan
*Pedro
*Rick
*Dave
*Smart

## Enter "Passed-Away" Angel Child and Suffer

Angel Child; Baby Frozen; Grandmother; Grandpa; Gwynn; Jane; John Perret; Mama; Martha Hoyt; Papa; Pat Wald; Sidney Altman.

■

DATE: 9/92
DISCUSSING: Fischer, diagnosis, and early childhood
PERSONALITIES: 105+

## My Observers

Alice; Beth; Cynthia; Donna; Gino Perrona; Giovanni Parry; Lydia; Marie Martin; Martin Caine; Rebecca Gwynn; Ruth; Sister Donna Pauline; Sister Dorothea Paul; Sister John Robert; Sister Josephine; Sister Luke; Sister Michael Marie; Sister Thomas; the Angel Child; Victoria La Mond; William Brown.

## My Creations of Power and My Students

Black Wolf; Carmine; Carol Seemore; Connie; Danie La Mond; Dark Men; Donna White; Eleanora Brown; Gina Perrona; Oya; Ronny; Selina; Sister Zoe Ann; the Angel Child; Virginia Zion.

## Eternal Protection

Frozen Baby; Oya; Rajon; Selina; Sharon I & II; the Angel Child; Baby/Core of the Angel Child; Two Guards.

## Guides and Friends Not in This Zone

Annie Lanette; Black Wolf; Bobbi Jo; Cassandra; Convent; Danielle La Mond; Heather; Juliette Leigh; Luke; Marie-Marie; Markus; Miss Beverly; Oya; Paul; Selina; the Angel Child; The Body; Zoe I, Presenting Patient; Zoe II, Host.

## Hell

Conven; Demon; Desesop; Patterson; Resuba; Rion; Selina; Slasher; the Angel Child.

## Pit of Death

Father; God's Child; Grandfather; John Perret; Others; Sidney Altman.

## My Subjects Resting in Limbo
### (But Always Ready to Protect Me)

Becky Jo; Doreen; Dr. Silverstein; Lonnie; Old Man; Old Woman; Sandra; Serena; the Angel Child.

## Those Under My Control to Keep Secrets

Agnes; Dr. Ashley; Mary Cora; Robert 6 months; Roberta; Selina; Sherry; Suzanna; the Angel Child; Zoe 6; Zoe 10.

*Turha (Turhapotsota) (1976) Does not speak about itself. Read backward is "a hurt" and "a to stop a hurt."

## Grief

Danielle La Mond.

## Those I Sent to Light

Ani; Chandra; Elizabeth; Mary; Mother Zoe; Rona; Sophie; the Angel Child; Zoe 2; Zoe 5.

## The Pit of Turha (To Be Handled.
### It Be Their Choice—Peaceful or ?????)

Gwynn; New York; Pat Wald.

■

DATE: 11/92
DISCUSSING: Middle Childhood
PERSONALITIES: 100+

## The Tunnel of Observers

Alice; Bobbi Jo; Carmine; Danielle La Mond; Donna White; Doreen; Elizabeth; Gino Perrona; Giovanni Parry; High Priest; Lydia; Marie Martin; Rajon; Ronny; Selina; Sister Michael Marie; Sister Zoe Ann; Two Guards.

*Diane (1992) Age 22.

## The Tunnel of Waiting

*No Names, Nameless Ones (1950) Also referred to as Lost Souls and Walk-ins. "They exist in Dena and are called forth to fill specific needs."

## The Tunnel of Power

Cenvent; Donna White; Gina Perrona; God Mother Aifam; God's Child; Oya; Patterson; Rona; Selina; Sharon Weissman I; Sharon Weissman II; Sister Donna Pauline; Virginia Zion.

*Debbie Roberta (1950) Age 5–12. "I'm my father's daughter. I'm not going to say anything bad about him or let anything bad be said about him."

*Blanche Steel (1992) Past-life impression, often coconscious with Donna. "I was raped as a child."

## The Tunnel of Past Lives

Blanche Steel; Martin Caine; Rajon; Ronny/Lillian; Selina; Suzanna; Victoria La Mond; William Brown.

## The Tunnel of Light

Ani; Black Wolf; Elizabeth; Mary; Mother Zoe; Rona; Sophie; the Angel Children; Zoe 2; Zoe 5 (Mazie); Zoe 7.

*Dream Wolf (1992) Ageless. "Spirit guide."

*Moon Shadow (1992) Ageless.

## The Tunnel of Guides

Cassandra; Heather; Juliette Leigh; Luke; Marie-Marie; Markus; Paul; Suzanna.

## The Tunnel of Secrets

Agnes Caine; Annie Lanette; Chandra; Closet Girl age 3; Danie La Mond; Debbie Roberta; Dr. Ashley; Juliet; Mary Cora; Sherry; Zoe 6; Zoe 10.

*Aunt Roberta (1977) Age 49. Does not further identify herself.

Sarrie Freed (1992) Age 6. Brown curly hair, feels she is Sarah Freed's daughter. "I love my mommy."

## The Tunnel of Limbo

Baby Robert; Becky Jo; Chandra; Connie; Conven; Demon; Desesop; Dr. Silverstein; Eleanor; Grandmother; Gwynn Fischer; Gwynnie Louise Fischer; Lonnie; Miss Beverly; Rebecca Gwynn; Resuba; Rion; Sandra; Slasher.

*Dark Man I (Sidney Altman) (1978) At first, he's an introject of any black man. Later, he becomes an introject of Sidney Altman. But he still has black skin.

*Dark Man II (Dave Bryant) (1978) Introject of Zoe's father. But he has black skin.

## The Tunnel of Protectors

Beth; Donna White; Eleanora Brown; Gina Perrona; Gino Perrona; God Mother Aifam; Lydia; Ruth.

## The Tunnel of Sorrow

Agnes Caine; Cynthia; Danie La Mond; Danielle La Mond; Mary Cora; Mother Zoe; Selina; Sherry; Zoe Host; Zoe Patient.

*Dora (1952) Age 6–19. "Serena says I'm dowdy."

■

DATE: 11/92 (Thanksgiving)
DISCUSSING: Late Childhood
PERSONALITIES: 130+

## Three Protectors

Janet; Sarah Freed; Sister Johanna.

## Selina

### The Tunnel of Waiting

*Golden Beach of Alters
*Each Alter Has an Alter
*No One Will Know Them
No Names, Layers 1–20, Desert Area

### The Tunnel of Observers, Guides, and Past Life

Agnes Caine; Annie Lanette; Blanche Steel; Cassandra; Cynthia; Heather; Juliet; Luke; Markus; Martin Caine; Paul; Rajon; Ronny/ Lillian; Selina/Black Wolf; Suzanna; Victoria La Mond; William G. Brown.

## The Angel Child

### The Tunnel of Observers from Darkness

Beth La Mond; Conven; Dark Man I: Sidney Altman; Dark Man II: Dave Bryant; Demon; Gwynn Louise Fischer; Resuba; Rion; Slasher; St. Paul "Saul, Saul, why doest thou persecute me?"

*Dark Man III: Henry Owens (1977) Chubby, 5'7". Introject of one of the workers at a hospital, who abused Zoe. Zoe's alters invited him to be High Priest of their coven.

*Ecrof (1976) Coven member. Gray hair, brown eyes. Tall, thin, looks sickly. Read backward, "force."

### Friends of System

Amelia Ellis; Barry Bertrand? (Not Everybody Likes Him); Father Kirkland; Jackie Austin; Janet Moore; Sally Ann Hough; Sandy Shenker, MD; Sarah Freed; Sister Johanna.

### The Tunnel of Light

Ani; Dora 6; Eleanora Brown; Julie; Marie-Marie; Marie Martin; Mazie 5; Mother Zoe; Rona; Zoe 2; Zoe 7; Zoe 10.

*Rose (1948) Age 3–13. "I'm retarded."

*St. Thérèse of Lisieux (1982) "This angel from Heaven appeared to help Zoe when things looked darkest. St. Thérèse is our favorite saint."

## The Tunnel of Power

Alice; Aunt Sophie; Black Wolf; Carmine; Carol Ann Seemore; Connie; Convent; Donna White; Elizabeth; Gino Perrona; Lonnie; Lydia; Oya; Ronny/Lillian; Ruth; Selina; Serena; Sister Donna Pauline; Sister Michael Marie; Sister Zoe Ann.

*Dr. Charles Blakemore and *Dr. Susan Watchman (1992) "We are Dr. Fischer's therapists. We are here to supervise her and to make sure there's no wrongdoing."

## The Tunnel of Limbo

Baby Robert; Becky Jo; Chandra; Doreen; Dr. Mildred Silverstein; Gwynn Fischer; Rebecca Gwynn; Roberta; Sandra Christian; Two Guards.

## The Tunnel of Patients

Mother Zoe; the Little Flower, Thérèse of Lisieux; Zoe; Zoe 3 months; Zoe Host.

*Other Baby

## The Tunnel of Secrets

Beth; Danie La Mond; Danielle La Mond; Debbie Roberta; Dora 6–19; Dr. Ashley; Eleanor; Gina Perrona; Giovanni Parry; Mary Cora; Patterson; Sarrie Freed 6; Sharon Weissman I; Sharon Weissman II; Sherry; the Angel Child; the Demon Child; Virginia Zion.

*Joey Freed (1992) Age 12½. "I protect Zoe Parry and Sarah Freed."

*Godmother Aifam (1982) Grandmother, protector. "Aifam," read backward is Mafia.

*Bobby (Bob) (1951) Age 6–16, male.

*Lonny (1953) Age 8–16. Male. "They've known about me since 1953."

DATE: 12/92 (Christmas)
DISCUSSING: Annual Christmas nervous breakdown
PERSONALITIES: 21

### Protection

Beth; Donna White; Elizabeth; Rona; Saint Thérèse; Selina; Sister Bridget Mary; Sister Donna Pauline; Sister Mary; Sister Michael Marie; Sister Zoe Ann; the Poor Johannas.

### Fear Tree

Ani; Mazie 5; Rose; Sherry; Zoe 2; Zoe 7; Zoe 10.

### Waiting Tree

Zoe Host

### Hope Tree

Jesus

### Panic Tree

Mother Zoe

### Isolation Tree

Baby Frozen

■

DATE: 5/93
DISCUSSING: Last therapy session with Gwynn Fischer
PERSONALITIES: 13+

### Woman with No Name

*Woman with No Name (1992) "She has no name. When she is there, no one can think."

"Everyone awake and asleep are now dead."

### Scream

Everyone

## Madness

Agnes; Cynthia; Zoe 10.
*Lost Woman
*The Other Zoe

## Pain

Ani; Mazie 5; Zoe 10.

## Fear

Ani; Zoe 2; Zoe 10.

## Panic

Ani; Zoe 2; Zoe 10.

## Confusion

Mother Zoe

## Tunnel of Lost Souls

■

DATE: 7/93
DISCUSSING: Zoe's future
PERSONALITIES: 130+

## Within the Bird

*Beak Area*
Debbie Roberta; Donna White; Gina Perrona; Serena.
*Inside Head*
Annie Lanette; Blanche Steel; Dora; Martin Caine; Ronny/Lillian; Suzanna.
*Throat Area*
The Angel Child
*Woman of Many Flight

*Breast Area*

Ani; Debbie; Lydia; Mary Cora; Ruthie; Zoe 2; Zoe 7; Zoe 10.

*Abdominal Area*

*The New Baby

*Wing Area*

Alice; Beth; Bobbi Jo; Danie; Julie; Lilly (Zoe 6); Marie-Marie; Mazie 5; Mother Zoe; Ronn; Ronny; Rose; Selina; Sherry.

*Starr Ship

*Claw Area*

Gino; Giovanni.

*Back Area*

Connie

*Peggy

*Tail Area*

Carol Seemore; Virginia Zion.

| | |
|---|---|
| Dena: | Zoe |
| | *Lana (1950) "In control of the Nameless." |
| | *Step In |
| Convents: | *Sister Zoe Paul (Spokesperson) |
| | *120 More Sisters |
| | *Four Convents |

## Outside of Bird

*Above Head*

Observer; Woman with No Name.

*In Air to Left of Head*

Daddy/Good; Dr. Watchman; Gwynn Fischer; Father/Bad; John Perret; Sidney Altman; Pat Wald.

*Dr. Waller

*In Air to Left of Beak*

Isis Bergeron; Sister Bernadette; the Bride.

*Crone
*Lynn
*Old Luke

*In Air to Left of Breast Area*

Danielle
Diane

Maiden
African Camp
Blue
Mark
Heather

*Carlin
*Daniel
*David
*Lukey
*Queens Cousin
*Trapper
*Jerry

*Luke Frank (1945) Age 20–29, male. "Spirit guide." I believe he's an introject of Zoe's dead fraternal twin brother.

*Dennis Stevens (1950) Age 30. Male. Black hair, black eyes. "Eat shit. I hate women."

*In Air to Left of Abdomen*

Cynthia; Agnes.

*Aggie
*Ams
*Paula
*Rems

*In Air to Right of Head*

Yorker Circle:  Sarrie age 6
               Joey age 16

               *Chance (Observer)
               *Eye Woman
               *Link
               *Mirror Woman
               *Secret Woman
               *Shadow Woman
               *Smiler
               *Witch Woman

*In Air at Back of Bird*

Cassandra; Paul.

*Fred McCabe
*Hattie Mac
*Lizzie McCabe
*Zanin

*Seventh Daughter. Family comment on Zoe's being the daughter of the seventh daughter, thus being born to special powers.

*In Center of Sunflower*

**Baby Frozen; Blanche Steel; Chandra; Dream Wolf; Elizabeth; Martin Caine; Rajon; Ronny; Selina; William Brown.**

**\*Owl Woman (1945)** Changeable appearance. "She's a prophet." Family story of owl hooting at Zoe's birth.

**\*Mask (1946)** Changeable appearance. No self-description.

**\*Ruby**

**\*Rula (1990)** Ageless. "Protects and watches."

## *Petals of Sunflower—counterclockwise*

*First Petal*

**Eleanor; Eleanora.**

**\*Mae**
**\*Nettie**

**\*Mist (1953)** Age 5–15. She's been around since the beginning of interviews, but this is her first appearance on a personality map. Her purpose seems to be to comfort and distract Zoe by constructing fantasies. But these fantasies have a way of getting out of hand and becoming violent.

*Second Petal*

**Baby Robert**

**\*Bright Eyes (1945)** Infant. Happy. "She's the second baby."

**\*Mence (1945)** Infant. "The third baby."

**\*Shoney (1948)** Also known as Closet Girl. Age 3. "Looking at Mother hanging up the laundry. I want to die."

*Third Petal*

**\*Dark One**
**\*Black One**
**\*Secret One**
**\*No Entrance to ONE**

**\*The Gang (1982)** First grouping-together of those male alters who appeared to protect Zoe against Dr. Sidney Altman. The Gang comprises **George**, 19; **Juan**, 17; **Pedro**, 17; **Rick**, 20; **Dave**, 22; and **Smart**, 16.

*Fourth Petal*

**Who Do They Say I Am?**

*Fifth Petal*

**Mrs. Patterson (Bad); Mrs. Patterson (Good).**

*****Granma Mattie** (1953) Age 93. Brown skin, brown eyes, white hair. Though this is her first appearance on a personality map, she spoke during interviews as early as mid-1992.

*****Granma Nettie** (1953) Age 75. China-doll complexion, white hair. She, like Granma Mattie, has been around, but has not written on the personality maps.

*Sixth Petal*

**Aunt Sophie; Sharon Weissman I; Sharon Weissman II.**

*****Mort**
*****Aaron**

## Below Flower

*****Eli**
*****Elijah**
*****Jesus**

## Alters Not on Any Map,
## Who've Also Appeared in Interviews

*****Agatha** (1993) "An alter of Agnes Caine's."

*****Endera** (1993) "An alter of Cynthia's."

*****Marnie** (1952) Age 30. Blonde hair, hazel eyes. "I'm the real mother of Zoe 7, and I look just like her."

*****Minnie**

*****Mr. Snow** (1947) Age 63. Scary-looking man. Zoe's alters talk about him and also refer to him as **Cookie Man.** Zoe has a related memory of a scary grocer offering her cookies.

*****Robot** (1969) Age 25. "She came to do what they wanted."

*****Torah** (1980) Mystic. Doesn't speak in interviews. Appears on one list Zoe hands me of her alters.

*****Zoe Parry** (1945) The newborn baby, the original self that Zoe and her therapists postulate. "She was almost destroyed by her parents."

# Acknowledgments
## Zoe Parry

Special thanks to my family, especially my husband, Carmine, who managed to live with many wives for thirty-plus years. With love, respect, and admiration. Hey, how did you do it?

My beloved son, David. You were always wanted and loved by all your mothers.

My granddaughter Janna Lynne. I love you. I hope that someday you will grow up and understand why Grandma did some of the unthinkable.

My friends—especially Janet, the best friend anyone could hope to have. Thanks for always being there for me.

Lillian and George, you showed the world what true forgiveness really is.

Diane, you came to my aid when most needed.

Cat, thank you. And you know why.

Sister Johanna and Father Kirkland, my spiritual advisers, thank you.

Barry, Suzi, Francie, Judy, and Gary, my attorneys, thank you for believing me.

Sarah, who is helping me find the missing pieces, "we" love you.

Gwynn, you opened the first door in the darkest room and shed some light.

Amelia, my dear friend, thank you for being the best listener.

Sandy S., my physician and friend, thank you for your gentle ways of healing.

Jane Dystel, my agent, who kept believing in this project, thank you.

Claire Zion, my editor, much appreciation.

Jackie Austin, my cowriter. You have been wonderful to work with. Your love, caring, and patience I shall always remember. I've learned so much from you.

*To my MPD brothers and sisters:*

*We all have a common bond. Dear ones, I know your suffering and pain. I want to let your little ones, your angry ones, and your constant observers know that my love and prayers will always be with you. Also, we don't have to integrate. For those who want to, I say "Go for it!" But for me and "us," we have made the choice not to. Ever.*

*Our goal is to function and to get along as a team.*
*Love,*
*Zoe, Donna, and everyone.*

# Acknowledgments
## Jacqueline Austin

Public thanks to Richard Levine, for being a good sport through four trying years. And thanks to Ivan Gabor, Nick Ingram, and "Sarah Freed" for thoughtful discussions on the nature of self; to Vicki Austin for the idea of body maps; to Dorothea Austin and Gerson Banner; and to Herman and Cecily Levine for their generous support on many levels.

Thanks to my agent, Sandy Dijkstra, for believing I could write a book at all, much less this one, and to Kathy Saidemann, Bob Schneider, Peg Haller, Lee Kravitz, and Constance Ahrons for sensible structural and textual suggestions. Thanks to my editor, Claire Zion, for adopting an orphan project and seeing it through, and thanks to Tom Spain for help in the final stages.

Thanks to the people who have dedicated their lives to learning how minds and bodies work together. Without Frank Putnam and Colin Ross's books on MPD, interviewing Zoe Parry would not have been possible. The personality maps are extensions of Bennett Braun's work (1986), as summarized by Frank Putnam. A wider view of multiplicity was provided by the philosophy of B. K. S. Iyengar, as taught by Mary Dunn, and by the works of R. B. Allison, Carolyn Bates, John Beahrs, Eugene Bliss, Bennett Braun, Truddi Chase, Ernest Hilgard, Karen Horney, R. P. Kluft, Janet Malcolm, Alice Miller, Virginia Satir, Florence Schreiber, and many others. Any wisdom in this book comes primarily from them.

Finally, Zoe's personality system, thanks to each and all. The effort, persistence, and spirit that you mustered during a time of enormous change, both internal and external, I profoundly and gratefully appreciate.

# To Patients

An informed client gets the best help. Have you asked your doctors about their professional orientation and qualifications? Have you researched the agreed-on treatment? Do you like your doctors? Though it's the therapist's responsibility to help, it's the client's to choose wisely.

Therapists' biographies are published in the annual directories of the professional organizations to which they belong, which are available in the library. So are descriptions of current, recognized therapies.

Check during and after each session: Are you meeting your stated goals, within an agreed-on time frame?

We feel that in most cases abuse can be prevented. But in some cases, litigation may be necessary.

Lawyers are professionally rated in *Martindale and Hubbell,* which is available in the library. The size of a lawyer's practice and its success rate are legitimate areas of inquiry for a prospective client.

Legal records concerning someone you suspect of wrongdoing are publicly available from both the civil and criminal courts. They are kept in your county clerk's office's department of records, which is listed in the phone book under the Government pages.

Records of completed disciplinary action against a doctor may be obtained from your state Medical Board. If you are considering filing a complaint, be aware that disciplinary action occurs only in a fraction of cases and can take years. But the client does not have to pay.

For ethical guidelines on psychotherapist-patient relations, consult the professional directory of the organization to which your therapist belongs (available at the library), or contact your state medical board, listed in the phone book under State Government.

Proactive measures for people with MPD can include, among other things, therapy, the formation of healthy relationships, and changes in work and education. A competent therapist should be able to point out appropriate venues.

Today, a social network does exist for multiples.

The International Society for the Study of Multiple Personality and Dissociation publishes a clients' newsletter, *Many Voices;* this contains personal memoirs as well as practical suggestions.